SCATTERED LIES II

"Lessons Can't Be Learned When Lies Prevail"

To Anna Draper Best Reviewer

Much Love Madison

WRITTEN BY
MADISON

Editor/Typesetter: Carla M. Dean (www.ucanmarkmyword.com)
Book Cover Designer: Kayon Cox (www.kcr8tions.com)
Images: Jupiter Images & SK Designz

Printed in the United States of America

First Edition

ISBN: 13-digit: 978-0-9825260-1-9
         10-digit: 0982526016

Library of Congress Control Number: 2010929953

Published by:
Influential Writers Publishing
621 Beverly Rancocas Road
PMB 145
Willingboro, NJ 08046

Websites: www.influentialwriterspublishing.com or iammadisontaylor.com

Follow Madison for the latest updates on *www.facebook.com /iammadisontaylor* and *twitter.com/madisonme*

Readers,

Thanks to you, *Scattered Lies* has been so well-received that I am both grateful and humbled by the experience.

I had hoped my first book would be an enjoyable read, but nothing prepared me for the exhilaration I would feel when I heard such positive feedback from the readers.

All the wonderful notes, e-mails, and reviews have let me know that the experiences of my characters are universal and relatable to a diverse audience.

So, if ***Scattered Lies: Where Lies Are the Reality of the Truth*** got you hooked, hold on to your seat, because this sequel is ready to reel you in.

Madison and her cohorts have even more to hide. So, of course, more will be revealed.

Secrets, subterfuges, and surprises are guaranteed to keep you on the edge of your seat.

I am confident you will not be disappointed.

Love,
Madison

Acknowledgements

As always, I would like to thank **GOD** for His blessings. Without Him, there would be no me. To my parents, thank you for always being there for me. Thanks to my mother for naming this book. To my sisters, I love you dearly. To my nephews and goddaughter, you guys make me so proud.

To reviewers **Joey Pinkney, Kisha Green, Leona Romich, OOAS Book Club (Anna Draper),** thank you for your reviews.

To the book blubs **Girls Bay Area (GBC)** and **Sister of Unity (SOU),** thank you for selecting my book.

I also give thanks to my team: **Editor Carla M Dean, Candice Coleman, Tonya Patterson, Keisha Green, Kayon Cox.** We did it again!

To my muse, the best is yet to come! Thank you for supporting and believing in me all these years.

SCATTERED LIES II

"Lessons Can't Be Learned When Lies Prevail"

INTRO

As the sun beamed down on her face, Morgan woke up the next morning, daze and confused, staring up at the ceiling. *It was just a bad dream,* she thought. She touched herself, and then frantically lifted up the blankets to find she was completely naked.

Ten minutes went by, and Morgan laid there motionless trying to remember what occurred last night. She decided to get out the bed. Lifting up, she fell back down. Her lower abdominal muscles were aching. For a few moments, she tried to figure out if they did crunches at dance practice yesterday. Again, she eased up, this time using her forearm and hand as a crutch.

"Owww," she mumbled, now in a sitting position.

She tossed the covers aside and sat on the edge of the bed, allowing only the heels of her feet to touch the floor. Pushing her long tresses off of her face and glancing around the room, she thought *everything appeared to be in order.* When she attempted to hop down from the bed though, she fell straight to the floor, her legs giving out from the soreness she was experiencing.

She sat there for a brief second collecting her thoughts, when suddenly the door flew wide open. It was Tony standing in the doorway dressed only in his boxers and a wife-beater tank top. It wasn't a dream. She was raped. Morgan dropped her head and started crying. *Oh God! Why?*

Tony walked over to her. "Ay, yo, get up and take a shower."

Immobile and trying to process his words, Morgan closed her eyes.

"Ay, yo, didn't you hear me?" Tony said, snatching her by the arm.

As Morgan slouched on the floor, refusing to move, he angrily yanked her by her feet. "Yo, stop playing with me and go take a fuckin' shower now!"

Naked and bemused, Morgan walked slowly to the bathroom. She turned around only to find Tony right on her heels. After adjusting the temperature of the water, she got in and began washing up.

Tony pushed back the shower curtains, causing Morgan to jump. "Hurry up so we can eat breakfast."

After Morgan finished, she grabbed a towel and returned to her bedroom with Tony closely monitoring her. Once she dried off, she went into the drawer to pull out something to wear.

"Here, put this on," Tony ordered, throwing a white tank top at her.

Confused and afraid, Morgan looked into his eyes and then dropped her head back down. She put the tank top on, and just when she was about to pull some panties out, Tony walked over to her and said, "No panties."

This time she didn't bother to look at him. She just closed the drawer.

"Come on, let's go downstairs and get something to eat."

Where's Denise? she wondered, as they walked out the room. She glanced to see if Denise was in her room, but Tony grabbed her, forcing her down the stairs.

As Morgan prepared breakfast, Tony stared at her. She looked gorgeous in the tank top. Getting an instant erection, he got up and walked over to her.

"Would you believe you got me hard again," he whispered in her ear, while standing behind her and touching her nipple.

Annoyed by his nasty comment and repulsed by his touch, she turned around quickly and pushed his hand away. Morgan tried to move away, but Tony pinned her up against the wall.

"Where are you going?" he mumbled.

Morgan pushed him back, hoping he would stop. "Get off of me."

Startled, Tony looked at her. *Is this little bitch crazy?* He furiously grabbed her by the arms and shook her. "Bitch, are you fucking crazy? Get off you?" He forced her over to the kitchen table. "Get off you, huh?" he grumbled, then flung her across the room so hard that her body collided with the refrigerator. He then charged toward her, picked her up by the waist, and slammed her down on top of the table.

However, Morgan wasn't going to allow him to violate her again. So, she shoved him away. "No! Stop it!"

In response to her act of courage, Tony knocked the shit out of her, causing her to see stars. "Fuckin' bitch! You wanna fight me?"

Still not willing to submit, Morgan kicked him in the chest. "Get off of me!''

For a split second, while he was racked with pain from her kick, he thought about giving up, but instead, he flew into a rage and started choking her. "Little bitch! I'm gonna kill you!"

Morgan frantically tried to pry his hands from around her neck. Gasping for air, Tony looked down, hoping she would stop fighting. When he realized she was struggling a little less, he released his grip on her neck, pulled her down to the edge of the table, whipped out his penis, and thrust it inside her.

"Take that, you little bitch," he groaned.

Defeated, Morgan surrendered.

Chapter One
Denise

D enise picked the wrong damn day to get locked up. It was Friday night, so she would be spending the night in central booking a.k.a. The Bullpen. Sadly, she wouldn't get to see the judge until Saturday night. *Damn, this place is fucking disgusting and the C.O.'s are so nasty.*

"I hope you don't lose your shit in here," one of the female correction officers said snidely, while looking Denise up and down.

"I hope not either, but if I do, you'll be the first to know," she responded in a condescending tone.

Losing her *shit* was the least of Denise's worries. In fact, she wanted them to try her so she could take out all of her frustration on their asses. After strip-searching her, they directed Denise into a holding cell where she found a small spot in the corner and chilled. She could not believe she was in jail. She hadn't been down this road in years, and she felt like a complete loser sitting in there.

She closed her eyes and tried to block out the conversations filtering the cell. It was sad listening to those young girls, most who thought being arrested was a badge of honor. *Was I that dense the first time I got locked up?*

As she rested her head on the cold wall, she heard the voice of a young girl. "I don't want any problems."

Glancing up, she saw two young black girls standing over a small Puerto Rican girl.

In general, Denise didn't get involved in other people's beef, but she hated bullies. If she didn't interrupt these chicks, they were going to beat the hell out of that girl and rob her, which would lead to the correction officers locking down the place and making their lives hell tonight. Hence, Denise decided to defuse the problem.

"Hey, chill out and leave her alone," she said, then closed her eyes again as if she didn't fear their presence.

When the girls turned around to see who said that, a crackhead pointed in Denise's direction. After walking over to her, the big fat nappy-headed one said, "Yo bitch, you said something?"

Denise sighed. *Why did I open my mouth?* Looking up at them, she replied, "I said leave her alone. Do you really wanna go there? If she screams, a crew of guards is going to come in here with riot gear and fuck us all up."

She was hoping to reason with them. Unfortunately, these girls were the new Pepsi generation. They didn't listen to advice; they were more reactionaries.

"You should've minded your fucking business then since your scared ass is worrying about police storming through here."

The other girl, who was staring Denise up and down, said, "How 'bout you give us your shit."

Denise smirked and took a quick glimpse at herself. Judging by the way she was dressed, she knew the girls assumed she wasn't from the hood. Another example of looks being deceiving. Denise tried to get up, when one of the girls pushed her back down.

"Bitch, did I say you can get up?"

Denise took a deep breath. She had to think quickly. She was outnumbered and unprepared.

"If you allow me to get up, I can take off my stuff."

After looking at each other, the girls stepped back so Denise could get up off the floor. Once Denise's feet were firmly planted on the ground, she swung at the larger of the two, knocking the shit out of her and causing her to fall right on her fat ass.

Denise was about to hook off on the other one, when the C.O. yelled, "Y'all fighting in there?"

The fat girl jumped to her feet and was about to charge Denise, when the C.O. said, "Denise Taylor, what the hell are you doing in here?"

Shocked by the mention of her full name, Denise turned her head towards the gate. It was Sonya Jefferson, a girl that she attended high school with.

While she was distracted, the girls were about to sneak Denise, until Sonya screamed, "Get the fuck back!"

That's when Denise diverted her attention back to the girls, who were glaring at her. She chuckled and walked over to the gate.

"You heard me, Denise. What are you doing in here?"

Denise lowered her head, ashamed to look Sonya in the face. "A gun charge, but it's registered."

Sonya laughed. She never would've thought she would see Denise Taylor in jail. "Well, it's going to be a long night, so I'm moving you to a cell by yourself. I don't feel like doing no paperwork, and knowing your ass, you would pop off in this bitch."

Denise laughed, while moving her eyebrows up and down. "You already know."

As Denise was walking out of the cell, she turned around and looked at the young Spanish girl sitting in the corner. She knew once she left those girl were going to start harassing her again, so she leaned over and whispered in Sonya's ear, "Listen,

15

you see that girl over there in the blue shirt? Move her, too."

Sonya gave Denise a confused look. "Why?"

"If you don't, they're going to rob and beat the shit out of her, causing you to do paperwork that you were trying to avoid doing by moving me."

Sonya looked into Denise eyes and then over at the girl who sat looking scared. "Hey you, in the blue shirt...come on, let's go."

The girl jumped up with a look of relief and walked out with Denise. Sonya put them in an empty cell next door.

"It's going to be a long night and dinner was already served. So, do you want something to eat and drink?" Sonya asked Denise.

"Yes, please," she replied, then looked over at the young girl who had her head down. "And bring her something, too."

Sonya rolled her eyes and screwed up her face. "Anything else, Mother Teresa?"

Denise chuckled. "Shut up!"

Once they were alone, the young girl looked up at Denise and said, "Thank you."

"You're welcome."

"My name is Lexis, and I'm not gay."

Denise looked at her from the corner of her eye. "Shit, neither am I. Your name is Lexis, as in the car Lexus?"

Lexis laughed. "Yeah, my mother named me after her first car."

Denise shook her head in disgust. "Now that's ghetto. My name is Denise."

They sat on separate sides of the cell. Lexis played with her hair, while Denise stretched out on the hard bench. Sonya returned with four cheeseburgers, two orders of French fries, and two bottles of water.

"Here," she said, shoving the bag in the cell. "You know I had to practically beg for this."

"Oh hush! Your ass didn't beg for shit. You think I don't

know how y'all C.O.'s do."

Sonya laughed. "Girl, take this food with your ungrateful ass."

Denise snatched the food, handed half of it to Lexis, and sat back down, while Sonya walked away.

"Thank you," Lexis said, breaking the silence.

"De nada." Denise winked, letting her know she knew Spanish, and then asked in a disappointed voice, "What are you doing in here?"

Lexis took a deep breath and put her head down once again. "Drugs and a gun."

Denise leaned forward, as if she didn't hear her. "You said drugs and guns? How old are you?"

"I just turned eighteen," she mumbled, looking away.

Denise eyes widened. She was just a baby. "You're eighteen years old selling drugs and carrying guns?" She was about to give her a lecture, but how could she when at that age, she had already committed her first murder.

"What made you start selling drugs?"

"That's the problem I don't sell drugs or guns. It's part of a gang initiation."

Denise frowned. "Gang?"

"Yes, I wanted to join this street gang called Murder for Fun, and the two ways for a girl to join was either have sex with about fifteen guys or transport some drugs and guns a few times for the leader."

Denise shook her head. She couldn't believe gangs still existed in New York. She heard about that gang shit in Los Angeles, but here in New York was crazy. "Why do you want to be in a gang anyway?"

"I don't know. This guy I was seeing wanted me to join. He wanted me to have sex with all of the guys, but I heard they take you in a room and make you take off all your clothes. Then you have to do whatever they want. I told him that I didn't wanna do that. At first, he was upset. So, he said that I had to transport their guns and drugs a couple of times."

Hearing that brought back many memories. Denise remembered when Grant was pimping her out to all his friends. *Bastard,* she thought. She wanted to comment, but she would sound like a hypocrite. So, she left the subject alone.

"I don't blame you for not wanting to have sex with that many guys, but these are serious charges you're facing. Well, I hope everything works out for you."

"Thanks. What are you in here for?"

Denise laughed. "A gun, but mine is registered."

Lexis tried to hide her shocked expression. "A gun! Wow, I thought you were in here for something else."

Denise busted out laughing, while looking herself up and down. She didn't look like she belonged in jail. If it was a couple years ago, hell yeah, but today she looked like a businesswoman. She had on some Alexander McQueen brown suede boots, Dolce & Gabbana jeans, a cashmere turtleneck, and mink poncho. She definitely didn't look like she belonged in there.

"Yeah, well, looks are very deceiving. Actually, I'm happy I did get caught because it probably would have been worse."

Lexis' eyes widened. She'd never heard of anyone being happy to be locked up. "Are you scared?"

"No, I'm not scared. I've been arrested before," Denise replied with a slight grin.

However, deep down inside she was. It had been years since she was on this side of the fence, and while it may have seemed good back then, it didn't now.

"Well, I wish you luck, Denise."

Denise giggled. "Thanks, Lexis."

She stared over at this young girl, and while she really didn't want to comment on the situation, a part of her felt like she had to. Maybe if someone would've taken the time out to talk to her, things would've been different.

Deep down inside, Lexis reminded Denise of herself when

she was younger, yearning for love and attention, trying to put on a brave face for the world. Denise sat there and thought for a second. *How should I approach this girl without sounding like her mother?* With teenagers, you have to meet them on their level in order for them to understand and then indirectly bring them up to yours, because if you don't, what you say will fall on deaf ears.

"Lexis, I know I don't have a right to be saying this, but you kinda remind me of my niece. I don't know how you feel about this guy, but trust me, he isn't worth it. Is he locked up, too?"

Lexis shook her head no. "He ran. When the cops ran up on us, he told me to say it was mine before he ran off with this other guy."

Damn, what a sucka, Denise thought. "Well, that right there should prove how much he loves you. No man should leave their girl or make her take the weight for his shit. But, we live and learn. What about your parents?"

"My moms doesn't really give a fuck about me because she's too busy trying to be a teenager herself. My dad robbed somebody and got caught, so he's upstate serving an 8½-15 year bid. Yo, my moms is grimy. That bitch is fucking with my pop's friend."

Denise suddenly became disgusted. She wasn't sure if it was from the story or the language. Although she was deep in the street, she never talked like that. She might've thought it, but to verbally refer to her mother as a bitch was totally disrespectful.

"You call your mother a bitch?"

Lexis looked at Denise and noticed the repulsive expression on her face. "I don't mean to, but she is. She treats me like shit. She's a bitch, yo."

Denise took a breath and tried to bite her tongue, but she couldn't. "Lexis, I don't give a shit how much you can't stand your mother or the things she does. Do not refer to her as a bitch! She gave you life, little girl. Therefore, you should be grateful for that."

Lexis put her head down. Suddenly, she didn't feel like talking anymore. Still staring at her, Denise felt somewhat sorry for her. She didn't mean to scream at her. "Hey, I didn't mean to sound so harsh, but you're a young lady, and while I don't know the relationship between you and your mother, you should never call her a bitch, especially to anyone. When you do that, it opens the door for others to say that, too. Now, she may be one at times, but don't call her one. That's all I'm saying."

Lexis peeked up at Denise, nodded her head, and smiled. "Okay, but she's doesn't act like my mother. You have to see how she dresses, like she's my age. That shit pisses me off, and to top it off, she's fucking my dad's best friend. I lost mad respect for her, yo."

Denise became more annoyed by the way she talked. "Lexis, what grade are you in?"

Caught off guard by the question, she stared at Denise for a second before lowering her head. "I didn't finish school, but I'm going back."

Denise figured that already. "What grade did you drop out?"

"Eighth grade. I plan on getting my GED. I just couldn't do high school. Yo, bitches be hating on me because I'm pretty and shit."

Denise sighed. "So you dropped out because of *bitches*?"

"Nah, but let's be real. What's high school gonna do for me? My moms didn't finish school, and we live in a nice condo, have a nice car, and mad niggas give her money because she's pretty."

Denise sat there amazed. *Does this little girl think her looks will be all she needs to the point that she doesn't need an education?* From where Denise was sitting, Lexis was average looking with a decent body, but she was certainly nothing to write home about. *If she thinks her looks are going to carry her through life, she's in for a short ride.*

"Well, I wish you the best of luck, but trust me, you will need an education because you will not look like that forever."

"I know, but hopefully, I will have already snagged my rich man."

Denise grinned. Lexis was hopeless. Therefore, she decided to leave that topic alone. Denise took her mink off and used it as a pillow so she could lie down. It was going to be a long night and she was tired. Denise closed her eyes and tried to go to sleep, while Lexis stood up.

"Denise?" Lexis called.

"Yes," she answered in a dry voice.

"Are you mad with me?"

Denise opened her eyes. "Huh? Why would you think that?"

"I don't know. You got quiet all of a sudden."

Denise sat up. "I'm not upset with you. However, I do feel sorry for you. If you think for one second that you don't need an education, then you're a fool. You stated you can't stand your mom because she tries to be young and messes with a lot guys. Well, she's doing that because she doesn't have anything else to fall back on. Once her looks fade, she's done, especially if she doesn't stash any money away. Do you want to be like your mother?"

Lexis frowned. She had never looked at it like that. "No, I don't wanna be like her."

"Well, if you don't go to school, then you will be just like her or maybe even worse. I have a niece. She's drop-dead gorgeous, but she works her ass off in school. When I asked her why, she said because she wants to be known for more than just her pretty face. Yeah, guys will treat you good and spoil you, until another pretty chick comes along," Denise emphasized.

"Yeah, I thought about that."

"Oh and another thing, a real man doesn't want a stupid girl. You're too pretty to talk like that. Using words like yo, bitch, and son...a lady should never talk like that. It's okay to talk slang, but at least try to refrain from using so much profanity."

Lexis lowered her head and stared at the floor. No one had ever talked to her about her behavior. All this time she assumed it was cute. Usually, she would put up a defense, but tonight, it seemed genuine coming from Denise. "I know, but when you grow up in the hood, it's hard."

Denise twisted her lips. "No, it's not. I ran with all dudes when I was younger, and yes, I spoke slang when it was necessary. However, I always carried myself like a lady. You see, Lexis, it's cool to hang out, but always remember you have to grow up. While I don't want to go too much into my past, I managed to finish school and even went on to obtain my Master's. Back in the day, I ran with a crew. Some might've called it a gang, but we didn't do stupid shit like y'all doing. We stuck together, and our leader made sure we at least graduated from high school. He told us in order to be rich, whether it's by selling drugs or buildings, you need to master reading, writing, and arithmetic. So, my point is whatever you do in life always make sure your education comes first."

Denise had a way with words. She just dropped a jewel on Lexis, something Greg did to her years ago. Hopefully, she planted the seed. Now it was up to Lexis to make it grow.

"Denise," Lexis said in a childlike voice

"Yeah, what's up?" Denise replied.

"I want to go back to school, but it's mad hard for me to read certain things. I watch my moms, who can't read for shit. She doesn't even know how to write. I don't wanna be like that."

"Well, don't be. Tomorrow explain to your lawyer your situation. Hopefully, since this is your first time getting arrested, they will give you a program and probation. If they do, get your ass back in school and leave that bum-ass nigga and gang alone. Get your life in order. Lexis, you're eighteen years old. It's time for you to grow up."

Lexis smiled. "I will...promise." She went over to Denise and hugged her. "Thank you."

Denise chuckled. "You're welcome, and start talking as if you got some sense. Don't go in there talking all that slang to your lawyer because they will think you're just another lowlife."

Lexis giggled, while walking back over to her side of the cell. "You talk slang?"

"Of course, I do," Denise replied. "I'm what you call a Phoenix. When you get a chance, look it up." "I'll remember that. Do you have any kids?"

"No, but hopefully, one day I will. Why?"

"Because you would make a great mom. I never had a conversation like that with my mother. We always end up arguing. Did you learn that from your mother?"

Denise laughed inside. She wished "Unfortunately, I didn't, but I learned you don't always learn things from your parents. They say it takes a village to raise a child, and fortunate for me, I had one."

Lexis, confused at the statement, just nodded. "Well, I'm happy we met, and I promise once I get outta here, I'm getting my shit together."

Denise leaned her head back against the wall. For the first time in a long time she felt good. She looked over at Lexis, who was making herself comfortable on the hard bench, and smiled. Even if Lexis doesn't do all the things Denise said, she knew Lexis would never forget this conversation.

It seemed like Denise only closed her eyes for five minutes, when Sonya banged on the cell.

"Here, I brought you guys some breakfast from McDonald's. Listen, I'm trying to get y'all paperwork moved up so y'all can get outta of here."

Denise yawned and stretched. Her body was killing her. She forgot how those damn benches felt and just being in that cage made her feel disgusted. She went up to the gate and grabbed the food.

"Thanks, Sonya," she said, then limped back over to the bench, separated the food, and handed Lexis a breakfast sandwich, hash brown, and small orange juice.

Just as Sonya was about to walk away, her relief entered the holding pen area.

"Oh, I see we have a celebrity up in here today," the C.O. commented with a smirk, while eyeing Denise's designer clothing.

Denise rolled her eyes. Female correction officers were the worse, and she figured they would fuck with her while she was in, giving them a reason to lose her paperwork. But, she wasn't going to give them the satisfaction. Besides, she was outnumbered. She was crazy, not stupid.

"Sonya, you better tell your friend her luck just ran out. This is my shift, and I don't do any favors."

Sonya looked at Evelyn and then at Denise, giving her a "don't even bother" look. The other C.O.'s had already put the word out about Denise.

"Evelyn, Dee will not give you any problems. Right, Dee?"

Denise almost choked on her juice, but she knew Sonya was warning her in a slick way. So, she glanced up at them and smiled.

After Evelyn and Sonya walked away to finish the count, Lexis whispered, "Why they don't like you?"

Denise giggled. "As I said, I've been locked up before. Besides, who knows why these bitches don't like me. I could care less. You see none of them came in here fucking with me, though."

Lexis' eyes widened. *Who is this chick?* she thought.

After Denise finished eating, she called Mr. Rubin, her attorney. He didn't pick up, so she left him a message on his cell phone with all the information. Then she laid back down on the bench and fell asleep, hoping that by the time she woke up they would be calling her for court.

When she finally did wake up, the shift had changed and another group of hoes was on duty. She looked around, but didn't see Lexis in the cell. *They must've called her for court.* She really hoped the young girl got her act together. *When the fuck are they going to call me?*

Having slept in her shoes, Denise's feet were killing her. The situation she was in reminded her of when she was out there hustling. She was scratching her head, when she heard, "Denise Taylor, let's go!" She jumped up and ran to the gate, where another C.O. was waiting.

"Don't come back here," were the C.O.'s departing words for her.

Denise was led downstairs and then upstairs to the courtroom. When she got there, Mr. Rubin's Jewish ass was standing there waiting for her. He glanced in her direction, and then motioned for her to give him one second because he was talking with the ADA about her case.

The court officer instructed Denise to have a seat until her lawyer came over to her. While waiting, she attempted to fix her hair and straighten out her clothing. She didn't want the judge to mistake her for a lowlife. When she looked over at Mr. Rubin, he signaled her to the lawyer and client booth.

She didn't even get to sit down, when Mr. Rubin yelled, "Jesus Christ, Denise! What the fuck are you doing with a gun?"

Denise slammed her hand on the desk. "I have a license for my gun."

Mr. Rubin fumbled through some papers. "Well, according to the serial numbers on the gun they found in the car, that's not it. Look over at the ADA. That's Assistant District Attorney Cox. She prosecuted Greg."

Denise knew her face looked familiar. She tried to charge Denise with accessory to murder and some other shit. *What the hell is she doing in the Manhattan Criminal Court?* she thought.

"She works here now?"

"Yeah, she left the Bronx a couple of months after Greg's trial, but I hear she's going back there."

Denise lowered her head and mumbled, "Great." This could not get any worse. "So what is she saying?" she asked with a frown.

"Dee, you know she wants you, but she doesn't have enough evidence. That's why she's asking for twenty thousand and another court date. Luckily, the gun is clean. It doesn't have any bodies on it. Still, she is trying to charge you with having a loaded weapon. We'll get the case dropped. Don't worry about that. I don't like the bitch either. In my opinion, she needs some dick," he said, then winked.

Denise felt relieved in a strange way. "So the gun was clean?"

"Yeah, why? It shouldn't be?"

Denise smiled. "No, I'm just surprised that the serial numbers didn't match since it is in fact registered."

"Let me tell you something. You're a smart girl who got another chance. Don't fuck it up. Greg busted his ass so people like you could make something of yourself. You owe it to him. Shit, you owe it to yourself. If you keep it up, there may not be a next time."

Denise glared at Mr. Rubin for a second, then threw her head back. He was so right. She might not get another chance. Unlike other snake-ass Jewish lawyers, Mr. Rubin did care about them. He was the one who actually helped Denise get a permit for her gun. She didn't know why Greg didn't use Mr. Rubin for his case. She was certain he would've beaten that trial.

"Dee, why didn't you call Gabrielle?" he asked, while handing her over a list of the criminal charges to review.

"Because I paid your ass a ton of money," she replied with a smile.

"That's true. Well, let's get you out of here, kiddo."

When Denise appeared in front of the judge, the court officer read off the charges. Then ADA Cox asked for one hundred thousand dollars in bail or some jail time.

Before Mr. Rubin could respond, the judge said, "Mrs. Taylor, I'm releasing you on your own recognizance, but you must report back to court on April 11, 2002, at nine thirty in the morning."

Denise turned to her lawyer, then looked over at ADA Cox and smiled. *That's what you get, bitch* Denise thought. After she was handed her court papers, she shook Mr. Rubin's hand, while he handed over the keys to her car, and she walked out.

Ahhh, the smell of fresh air. Denise smiled when she exited the courthouse. Being locked up for a day made her feel like she had missed so much. Just as she was about to flag down a cab, a black truck pulled up and the passenger side window was lowered. It was Perry.

"You need a ride?"

Denise frowned. "What are you doing around here?"

"I had some business to take care of. Do you need a lift or what?"

"Yes. Take me to the police impound. I need to get my car."

"Where the fuck are you coming from?"

Disgusted, Denise shook her head. "I was locked up."

"For what?" Perry snapped.

"A gun," she exhaled.

"Yo, Dee…"

"I know, Perry…" Denise sighed. "I know."

"Listen, sis, you made it. I mean, what does it take for you to leave them streets alone?"

"It had nothing to do with the streets. A dude…"

Before she could finish, Perry angrily interrupted her. "A fucking dude! What, is he tryna extort you?"

With her head lowered like an ashamed child, she replied, "No, it was over some bullshit. Let's just leave it alone."

"A nigga isn't worth your life or freedom, ma. You see the end results. I mean, what? You wanna join Greg in prison?"

"No, Perry…" Denise responded, getting aggravated. "Let's just leave it alone."

He looked at her and nodded. "A'ight, I'll leave it alone, but if you need me to step to someone, you let me know. You have too much shit going for yourself to fuck up."

"I know," Denise mumbled, her eyes filling up with tears.

After Perry dropped her off at the impound, she thanked him, then went inside the office to handle the paperwork before hopping into her car and speeding off. She couldn't wait to get home to take a bath and eat some good food. Thirty minutes later, she pulled into her building's garage. She looked at her clock on the dashboard and saw it was almost 9:00 p.m. Exhausted, Denise placed her head against the headrest. *This has been one helleva day. How the hell did the serial numbers on the gun not match?* This made Denise nervous. She felt like she was slipping, and when slip, you slide.

She looked in the glove compartment and saw her cell phone and small clutch purse were there. *Wow, I guess not all police are thieves.* Grabbing the items, she jumped out and proceeded to the elevator. While walking, she looked at her phone and saw she had about thirty missed calls. She didn't even bother listening to her messages. Instead, she threw the phone back in her clutch and got on the elevator.

Denise opened the door to her apartment and found Tony coming out of the living room.

"You're home, sis. I was worried about your ass," he said.

Denise looked confused. *What the fuck is he still doing here?*

"I'm alright. Why you are still here? Is Morgan alright?" she asked, while placing her keys and bag on the table.

Surprised by her question, Tony replied, "Yeah, I think she's upstairs sleeping. I haven't seen her since she came home from school. I chilled here all day just in case your ass called. Come on, you know I wasn't gonna leave Morgan by herself."

Denise sighed. "I didn't mean it like that. It's been a long day and I'm tired. Thanks for looking after Morgan for me. Does she suspect anything?"

Tony smiled and folded his arms. "She asked where you were when she came home from school, and I told her that you probably were still at Morris' crib. Listen, I have to go. Mike is downstairs. If there's anything you need, just holla."

Tony reached out to hug Denise, but she backed away from him.

"I stink."

He reached out and yanked her anyway. "Fuck outta here! You're my sister. I don't care if you stink," he said, hugging her tightly.

Denise pulled away and walked into the kitchen. She was starving. Tony looked up to see if Morgan was coming downstairs. When he noticed she wasn't, he walked into the kitchen.

"Dee, I'm out, and oh yeah, go wash that ass," he laughed before walking out of the door.

Denise poured some cranberry juice and walked upstairs to Morgan. She knocked on the door, but Morgan didn't answer. After knocking a little harder, Morgan called out for her to come in. Denise opened the door and turned on the light. Morgan had the window cracked open and was lying in bed.

"Hey, niece! What's up?"

"Hi, Auntie. Where were you?" Morgan asked, trying to sit up.

Denise entered the room and went to sit in the chair, when she noticed Morgan's cheeks were red and puffy.

"Why do you have the window open? It's freezing outside. And what happened to your face?"

Morgan pretended not to know what Denise was talking about. "Because I have gas. What's wrong with my face?" she asked, while rubbing her cheek.

Denise walked over to Morgan and touched her face. "Why is your face red and swollen?"

Morgan tried to jump up, but she fell back down. Her vagina was killing her. Still, she forced herself up. She was in so much pain that she limped over to the mirror. Denise noticed.

"Morgan, what's wrong with you? Your face is red and

you're limping. What happened?"

Morgan looked down, her eyes getting watery. "Nothing happened. I was working out and busted my butt, that's all. I was limping yesterday. Didn't you notice?"

Denise was tipsy and had run out of the house so quick that she figured she didn't notice. So, she decided to leave the conversation alone, especially since she didn't want Morgan to ask her any questions.

"Well, be careful. You're messing up your pretty face. I'm going to take a shower and take my ass to sleep. See you in the morning." When she turned to walk out, she noticed the sheets were changed. "Morgan, who changed the sheets?"

"I did. We change them every Saturday, remember?"

Denise slapped her forehead. "Oh yeah...sorry. It's been a long day."

Usually, Denise would kiss Morgan goodnight, but instead, she just walked out because she didn't want Morgan to smell her body odor. Once she was in her bathroom, she kicked off her shoes, removed her clothes, and jumped in the shower. After washing off the stench of the jail, she stepped out off the shower, grabbed a towel, and went into her bedroom. She was so exhausted that she didn't even both to apply lotion to her body. She snatched a t-shirt and some boy shorts out of the drawer, put them on, and jumped in the bed.

Although covered with the fatigue of the day, she couldn't sleep. She was still puzzled by the fact that the serial number of the gun she was caught with didn't match the gun she had registered. So, she got out of bed and went over to her safe where she kept her gun. She entered the code and opened it. The only thing inside was the money Tony gave her.

Baffled, she thought, *Where the hell is my gun?*

Chapter Two
Gabrielle

G abrielle lay in the bed thinking about Britney, playing her words over and over in her mind. Greg was messing with both of them at the same time. Maybe that's why Britney backed out of the deal.

She rolled over and looked at the clock. It was 4:30 a.m., and time for her to get up so she could prepare for her drive up to visit Greg. It had been two weeks since she'd visited him. Even though she missed the hell out of him, she couldn't help wondering how he felt about Britney.

Knowing there would be mountains of snow along the way, Gabrielle decided to drive her Tahoe. During the drive, a feeling she couldn't understand came over her. She never imagined she would be the other woman and always assumed if she found out Greg had been unfaithful, she would be angry. However, she wasn't. Instead, she actually felt sorry for Britney. Lost in her thoughts, before she knew it, she was pulling up to the facility.

As usual, she was processed and escorted to the visiting floor. Generally, she would walk into the vending machine area and purchase food, but today, she didn't. She sat there with her hands folded and hid her indignation. When Greg entered the visiting area with his face lit up, she stood up to greet him with a kiss and forced smile.

"Ah, baby, I miss you so much."

"Yeah, I miss you, too, boo," she responded, staring intensely at him.

"Is the vending area closed," he asked, noticing there wasn't any food on the table.

She took a deep breath and decided not to broach the subject at the present time. "No. What do you want?"

Beaming, he replied, "My usual, and if they have orange juice, get me one."

Gabrielle flashed her trademark smile and then switched away. After she was a few feet away, she turned around only to find Greg staring at her and smiling. *Cheating bastard,* she thought

Greg and Gabrielle always had good visits. They would laugh and talk like they were in the comfort of their own home, tuning the world out. However, today, Gabrielle seemed a little aloof.

"Boo, are you alright? Seems like something is on your mind," he asked when he noticed himself having to repeat himself a lot.

"No, I guess I'm a little tired. Didn't get much sleep last night because I was out with Denise."

"Oh, so you were chilling with Dee? How is my sis?" he inquired.

"She's fine. I told you that she's in the process of purchasing some building around y'all's old neighborhood."

Greg smiled like a proud father. Out of everyone on his team, he respected Denise the most. She was a triple threat. A phoenix, revolutionary, and the truth, just like his wife.

"That's good. I know it's only a matter of time before she takes over the real estate business. Which brings me to ask when are we gonna purchase some additional property?"

Gabrielle shrugged her shoulders. While she thought about

investing in real estate, she didn't feel like dealing with tenants. Before Greg got locked up, he owned two small buildings, and it seemed like once his tenants found out he was in jail, all hell broke loose. Gabrielle spent more money taking their asses to court than she received in rent. So, she finally sold the buildings.

"I don't know. I'm still recovering from the last building," she joked.

Greg laughed. "Well, let's look into Jersey or other states. Only New York allows that shit. Baby, real estate is a great investment."

"Alright, I'll look into it," she replied, brushing him off.

While Gabrielle watched him eat his breakfast sandwich, she thought about Britney, wondering if she ever visited Greg and why he still hadn't brought her up. Troubled by all of this, Gabrielle's mind started playing tricks on her. With all kinds of thoughts racing through her head, her eyes watered up, she started gasping for air, and she suddenly felt hot. Gabrielle jumped up and ran to the ladies' room to vomit. She didn't realize that hiding one's emotions wasn't easy, and that no matter how hard a person tried to bury the truth, it would always find a way to come out...literally.

After washing her face, Gabrielle returned to the visiting room and enjoyed the rest of the day with her husband. There were moments when she had to catch herself from saying slick shit to him. However, she decided if she was going to confront him, she would need more proof than some dumb-ass love letter. If it's one thing she learned it's what doesn't come out in the wash always comes out in the rinse.

As the visit came to an end, Greg embraced his wife. "Boo, you know I love you. Have a safe trip home, and I'll call you in the morning."

Gabrielle couldn't help but wonder if his words were sincere. Did Greg really love her?

"I love you, too," was all she could say.

As she turned around to smile and wave goodbye, she saw Britney's face, and immediately, her expression changed. She jetted out of the visiting room before she ended up blurting out something she would regret.

Four hours later, she pulled into her driveway. As she entered the house, her cell phone started ringing. It was her girl, Stevie.

"Hey, Stevie," she answered in a dry tone

"Gabby? Girl, what's wrong with you? Why the hell do you sound like that?"

"Sound like what?"

"Like you lost your best friend."

Only if you knew, she thought. "I just have a lot on my mind I guess," Gabrielle replied instead.

"Anything I can do to help?" Stevie asked. "You know I'm always here for ya."

Gabrielle took a deep breath. She really needed someone to talk to, and Stevie was just the person. So why was she reluctant to confide in her? Perhaps, deep down inside, Gabrielle was embarrassed that Greg could love someone else. Everyone always assumed her life was perfect. Hesitating for a second, she remembered the image her parents portrayed. Was she slowly turning into that? Is it true what they say about the apple not falling far from the tree? How could she be ashamed to tell her best friend about her marriage?

"Stevie, I found a love letter from one of Greg's ex."

"Okay. So what?"

"She wrote to him saying how sorry she was and how much she loved him."

"And, you're upset because she wrote him a love letter? Gabby, please! I'm sure a lot of women wrote him letters. You know women are sick. Don't get upset over stupid shit like that."

Gabrielle slid off her shoes in the foyer and walked into her lavish living room "That's not why I'm upset. It seems that

Britney and Greg had a relationship. She was his ride-or-die chick. She transported his drugs in and out of state. She was busted a few times…and gct this. The ADA that prosecuted Greg was her mother," Gabrielle explained in one breath.

Stevie was stunned and couldn't believe what she just heard. "Damn! Are you kidding me? How the hell did you find out all that shit?"

"Well, after I found the letter from her, I confronted Denise. You know she gave me some bullshit excuse at first, but she finally told me the truth. That's not the bad part, though. I tracked the girl down to a house in Queens and…" She paused to sigh. "I went to see her."

"You did WHAT! Gabrielle, are you crazy? You tracked her down and went to see her? You wanna join Greg in prison, don't you?" Stevie angrily stated.

"No! Nothing happened. We just talked. Somehow, I felt bad for her, even though she knew about me and was aware that Greg was married."

"Girl, you have lost your damn mind. So what happened?"

"Nothing. She slammed the door in my face and basically told me to leave her the fuck alone," Gabrielle chuckled, as she walked into the kitchen.

"Good. Leave her ass alone. Gabrielle, one thing I've learned is that some things are best left alone. Now I'm not saying to forgive Greg, but just don't jump to conclusions. You know us woman act on our emotions. You know we are emotionally unbalanced."

Both laughed

"Just don't ruin your marriage over something that happened years ago. I know one thing. You and Greg were meant for each other. He loves you…"

"Yeah, I know, but why didn't he tell me about her?"

"Because 'Y' is a crooked letter. Gotdamnit! Listen, if she can help your husband come home, I say go for it, but if you're upset because he slept with her, then you need to divorce him now. You knew you weren't Greg's first. Maybe his first love, but that man was fucking before y'all were married. Let it go!" Stevie said in an annoyed voice

"I am. I just needed to vent. Anyway, enough about me. What's going on with you?"

"I'm fine, girl," Stevie replied. "I forgot to tell you that I ran into Tony and his girlfriend. Talk about insecure. She had the nerve to walk up on us and introduce herself to me as his girl. Gabby, I almost died. Tony's cheating, abusive ass...girl, only if she knew!"

"What! So what did you do?" Gabrielle said, laughing her ass off

"Nothing. Shit, he's not my man. I smiled and went back over to my husband. Please, the only thing I care about is when the checks he sends me don't clear. Then we have a problem"

Again, both laughed.

"I know that's right. Well, he called me about a month ago wanting to visit Greg. You know I didn't pay his ass any mind. I told Denise she better watch him, but she claims they are like brother and sister."

"Yeah, well, Cane killed Abel. So, go figure."

Gabrielle chuckled. "Well, girl, I just got in. I'll call you later in the week."

"Alright, and listen, don't worry about that girl. You have too much to lose."

"Yeah, I know. Love ya."

"Love ya, too. Bye," Stevie said before hanging up.

While walking into her office, Gabrielle thought about what Stevie said. *Am I overreacting?* She went over to a file cabinet that contained Greg's trial transcripts. Until now, she never thought about going through it. She always felt it was too painful. She opened up the file drawer and pulled a big envelope that was sealed with thick tape. Taking a letter opener from inside her desk, she opened it.

As she read through the transcripts, her blood started

boiling. All of the prosecutor's witnesses testified that they had seen Greg shoot Charlie on August 25, 1992, but that was impossible because Greg wasn't even in New York. Gabrielle remembered that day. Greg had driven her down to Massachusetts to Harvard University for a seminar. *Why didn't Greg tell them he wasn't here?* The more she read, the angrier she became. Nothing added up.

Gabrielle tossed the file across the room. She'd had enough. It was time to expose this injustice, even if it meant losing her husband. Shit, she wasn't from the street. So, all of that "keeping it real" shit fell on deaf ears. *What's so great about keeping it real when you're serving life in prison?*

*****

It was Monday morning, and Gabrielle was sitting in her office determined to come up with a plan. However, she needed some assistance, and Tommy was just the person. With Tommy being a private investigator, he could dig up shit on the presidents. She wanted him to find all the witnesses that had testified against Greg and re-interview them because something about their testimony didn't add up. She also needed the gun ballistic report.

Greg had kept her in the dark about his case all these years, giving her false hope, and like the good naïve wife, she smiled and agreed. Well, today was a new day. Gabrielle was not that little upscale dick-crazy girl he met fifteen years ago. She wanted answers, and gotdamnit, she was going to get them.

Contemplating if she should tell Denise, Gabrielle decided not to. Knowing Denise, she would either talk her out of it or warn Greg. Just as Gabrielle was about to make a phone call, Abigail knocked on the door.

"Gabby, are you busy?" she asked, opening the door.

Gabrielle looked up. "No, come in."

Abigail entered and sat down. "Gabrielle, I need to take some time off. Most of my cases are settled. The ones that aren't I already briefed Thomas on them. I'm going through so much with my mother. She's back out there again."

Gabrielle was confused by Abigail's admission. *Her mother is back out there,* she thought.

"Okay. Well, family comes first. But, may I ask what do you mean by 'out there'?"

Abigail took a deep breath. She didn't like discussing her mother's addiction. "Gabrielle," she sighed, "my mother is a heroin addict. She's been using since I was a teenager. My dad introduced it to her. She stops every now and then. But, she's back out there using."

Gabrielle eyes widened. She always assumed Abigail came from a prestigious family. *Guess you can't judge a book by its cover,* she thought.

"Sorry to hear that. Where did you grow up?"

Abigail smirked. She knew Gabrielle would be shocked at her confession. "I grew up in Alpine, New Jersey. My father was a top surgeon at NYU, and my mother…well, before the drugs, she was one of Forbes best real estate agents. I know you're wondering how the drugs got into my home. Well, my father's mistresses turned him on to crack and then heroin. When my mother found out, instead of leaving him, she joined him. She thought maybe if she participated it would make him love her more. Instead, she became an addict. You would think after my dad died of an overdose my mother would stop, but she hasn't. "

"Tragic. Abby, I had no idea. Well, take as much time as you need," Gabrielle said, reaching for Abigail's hand.

Abigail thanked Gabrielle and started to walk out, when she turned around and said, "You know, love makes you do the craziest things."

Gabrielle nodded. "Indeed it does."

Abigail shook her head in agreement and walked out. Her words penetrated Gabrielle's soul. Was she that in love with Greg that she overlooked his flaws? Gabrielle stood and walked over to the window. She often wondered what her life would be like if she didn't meet Greg. She leaned her head against the window as a single tear rolled down her face. *How did I get here?*

Knock...knock!

Gabrielle wiped her eyes and answered, "Yes."

Nancy walked in. "Boss lady, Kyle is here to see you."

Gabrielle exhaled noisily, rolled her eyes, and said, "Send him in."

"Okay." Nancy giggled before closing the door.

Gabrielle looked herself over and walked to her desk. She forgot about her meeting with him. She searched for his file on her desk. She wanted this to be a quick meeting. *Yes, I found it.*

Kyle walked in. "Gabrielle, it's always a pleasure."

Forming a pathetic smile, she replied, "The pleasure is all mine, Kyle. I have all of your paperwork here, and it's signed I might add. In addition, I've contacted a bank in London who has agreed to take your money. A colleague of mine works out there. He's good and will personally handle all of your business affairs," Gabrielle beamed.

Kyle smiled. He knew she would come through for him. "Wow! I'm impressed, Gabrielle. And to think I almost doubted you."

Gabrielle rubbed the bottom of her chin. "Why in the world would you do that?"

"You're a gem! However, I'm curious why you're not handling my London affairs. You know I don't like dealing with new lawyers?"

Is this motherfucker crazy? After all the shit I had to go through to set up his accounts?

"Kyle, I am not an international attorney...yet. That's why it's always good to do your homework first. Nonetheless, he's one of the best attorneys in the United Kingdom. Don't you trust me?" she stated with an impish grin.

"Hmmm…is that a rhetorical question? I trust you. However, if I didn't know any better, I would guess you're trying to get rid of me," he responded as a remark, but really wanting an answer.

"Well, Kyle, the thought has crossed my mind," she laughed, "but you're one of my best clients. A pain in the ass, but you believe in me. Therefore, I will be forever grateful."

Kyle smiled.

"Don't worry. I will still handle all of your U.S. affairs. Who else is gonna put up with your shit?" she said, then winked.

There was something about Gabrielle's aura that captivated Kyle. He wanted her so badly that he could feel an erection coming on. Kyle reached across the desk and snatched Gabrielle's hands.

"Let's fly to Brazil for the weekend."

Gabrielle snatched her hand away from him. "Have you lost your mind? First of all, I'm married, and secondly, I do not date my clients."

"So drop me as your client."

"Kyle, get the hell out of here."

"You know I'm so attracted to you," he boasted.

"So noted," Gabrielle replied, as she gathered his papers together.

Kyle leaned back in the chair. He hated when she rejected him in a subdued way. "Can I at least take you to dinner?"

Gabrielle looked up at him, trying to see if there was something appealing about him. She never really looked at him, so maybe she missed it. He was scrawny looking, had stringy hair, and you could see his brains through his nostrils. He did wear some expensive suits, but it was too bad he didn't have the body to fill them out. *Nah,* she thought

"I'll tell you what. Go to London, check it out first, and

when you come back, we'll go out to dinner."

Kyle grinned. He knew she was brushing him off. He stood up and leaned forward over the desk. "Don't knock it until you try it, babe."

Gabrielle rolled her eyes. *Is he serious?* She stood up and handed Kyle a file with all of the information in it, trying not to show her disgust. "Have a safe trip" she said, while escorting him to the door.

Just then, Nancy announced over the intercom that Joan was on the other line.

"Hello, Joan."

"Gabrielle, did you reach out to their attorney?"

"Yes, and given the incriminating evidence, they have agreed to our terms, providing we turn over all material to them and sign a confidentiality agreement."

"What are they giving me for all of this?" Joan asked in a disappointing voice.

"You're getting three years' worth of salary, an additional ten million, five percent of the stocks, health benefits for the next five years, and a recommendation letter. I think you made out great."

"Um, I beg to differ. But, oh well."

"What do you mean, Joan? Speak your mind," Gabrielle said, rolling her eyes.

"Well, I'm not happy with the deal. I think we could have gotten more."

"What exactly were you hoping to get? You were blackmailing them, which is a crime itself. Joan, getting fired from a job isn't a crime, and trust me, I'm pretty sure they have some dirt on you."

Joan remained silent. Gabrielle did have a point. Just by being associated with them, it could ruin her reputation, not to mention her family.

"I guess. I just hate that these fuckers are getting away with shit like this," she finally said.

"Who said they're getting away with it?"

Both chuckled.

"I knew you wouldn't. Well, send the papers over to me so I can sign them. And, Gabby, make sure you bring those sick bastards down."

"With pleasure," Gabrielle replied with a laugh.

Chapter Three
Morgan

It had been a couple of weeks since Morgan was raped. While trying to be strong, there were days when she would burst into tears. Every time she closed her eyes, she replayed the scene over and over in her head, oftentimes blaming herself and figuring she had led him on.

This vibrant, outgoing young lady was gradually sinking into a depression. There were mornings when she'd force herself out of bed, and she became so withdrawn from the world that she didn't feel like doing anything. All her dreams were washed away when Tony sexually assaulted her. Automatically assuming her classmates knew what happened, Morgan would walk in the opposite direction when she saw them. When she did bump into any of them, she avoided eye contact.

One gloomy afternoon, Morgan decided to skip dance practice and go home. On her way out of the school's doors, she ran into Chloe.

"Hey, girl, are you okay? You've been a little reserved lately."

"Hi, Chloe! I'm fine. Just have a lot on my mind. Why, do I

look different?" Morgan inquired.

"No, you look good. You just look like you don't want to be bothered. Did I do something wrong?" Chloe asked.

Suddenly, Morgan's eyes filled with tears. *Maybe I should tell Chloe what happened,* she thought, but then she remembered what Tony said about hurting her family.

"No, girl, I've just been going through something."

"Well, let me know if you need to talk," Chloe said as she walked off.

Noticing a group of kids coming towards her, Morgan immediately went in the other direction, walking towards the FDR highway. Even though it was only four o clock, it was getting dark outside. She stood on the corner waiting for the signal for her to cross the street, when a black SUV pulled up beside her. She quickly backed up from the curb, thinking it was trying to park. However, a tall guy jumped out and walked over to her. She glanced at the guy and was about to cross the street, when he grabbed her arm.

"Someone wants to talk to you," he whispered.

Morgan frantically looked around. *Great! No one would hear me scream,* she thought, realizing she was one block away from the highway. She had to think fast.

"Get off of me," she said, snatching her arm away.

The big, tall, white guy released her arm and looked over at the truck as the window rolled down. Morgan looked over, as well, and her nightmare came back to haunt her. It was Tony. He poked his head out just enough so she could see him. She wanted to run but couldn't. She appeared to be brave but was trembling inside. Tony's driver looked around, then escorted her to the car. Morgan was so scared that she didn't bother putting up a fight. Once she was inside, the driver stood outside and smoked a cigarette.

"What's up?" Tony said, staring straight ahead.

"Hello, Tony," she mumbled, while staring at the floor.

He smiled and touched her knee. "I missed you."

Morgan jumped. "Tony, I really have to go. Denise is meeting me here."

Tony looked around. "Denise is meeting you on the FDR?"

Shit! Morgan forgot she was near the highway. "No, not here, but I have to go," she said, trying to open the door.

Tony grabbed her by the wrist. "Why are you lying? Since when does Denise pick you up? What, you scared of me now?" Tony asked with an impish grin.

Morgan shook her head, praying it was a dream. "Tony, I really have to go," she repeated in a scared tone.

"A'ight, well, let's go." He tapped on the window, letting his driver know he was ready.

Morgan was about to get out, when Tony grabbed her.

"You're not going anywhere."

She peeked over her shoulder and fell back in her seat as the SUV pulled off.

Morgan was sure they had driven for at least an hour, ending up at a house in a wooded area of New Jersey. When they pulled up, Tony instructed his driver to come back in a couple of hours. Then he opened the door to the house and led her inside.

"You want something to drink?" he asked.

Petrified, Morgan shook her head no and just stood in the middle of the hallway with her book bag on her back. "Tony, I really have to go," she explained.

Tony went up to her. "You'll leave when I say so."

Morgan dropped her head. She could not believe this was happening again. As tears started to roll down her face, she begged Tony to let her go, but he ignored her.

Tony snatched Morgan's book bag off of her. "Chill out and go sit the fuck down," he commanded.

Morgan went into the living room and sat on the couch. She took a deep breath and prayed that she was just overreacting. *He probably wants to apologize,* she hoped.

After Tony finished checking the rooms and closets, he sat

beside Morgan and grabbed her face. "Did you tell anyone about what happened? Because I meant what I said about killing your family," he mumbled in a calm tone.

"I haven't said anything," Morgan wept.

"You see, I knew you were smart," he stated, pushing her head back.

Why is he doing this to me? she thought, as she started to cry harder. She tried to get up off the couch, but Tony yanked her back down.

"Did I say you could move?"

She glanced over at him and saw that his eyes were filled with rage.

"No, sorry," she mumbled.

Tony got up and stood over her. "Take off your clothes." When Morgan just looked at him, he immediately became annoyed. "Yo, did you hear what I said?" He snatched her up to her feet. "Take off your fucking clothes."

She closed her eyes and prayed it was a bad dream. "Tony, please," she cried. "I haven't said anything."

Without warning, Tony backhanded her, sending her flying over the couch.

"Get the fuck up and take off your clothes!"

Traumatized, Morgan held her face and then immediately started removing her clothes as quickly as possible, but she wasn't moving fast enough because Tony flew into a rage. He grabbed her up by the neck and dragged her into the bedroom. In just her panties and a bra, she tried to wiggle away, while blocking her face at the same time.

"Tony, I'm sorry," she cried.

"Nah, you think I'm playing with you. I'm gonna teach you a lesson."

"No, please!" she screamed fearfully.

Tony slammed Morgan against the wall. "The next time I tell you to do something, you better do it. You fucking hear me!"

With her hand covering her face, she nodded yes.

Tony grabbed her and flung her on the bed. Then he jumped on her, putting his knee between her legs while huffing and puffing. She tried to squirm from underneath him, but he overpowered her.

"Please stop! I'll do it...whatever you want me to do," she sobbed.

"That's what I like to hear," he said, out of breath.

Tony took off his clothes, while Morgan removed her underwear. Uncertain of what to do next, she sat on the edge of the bed scared to death.

"You better not ever deny me. You understand?" he walked over to her and said.

Morgan nodded, while crying and shaking uncontrollably. Frightened to move, she asked could she use the bathroom. Tony said yes, and she walked in the bathroom to look in the mirror at her lip that was bleeding. She tried to clean it up, but Tony busted through the door butt-naked.

"What the fuck is taking you so long?" he snapped.

Morgan jumped and tried to explain, but Tony just dragged her by the hair into the bedroom.

"I don't have all fucking day." He pushed her on the bed and jumped on her.

Before she knew it, he was inside of her. Morgan closed her eyes and prayed it would soon be over.

Once he finished, Morgan asked if it was okay to take a shower since she couldn't go home looking disheveled and smelling like sex. Tony agreed, but she had to leave the bathroom door open. When she stepped into the shower and began to wash, she noticed she was bleeding. *Oh no,* she thought.

Tony walked in and saw this, as well. "That's why I need to fuck you everyday so you can stop bleeding."

Ignoring his comment, she got out of the shower and started to put her clothes back on.

"If you breathe one fucking word, I'll kill you. You understand?" he mumbled, while grabbing her by the neck.

Unable to breathe, Morgan nodded her head in agreement. When he released her, she dropped to the floor gasping for air.

Tony kneeled down and lifted her up. "Finish getting dressed. We have to go."

While dressing, he informed her that someone would pick her up on the same corner around two o'clock the next day.

"Tony, I can't. I'm going out to dinner with my mother. It's my little brother's birthday."

He walked over to her. "Have your ass out there at two."

"Tony, I..." Before she could finish, he slapped her across the face, causing her to fall back into the dresser.

Tony charged at her and said, "You want me to put my hands on you, huh? You better have your ass out there tomorrow. You hear me!"

Morgan covered to shield herself from his blows. "Yes, Tony," she cried, while trembling.

Tony grabbed her up by the hair, forcing her to look directly into his face. He wanted her to see the fury in his eyes; he needed to instill fear in her. Before they left out the door, Tony ordered her to go and wash her face.

On their way back to the city, Tony talked on the phone, conducting business as if nothing happened, while Morgan sat there in trepidation. Afraid to look up at him, she stared out the window until they were a block away from her building, where Tony ordered his driver to pull over and get out.

He turned towards Morgan. "I'll see you tomorrow. Don't be late. Oh, and remember what I said about not telling anyone."

"Tony...I can't."

Tony looked at her, then glanced down at his Rolex. "You need to get going so you can call your mother and cancel."

Morgan lowered her head. It was pointless talking to him. Just as she was about to exit the vehicle, Tony yanked her back by the nape of her neck and forced his tongue down her throat.

"Goodnight," he said with a smile, as Morgan got out and slowly walked into the apartment.

*****

The next morning when Morgan woke up, she decided she'd had enough of Tony's crap. Denise offered her breakfast, but Morgan declined. She was already late for track practice. As she jetted out the door to avoid her aunt from seeing her slightly bruised face, Morgan yelled, "Don't forget I'm having dinner with Mommy tonight, so I'll be home late."

"Alright. Call me when you get to your mother's house."

"Okay."

Even though she didn't feel up to it, Morgan went to practice. She really needed something to take her mind off of this horrific situation she found herself in. After practice, she headed to class, and while on her way, she ran into Julissa.

"Hey, Morgan, what's up? Girl, what happened to your face?" Julissa asked, trying to get a better look.

Morgan turned white. She didn't think it was that noticeable. "It's no biggie. I hit my face on the cabinet while reaching for some sugar."

Julissa laughed. "Girl, I do that shit all the time. Hey, are you coming to Monica's party? You should come. It's going to be nice. It's at Chelsea Piers."

Not wanting to say no, she replied, "I'll see," before running off to class.

Throughout the day, Morgan kept looking at the time. It seemed like it was going by so fast. It was already lunchtime, and since she knew Tony would be outside waiting for her, she decided to leave at one o'clock. She grabbed her book bag and snuck out the side door. Once outside, she pulled out her cell phone and called her mother.

"Hey, Mommy, I got out of school early, so I was thinking

maybe I could meet you out in Brooklyn."

Surprised by the offer, Jasmine responded, "You don't have dance practice? You know your sister and brother aren't even home from school yet."

Morgan looked around nervously to make sure no one was watching her. "I don't have practice today," she replied, praying her mother would say yes.

"Okay, sweetie. You remember how to get here? Don't talk to no one and get in the conductor cart. I'll meet you at the train station," Jasmine told her.

With a sigh of relief, Morgan said, "Thank you. I'm on my way," and hung up.

Before she knew it, the train pulled into her stop, so she got off and headed for the exit. When she reached outside, she saw her mother walking towards her.

Excitedly, she waved and yelled, "Mommy!"

Her mother waved back. When they got face to face, Jasmine reached out to kiss Morgan and hug her tightly. "Hi, baby. I missed you so much."

"I missed you, too, Mommy."

Jasmine took a step back to look at her firstborn. Morgan was growing into a beautiful young lady.

"What happened to your face?" she asked, touching her cheek.

At first, Morgan pretended not to know what she was talking about. "What?"

"Here!" Jasmine pointed.

Morgan started to tell her mother what happened, but she remembered what Tony had said. "Nothing. I fell dancing."

Jasmine hugged her again. "Next time, be careful."

Morgan and her mother went to pick up her brother and sister from school because they wanted to surprise them.

"So what's new?" Jasmine asked.

Morgan sighed and put her head down. *Besides being raped and beaten?* she thought.

"Nothing's new. School is kicking my butt. Oh, and I got into Harvard Law School for the summer. Remember that program I was telling you about for inner-city kids," she replied, flashing a fake smile.

"Yeah, I remember. That's great. I'm so proud of you."

"Thanks."

"Listen, I have some wonderful news, too. Remember when I told you that I couldn't attend your dance recital because I had to go visit a school I found for your brother? Well, it's affordable, and his father's insurance will cover eighty percent of it," Jasmine informed her.

Morgan paused in her tracks. "Really?" Her eyes widened.

Jasmine chuckled. "Yep. It's the school in Atlanta that I was telling you about. He was interviewed and accepted for the fall. So, we have to move down there."

"Atlanta? All of us?" Morgan asked.

"Well, your brother and sister yes. That's why I wanted to talk to you…to see if you wanted to come with us."

"Atlanta?" Morgan repeated.

"Yeah, and like I told you before, I would love for all of my children to be with me, but I know you just started at Dalton. So, I would understand if you wanna stay here with Denise until you graduate. It's fine. But, remember, I'm still your mother and have the final say."

Morgan giggled. "I know, Mommy, but I wanna come with you. I don't want to live up here no more."

Jasmine was surprised my Morgan's statement. She looked at her child with one eyebrow raised. "Is this my child Morgan, the one that begged me to live in Manhattan?"

Morgan busted out laughing. "Yes, it's me. I just wanna be with you." *And away from Tony,* she thought.

"Okay, but I want you to think about it first before making your final decision."

"Alright," Morgan whined.

As they approached Michael and Monique's school, Morgan

could hear her sister screaming her name from afar. While Monique ran towards them, with Michael right behind her, Morgan and her mother looked at each other and laughed. Her little sister wrapped her arms around Morgan as soon as she reached her.

"Morgan, you're here!"

Morgan's eyes filled up with tears. "Yes, I'm here. I wanted to surprise you. Surprise!"

Michael grabbed Morgan by the waist. "Hey, big sis," he said with a broad smile.

After walking back to the train station, they took it to 42nd Street. Since it was Michael's birthday, he wanted to see a movie and have dinner in Times Square. When they reached their destination, Michael and Monique almost lost their minds, screaming and pointing at the big, bright buildings.

Jasmine purchased four tickets to the 5:30 p.m. showing for *Shrek*. After the movie, they went across the street to Applebee's, where Jasmine had already arranged for a cake to be delivered. Happy to be with her family, Morgan smiled and enjoyed their time together.

When Jasmine looked at her watch, she saw it was almost nine o'clock. Therefore, she asked the waiter to bring the cake so they could sing happy birthday. She had a long train ride home and didn't want the kids out too late, not to mention she had to take Morgan home first.

After they sang happy birthday and had a small slice of cake, Jasmine had the leftover cake packaged to take home with them, and once they exited the restaurant, she flagged down a cab to Denise's house. As the driver sped through traffic, Morgan thought about Tony, wondering if he showed up at her school today.

When the cab pulled in front of building, Morgan thought her mother was just going to drop her off, but instead, Jasmine told Michael and Monique to get out. As Morgan unlocked the door and entered, Denise was walking back into the living room.

"Hey, niece." She didn't see the rest of them behind Morgan until she opened the door wider. "Jas, Michael, Monique...hey, guys." Denise walked over and hugged them. She and Jasmine exchanged kisses on the cheek, and then she diverted her attention back to her niece and nephew. "What's up, Mike? Did you enjoy your birthday? Auntie is going to take you out this weekend so you can pick out a gift. Okay? Tony, guess who's here."

Morgan froze as Tony emerged from the living room.

"Jas, what's up? Oh shit, you brought the gang with ya." He smiled and extended his arms to give her a hug.

"Tony, I didn't know you were here. Yeah, today's Michael's birthday, so I took the kids out to the movies and dinner."

Morgan felt like sprinting out of there, but her feet felt like they were cemented to the floor. Avoiding his stares, she tried to sneak up stairs, but Michael called out to her.

"Morgan, where are you going?"

Morgan turned around. "Up to my room. You wanna come?"

"I wanna come, too," Monique screamed.

"She wasn't talking to you," Michael teased.

"I can go, right, Morgan?" her sister asked.

Morgan threw her head back. "Both of you can come."

Michael ran first towards the stairs, pushing Monique along the way.

"Stop it, Michael! Mommy!"

Jasmine walked over and in a stern voice said, "Cut it out, you two...now."

Denise laughed. "And your ass wonders why I don't have any."

"Don't remind me," Jasmine replied, while shaking her head.

As Tony followed them into the living room, he asked, "So,

Jas, you took the kids out, eh? That's what's up. Did Michael's dad go with y'all?"

Taking off her coat, she replied, "No, Big Mike had to work, but he's taking Michael to the space museum this weekend. I just wanted the kids to be with Morgan since they don't see her often."

Tony nodded. *So she was telling the truth.*

After a few minutes, Jasmine announced that she should be going since it was nearly eleven o'clock and they had to take the train back home.

"Why didn't you drive?" Denise asked.

"Because I didn't feel like dealing with traffic," she replied.

"You know what, take my car. I'll pick it up this weekend," Denise offered.

"No, Dee. I'll just take a cab back to the train station."

"Jas, let my driver take you home. He can drop me off and then take you guys straight to Brooklyn. Don't get on the subway this late with the kids," Tony stated.

She looked over at Tony and Denise. "Alright," she finally replied.

Jasmine was about to call her children downstairs, when Tony offered to get them since he needed to use the bathroom. When he reached the top of the stairs, he heard the kids in the bedroom fighting. Then hearing someone in bathroom, he turned and looked in that direction. He knew it had to be Morgan.

When Morgan opened the door, Tony bum-rushed her, forcing her back inside.

"You think you're real fucking funny."

Morgan almost passed out. "Oh my god, Tony," she mumbled. "I told you that I was going out to dinner with my family."

Tony grabbed her by the shoulder. "And I told you to cancel. Ay yo, have your ass out there tomorrow. If you don't, you'll see what can happen," he said in an angry tone and walked out. "Michael and Monique, let's go!" he yelled, knocking on Morgan's bedroom door.

"Where are we going?" they asked in unison after opening the door.

Tony glanced over at Morgan and smiled. "I'm taking you home."

Morgan trembled. *Oh no! He's going to hurt them.* She reached out and touched his hand. "Tony, please don't hurt them. I will be out there tomorrow. Please," she cried.

As the kids ran down the stairs, Tony went back over to Morgan and said, "You better." Then he left without another word.

That night, Morgan didn't get any sleep. Instead, she lay wide awake crying. The next day, she didn't want to go to school, but she knew Denise would ask her a bunch of questions. She also thought about what would happen to her family if she didn't show up. So, she got dressed and headed to school.

As the day went by, Morgan thought about Tony, and every time she contemplated leaving school she remembered his threatening words. Walking to the vending machine to get a bottle of cranberry juice, she realized it was almost two o'clock. *Oh no! Tony will be mad if I'm late.* Worried, she ran down the block, but when she got to the corner, she didn't see the truck. Just as she was about to walk away, a black car came speeding down the street. It was Al; he was running late.

"Get in," he ordered.

Initially, Morgan was reluctant to get in. *What if Tony's not in the car?* She looked around and hesitated.

"Get in," Al yelled, causing her to flinch.

Afraid of the consequences if she didn't, Morgan got in. Once inside, she noticed Tony wasn't in there. She tried to get out, but Al sped off onto the highway.

"Where's Tony?" Morgan asked, but the driver ignored her. "Hello! Where's Tony?" she repeated louder.

"I'm taking you to him," he mumbled.

Morgan took a deep breath, sat back, and looked out the window. Before she knew it, Al was pulling up to the house. Since Tony wasn't in the car, she was able to get a good look at the area. The house was surrounded by trees and sat right off a dead-end road. Morgan swallowed hard and took a deep breath. No wonder he brought her here. No one could hear her scream. She looked out the window and noticed the front door open. After getting out the car, she turned and watched as Al drove away, leaving her standing there alone. She then looked at the house and started walking slowly to it. A part of her felt like turning around and running, but where could she run to. The closer she got to the house, the faster her heart started beating.

When she got inside, Tony was standing there with his arms folded. "Took you long enough."

"Sorry," she mumbled, as if she had control over the driver's arrival.

Morgan dropped her bag on the floor and was about to sit down, but she remembered what happened the last time she moved without permission. While staring at the floor and waiting for his instructions, she saw his shadow moving from her peripheral vision. She was about to look up, when everything went dark momentarily. The force of Tony's hand sent her flying back into the door, damn near knocking her out of her shoes.

"The next time you disobey me, I'm going to fuck you up. You understand me?" he shouted, walking away.

With her hand covering her face, Morgan cried in pain. "Yes."

Tony looked over, and seeing that she was still on the floor, he immediately went over to her and dragged her by the hair.

"I'm gonna teach you a lesson. You're gonna learn to respect me."

Morgan tried desperately to plant her feet on the ground so she could pull away from him, but he was too strong. "Tony, please, I'm sorry."

He turned around and threw her up against the wall. "The next time I tell you something and you don't do it, I'm gonna beat the shit out of you. You fucking hear me?"

With mucus running from her nose and tears rolling down her face, Morgan shook her head yes.

He backed away from her. "Undress."

Sobbing, Morgan instantly took off her clothes. She was about to leave her underwear on, but removed that, too.

With a ferocious glare, Tony grabbed her by the neck and threw her on the bed. As he started to remove his clothes, his cell phone rang. It was Christina, his girlfriend.

"Yo, I'm in the middle of something right now. I'll call you back," he told her, then hung up before she could respond.

Morgan just laid there and watched as Tony continued to take off his clothes. Just looking at Morgan made him rock hard. He was bulging out of his boxers. When he caught her peeking at it, he said, "It's big, right," while smiling and rubbing it. He then got on top of Morgan and spread her legs. She wanted to close them but was scared. As he shoved inside of her, she began to cry silently.

"Ahhh, this is sweet," he moaned.

Morgan tightened her stomach, trying to hold in the pain, but it was unbearable. So, she tried to close her legs.

Tony lifted up a little. "Ay, yo, open your legs. You want me to beat the shit out of you?"

Morgan mumbled, "No."

"Then open them. I want them open wide like you're doing that yoga shit."

She turned her head so she was facing the window and opened her legs wider.

"Yeah, like that. I knew them legs could open wider." Tony slid back in and pounded her so hard that her body jerked. She was in too much pain to say anything. She just laid there with tears rolling down her face.

Oddly, he couldn't last long inside her, and once it was over, she laid there with her vagina numb and throbbing from the horrendous amount of pain. She wanted to go to the bathroom but was afraid to move.

Tony laid there next to her trying to catch his breath, while Morgan curled up in a fetus position. To her horror, he turned her back over and was on top of her again. They had sex for another forty-five minutes, and by the time they were done, she couldn't even stand up. Her inner thighs were black and blue.

Exhausted, Tony looked at the time and saw it was almost eight-thirty. He didn't realize it was that late. They didn't even have time to take a shower.

"Yo, get dressed."

Morgan tried to get up, but collapsed back on the bed due to the numbness of her legs. She tried again, this time using her hand as leverage.

Tony jumped out to go urinate. "Morgan, let's go!"

Barely able to stand, Morgan staggered a few times, causing Tony to notice it.

"What's wrong with you?" he asked.

"Nothing," she mumbled, while putting on her shoes.

Tony pulled out his cell phone. "We're ready," he told Al, while walking over to Morgan. "Make sure you have your ass out there tomorrow."

No, not again, she thought.

"I have practice tomorrow. I can't afford to miss it."

Tony lifted her face up by her chin. "Sorry, I didn't hear you."

Morgan glanced down at the floor. "Nothing," she replied, knowing if she would've repeated it, he would knock the shit out of her.

While grabbing his jacket off the chair, he glanced over at Morgan, who was leaning against the wall. "I'm going to bring some porno tapes so you can learn," he said, walking over to her.

Not knowing how to respond, she stared at the floor.

Tony touched her face. "Don't worry. After a few more sessions, it won't hurt anymore.

Afraid to say anything, she just ignored his comment.

"Yo, let's go. He's here," he told her when he saw his driver coming up the road.

On the car ride home, Morgan looked out the window or down at the floor while Tony conducted business on his cell phone. During the ride, he reached over and rubbed her legs. When she flinched, he shot her a nasty look and forced her legs open. She wanted to push his hands away, but knew it would cause her to get hit again. So, she just allowed him to rub his hand up her thighs.

After Al pulled over once they were a block away from Morgan's apartment, he got back to smoke a cigarette and to give Tony some privacy.

"Morgan, I'm not playing with you. I wanna see you tomorrow. If you have me waiting…"

Before he could finish, Morgan interrupted. "Tony, I have practice. Can I come at four instead of two-thirty? I promise I'll be out there. If I don't go to practice, they'll call Aunt Denise or my mother."

Tony thought about it. She did have a point. He did not want them to start speculating anything.

"A'ight. I'll pick you up at four, but you better have your ass out there."

Morgan nodded and was about to get out of the car, when Tony snatched her by the arm and forced his tongue down her throat like he had done before. Still in pain, she exited the car and proceeded to limp the rest of the way home. When she got inside the apartment, she found Denise in the living room reading some papers. After quickly saying hello to Denise, she went straight upstairs.

Chapter Four
Tony

After dropping Morgan off, Tony instructed Al to take him to the studio on 58th Street, where Christina was doing a photo shoot. He decided he would go see her since he had been neglecting her lately. He wondered how much longer Christina would put up with his bullshit. In truth, he didn't know how much longer he would tolerate hers. Tony had a huge sexual appetite that Christina couldn't satisfy, which caused him to think about Morgan, who he called a *phenomenal woman*: beauty, brains, and a sexy body. Because she possessed those attributes, Tony couldn't get enough of her.

He leaned back, closed his eyes, and thought of Morgan. In a disturbing way, her fear was a boost to his ego. Not only did it help his self-esteem, he also felt respect. All his life, Tony had been labeled a sucker, and no one really respected him because they knew he was a chump. But, Morgan knew different. He saw the fear in her eyes and loved it. Tony wanted to love Morgan. She was everything he had ever wanted, and he hoped to marry her someday. So why was he doing this to her? He decided he would make it up to her the next day by showing her that's he's not such a monster after all.

When Tony arrived at the studio, a security guard led him upstairs to where Christina was located. Just as he was about to enter the suite, Christina and her entourage were on their way out. Tony noticed Mookie, his right-hand man and business partner, was with them.

"I didn't know you were coming," Christina said, trying not to appear shocked.

"Yeah, I called and Joyce answered your phone. What's up, Mook?" Tony said in a snide tone and a wary look on his face.

"Hey, I just stopped by to check on Chris, you know," Mookie explained, while Tony nodded.

Christina grabbed Tony's arm and started beaming. She loved when he got jealous. Leaning her head on his shoulders, she guided him back to the elevator.

"Baby, I'm so happy you're here. You should've seen your girl. I was killin it," she grinned.

As they rode down in the elevator, Tony held Christina around her waist while glancing at Mookie from the corner of his eye. Mookie must've felt Tony's vibe because as soon as the door opened, he hurried out saying he had to stop by the office to catch up on some paperwork.

Tony flashed a fake smile and continued to walk to his car with Christina. Once inside, Christina snuggled under his arm.

"Tony, I missed you. I'm so glad you stopped by."

Tony, who was still puzzled about Mookie with Christina, replied in a laid-back tone, "Yeah, I'm glad, too. What was Mookie doing there?"

Christina sat up straight in her seat and took a deep breath. *Why the fuck do you care? You haven't been spending time with me,* she thought.

"He was in the building with Addotta, and when he found out I was there, he decided to stop by," she explained in a sweet tone. "Tony, it's nothing."

"I know. I just wanted to make sure," he responded, then

gave her a peck on top of her head. Still, he didn't trust dudes in the business. He knew they wanted Christina.

Once they arrived at Tony's apartment building, they were escorted upstairs. Tony held Christina close by his side as they walked. She loved when he showed affection in public, which was something he rarely did. Wanting to surprise him, she went upstairs to the bathroom as soon as they walked in the door. She ran water in the tub, placed a drop of bath oil in it, and lit some scented candles. She then went back downstairs to grab a bottle of champagne and two glasses. Although she was being spontaneous, she wanted to make everything perfect. So, she went into the kitchen and fixed a fruit platter. On her way back upstairs, she bumped into Tony, who had just ended a business call.

Seeing the puzzled look on his face, she chuckled and said, "I have a surprise for you."

"Oh yeah?" he replied with a smile.

"Yes…"

After they walked into the bedroom, Christina rushed into the bathroom, while Tony sat on the edge of the bed. He was exhausted and about to lie down, when she emerged from the bathroom naked. Instantly, Tony should've been sexually aroused, but he wasn't.

"Come, baby. I just ran us a nice, hot bubble bath," she said in a seductive tone, while playing with her nipples.

Oh boy, Tony thought. He really didn't have the desire to have sex with her, but to avoid an argument, he replied, "Sure," while following her into his luxurious bathroom.

Just as Tony was about to undress, she said, "Let me take that off for you," then gently removed his shirt, while kissing his pecks and staring into his eyes.

Tony smirked. *Oh, now you wanna freak off,* he thought.

Christina dropped to her knees and unbuckled his pants. Sadly, Tony still wasn't hard. So, she pulled out his penis and started teasing it with the tip of her tongue, which caused it to jump a little.

Standing with his eyes closed, he moaned, "Yeah, ma," as he tried to get in the mood.

"Is that how you want it, daddy?" she asked, while licking it up and down slowly.

"Yes, baby, that's how daddy likes it."

Christina was just about to put his penis in her mouth, when she swallowed and noticed a funny taste. Pausing, she took a sniff, and sure enough, it smelled like cum. She was about to stand up, when Tony looked down.

"Why are you stopping? That shit was feeling good."

She wanted to say something, but didn't want to risk having a heated argument with him. Desperately wanting to please him, she continued giving him head, while trying not to gag. However, as she was putting it in her mouth, she saw brownish red scales on his cock. Inspecting it closer, she noticed some on his pubic hair, too. *Oh my God, is that blood?* she thought, while pulling his penis out of her mouth. Quickly, Christina got up and went over to the sink to rinse out her mouth.

Semi-hard, Tony followed her. "Why you stop?" he whispered.

Christina was hurt. She couldn't believe he would have sex with someone else and allow her to perform oral sex on him, especially without washing up first.

"My mouth was hurting," she replied, looking away.

Tony grabbed her by her chin, forcing her to look into his eyes. "Baby, you was doing a great job," he told her, then stuck his tongue down her throat.

She tried to turn her head, but he was a great kisser and she had yearned for his touch for so long. His soft, wet lips and thick tongue tingled inside her mouth. Soon, she let down her guard and surrendered as he kissed her passionately and caressed her soft body.

"Tony, please fuck me," Christina moaned, while gazing into his eyes.

After lifting her up on the sink, he started licking her neck and traveled slowly down to her navel. Arriving at her bikini line, he massaged her thighs.

"Oh, Tony," she moaned, as she licked her lips and rubbed on her breasts.

Christina directed his head to her vagina, spread her lips, and seductively said, "It's yours."

Tony grinned. He had never seen her so freaky. Suddenly, he started to think about Morgan. He wanted to stop, but knew it would lead to accusations. Therefore, he continued, but with limited touches. He licked and kissed around her juice box, but never allowed his tongue to come into direct contact with her clit. Christina was a little upset that he didn't taste her, but continued to enjoy his touches. Gently, he grabbed her small waist and moved her to the edge of the sink, and while lustfully gazing into each other's eyes, he slowly slid inside of her.

As Tony gradually pushed inside of her, Christina mumbled, "Slow, baby."

Nodding his head, Tony continued to push, but Christina moved back.

"I don't think I'm wet, Tony."

Annoyed by her comment, he faked an orgasm just to put an end to it. "Damn, baby, I'm about to nut," he lied, while holding her waist tightly and kissing on her neck as he pretended to catch his breath. Then, he pulled out and walked over to the shower, overlooking the hot water in the Jacuzzi.

Christina hugged him from behind and kissed him on his back. "I love you," she whispered.

"I love you, too," he replied, not upset in the least because Morgan had drained him earlier that day.

After showering, he dried off, threw on a wife beater and a pair of shorts, then told Christina, who was lying across the bed, that he was going downstairs to his office to look over some contracts. Truthfully, he used that as an excuse not to be in her presence. By the time he returned to the room, she was fast asleep. So, he slid into the bed slowly while trying hard not to wake her, closed his eyes, and drifted off to sleep with sweet thoughts of Morgan floating through his mind.

*****

The next morning, Christina and Tony woke up and worked out together, which was something they hadn't done in a long time. Christina ran on the treadmill, while Tony used the elliptical machine.

"How does your schedule look later? I was thinking we could have dinner together?" she offered, out of breath.

Listening to some songs off his new album, he didn't hear her. Once she realized he didn't respond because he had headphones on, she stopped the treadmill, went over to him, and clapped her hands loudly.

Tony removed his earphones. "What's up, babe?"

Standing there sweaty, Christina wiped the baby hair from her forehead. "I was thinking we could have dinner tonight at the Waverly Inn."

Tony got off the elliptical and grabbed his hand towel. "Maybe," he replied before leaving the gym.

"Maybe?" she mumbled to herself, while still standing there. "Is this a fucking joke?" Snatching her towel off the treadmill, Christina stormed behind him. "Did you just say maybe?" she asked.

Just as Tony turned around to respond, Tia and Mookie walked in the door.

"What's up, guys? Give me a second to get ready," he told them, completely ignoring Christina.

"Tony, I asked you a fucking question. And if your answer is maybe, then *maybe* you need another girlfriend," Christina barked, with her arms folded across her chest.

Tia and Mookie looked at Christina and then back at Tony, wondering what they had walked in on.

"I asked you a fucking question. I'm sick of your slick comments, Tony!" she yelled, throwing the towel at him.

Tony felt like beating her ass, but instead, he fell back and smiled. *Bitch, you just played yourself,* he thought.

Directing his attention back to his staff, Tony jokingly screamed, "Good fucking morning! Let me get ready and I'll meet y'all in the living room. A'ight?" This was the only way he could control his anger, or else he would have sent Christina to the hospital.

Christina stood there fuming. After brushing past him, she stomped up the stairs. "Fucking faggot," she mumbled.

Tony went upstairs behind her and jumped in the shower. A half an hour later, he returned to the living room and asked Tia for his daily agenda.

"Your album is dropping in three weeks. The single is number one on the hip-hop charts, so we need to start promoting it," she informed him after pulling out the agenda sheet.

Tony nodded. "Okay. Well, book some shit up. Just don't have my ass all around the world like the last time," he replied, while frowning.

He's such an asshole, Tia thought, but had to remind herself not to express it verbally since he paid her bills.

As they were about to leave, Christina came down the stairs dressed in a pair of Vintage skinny jeans, a Marc Jacob fitted sweater, a pair of five-inch Jimmy Choo animal-print shoes, a Fendi mink jacket, and Cartier shades to complete the look.

Strutting down the stairs, she flung her hair and announced, "I'm ready."

Everyone shook their heads. One thing was for sure, Christina was a bad chick. On the elevator ride down, everyone was silent. Christina stared at Tony through her shades and knew he was checking her out. When the elevator reached the lobby, they all walked out, with Tony and Mookie leading the way. The doorman informed Tony that his driver and bodyguards were out front. Tony nodded and gave the man a pound in response. As they got closer to front door, Tony saw Paul and Mike waiting there. He smiled because Christina was about to be in for a rude awakening.

"Morning, fam," Tony said, giving Mike and Paul a hug. Then he turned around to face Christina. "From now on, Mike will be your driver and Paul will be your bodyguard."

Everyone was shocked by what Tony had just said. Mookie and Tia glanced at each other, then at Christina, and then back at Tony. Tony ignored the stares and walked over to his new driver.

"Tia and Mookie, let's go," he said, jumping in his Mercedes Benz CL 600.

Christina stood there with a stupid look on her face for a few moments, before shaking her head and walking over to the black Suburban. She knew Tony had done that shit on purpose. Paul, who could tell she was embarrassed and pissed off, opened the door for her.

He flashed a fake smile. "Sorry, Christina," he said before closing the door and jumping in the front with Mike, who was in the driver's seat.

Still confused about Tony's actions, Tia and Mookie jumped in his car behind him.

Just as Al was about to pull off, though, Tony said, "Mookie, do me a favor. Ride with Christina today. I mean, if you don't mind," he said in a condescending tone.

Mookie looked over at Tia and frowned. He didn't know if Tony was being for real or just trying to be funny. Mookie sat there for a moment and then responded back in a sarcastic tone, "Nah, I don't mind."

He jumped out and waved for Mike to stop so he could jump in with them. The whole time, Tia glanced at Tony from the corner of her eye. She wanted to say something, but opted not to. Tony could feel Tia's eyes on him.

Looking out the window, he smirked. "Isn't life great?"

Chapter Five
Christina

Christina laid her head back and closed her eyes. Tony was really acting up and she didn't know what to do. Mookie sat next to her, not believing Tony would pull some sucka shit like that.

"Sorry, Chris, I didn't know this was gonna happen."

Taking off her shades, she replied, "It's fine, Mookie. I need to start doing things for myself."

He was about to make a snide comment, but with Mike and Paul in the car, he decided it was best to remain silent. So, he just nodded.

Christina pulled out her cell phone and called her best friend Asia, who she hadn't spoken in weeks because of her demanding schedule. Whenever she had a little free time, she spent it with Tony. But, today, she was going to start making time for herself.

"Asia...it's Chris, girl." Christina crossed her legs and smiled. She missed her best friend. "I was wondering are you free for dinner tonight. I wanna hang out."

"Yes, girl," Asia responded, excited by the offer. "Maybe

after dinner, we can hit the club and get our dance on."

Christina laughed. "Sounds like I plan. Lord knows I need to get my drink on and live my life," she sang, throwing her hand up in the air.

Asia looked at the phone. "Uh oh, trouble in paradise?"

Christina sighed. "Like always, girl, but we can talk about it over dinner. I have to go. Okay?"

"Well, you know I'm here for ya. Do you have a place in mind?"

"Waverly Inn located in the city on 16 Banks Street," Christina replied.

"Okay, I know that place. So are we meeting there or your place?"

Since she had been staying at Tony's place a lot lately, most of her clothes were there and not at her loft in Tribeca. So, she decided to have Asia meet her at Tony's, even though she knew he didn't like people in his house.

"Asia, you know where Tony lives, right? Meet me there around seven o'clock."

"Sounds like a plan. Later," Asia said before hanging up.

Next, Christina dialed the number for her assistant. "Morning, Joyce. What do I have planned for today?" she asked, flinging her hair back.

"Hello, Chris! You're supposed to be on your way to make a brief appearance at the Teen Summit being held at the Jacob Javits convention center. After that, you have to go view your pictures for the Guess ads."

"Okay, I'm on my way to the convention center. Oh, and I'm having dinner with Asia tonight. So, can you pick me up something to wear and drop it off at Tony's? I want something tight and sexy. Nothing off the rack," Christina said in a sexy tone.

Joyce laughed. "Okay, I will make a few calls to the top designers. Shall I alert the paparazzi for the publicity?"

"Of course," Christina replied with a laugh, preparing to

show her ass that evening.

After she hung up, Mookie looked over at her and shook his head.

Christina smiled. "What?"

Mookie laughed. "I ain't mad at 'cha"

Christina faced him. "Come with me. I could use the support."

Caught off guard, Mookie laughed again. He didn't feel comfortable being with Christina in public. Besides, he didn't need the speculation. "Thanks, but you know I can't. Tony is my man. How would that look?"

"Oh please, we're friends, Mookie. It's not a big thing."

When Mookie glanced up, he noticed Mike was staring at him through the rearview mirror. Then he looked back at Christina who was smiling and waiting for an answer. "A'ight, you're gonna get us both in trouble," he laughed.

Christina did a little dance in her seat. "Shit, it's not like he cares. Mike, to the Javits Convention Center please."

Mookie looked up and saw Paul and Mike shaking their head. He knew he just fucked up. *Oh well, I'll deal with Tony later.*

*****

After Christina's appearance, they dropped Mookie off at his office. She had used him enough for today "Mookie, thank you so much," she said before giving him a peck on the cheek.

Mookie smirked. He was aware of her hidden motive. "Anytime, Chris," he replied, then jumped out and walked into the office building.

Usually, Christina would go upstairs to see Tony, but not today. She was going to teach him a lesson. Instead, she headed over to her record label to meet with Aaron Styles, the CEO. Since she had been number one on the charts for the last couple of weeks, the executives wanted to meet with her to discuss another video and a third single.

Christina was greeted by some people that worked in the building. "Hi, Ms. Carrington!" someone yelled. Christina just smiled as she got on the elevator, with Joyce right behind her. *What has gotten into her?* Joyce thought while looking at her.

When they stepped off the elevator, they were greeted by Aaron. "Chris, glad you could stop by. I spoke to Tony a couple of weeks ago, and he had some great ideas for the next single," he said, while leading her into his office.

Immediately, she frowned. She didn't want Aaron to discuss anything with Tony. Once they got inside his office, Christina said, "That's great, Aaron, but from now on, please discuss my career with Elisa, my manager, and me. Tony is no longer involved with my career. And before you alert the media, we're still together, but decided to keep our business lives separated," she snidely told him.

Surprised by her comment, Aaron replied, "Why certainly, Christina. So should I share what he and I discussed?"

Removing her shades, she said, "Sure, why not? No offense, Aaron. I just need you to communicate with my manager first. Okay?"

Aaron nodded. "No problem," he responded. Then with a puzzled look, he glanced over at Joyce who was sitting on the sofa behind Christina. Joyce simply shrugged her shoulders and shook her head.

He shared his ideas with Christina. Thrilled, she advised him to meet with Elisa that week. Since her album dropped, Christina was heading out to the west coast for a couple of performances. She was expected to sweep the music award shows. Christina Carrington had locked down the game. In addition, she had just renewed her modeling contract with Express Modeling Agency. Her career was taking off and she loved it.

After she and Joyce left Boston Records, they went over to Harrod Marketing to review her photo layout. She was impressed with most of the photos. She was photogenic, it was hard for her to take a bad picture. Next, they went to Da Silvano's for lunch. Once seated, Christina ordered ginger ale, while Joyce had grapefruit juice.

"Hey, what's up with you today?" Joyce asked once the waiter left.

"I don't know what you're talking about," Christina replied in a spiteful tone.

Joyce stayed quiet.

"What do you mean, Joyce?" she asked, flinging her hair back.

Before speaking, Joyce looked around to make sure no one was listening. "You're acting funny today… showing up with Mookie at the convention center, telling Aaron to only talk with you or Elisa. Tony was always involved in your music business, Christina. Why the change now? Have you told him?"

Christina tilted her head, rolled her eyes, and sighed. "First of all, what's with all the questions? I am not acting funny today. It's just time for me to take control of my life and career. Secondly, it was Tony's idea for Mookie to ride with me. If you must know, Paul and Mike are now a part of my team. Yes, Tony has helped me with my music career, not my modeling career. But, it's time that we keep our personal and business lives separate. Joyce, I don't need permission from you or anyone else when it comes to my career. If you have a problem with it, maybe you should work for Tony," she said with a stern look.

Joyce sipped her drink and narrowed her eyes. "Christina, I didn't mean anything by it," she explained. "You just always seek advice from Tony. I guess I'm not used to you taking control of things. Sorry if I offended you. Girl, I always got your back. Just warn me first." Joyce laughed.

Christina reached out for Joyce's hand, feeling bad for being so harsh. "I'm sorry, too. I didn't mean to snap at you. It's just that Tony and I are going through a rough time right now.

We're not connecting anymore. He's acting different. Joyce, we're not even having sex anymore. I know he's cheating on me, but I love him. I just feel like it's time for me to start taking control of my life."

Joyce nodded and then changed the subject. "So what do you want to wear tonight?"

With a devilish smile, Christina replied, "Something that will make the front page of every major newspaper."

Joyce laughed. Christina was playing with fire, but what could Joyce do about it?

After they ate lunch, Christina went to get her hair done at Tracey's Salon on the upper Westside, while Joyce went to find an outfit for Christina to wear that evening. As she was getting a wash and set, Christina checked her cell phone. It was going on four o'clock and Tony hadn't called. She couldn't believe she was in love with such an ass of a man. She finally decided to call him and break the ice, but the phone rang three times before going to voicemail.

"Hey, it's me. Call me."

Christina was about to call again, when Joyce came through the door. "What's up, Joyce? Did you find me anything to wear?" she asked after taking her head from underneath the dryer.

Joyce sat next to her. "Yes, I found several things for you to choose from. They are at the cleaners being pressed. I'm picking them up in an hour."

"Cool. Have you heard from Tony today? I've been trying to reach him, but he's not picking up."

Joyce glanced around the salon before responding. "No, haven't heard anything from Tony. However, I was going over your calendar with Tia and I see where he's pulled out of a lot of engagements, something about schedule conflict."

Christina rolled her eyes. *He's such a bitch.* It was fucking payback time. "Fine, you know what? Call Tia back and cancel all appearances together. Fuck him!"

Joyce nodded.

While getting her hair blow dried, she asked Joyce to call Paul and Mike to let them know she was ready. By the time they left the salon, it was 5:30 p.m., and Tony still hadn't called. Christina hopped into her awaiting car service. She wanted to ask Paul had he heard from Tony, but decided not to. She would just let things ride out.

After arriving at Tony's pad and entering with Joyce, Christina realized Tony wasn't there. She made her way to the kitchen. "Carmen, has Tony been here?"

"No, Senora Christina," Carmen responded, as she put away some groceries. "Can I get you anything?"

"No, thank you, Carmen. I'm expecting a friend to stop by. Okay?" Christina said, while exiting the kitchen.

"Si, Senora Christina."

Christina went into the living room, grabbed her clothes from Joyce, and went upstairs. Joyce offered to help her get ready, but Christina declined. She felt like being alone. Christina laid across the bed with tears rolling down her face. She was hopelessly in love with Tony. Looking over at the clock, she noticed it was almost seven o'clock. So, she jumped up and started getting dressed. A few minutes later, she heard voices downstairs.

"Asia, is that you?" Christina opened the bedroom door and yelled out.

"Yeah, girl. I'm going into the living room with Joyce and the others."

"No, come up here. I need your help."

Asia ran up the stairs. "Child, this penthouse is off the fucking hook. Tony has a great sense of style," she said, huffing from her jog up the stairs.

Christina laughed. "Yeah, he does have great taste," she replied snidely.

After Asia helped her decide on the black Gucci dress with the back out and a pair of Alexander McQueen satin pumps, the two women laughed and talked shit while Christina got dressed. She forgot how much fun Asia was, and she missed her best friend.

As they headed downstairs, the front door opened and Tony entered. Christina almost tripped. When he looked up and noticed Asia coming down the stairs behind Christina, he glared at her.

"Hi, Tony," Asia said cheerfully.

With a pissed-off look, he stared her up and down and then said, "What's up, Asia?"

Asia brushed past him and proceeded to the living room. Christina tried to do the same, but Tony snatched her by the arm. At first, they just glared at each other.

Then Tony angrily muttered, "You brought someone into my fucking house? Have you lost your mind?"

Christina yanked her arm away from him. "Get the fuck off of me. Asia isn't *someone*; she's my friend, asshole!"

In an attempt to calm himself, Tony wiped his face with his hand. He was close to slapping the shit out of her when Paul interrupted.

"Sorry, Tony. Chris, are you ready?"

Christina turned around. "Yes, Paul. Asia and Joyce, let's get the fuck outta here," she said, while snatching her mink out of Joyce's hand.

Tony stood there with a smirk on his face. *So Christina has a backbone in her after all. Good, because she's gonna need it*, he thought. "Have a good night," he said, then started walking up the stairs. He paused midway. "Yo Paul, after they're done, please take that bird to her nest." .

Paul wanted to burst out laughing, but he couldn't. He looked over at Christina who had smoke coming out her ears.

"Fuck you, Tony." Embarrassed, Christina yelled, "Get me the fuck outta this place!"

*****

When Paul pulled the car up in front of the Waverly Inn, the paparazzi was already out there. Christina beamed. Joyce had done her job and alerted them. Paul jumped out and went inside to notify the hostess she was there. Then he came back to the car, opened the door, and ushered her and Asia inside.

"Christina! Christina, over here!" the paparazzi yelled, as Christina smiled and waved while being led inside to the private seating area.

When she looked around and noticed there were no other guests in that area, she summoned for the manager. "Max, I would like to be seated in the public section. Don't feel like eating in the VIP tonight."

Surprised by her request, Max asked, "Are you sure, Ms. Carrington?"

Christina smiled. "Yes, I'm sure."

Max nodded. "Very well, let me take you to the public section."

Once seated in the open area, Christina and Asia ordered some drinks and reminisced about the good ole days. Of course, Tony popped into Christina's head a few times. She wondered what he was doing and if he missed her, because she missed him.

Asia took a sip of her Cristal and asked, "So what's going on with you and Mr. Tony?"

Exhaling, Christina replied, "I don't know. He's been acting up lately. He says it's work, but it's more than that. I think he has someone else."

"Tony may have slipped up a few times, but I seriously doubt he has someone else, Chris. He would be a fool. You're gorgeous, rich, and smart. What man doesn't want that? Maybe he's going through something. You know a lot of men have a problem with women on their level. Maybe he's feeling a little jealous of your success."

Christina never thought about it like that. Maybe she was

overreacting. She had to admit that she hadn't been spending time with him lately. When she was with him, she was always tired. "You may be right, Asia. When I get back from the west coast, I'm gonna plan a romantic getaway for the two of us. He's been under a lot of stress, too."

"Work it out, girl. Tony is the perfect man. He's rich, sexy, and did I mention rich?"

Both laughed.

"Yeah, you did, but it's not about money, Asia."

"According to who? Christina, a relationship requires two things: a woman with good pussy and a man with long money."

Christina shook her head. "You're a fool."

Once they finished eating, Christina called Paul to let him know they were ready. While waiting for him, the two women decided to freshen up their makeup.

"Oh Paul, you scared the hell out of me," Christina said, while coming out of the private bathroom.

"Sorry, Chris. Are you ready to leave?"

Christina looked him up and down. Even though Paul always had a stern look on his face, there was something sexy about him. She wished he would just smile sometimes. "Yes, we're ready. You know where we're going, right?"

"No, but I was gonna take you to NV on Houston Street. It's a hot spot where all the celebs go."

Acting like a couple of schoolgirls, Christina and Asia giggled while holding each other's hand.

"Let's go!" Even though it was nighttime, Christina paused for a second to put on her shades. "Now I'm ready," she said with a grin.

After getting in the car, Paul called the club owner to inform him that they were on their way. Once there, Paul got out and spoke to the bouncer.

The manager welcomed Christina. "It's a pleasure to have you here. We have arranged a special VIP area for you."

"Thank you," she responded, flashing a seductive smile and strutting inside like she was on a catwalk.

She wasn't even in the club good before the DJ announced, "The hottest chick in the game, Christina Carrington, is in the house y'all!" and started playing "Trauma", her new single.

Christina waved to the crowd that went crazy as she was led to her private section.

"Ms. Carrington, can I get you anything?" the waitress asked.

While grooving to her new joint, Christina told her, "Yes, get me a bottle of Cristal, Dom P., and oh, bring some bottled water."

Asia and Christina danced to the music. The vibe was crazy. Christina pinned her hair up and started shaking her ass, giving the crowd something to look at. Suddenly, the DJ announced, "NBA player Rashid Williams is in the building!" Christina stopped and looked at Asia. She wasn't familiar with sports, so she didn't know who he was. However, he was the MVP all-star rookie of the year who was moving up fast. He just signed a multi-million dollar deal with Nike.

While Christina and Asia danced, the club owner led Rashid over to the VIP area. "Rashid, this Christina. Christina, meet Rashid. Please enjoy," he said before walking off.

Christina and Rashid extended their hands to shake, and then she turned her attention back to Asia, who was standing there like a bump on a log,

"Girl, he's fucking sexy," Asia whispered.

Christina grinned. "I guess," she replied and continued dancing. When she looked from the corner of her eye, she saw Rashid doing his two-step with a drink in his hands, while checking her out. Tired from dancing, she sat down. The waitress came over and was about to pour Christina another glass, when Rashid grabbed the bottle from her.

"I got this, ma."

Christina looked up and blushed. *Oh god,* she thought.

"Cristal or Dom P.?" Rashid asked, lifting both bottles up. She pointed to the Dom P. "So you come here often?" he asked, while pouring them both a glass and handing her one of the drinks.

Christina glanced around to make sure they weren't being watched. "No, this is my first time. I haven't been out in a long time," she replied, sipping on her champagne.

"Yeah, I feel you on that one. I haven't been out in a long time either."

Unexpectedly, they both felt awkward and tried not to stare into each other's face.

"So you're a basketball player?"

Rashid chuckled. She was sexy as hell and even prettier in person. "Something like that," he responded with seductive eyes.

Christina blushed, trying to avoid eye contact. *Damn! Asia was right. He is sexy,* she thought. She couldn't help staring at him. Rashid was 6'7", with glowing chestnut skin, beady-eyes, and a sexy smile. His bald head complemented his look. It seemed like his V-neck sweater was tailored to expose biceps, triceps, and washboard abs. She loved the way he licked his full, moist lips. She looked down at his hands, which were big, strong, and manicured.

Rashid caught Christina checking him out and laughed; he was flattered. When one of his homeboys whispered in his ear that she was Tony's girl, he just nodded his acknowledgment. That didn't stop him from flirting with her, though.

"So Christina, has Tony lost his mind letting you out looking this sexy? Ma, you're killing it in that dress, for real."

Christina giggled. She loved the attention "Tony let me out? Rashid, I'm a grown woman who is hanging out with my girl. Is that okay?"

Throwing his hands up, he said, "It's cool, ma." Then he leaned over, licked his lips, and mumbled, "But if you were mine, I'd be home loving you."

Christina suddenly felt warm inside. She should've been offended, but wasn't. In fact, it turned her on. She wasn't sure if it was his deep, sexy voice or cologne. All she could do was giggle and sip her drink.

Since she didn't curse him out, Rashid decided to ask her to dance. "You're enjoying the music, so let's go down there and get our dance on."

He extended his hand, waiting for her to take it. At first, Christina was reluctant. She knew it wouldn't look right, but then again, it was only a dance. After contemplating it for a few seconds, she allowed him to lead her to the dance floor. Before she could walk off, Asia snatched her by the arm.

"Girl, are you fucking crazy? This will be all over the papers tomorrow. Think about what you have at home."

Feeling a little tipsy, Christina yanked her arm away. "Since you're so worried about my home, maybe we should trade places. It's not like you haven't slept there before."

Asia stood there humiliated, as the two made their way to the dance floor.

At first, Rashid and Christina did a simple two-step because the crowd was staring at them. However, when "Shake What Your Momma Gave Ya" came on, everyone went wild, bumping and grinding on each other. Joining them, Christina shook her ass on Rashid. Loving it, Rashid held her by the waist and even slipped up and kissed her on the neck a few times. Aroused in a subdued way, Rashid rubbed Christina's thighs. Hating, Asia alerted Paul as to what was going down on the dance floor.

"Fam, easy with the hands," Paul warned after walking over to them.

Rashid smiled and backed up. "She doesn't seem to mind, fam, but don't worry. I won't disrespect her like that."

"What the fuck are you doing?" Christina screamed at Paul once she turned around to see why Rashid had stopped dancing. "Go over there and watch. Isn't that what you get paid for?"

Completely humiliated, Paul glared at her for a moment. She was lucky he needed his job. Without saying a word, he went back over to the VIP section, while Christina and Rashid continued to dance and talk.

"I didn't know basketball players could dance."

"That's not all we can do," he stated, winking.

"I bet," she said, licking her lips and slow whining down to the floor.

Rashid stood there in awe. She was so sexy. Becoming aroused, he pulled her closer to him. As they danced, Christina felt his cock pressing against her ass.

"Come with me back to my place," he mumbled, grinding against her harder.

When Christina turned around, that's when it hit her that she was acting like a whore. "I can't, Rashid," she said, then started to walk away.

He pulled her back. "What's up? Did I do something wrong?"

Christina took a deep breath. *Yeah, you're being too damn sexy and tempting for one,* she thought. "No. I just can't. You know I'm with Tony." Her eyes became watery. "It's difficult," she mumbled, holding back her tears.

Rashid gently held her hand as they returned to their private area. "Listen, ma, I didn't mean it like that."

Christina stared into his sexy eyes, wanting to get lost in them.

"I'm gonna slip my card in this tissue. If you ever need to talk, just call. A'ight?"

Christina giggled. "I will. Thank you."

"Nah, thank you."

She took the tissue, tucked it in her purse, and walked over to Paul. "I'm ready."

While they waited for Mike, Rashid walked by and whispered in her ear, "If anyone asks, I was tryna holla at your friend."

Both laughed.

There was silence during the ride home. Everyone was in their own little world. Asia was sleep, Mike focused on the driving, and Paul thought about Christina. With her shades on, Christina rested her head back on the seat. She was so disappointed with herself.

Ironically, Christina hesitated when they arrived at her place. Somehow it did not feel like home. Paul opened the door and walked her upstairs. After unlocking her door with the touchpad lock, she allowed Paul to do a security walk-thru. The loft was so empty and gloomy. She went into the kitchen and grabbed a bottle of water out of the fridge.

As he headed out, Paul said, "Everything is clear. Do you want me to stay the night or are you cool?"

Christina looked around. "I'll be fine. Thanks."

Paul nodded. "I'll be here around ten. Okay?"

Christina nodded in response, locked the door behind him, and then leaned her head against it.

What the fuck have I done?

Chapter Six
Denise

Two months had gone by and Denise continued avoiding Morris. She missed him miserably, but blamed him for her arrest. She thought about Mr. Rubin and Perry's words. They were right. If she didn't change her life, there would not be a next time. Maybe this was a sign from God that she had better get her act together. While typing her project report for work, Denise couldn't shake Felicia's words out of her head. What did she mean by her brother? Most of all, where was her gun? Her thoughts were interrupted by her office phone.

"Denise Taylor speaking."

"Hello, Denise. It's Derrick."

Denise was silent for a second. *Who the hell is Derrick?* she thought.

"Derrick…?"

"We met at the book store a couple of months ago," he stated.

"Oh Derrick, the guy who reads!" she said, smiling over the phone.

"Yep, that's me. How are you doing?"

"I've had better days. And you?"

"Great now that I've heard your voice," he charmed.

"Awww, thank you! Such a bullshitter!"

"Bullshiter?" he repeated, chuckling in a sexy voice.

"Yes, until proven otherwise."

Derrick laughed. "Fair enough. So, Ms. Taylor, I would love to take you out to dinner. Would that be possible?"

"Um, it depends."

"On?"

Denise giggled. She didn't know why she was giving him a hard time. "It depends on if you're still in that same relationship."

"That depends. Are you in the same one?"

Both laughed.

"True! When would you like to see me?"

"I was hoping this evening. Maybe we could go out to dinner or read a good book."

"Funny! And spontaneous!"

"Well, I try. So what do you say?"

Denise sighed. She really wasn't in the mood to hang out, but she gave in. "Alright, where shall I meet you?"

"You tell me. You're in control"

Since she didn't know what his budget was like, she decided to keep it simple. "How about we meet at Philippe Chow? You know the place?"

"Sure do! It's on 60th Street on the east side."

"That's the place"

"Let's say seven," he suggested.

"That's fine."

"See you then"

"Okay, goodbye," she said.

After hanging up from Derrick, Denise felt tingly inside, but determined not to be distracted by her thoughts, she continued working on her report, until the phone rang again! *Who the hell is this now?*

"Denise Taylor."

"Ay yo, what's up?" Morris yelled.

"How did you get my work number?" she asked in a nasty tone.

"Don't worry about that. Yo! What's up with you, Dee? I feel like lately, you've been ducking a nigga. I told you about homegirl. You know I'm not fucking her," he explained.

Denise rested the phone against her chest, closed her eyes, and took a deep breath. She missed him so much. "I've been busy, Morris."

"Word? That busy that you can't return my calls?" he responded in an annoyed tone.

"Yes. Anyway what do you want? I'm busy." Denise started to get frustrated.

"Yo, Dee, I miss you! You got me open. We need to talk."

"No, we don't. I can't do this anymore," she blurted out.

Morris moaned. "You can't do this no more? Nah, fuck that. Tell me to my face. Leave work now and let's talk."

"Hell no! I'm not leaving work now. Morris, it's over. What the fuck is your problem?" Denise shouted.

"Don't come with that bullshit about it being over! Denise, for real, that's how we do each other? A'ight, let's see when I come up there to your job."

Denise eyes widened. "You're not coming to my job."

"Don't tell me what the fuck I'm not gonna do. Either you come to me or I'm coming to you. And you know I don't give a fuck."

Denise sighed. She knew Morris' ass was crazy; he would pop up and make a scene for sure. *Fuck! I don't need this shit today.* She glanced at the time on her computer. "Alright, I'll be downstairs in fifteen minutes." "

"Fifteen minutes, Denise, or I'm coming up," he said, then hung up.

Denise shook her head.

Again, her phone rang, but this time, it was her real estate agent, Josh.

"Josh, where the hell have you been? I left several messages for you."

"Hello to you, too!"

"Don't play with me. Why hasn't Gabrielle received the contracts yet?" Denise yelled, while shutting down her computer.

"I was working on them. Your ass needs to have a little more faith in me."

"I do. That's the fucking problem."

"Anyway, I have some wonderful news for you," Josh stated. "I was able to get you approved for all the properties. Your credit score is great, but considering this is an investment, the bank requires a minimum of twenty percent of the total purchase price. In your case, it's two million."

Denise got silent. She didn't think it would cost that much. Two million was a lot of money, and she would still need some cash to fix up the buildings. If she made the investment, it would take her entire savings and then some. She started to reconsider if it was something she really wanted to do.

"Shit, Josh, I'm not hustling anymore," she joked, tapping her French-manicured fingers on the desk.

"Yeah, I know. Maybe we can do a few at a time. I'm pretty sure they will still be there," he replied, trying to comfort her.

Denise bit down on her bottom lip and thought about it for a second. "You know what? Send me the paperwork. I have the money," she said, looking at her Rolex watch.

"Denise, two million dollars is a lot of money. You would have to mortgage all of your properties and put some money in cash," Josh explained.

By now, Denise was cleaning off her desk so she could meet Morris downstairs. "Okay, so let's do that. I'll have the money. Just tell me how much." Denise waited as Josh did the figures on his calculator.

"Your properties are worth well over two million. So, if you mortgage at least two of them, it will cover most of the down payment. However, the bank is still going to want some in cash."

"How much?"

"Around seven hundred thousand."

"Does that include your fee?" Denise snidely replied.

Ignoring her slick comment, Josh asked, "So what are we going to do? Do we have a deal or not?"

"Well, I don't have seven hundred thousand. I have four hundred thousand. Make it work."

Josh sighed. "You're such a fucking bitch. Let me see what I can do. So you have that amount in the bank now?"

"Not exactly," she replied with a giggle.

"What do you mean not exactly?"

Denise looked at the time. She had about ten more minutes. "Not exactly, like I said."

"You know the bank has to have a record of where the money came from," he informed her.

"Uh, don't you think I know that? Listen, if you must know, the money is in my apartment."

Josh's face lit up and he almost fell out of his chair. "You have four hundred thousand in cash. My god, Denise! Please don't tell me how you got it."

"Don't ask," she replied sarcastically, grabbing her bag. "Listen, Josh, I have to run. Send Gabrielle the paperwork and let's make it happen."

"Okay, I'll try to make sure everything runs smooth, but it will cost ya."

"With you, it always does. Later!"

Denise hung up the phone and jetted out of her office. The last thing she needed was Morris' ghetto ass to pop up at her job. In the elevator, she applied some lip gloss and straightened out her clothes. When the door opened up, Morris was right there.

"What are you doing?" she asked, rolling her eyes and pushing past him.

Morris stood there with a stern look. "You're late. I was about to come up there."

Denise glared at him. "Let's go, fool."

Once in the car, she was about to ask him where they were going, but she didn't bother. In truth, she was happy to see him. She put her Gucci shades on and closed her eyes. As Morris jumped on the FDR heading toward the Brooklyn Bridge, he glanced over at her. He couldn't wait to stick some dick in her. Denise wasn't drop-dead gorgeous, but she was very attractive. Her nicely toned legs, plump ass, and perfect size breast made Denise sexy. Her feisty attitude was an added bonus.

After pulling up in front of a brownstone, they got out. Noticing it wasn't Morris' house, Denise asked, "Where are we?"

Ignoring her question, he walked up the stairs, leaving her standing at the bottom with her arms folded.

"Morris, where the hell are we?" Denise yelled.

Morris looked around and opened the door. "Get the fuck in here."

Denise frowned and ran up the stairs. Before she had a chance to remove her coat, he grabbed her from behind and kissed her on the neck. "Why are you ducking me, huh?"

Caught off guard, Denise jumped. "No one is ducking your ass. I've been busy."

"Oh, that's what you call it," he replied, pressing his penis against her round ass.

Denise closed her eyes. She yearned for him. "Morris..."

He pushed the front of her body up against the wall and started fondling her, sending chills through her body. "Damn, I missed you so much."

Denise, breathing heavy, bit on her bottle lip and inhaled his cologne. "I missed you, too," she moaned. She was so caught up in the moment that she didn't even realize she still had her purse in her hand. They removed their coats, letting them fall to the floor.

"Morris, wait," she said, trying to turn around. "Morris!"

He stepped back, and Denise turned around. "I thought you said we needed to talk? This is not talking," she stated, staring into his eyes as he undressed her with his.

"Denise, I missed you, ma. For the last couple of weeks, I've been miserable without you. I know you think I'm out here fucking other chicks, but I'm not."

She just stared into his eyes while listening. *Oh God, what do I love about this man?* She reached out, gently pulled him to her, and started rubbing her head up against his chest. "You get on my nerves."

Morris lifted her face up by her chin. "Likewise," he said, and with that, it was on.

She ripped open his shirt, lifted his wife beater, and began kissing on the smooth, dark-chocolate skin of his chest, as he massaged the back of her head.

"I'm gonna fuck the shit out of you," he moaned.

Denise slowly licked his brown nipples, while rubbing her hands up and down his back. One thing was for sure, Denise and Morris' chemistry was crazy. Their foreplay was always intense.

Kissing him all over his chest, Denise moaned, "I missed you, daddy."

Morris snatched opened her maroon, double-breasted Elie Tahari suit jacket and cream DKNY blouse. He suddenly stopped and stared into her eyes. "You know I love you."

Denise closed her eyes. She waited so long to hear those words. "I love you, too."

He leaned forward and gently sucked her bottom lip, causing Denise to moan. She shoved her hand down his pants and felt his hard cock.

Morris smiled. "He's happy to see you, too." He then lifted Denise's skirt up and literally ripped her stockings off. He moved her thong to the side and stuck his two fingers inside of her. Holy shit! She was dripping wet.

"Fuck me!" Denise screamed.

He unbuckled his pants, letting them drop to the floor. After removing what was left of her stockings, Morris grabbed her legs and lifted her up against the wall. Denise wrapped her legs around him, squeezing his ribcage. Like a caveman, Morris snatched her thong off and tossed them on the floor.

Denise giggled. "Aren't we anxious?" she commented, breathing heavy.

Since Morris was a thug, he shoved inside of her, causing Denise's body to jerk. She let out a soft groan. She forgot how big Morris was. "Awww shit! I missed you so much, daddy."

Morris pumped in and out of her, while grabbing her ass. "You missed it, huh?"

Lost in the moment, she was unable to respond. Her body trembled, and her back was hot from the friction of the wall. He wasn't inside her ten minutes before he busted off. "Shit," he moaned, with one hand on the wall to balance them and the other still on her ass.

Trying to catch their breath, Denise rested her head on his shoulder. *Damn, he's never busted that quick, but I guess he missed it,* she thought. A few second passed before Morris pulled out and guided her over to a raggedy couch. Reluctantly, she followed him. When she tried to pull down her skirt, he turned around and shook his head no. With a seductive grin on her face, she unzipped her skirt and let it drop to the floor. Next, she removed her shirt and bra, and then she started playing with her nipples.

Morris licked his lips. "Come here," he said, rubbing his penis and getting it hard. "You're too much," he added, yanking her into his arms.

Before you knew it, they were at it again. Morris brought Denise to a climax about five times before they passed out on the sofa in each other's arms.

When Denise woke up, she jumped up off the couch and looked around. *Where the hell am I?* She looked down and saw Morris butt-naked sleeping. That's when she realized what happened. She sat there for a moment to collect her thoughts. She glanced at her watch; it was five-thirty. *Oh shit!* She remembered she was meeting Derrick for dinner. Quickly, she scrambled around the room to collect her clothes that were strewn all over the place. Tiptoeing around in search of her suede pumps, Denise tried not to wake him. She finally found them behind the couch. *How the hell did they get back there?* She looked down at Morris and giggled to herself. She then went upstairs to the bathroom. Since she was pressed for time, she couldn't snoop around the house, but one thing for sure, it wasn't Morris' crib. Knowing his sneaky ass, it was probably one of his other chicks' houses. *Bastard!* She just shook her head and got dressed. *Damn, I don't have any stocking now and it's cold as hell outside. Fuck it. I'll get some at the bodega.* She went back downstairs, picked up her coat, turned around, and looked at Morris. She thought about waking him, but knew it would lead to another sex episode. Standing with a big grin on her face, she thought about Morris saying he loved her.

She took a deep breath. "Goodbye, Morris," she whispered and then walked out the door to grab a cab to meet Derrick.

By the time she arrived at the restaurant, it was a quarter to seven. She called Derrick, and it rang three times before he picked up.

"Hey."

"I'll be there in ten minutes," he blurted out.

"That's fine. I'll get us a table in the meantime."

"You're there?"

"Yes, I just got here."

"Okay, babe. See you in ten."

Since Denise couldn't remember how Derrick looked, she notified the hostess that she was expecting a male friend. Suddenly, Denise started to feel anxious. *What if he's ugly and fat?* In an attempt to calm down, she picked up a menu. As she scanned through the restaurant's selections, a tall handsome gentleman walked over and stood over her.

"Denise," he said.

She looked up. *WOW!* she thought. For a second, she was speechless. She took a deep breath, trying not to fumble when she spoke. "Derrick?"

Both laughed and shook hands.

"Sorry I'm late. I got caught up at work."

Denise nodded and tried not to stare. Growing up, Denise always admired men in suits, but she always assumed they only dated conservative women.

"You look lovely," Derrick complimented.

"Thank you. You don't look so bad yourself."

Derrick looked over at Denise, causing her to blush. "Why are you staring at me?" she asked him.

"Because I like what I see."

Denise giggled. "Really?"

"Yeah, really," he teased.

They got lost in each other's eyes for a moment until the waiter came over to take their order.

Grinning from ear to ear, Denise couldn't remember the last time she had this much fun on a date. Unlike the usual suspects Denise dated in the past, Derrick was like a breath of fresh air. Throughout dinner, they got to know each other. Derrick grew up in Astoria, Queens. He went to Baruch College and got his Master's in Computer Science at Massachusetts Institute of Technology. He was thirty-seven years old with no children and worked on Wall Street for ten years before branching out into his own business, which was a commercial consultant firm. He loved to cook, workout, and of course, read.

"Now that you know about me, tell me a little about yourself."

Denise gave him a brief history of her life, leaving out sex, money, and murder. She didn't want him to run away before paying for dinner.

"Sounds like you lived a life," he said, sipping on his glass of water.

"You can say that."

"So tell me one thing, Denise. Why is someone who is sexy, beautiful, smart, and classy like you single?"

"The same reason why you're single," she replied, causing them both to laugh.

"Fair enough," he replied, clearing his throat. "Well, I was engaged for three years. It was good at first. I mean, we were good together. You know, while growing up, your parents tell you to finish school, marry a pretty girl, and start a family."

"Yeah, the American Dream," Denise muttered.

"Exactly! Well, like I said, it was good at first. She's a savvy attorney who made six figures, and I'm this powerful stockbroker. With our prestigious careers, we were the American Dream. While most people would probably kill to live like that, I got tired of putting up the façade. So, one day, I woke up and said I couldn't do it anymore. Called off the engagement and never looked back."

"Sorry to hear that. It's funny. When you meet a person for the first time, you meet their representative," Denise stated.

He chuckled. "Now that's true. So who am I meeting with tonight?"

Denise seductively stared into his eyes. "You know what, Derrick. I don't even know," she said before turning away.

Reaching out, he gently touched her hand. "I've been there before. So why are you single again?"

Denise giggled. When she felt her phone vibrating in her bag, she knew it was Morris. She chose to ignore it and let his call go to voicemail. "You know I really don't know. I'm not exactly single, but I'm not in a relationship either. We're kinda like fuck partners, if that's what you call it nowadays."

Stunned by her words, Derrick laughed. "Yeah...or a booty call."

Both chuckled.

Something about Derrick brought comfort to her. After dinner, Denise and Derrick left the restaurant. They were so intrigued with each other that even though it was freezing cold outside, they walked all the way to Denise's house. She felt like a schoolgirl on a first date. Derrick had on a long, black, wool trench coat, a cashmere scarf, and a black knitted Polo hat. As they walked, she held him by his arm, something she never did before, and they stopped in front of a couple of stores along the way. Denise was so overwhelmed with joy that she wasn't even cold anymore.

"So this is where you live?" he said, smiling when they arrived in front of her building.

"Yeah, this is me."

"Well, Ms. Denise, I really enjoyed your company. Will it be possible to see you again?"

"Likewise and I would love that."

Leaning over, Derrick kissed her on the cheek. "Goodnight, sexy."

Chills went through her body, and it wasn't because of the cold. "Goodnight."

Denise walked into her building. *So this is what Jasmine meant by change.*

Chapter Seven
Gabrielle

On the train ride back to her office from One Police Plaza, Gabrielle had her head so buried in the ballistic reports from Greg's case that she almost missed her stop. She jumped up, threw the folder in her bag, and ran out just before the doors closed. Before reaching her office that was a half block away from the train station, she stopped at the bakery next door to pick up some lemon tarts. It was only one o'clock and she was exhausted.

"Good afternoon, Nancy. Do I have any messages?" she asked, entering the office.

"Hello, boss lady. You have several. I left them on your desk. And a young lady came to see you this morning. I told her that you were not expected back into the office until this afternoon."

"Did she say what she wanted?" Gabrielle said, hanging up her coat.

"No. I even offered to make an appointment."

"Hmmm, that's strange. Hopefully, she will come back. Here, I brought the office some desserts. Please put them in the pantry. Also, order us some lunch and let's go over some of these cases. Tell Thomas to give you the Bergen file," she instructed, then walked into her office.

"Oh, Josh from Wells Fargo dropped this off for you." Nancy handed her a huge envelope.

Gabrielle reached out and took it. "This must be Denise's contracts. Thanks. Get Denise on the phone for me please."

Gabrielle sat down at her desk and pulled out the report again. Something didn't add up. According to the report she got from the police station, it wasn't the same information presented at Greg's trial. After carefully reviewing it again, Gabrielle sat back and closed her eyes. This report was the one assigned to Charlie Chapman's murder case. *Someone intentionally fucked this report up,* she thought. Gabrielle sat there thinking, when her private line rang.

"Gabrielle Brightman," she answered.

It was her husband calling from prison. *Shit!* She forgot she had forwarded the house line to her office. She accepted the charges.

"Hi, boo."

"Baby, what's up? Where were you? I was calling you all morning."

"I was in court," she lied.

"Oh! Boo, what's going on with you? For the last couple of weeks, you've been really distant, as if something or someone is occupying your time. When I call you, you're always busy or don't answer. Then when you come up here, it's like you don't wanna be here. What's up? If it's getting to be a little too much for you, tell me and I'll leave you alone."

"Leave me alone?" she repeated.

Greg was right. Lately, Gabrielle had become distant. There were so many things she wanted to discuss with him — from Britney to the false ballistic report — but she made a promise to Denise that she would keep her mouth shut. Besides, she didn't want to sound like a jealous wife. Instead, she took a deep breath and decided to wait for the other shoe to drop.

"Yes, I'm tired. And I can't lie; our situation is taking a toll on me. But, that doesn't mean I'm messing around with someone. Business has picked up, and that's why I've been stressed. You know it's me supporting the both of us."

Greg wasn't buying her excuses. He knew his wife better than that. He knew something wasn't right.

"Boo, you know you're not a good liar. You've always been busy with work, so I know it can't be that. Talk to me."

Gabrielle looked at the phone and shook her head at the fact that he knew her so well "You're right. I'm not a good liar like some people."

"What's that suppose to mean?"

"Nothing," she responded, trying to hold back her emotions.

"Yeah, okay. You know lawyers are the best liars. They do that shit for a living."

"So do men."

"And women."

Gabrielle could see the direction their conversation was going. So, it was time to change the subject before some hurtful things were said. "Anyway, did you get the food package I sent you?"

"Yeah, thanks," he responded in an angry tone.

They both remained silent for several seconds.

"Boo, if something's on your mind, you need to tell me. I'm not the one for playing mind games," Greg told her.

"What are you talking about mind games?"

"That reverse psychology you're playing. If you have something to say, just say it."

How about you tell me about Britney Cox? she thought. "Greg, when I do, you'll be the first one to know. Trust me"

"Yeah, okay. Innocent until proven guilty."

"Whatever! You're over-analytical anyway."

"Nah, I'm just always on point."

Umm, if you were so on point, your ass wouldn't be in

prison, dick, she thought. "If you say so."

"I know so," he retorted.

Again, they both got quiet on the phone. Gabrielle was steaming. She couldn't believe that bastard. After all the years they've been together, he still didn't trust her.

"Yeah, well, I'm not the one..." Then she caught herself. "You know what? Let's drop it. If you think I'm out here fucking around, then divorce me."

"Send me the papers!" he replied angrily.

"I will!" she shouted.

Both laughed.

"You're not going anywhere. You were made for me," Greg stated.

"Oh really? What makes you think I was made for you?"

"Because you're the only one I have ever loved besides my mother and sister. I never loved a broad."

Yeah, right! Keep lying, muthafucka, she thought. "Are you sure?"

"What the fuck is that suppose to mean? Of course, I'm sure. Anyway, did you speak to Mr. England about our next family visit?"

"Yes. It's next week."

"That's good. I need one."

Gabrielle stayed quiet; she was still upset at Greg's comment. The nerve of him to accuse her of cheating when his black ass was fucking some white chick. Just then, Nancy called her name through the intercom.

"Boo, hold on. Yes, Nancy!"

"Boss lady, the food is here, and I have Denise on the line for you."

"Alright, tell her to hold on."

"Sorry, boo, but I have to take this call," Gabrielle told Greg.

"It's cool, baby. I'll call you tonight. Listen, did Lawrence say anything about my case?"

"I haven't spoken to him since the last time I told you. I'll give him a call and see if he found anything. Maybe we should hire another attorney."

"Nah, Lawrence is good. He's the best in the business. Trust me, we're in good hands."

"If you say so. Hey, I have to go."

Gabrielle clicked over. "Hey, Dee."

"Mrs. Brightman."

"Where the hell have you been?"

"Work; it's been kicking my ass."

"Tell me about it. Anyway, I received the contracts from Josh today. I'll review them and get back to you."

"I bet you did after I lit a fire under his ass. He's so fucking slow."

Gabrielle giggled. "That's Josh for ya! How much is he charging?"

"Who the hell knows? Sometimes I think it's better to kill that son-of-a-bitch?"

Both laughed.

"Denise, you're a mess. You better stop talking like that."

"It's the truth. He's worse than the IRS, and the sad thing about it is if he ever gets caught, he will be sent to a country club prison while my black ass goes to Bedford. He's lucky I'm not the old Denise. He would have been paying me."

Gabrielle was cracking up. "Anyway, girl," she said, wiping the tears from her eyes, "when are you going to come to my office?"

"I don't know. Sometime this week. If not, we can meet for dinner."

"Sounds great! How are you otherwise?"

"I'm great. I just started seeing this guy named Derrick."

Gabrielle sighed. She hoped it wasn't another lowlife. "Derrick?"

"Yeah, but don't worry. He's not a thug."

Both laughed.

"Really! Well, that's good to know."

"Yeah, I met him at the bookstore. Would you believe he reads? We've went on a few dates and it's been good. I'm still waiting for the bullshit to surface, though. You know, child support, bad credit, dumb-ass girlfriend…the usual."

Again, both women laughed.

"Where's Morris, your black buck?"

Denise giggled. "His ass is still around. Blowing my back out when I want him to."

"Well, be careful. You know how men are if they find out their chick is cheating."

"No, I don't."

"They act crazy and wanna beat the girl up."

"I wish one of them would. I'll come out of retirement…early. Anyway, Gabby, he's different. Derrick is handsome, smart, has a good job, and is sexy as hell. "

"That's great! You know, Dee, we're older now. So, all that thug shit is not cute. You need a real man that's going to bring something to the table."

"Who are you telling? Shit, I almost forgot what it felt like to be taken out."

Gabrielle laughed. "I know that's right! I don't know about Greg and me."

"Oh Gabby, don't start that shit. You and Greg are fine."

"No, we're not, Denise. Look at our marriage. You tell me what's normal about it?"

"Gabrielle, please. No one has a normal marriage. What y'all have is rare. People search their whole lives looking for love. Be grateful you found it. The only difference is your husband is in prison. That doesn't mean he don't love you."

Gabrielle smiled. Denise did have a point. She knew Greg loved her. "I know, but I just want him home."

"I'm sure you do and he's coming soon. Just think of it as Greg is in the army fighting for his country."

Laughter erupted from the women.

"Yeah, I could envision him with an M-60 in his hand," Gabrielle said.

"Yep! Blowing muthafuckas away. Hey, I gotta go. Let's hook up for dinner."

"Sound like a plan to me. Love ya!"

"Love ya, too! And stop worrying so much. You're stressing me out."

Gabrielle hung up laughing. Denise was a bitch at times, but she was always there for her. She shook her head and got back to work. Since Abigail took a family leave, everyone pitched in on her workload. Gabrielle's head was buried in her work, when Nancy poked her head in.

"Boss lady, you're not leaving?"

She glanced over at the time. "Wow, I didn't know it was that late." She stretched. "I'll leave in a while. Just wanna finish up this case."

"Okay. Well, everyone is gone. So lock up and make sure you put the alarm on."

"Will do! Goodnight."

"Night."

Gabrielle went back to reading the brief. Minutes later, the bell rang. At first, she ignored it, assuming someone rang the wrong bell. However, the bell rang again. She got up thinking it was Nancy. *Maybe she forgot her keys.* She buzzed the door and went back into her office. Moments later, she heard a knock on the door.

"Nancy, did you leave your keys?" she said, walking to open it.

Gabrielle almost shit on herself. It was Britney. She stood there for a second with a surprised look on her face that soon turned to a look of anger.

"Hi! Can we talk?" Britney asked in a scared voice.

Standing in the doorway, Gabrielle took a deep breath and rolled her eyes.

"Please, I need you to understand," Britney said.

Gabrielle moved to the side, allowing her to come in.

"Thank you."

They walked into Gabrielle's office, where Britney removed her coat and sat on the sofa. Gabrielle sat in the chair. Britney glanced around the room and saw a picture of Greg and Gabrielle on the wall. She immediately got angry and sucked her teeth.

Noticing Britney's demeanor, Gabrielle asked, "So what would you like to talk about?"

Britney exhaled. "Well, when you popped up at my house, I was angry."

"Why?"

"Because you have the man I love. Greg was supposed to be with me."

"You came all the way here to tell me that? I don't understand," Gabrielle replied in an annoyed tone.

"I met Greg while I was in Lehman College studying to become a RN. He was taking some real estate courses at night there. I fell hard for him. He was different than the rest of the guys, very smooth and laid back."

Gabrielle smirked. *Yeah, I know that's right.*

"One night, I asked him could I hang out with him. At first, he said no. When I asked why, he said I really wasn't his type. That attracted me to him more. After weeks of begging, he finally agreed to take me out. But something happened where he had to leave and go out of town immediately. I was so infatuated with him that I asked him was there anything I could do to help. I knew he was into selling drugs. He told me no, saying it was too risky. Needless to say, I convinced him to let me help."

"Help him how?"

"At that time, it was carrying his drugs and guns."

"Greg had you carrying his guns and drugs and you did it?" Gabrielle snidely replied.

"He didn't make me. I wanted to," Britney stated, trying to

defend Greg. "I practically had to beg him to let me. I was so in love with him that I probably would have done anything."

"How could you be in love with someone who put your life at risk?"

"It wasn't Greg's fault. I chose to at that time. I thought it would bring us closer. I wanted him to love and trust me."

"Okay, so what happened?" Gabrielle asked in an irritated tone.

"You! I was with Greg for three years before he met you. One day, I followed him to your job at Kosher Delight. When you came out to meet him, I saw the way he embraced you. That's when I realized he'd never done that with me. All these years, Greg never kissed me or hugged me the way he did with you. His face never lit up like that."

Gabrielle lowered her eyes to the floor. She felt like a fool.

"I confronted him a week later, and he told me that you were his girl," she continued, while wiping tears from her rosy-red cheeks. "I was devastated. When I asked him why you and not me, he said because you're everything he's ever wanted. He will always love me, but as a friend only. I was so in love with him that I was still willing to see him even though he was with you. But, he told me no because it would only complicate things." Britney had to pause for a second and took a deep breath. This was indeed painful for her. "So, I begged him to make love to me for the last time. I wanted something to remember him by. He agreed, and we made love for several hours. I didn't want him to go. After we were done, though, he left. I went into the bathroom and found the condoms in the wastebasket. I took a syringe and injected his sperm into me."

Gabrielle rubbed her forehead, as her heart started beating fast. "Did you get pregnant?" she said, swallowing hard.

"Yes, I did, but I had a miscarriage. Greg never knew. After he left me, I dropped out of school and started using drugs frequently. My life took a turn for the worse. I was transporting drugs for anyone just to make a buck."

Gabrielle was confused. "Britney, I was told you were caught carrying my husband's drugs and your mother bailed you out."

"No. Where did you get that from? My mother found out about Greg by reading my journal. I left it out and she found it. One evening, she popped up on me at school and caught us together. It's strange because at first, she adored him. Then, a year later, she forbids me to see him. When I asked her why, she said because it's dangerous."

"So how did she know he was into selling drugs?"

"I was busted in Florida. Greg flew all the way down there to bail me out, even though it wasn't his drugs I was carrying. The authorities notified my mother, and once she found out it was Greg who bailed me out, she assumed it was his drugs."

"So that's why she went after him?"

"I guess. She said he was gonna ruin everything. She even accused him of introducing me to drugs. I tried to explain, but she wouldn't listen. She had Greg followed. It's funny because her plan was to run up in Greg's stash house and arrest him. But, then she got wind that one of Greg's workers was locked up and charged with murder. She was ecstatic. When she first met with Alex, he told her nothing. She kept asking him had he ever seen Greg kill anyone, and Alex told her no. That's when they started showing him bodies of drug dealers. They gave him inside information about the killing. Alex stuck to his story for about month. Eventually, they came up with a plan to offer him a lesser charge if he agreed to testify against Greg. Alex agreed."

Gabrielle's blood was boiling. "So where did you come in at?"

"I didn't. When I found out what my mother was doing, I immediately called Jake, Greg's lawyer."

"You mean Jake knew about this before Greg went to trial?"

Britney nodded. "Yes. I went to his office and told him who I was."

"I don't understand how Jake allowed this to go to trial knowing this information. It doesn't make sense. That was grounds for an immediate dismissal."

"I know. So, when I found out they indicted Greg, I went to see him on Rikers Island. Greg spoke to Jake, and I was supposed to testify. But, my mother got wind of this and hit the roof. She threatened me by saying she would put me in jail, too. Even with that, I was still going to take the stand. Two days before I was supposed to appear in court, I was kidnapped and taken out of the country until the trial was over. I didn't even know they found him guilty until six months later."

"Where did they take you?"

"Cayman Islands. I was in rehab over there. After the trial was over, my mother flew out there to see me. She told me that she received word that some people from Greg's team were going to kill me after I took the stand. That's why she snatched me away."

"What! Why would they do that?"

"I don't know, but I believed her."

Gabrielle sat there puzzled. She couldn't believe what she had just heard. "Your mother did all of this to stop you from seeing a man?"

Britney nodded. "Yep. She ruined my life."

Somehow, Gabrielle wasn't buying it. There was more to the story Britney didn't know.

"Was it because Greg was black?"

Britney shook her head no. "I don't think so. My mother has dated lots of black men, so I don't think it was because of that. I think it was because of this," she said, reaching into her bag and handing Gabrielle two huge envelopes. "After I got back into the States, I stumbled across this."

Gabrielle reached for it. "What is it?"

"It's tapes and documents that prove Greg was set up. Gabrielle, someone forged all the reports in Greg's case. They said Greg killed Charlie Chapman, but he didn't. Charlie was killed by Larry Stevens, a corrupt detective at the fortieth precinct. Word on the street was Larry and his partner Miguel was extorting dealers. They killed Charlie to send a message. But, just before Charlie was killed, he and Greg had an argument over a basketball game bet. So, everyone assumed it was Greg."

Gabrielle thought she was going to faint. This was too much for her.

"So this detective framed Greg?"

"He was one of them. Greg was the only dealer in the Bronx that was grossing two million dollars a month. He kept his shop tight, small, and wasn't flashy like most dealers. But, most of his money came from out-of-town connections. When Larry heard this, he tried to shake Greg down. But, it didn't work. He thought about killing Greg, but knew Greg's team was ruthless and loyal. It would've been a war. So, he did the next best thing: set him up. Greg was supplying every law official with something, whether it was drugs or women. He was the man, and Larry knew this. So, instead of killing him, he put the word out that Greg was working with the FEDS. Of course, no one believed that. So, along with my mother, Judge Barron, and a few others, they framed him. Alex was a plus. All they had to do was change the ballistics report and everything else fell into place."

"Judge Barron!"

"Yep! Gabrielle, half of the Bronx's law enforcement was Greg's clients."

"But he had Jake Lawrence, one of the best attorneys in the world."

"Jake was involved."

Gabrielle got up and paced back and forth. This was so surreal. The entire Bronx judicial system was corrupt. She looked over at Britney and thought, *What if she's lying? But for what?* Gabrielle stopped pacing and stood there with her arms folded. "Why Jake?" she finally asked.

Britney shrugged her shoulders. "They threatened to expose him because of something he did years ago on a case. They boxed him in, and he had no choice but to agree."

So that's why the muthafucka keeps giving me the runaround. He had not intentions on helping Greg come home.

"Did Greg know this?"

"No. Greg thinks it's because of me. He believed I betrayed him, but I didn't. I wanted to help him," she cried.

Gabrielle sat down next to Britney and hugged her. "Britney, it's not your fault."

Britney sobbed. "Believe me, I wanted to help him, even when I found out he was married to you. I know you may not want to hear this, but I loved him. He was the only person who really believed in me. My mother thinks he was the one who turned me on to drugs, but she was so wrong. I started using drugs at the age of thirteen. It started with marijuana and escalated from there. It was Greg who tried to help me get off."

Gabrielle looked away. "Yeah, my parents tried to prevent me from being with him, too."

"Well, at least you had the guts to stand up to them," Britney replied, sniffling. "Gabrielle, I was distraught when I found out about you. I couldn't believe he was with someone else. After his case was over, I wrote him and apologized for not being there. I also told him how much I loved him. I even asked him if we could be together, assuming you would have left him after he went to jail. He wrote me back saying he forgave me, but the only thing I could do for him was pray for him to come home. He also made me promise that I would take care of myself, stop using drugs, and pursue my nursing degree. He then went on to say that he was married to the love of his life, and although some might believe he was cursed, he felt blessed because he had you in his life."

Gabrielle's eyes filled with tears. She couldn't believe she doubted his love. Unable to hold her emotions back, tears rolled down her cheeks. "Excuse me. This is all too much for me.

Britney, I'm sorry for all of this. I had no idea you felt this way."

Britney's tears continued to roll down her face as she waved Gabrielle off. "Girl, don't be. I'm just happy he found someone like you. I tracked you for years. You are one of a kind, Gabrielle. He's lucky to have you in his life."

Not expecting the comment, Gabrielle blushed. "Awww, thank you. Well, I'm happy you got yourself together. Britney, I don't know what to say."

Britney stood up and put on her coat. "I wasn't able to help him back then, but today, I can," she said, while staring at the envelopes on the desk.

Gabrielle nodded and stood up. "I'll read over it," she told her, walking her to the front door.

Britney turned around. "If there is anything I can do to help, please don't hesitate to call me."

Gabrielle smiled. "I won't, and thank you again."

"May I ask what you're going to do?"

Gabrielle smirked. "I'm going to do what I do best...seek justice."

Both smiled.

Britney hugged her. "You do that, and be sure to add my dearest mother to the list." And with that, she left.

Gabrielle walked back into her office, picked up the envelopes, and sat down at her desk. She took a deep breath before opening the first one. Was she ready?

Fuck it, she thought.

Chapter Eight
Morgan

*I*t seemed like only yesterday there was snow on the ground, Morgan thought, while staring out her bedroom window. It had been almost three months since she started living her double life. During the day, she was an outstanding student, but at night, she turned into Tony's sex slave. Sometimes she felt like giving up and telling someone, but then she thought about the end results. Tony assured her that as long she did what he said, her family would remain safe.

Although she was raised never to question God's decision, she sometimes asked what she did to deserve this. There were times when Morgan was sure Tony would kill her in that house. He controlled every aspect of her life, from visiting her family on weekends to dance rehearsals. She wasn't allowed to do anything unless he approved it.

To avoid getting beaten when they got to his Cape Cod house, she would cook him a full-course gourmet meal, which was followed by painful sex. However, it really didn't matter what she did. If Tony got irritated, he would hit her anyway.

"When will it end?" she asked herself, as she grabbed her

bag off the floor and headed out to school.

Since practice was cancelled, Morgan went to the library to catch up on her studies. Surprisingly, she hadn't fallen behind. As she pulled out her book *Darwin Theory of Evolution,* she heard snickering and laughing coming from the other table. She looked up and saw two teenagers kissing and hugging. Morgan instantly became depressed. *Will I ever have a boyfriend?* Sighing, she diverted her attention back to the book.

As usual, Al picked her up after school to meet with Tony. On the car ride over to Tony's office, Morgan dozed off and was awakened by the sound of his voice when he got in.

"Sorry," she mumbled, trying to keep her eyes open.

Tony glanced over at her and his heart lit up. He leaned over and gently kissed her on the cheek. "Go back to sleep. I'll tell you when we get there," he told her, while resting his hand on her thigh.

After pulling up to the house, Al asked, "Same time, Tony?"

"Yep," Tony replied, then grabbed Morgan's book bag to help her out. Once inside, he hugged Morgan. "You know, all I do is think about you."

While most women would be flattered, Morgan frowned. She didn't want him to think about her. Tony leaned forward and kissed her passionately. She was going to turn her face away, but she feared getting hit.

"Mmm, you smell so good. What are you wearing?"

"Gucci Rush," she replied.

"That shit smells good."

Astonished by Tony's behavior, Morgan looked away. He had never been this nice. Generally, he ordered her to remove her clothes and open her legs. *What has gotten into him?*

Tony pulled out a few pornography tapes and waved them in the air. "I finally remembered to bring them. We're going to watch these so you can learn."

Morgan sighed. She could not believe he was going to make her watch them.

He popped in a tape of a girl riding and sucking some guy off. Morgan was so sickened by it that she jumped up and offered to start dinner. However, Tony yanked her back down.

"Chill out! You need to watch this and learn," he snapped, rolling his eyes.

Glaring at him, she sat back down, but tried to avoid watching it by looking all around the room.

Tony noticed and asked, "Are you watching this?"

The tape had only been playing for ten minutes before Tony got aroused. "You see how she's riding that nigga's dick? Why don't you do that to me? Come over here and ride this dick like a cowgirl."

Appalled by his comments, she sucked her teeth and rolled her eyes. *Is he for real?* She'd never heard anyone talk like that. Morgan just sat there in a daze.

"Yo, did you hear what I said? Take your clothes off and jump on this dick!" he yelled.

Taking a deep breath, Morgan stood up from the couch and pinned her hair up. She was about to go to the bathroom to take off her clothes, but Tony grabbed her.

"Nah, I want you to take it off right here, and look at me when you do it," he told her, while touching his penis.

She glanced over at the tape playing on the television screen. "I don't..." Then she stopped. She could see Tony getting frustrated and knew it would only be a matter of time before he would jump up and hit her.

So, she strutted in front of him and gazed into his eyes. Obliging, slowly and sexually she unbuttoned her blouse, exposing her satin tangerine push-up bra. Unzipping her pleated skirt, Morgan allowed it to drop to the floor, revealing her matching panties. Tony lost his mind. Morgan seductively looked up at him with her bluish-grey bedroom eyes and removed the clip from her hair, allowing her tresses to fall. Tony sat there in awe. She was the most gorgeous thing he'd ever seen. Incapable of controlling himself any longer, he got up and went over to her.

"God, you're so fucking sexy," he said, before shoving his tongue down her throat.

He then guided her back over to the couch and removed his pants. That day, Morgan rode Tony into heaven.

It was almost nine o'clock when she arrived home exhausted. She dropped her bag on the floor and headed for the shower. Once she finished, she laid across the bed. Even though it had been months, she still wasn't use to Tony's penis. Dragging her throbbing body off the bed, she pulled out a nightgown. *When will this nightmare end?*

As she was getting ready for bed, the phone rang. Since it was rarely for her, she didn't bother to answer it. Moments later, Denise knocked on her door. "Morgan, the phone," she announced, opening the door.

Morgan hesitated for a second. "Who is it?"

With a poker face, Denise replied, "I don't know."

Morgan stood there for a second. *God, I hope it's not Tony.* She took a deep breath and grabbed it. "Hello," she said in a timid voice.

"Hello, Princess."

"Daddy!" She immediately recognized his voice.

"Yes, baby. How are you?"

"Daddy, I miss you so much," Morgan said, bursting into tears.

Denise had never seen Morgan so happy. She walked over and rubbed her back. "It's okay. I know you miss him."

With tears in her eyes, Morgan smiled at Denise, who then exited the room to give Morgan some privacy.

"I miss you, too. Guess what? I have a surprise for you," her father said.

"What is it?" she asked with excitement.

"Remember the last time I talked to you and said your mother and I would discuss letting you come out here?"

"Yes!"

"Well, your mother has agreed to let you come for your birthday."

"Oh my God!" Morgan screamed and jumped for joy. "Daddy, for real?"

"Yep, but that's not all. I want you to invite some of your friends so you can have a party here."

"Get out! A birthday party in Italy?"

"Yes! Whatever you want, and Denise has agreed to bring you out here."

"Alright! I can't wait to see you and Grandma," she replied, while dancing around her room.

"Neither can I, Morgan. I miss my Princess so much."

Morgan tried to calm down, but she couldn't. This was the best news she had gotten in a long time. "So when am I leaving?"

"Next week when school is out."

Oh yeah, spring recess, she thought. Ever since she'd been seeing Tony, Morgan didn't know if she was coming or going.

"Wait! My friends can't afford to travel out there."

"I'll pay for them. Don't worry, Princess. Just ask them and let me know."

"Okay."

"So how are you otherwise?" he asked. "Your mother told me that you were accepted into a Harvard Law School summer program."

Morgan smiled. "Yeah, the program starts in the summer, but don't worry, I still can visit you."

Both laughed.

"Alright, because I have a lot of stuff planned for us this summer."

"Yay, Daddy!"

Morgan and her father talked for another forty-five minutes to do some catching up. She told him about her studies, while her father updated her on the family. After they hung up, Morgan bolted out the room.

"Denise, why didn't you tell me that Mommy said I could fly out to see my father?" she asked, busting into her aunt's bedroom

Denise laughed. "Because I wanted it to be a surprise. So, surprise!"

Morgan stood there with her arms folded and trying to act mad, but she couldn't help but to burst into laughter.

"So you're taking me?" Morgan said, while taking a seat on the edge of the bed.

Denise sighed. "Maybe."

"But Daddy already told me that you would."

"Yeah, kiddo, I'm taking you," Denise replied with a smile.

"Awww, Aunt Dee, thank you." She smiled and reached out to hug her.

"You're welcome. I know how much you miss your father."

"Guess what? Daddy said I could invite some of my friends out there and he'll pay for it. He wants to give me a birthday party out there. Isn't that cool?"

Denise giggled. Morgan was such a little girl. "Yeah, that's cool," she said, mimicking her niece.

As Morgan was stretched out across the bed, Denise noticed the bruises on Morgan's body. Her shoulder was black and blue. "What's up with all of these bruises?"

"I don't know. What bruises are you talking about?"

"This mark," Denise said, touching her shoulder, "and look at your neck. Was someone choking you? Go look in the mirror. Were you in a fight? "

Yeah, and I got my ass whipped by your best friend, she thought.

Morgan tried to play stupid, but once she saw how serious Denise was, she went over to the mirror. "Oh, you know I dance. I probably hit my shoulder against something."

"Alright, well be careful next time," Denise said before laying back down.

Once again, Morgan allowed the opportunity to tell her aunt

about the abuse she was suffering at the hands of her best friend slip by because of her fear. *When will this ever end?*

Before going to bed, Morgan got down on her knees and prayed to God. She thanked him for everything, but she asked him to remove the pain from her life.

*****

The next morning, Morgan woke up excited. She couldn't wait to get to school and tell her friends about the good news. After running the few extra laps at practice that the coach made her do since she had been slacking on the field lately, Morgan looked up and saw Chloe and Julissa sitting in the bleachers. She waved at them, and they waved back.

Trying to catch her breath, Morgan went over to them. "Hey, guys."

"Hey, Morgan. You look good out there, girl," Chloe cheered.

"Yeah, your ass and legs look good. I didn't know running track could do that for the body. Maybe I should tryout next year," Julissa teased

They all laughed.

Morgan couldn't hold out telling them about her father's offer any longer. "Guys, guess what? I'm going to see my dad in Italy, and he told me that I could bring some of my friends," she said, beaming.

"For real?" Chloe asked.

"Yep."

"That's cool, but who has the money to go to Italy?" Julissa asked in a snide tone.

"No, silly, my dad is going to pay for it. All you have to do is bring some clothes and get your passport."

"Get the fuck outta of here. Italy? You know I want to go!" Chloe jumped up and yelled excitedly.

"I wanna go, too," Julissa whined.

Morgan was cracking up. "Both of you can go. You just have to ask your parents and let me know by tomorrow. It's during spring break, so we're staying out there for a week."

"Okay. I'm asking my mom tonight," Chloe boasted, with her hands on her hips and poking her lips out.

"Me, too," Julissa said.

Morgan shook her head. She was happy they didn't turn their nose up at her offer. "Great! I guess we're going to Italy then."

They all screamed like schoolgirls. After they gossiped a little, Morgan headed to the locker room to shower and get ready for her first-period class. Morgan beamed while getting dressed. Life was almost bearable. Next week, she was going to see her dad and her friends were joining her. Then Tony popped into her head. *Damn!* She almost forgot he was picking her up this afternoon. Morgan sighed. She didn't know how much more she could take. She closed her locker and headed to class.

As Morgan was leaving her calculus class, she started to feel lightheaded. So, she went to the cafeteria to get something eat, hoping that would make her feel better. However, when she got there, the smell of the food turned her stomach. She immediately became sick and ran to the bathroom, where she busted into one of the stalls and threw up. Afterwards, she splashed some water on her face and rinsed out her mouth. *What the hell did I eat?*

Throughout the day, Morgan had a slight headache and felt nauseous. She wanted to go home, but remembered what happened the last time she disobeyed Tony. Therefore, she ate a banana and went to her next class. On her way out to meet Tony's car, she ran into two guys that were in her dance class. They thought she had dropped out. Lying, she told them that she had just been busy with school, but after spring break she would be back. As usual, the car was waiting at the end of the block. Before getting in, Morgan quickly looked around.

"Yo, what's wrong with you?" Tony asked, when he noticed

her flustered face.

Morgan rested her head against the window and replied, "Nothing. I just don't feel good today." She hoped he would take her home. Feeling like something wasn't right, Tony considered it when he peeked over at her, but then changed his mind. *She'll be alright once we get to the crib,* he thought.

During the drive, Morgan slept, while Tony talked on the phone.

When they pulled in front of the house, Tony tapped Morgan. "We're here."

"Same time, Tony?" Al asked.

"Yeah, Al."

Once in the house, Morgan went straight into the bedroom to lie across the bed. She felt so tired. After walking into the room, Tony put his keys and phone on the dresser, then went over to Morgan. A part of him felt awful. He didn't understand why he was abusing her.

He sat on the bed. "Are you sure you're okay?"

Afraid of what he might do, Morgan got up. "I'm fine," she replied and started removing her clothing.

Today, she didn't have the strength to fight him. So, instead of waiting for him to give the orders, she did the usual and went into the kitchen to prepare his dinner. Following dinner, they went into the bedroom and she proceeded to give him sexual gratification. He couldn't get enough of her.

On the way home, they slept, with Tony holding Morgan in his arms. They both were exhausted. He woke a few times and glanced over at her to make sure she was comfortable. He even leaned over, kissed her plump cheek, and whispered, "I love you."

They parked down the block from her building, and like always, Al got out to, giving them some privacy.

Gently moving Morgan's hair off her face, Tony whispered, "See you tomorrow."

As soon as Morgan walked in the door, Denise yelled from

upstairs. "Morgan, where in the hell was you?"

Oh no, Morgan thought, as she ran upstairs and into Denise's room. "I was at practice," she quickly explained.

Denise looked at the time on the cable box. "This late?"

"Yes. A group of us decided to walk home since it wasn't cold outside."

"Okay, but is something wrong with your cell phone?"

"No."

Denise hopped off the bed and walked up to Morgan. "The next time your ass walks in here late without calling, I'm gonna smack the shit out of you. Understand!" she yelled, pointing in her face.

Morgan's eyes widened. She was astonished. Denise had never spoken to her like that. Frightened, she stared into her aunt's somber face and replied, "Yes."

Denise got back into the bed, but Morgan, who was afraid to move, stood there for a few seconds before lowering her head and going to her room. *Great! Now Auntie is upset with me.* Dropping her bag on the floor, Morgan plopped down on the bed and cried. It seemed like just yesterday she had a bright future ahead of her.

As tears rolled down Morgan's face, Denise tapped on the door and walked in. "Hey."

Morgan looked up, while wiping away her tears. "I'm sorry, Auntie," she said, then started crying again.

"It's fine. I didn't mean to snap at you. I just had a bad day," Denise replied, embracing her.

"I promise I'll call next time."

"I know. Listen, I just don't want anything to happen to you. There are a lot of sick people in this world."

Like Tony, Morgan thought, as she collapsed into her aunt's arms and continued to sob.

"Hey," Denise said, lifting her face up by her chin. "Cheer up, niece. In a couple of days, we're going to Italy."

"I will. I just don't like it when you're mad at me."

Denise laughed. Morgan was so sensitive. "Girl, please. As you get older, I will continue to yell at your ass." While walking out, Denise sniffed the air. "Why do I smell Tony's cologne all of sudden?"

Oh lord, she thought, stricken with panic. "Beats me," she managed to calmly say.

Denise sniffed one more time. "Maybe it's just me," she said, then walked out.

Morgan fell back on the bed. "Whew," she mumbled.

Chapter Nine
Tony

Tony and Christina's relationship had been different ever since he read about her and Rashid in the tabloids. While deep down inside he was hurt, a part of him was happy. When they first started out, Tony adored Christina. She was beautiful, young, and sexy. However, as time went on, he slowly began to resent her. Even with all her attributes, Tony wasn't in love with her anymore. There were days when he just felt like telling her it was over, but didn't. Tony entered his apartment and found Christina in the living room with her hands folded.

"Hey, what's up?" he said, standing over her.

Reluctant to respond, Christina replied, "Hello," in a snide voice and brushed past him. Tony smirked. He knew Christina was only acting out because her ass got caught. Her little publicity stunt backfired on her, and the media ate her ass up.

Tony felt it served her right. Lately, he had been completely disregarding her childish behavior. One would think she would tip-toe around him since she was wrong, but not Christina. She blamed Tony for her actions. Every day he came home, she would try to read his body language, trying to figure out what mood he was in. Unfortunately for her, Tony didn't give her one. If Christina wanted to run around acting like a whore, that was her fucking problem. All Tony cared about now was Morgan.

Tony glared at Christina as she left the room. He shook his head and mumbled, "Silly broad." He didn't bother to follow her. Instead, he went into his private office. It had been months since he sent Stevie a business contract regarding the sale of his company, and he wondered if she had a chance to review them. So, he decided to call her. After two rings, she answered.

"Hey, Mr. Flowers," she giggled.

Tony smiled. Her voice was comforting. "Stacey Jackson," he said, using her real name.

"No, it's Stacey Strong now," she replied, correcting him.

He forgot Stevie had gotten married. "My bad, Mrs. Strong. Did you have chance to review the contracts?"

"Yes, I did. I was gonna call you, but I got tied up. Tony, give me a second. I made some notes."

As Tony waited while Stevie searched for the paper, Christina walked in and asked, "Tony, did you eat?"

Looking up at her, he replied, "Yes."

Christina noticed he was on the phone, so she started to walk out when Stevie came back on the line.

"I found it. Sorry…okay, my only concern is will they pay you in a lump sum or in payments because I don't see where that's outlined in the contract. I sent it to Gabrielle so she could revise it for you. Tony, as long as you own the majority of the company, I say go for it."

That voice sounds so familiar, Christina thought.

Tony was about to respond when he noticed Christina standing there with her hand on her hip glaring at him. He shook his head in disgust and diverted his attention back to the phone. "Yeah, I was thinking about that, too. That's why I had my girl look at it before I signed. "

"Oh hush! How are things with you otherwise? Congrats on your album. They're playing it like crazy down here."

Just as Tony was about to respond, Christina blurted out, "When you're done, I need to talk to you."

This time, Tony glared up at her and rolled his eyes. *She's such a fucking kid,* he thought. As soon as Stevie heard Christina's voice in the background, she immediately cut their conversation short. She didn't want her getting the wrong idea about them. She started to say goodnight, when Tony picked up the receiver, taking the call off of speakerphone, and whispered, "You see, if I was with you, I wouldn't be going through this shit."

"Oh really? Well, when you had me, you didn't know how to treat me."

Tony remained silent because it was true. Stevie was the best girlfriend any man could have asked for. She was smart, sexy, and supportive, but most of all secure. She never acted out like Christina.

"So when are you coming to New York? Maybe we can have dinner," he said, changing the subject.

"I don't know, Tony. I've been so busy with my company that I don't have time. However, I do plan on visiting within the next few weeks. But, it's going to be more of a business visit," she responded, ignoring his invitation.

"That's what's up, Mrs. Strong. Well, if your schedule permits, holla at me," he said, trying to sound intelligent.

"Okay, sounds like a plan. If you have any more questions, feel free to call me. "I'll do my best to help you out."

"I'll keep that in mind. Goodnight."

"Goodnight"

Tony glanced up at Christina, who was still standing with a pissed-off expression on her face.

"Who was that?" she asked in a nasty tone.

"A good-ass woman," he retorted, while rolling his eyes.

"If she's so good, why aren't you with her?"

"Don't come in here asking me no fucking questions, when your stinkin' ass was acting like a whore a couple of months ago. Yeah, you thought I forgot. Maybe you should be with that nigga," he proclaimed and walked out.

"Maybe I should. At least he knows how to treat a woman."

"Well, when I get a woman, I'll know how to treat her, too."

"Yeah, whatever, asshole!"

Tony glared at her. He didn't even bother to comment. In fact, he didn't need this shit tonight. He had too much going on. "Why are you even here? Go model or sing some shit. Get the fuck outta my face."

"Whatever!" she said, then sucked her teeth and walked off.

Tony went into the kitchen and grabbed a bottle of apple juice out of the fridge. On his way up to the bedroom, his cell phone rang. It was one of his jump-offs.

"Yo," he answered.

"Tony, you don't love me anymore?"

Tony giggled. "Nah, I've just been crazy busy. What's good with you?"

"Nothing. Missing my Tony," she moaned.

"Hmmm, how much?"

"Come over here and let me show you."

Tony was about to say something nasty, when he looked up and saw Christina standing at the top of the stair. "Listen, let me hit you back."

Click!

"Another one of your groupies calling?" Christina asked in a sarcastic tone.

Tony disregarded the slick remark and brushed past her.

Christina placed her hand on her hip. "Oh, so now you gonna ignore me? I have to be crazy to stay with your ugly ass."

Tony turned around and glowered at her, wanting to strangle her ass. Christina didn't know it, but Tony was very sensitive about his looks. He knew he wasn't attractive, but to hear someone say it to his face was more than he was willing to take.

All he could do was take a deep breath and reply, "If you feel like I'm too ugly for your ass, maybe you need to be with someone else. I'll still get paid."

They angrily stared at each other for a few moments before Christina turned away and walked into the bedroom, while Tony went back downstairs into the living room to watch TV. In order to avoid any more arguments, Tony slept on the couch that night.

The next morning, he got up to find Tia standing over him. "What?" he said.

Tapping her feet and shaking her head, she said, "So you're sleeping on the couch now?"

"Morning to you, too," he replied, while getting up and stretching. "Fucking girl is getting on my nerves, for real."

"Hmmm, I guess the feeling is mutual," Tia stated, handing him a paper.

"What's this?" he asked, while snatching it.

"It's a letter from Elisa, prohibiting you from negotiating any deals for Christina. Apparently, she went to her record label and told them not to discuss anything with you anymore."

Tony frowned. "Fucking bitch," he mumbled. Then he smiled because Christina had just fucked herself.
"You know what, Tia? It's cool. If Christina doesn't want me to be involved, that's a'ight. I'm gonna give her what she asked for," he stated with a smirk.

Tia shook her head because she knew Tony was about to teach Christina a lesson she would never forget. He read the paper and was handing it back to Tia just when Christina walked in.

"Morning, Tia," she greeted cheerfully.

Tony and Tia both looked at Christina.

"Morning, Chris." Tia peeked at Tony from the corner of her eyes, hoping he wouldn't say anything about the letter.

Tony walked over to Christina, said, "Morning, baby," and then went upstairs to get dressed.

Both women, who were surprised by his actions, just stood there and thought, *What the hell has gotten into him?*

Tony was buttoning up his Polo shirt, when Christina came in the room. "Since we're both getting ready to go on tour, I was thinking maybe we could fly away for a few days. We've been under a lot of stress, and it's taking a toll on our relationship. What do you think?" she suggested.

Tony wanted to tell her to go to hell, but he chose not to…at least not yet. "A'ight! Set it up," he said, kissing her on the cheek and walking out.

Skeptical about his response, she ran behind him and asked, "Are you sure?"

Tony turned on the stairs. "Yes, Chris, I'm sure. Let's keep it local, though."

Smiling, Christina jumped up and down. She was finally going to get her man back.

Tia was waiting in the living room for him.

"You ready?" he said, while putting on his shades.

"Yes, but where's Chris?"

Tony walked towards the door. "She doesn't ride with us no more, remember?"

Tia nodded. She had forgotten that quickly.

On the way over to the office, Tia handed Tony a schedule of his performances. After reviewing it, Tony tossed the paper at her. "What's this? What kind of shit is that, Tia?" he asked, clearly upset.

"What do you mean? We sat down and talked about this months ago. You're scheduled to be in Europe for a week. Then you'll come back for a few days before you're off to the west coast. After that, the *Flower's and Company* tour starts. You gave me the dates. Remember, you wanted to be on tour around the same time as Christina? What's the problem now?" she snapped.

Tia was right. He did discuss those dates with her months ago, but that was before Morgan came into his life. Tony closed his eyes. *What the hell am I gonna do now?* Tony sighed. He could not be away from Morgan that long.

"We can't cancel some of these performances?"

Tia frowned. After all the hard work she had done to arrange these appearances, now he wanted to back out. "Cancel? Hell no, Tony, you can't cancel. What has gotten into you lately? You leave the office early everyday now. No one can reach you after three o'clock. I mean, what's the problem? You were the one who gave me the dates, and now you're saying cancel some of them."

"It's none of your fucking business if I leave early. Last time I checked, I'm the fucking CEO. Fuck it! Don't cancel it. I'll be there, but next time, tell me beforehand and not the day before. How the fuck you didn't know I had something planned?"

"You gave the fucking dates to me. No one cares where the hell you go. All I'm saying is I've been trying to meet with you for the last couple of days and your ass has been jetting outta there. You know what? Fuck it!" she snapped.

Tony glanced over at Tia; she had never spoken to him like that.

He took a deep breath. "I don't have shit packed," he said, grumbling. "Do Mookie and the others know I'm leaving tomorrow? What about my meetings?"

Tia stared at him in repugnance "If your ass was around more, you would've known that everyone knows you're leaving tomorrow. Mookie will handle the meetings and then meet us there. Kareem is coming by to line you up. Carmen has already packed your bag. Just because you're not on point doesn't mean everyone else isn't," she stated in a spiteful tone.

Tony laughed because Tia was right. He did have one helluva team. Being his manager and personal assistant, she was the best at keeping it sharp.

"A'ight, that's what I'm talking about. Shit, that's what y'all get paid to do," he replied, laughing to break the ice.

She didn't crack a smile, though. She found nothing funny.

When they pulled up to the office of the record label, Tony glanced over at Tia, who was still pissed. He pulled her arm. "Ay yo, fix your face. You know I'm sorry."

She playfully smacked his hand away. "You're too fucking much, you know that? I want a raise just for dealing with your shit."

They both laughed.

Tony stopped in the office before heading over to the studio to listen to his new group, Wild Child. Tia was right. Tony had become so addicted to Morgan that he had been neglecting his company lately. After leaving the studio, he went back to his office so Kareem could line up his Caesar. He also had two conference calls with Society Records, and Jamal had scheduled a meeting with this young cat named Bishop from Mississippi.

It was about 3:30 p.m. when Al called. "Am I picking her up today?" his driver asked.

Tony looked at his watch. *Damn, how time flies,* he thought. He thought about saying no because he still had a lot of things to do before flying out the next morning, but at the same time, he didn't want to leave town without being with her again.

"Yeah, pick her up, take her to the house, and then come get me."

"Okay, Tony."

Just as Al was about to hang up, Tony said, "Wait, Al. Are you downstairs?"

"Yes."

"Never mind, I'm on my way down."

Tony called Tia and told her to reschedule his meetings for tonight because he had to step out for a few hours. Before she could ask him any questions, Tony had hung up. On his way down to the lobby of the building, Mookie called his phone.

"Tony, what's up? You're not jumping in on the conference call?"

"Are they on the phone now?" he asked, while jumping in

his black CL 500.

"Yeah."

"A'ight, conference me in, fam."

While discussing the direction of his company, Tony saw Morgan from afar. He instantly lost his train of thought; he dropped the phone in his lap to focus on her. The wind gently blew her long, silky hair as the sun shined on her flawless skin. She was beautiful. Morgan had on a khaki skirt, white Polo shirt, dark brown camisole, and brown suede flat shoes. Tony just stared at her in admiration. She looked so young and fresh.

"Yo, Tony, you there" Mookie screamed into the phone.

Oh shit! Tony picked up the phone and jumped back on the call. "Sorry, I was distracted for a moment."

"It's cool."

"Listen, Mookie, I gotta go. Let's hook up tonight around nine. Okay?"

"A'ight, son. One."

"One."

Click!

Morgan opened the door and got in.

"What's up, baby?"

"Nothing."

Like always, they went to the house, Morgan cooked dinner, and then she served Tony dessert in the bedroom. Afterwards, they cleaned themselves up and waited for Al.

As they were going out the door, Tony said, "Oh, I forgot to tell you. I'm not picking you up tomorrow or next week. But, I better not hear no shit about you."

Yes! Morgan was so relieved. Tony wasn't aware that she was leaving the following week to Italy.

Since there was no traffic coming into the city, they got to Morgan's apartment in thirty-five minutes. As usual, Al got out and smoked a cigarette. Tony leaned toward Morgan and said, "I meant what I said. I will hurt you. Understand?"

Morgan nodded. "Yes, Tony."

"Trust me, I have eyes and ears all over. Fuck up and that's your ass."

"Okay," she said, while preparing to open the door to exit. However, Tony grabbed her by the arm and pulled her back. For a second, she was confused, but then it dawned on her that he wanted a kiss goodnight. So, she leaned forward and forced herself to give him a passionate kiss. He smiled, licking his lips.

"That's what I'm talking about. Take care of daddy," he moaned, before pulling her on top of him.

What started as a goodnight kiss turned in to a quickie in the backseat. Morgan was already sore from earlier and wanted to say no, but she knew it would have led to a fight.

*****

For the next week, Tony promoted his album throughout Europe. It was the last night before he was to fly back home, and he couldn't wait to be with Morgan. Sadly, he'd only spoken to Christina about three times the entire trip. Strangely, he didn't miss her. While she was every man's dream, for Tony, she was becoming a nightmare.

When he wasn't promoting in Europe, Tony partied. However, no matter what he was doing, Morgan was never far from his mind. His entourage brought back a different group of girls to their suite every night. While his team loved it, Tony declined. Though the women were gorgeous, they didn't measure up to Morgan. Screwing them would be a waste of his time. Morgan had Tony Flowers whipped.

Since he couldn't be with Morgan physically at the moment, he decided to place a call to Denise, and during the conversation, he innocently asked about Morgan. While talking to Denise, she informed him that she and Morgan were going to Italy the following week to visit Morgan's father. When he learned of this, he almost shit on himself. He knew of Felix and how dangerous a man he could be when provoked. Before,

Tony didn't fear Felix since he lived out of the country and never saw Morgan. However, now things had changed. Suddenly, he became aware of the consequences he would face if anyone found out about his sexual involvement with Morgan. Certainly, Felix would be upset if he knew Morgan was having sex, and more importantly, he would kill Tony if he found out he had raped his little girl. Tony knew how Denise got down. If she ever found out, she would just kill him. But, Felix operated on a different level. Not only would he kill Tony, but he would murder Tony's family, too. In a blink of an eye, Tony's entire generation would be sent back to their essence. Therefore, Tony made a deal with God. If God would protect him, he promised to never touch Morgan in a sexual way again.

Chapter Ten
Christina

Today was Tony and Christina's second-year anniversary. Although exhausted from promoting her album throughout the west coast, Christina still wanted to spend time with Tony. On the ride over to his place, she thought about the last time they were together. It wasn't good. Something in Tony's eyes expressed he'd had enough. He didn't even bother to kiss her goodbye.

Entering Tony's apartment with Joyce and Paul, Christina was happy to be home. Sure, she was glad about her career taking off, but more excited about seeing her man. The last couple of months had been tough for them. Tony was slowly drifting away. To make matters worse, they had been in different parts of the world promoting their albums and were barely speaking. When they did, it was no more than a five-minute conversation. She began to think it was a mistake excluding him from her career. At least then she could see him at meetings and arranged lunch dates. Deep down inside, Christina felt like she was losing him.

Christina went upstairs to the bedroom thinking Tony was up there getting ready, but he wasn't. When she inquired to

Carmen about Tony's whereabouts, Carmen told her that Tony hadn't been home all day. Immediately, she assumed he forgot about their dinner date and was with another girl. She sighed and went into living room where Paul and Joyce were seated.

"Joyce, please help me unpack."

Her assistant peeked at her from the corner of her eye. "I thought you were going out to dinner with Tony?" she said with a confused expression on her face.

Christina frowned. "I thought the same thing."

After they went upstairs to start unpacking, Joyce glanced over at Christina, whose face was red and eyes watery. She shook her head. She didn't know why Christina allowed Tony to treat her the way he did. Instantaneously, Christina stopped unpacking and sat on the bed in a daze. *What am I doing wrong?*

Joyce was about to say something, when Paul knocked on the door. "Excuse me, Christina. Tony just called. He wants us to meet him at the restaurant."

Joyce and Christina looked at each other and then back at Paul.

"Where is he?" she asked.

"He didn't say."

Christina took a deep breath. "Give me a second, Paul."

"A'ight," he said, closing the door.

If that's what they call love, then they can keep it, Joyce thought.

"Chris, why don't you go and freshen up while I finish unpacking for you," Joyce offered.

"Thanks," Christina replied, flashing a fake smile and then going into the bathroom. Minutes later, she walked into the living room. "I'm ready. Where are we supposed to meet him?"

"At Bar Pitti," he replied, walking out the door.

Christina shook her head and followed Paul. It was pointless getting upset with Tony.

In the car ride over to the restaurant, Christina stared up at the stars. *This can't be love,* she thought, while fighting back tears. Feeling someone staring at her, she looked up and saw Mike watching her through the rearview mirror. Their eyes briefly met, before she turned away ashamed. Something about Mike's eyes said it all.

When they arrived, Paul phoned Tony, who was already inside.

On their way in, a fan passing by yelled, "Oh my God! That's Christina." The young girl ran up to her and asked, "May I have your autograph?"

Thrilled, Christina smiled and said, "Sure. What's your name?" After signing a piece of paper, she continued inside.

Tony was waiting at the bar. When he saw Christina, he came over to her. "What's up?" he whispered in her ear.

Trying not to show her emotions, she simply replied, "Nothing."

The hostess greeted them and led Tony and Christina to their table. Once seated, Tony's cell phone rang and he excused himself before answering it. Christina shook her head. *He didn't even say happy anniversary.* Since she was in the public and afraid the paparazzi were lurking in the shadows, she grabbed the menu and pretended not to be displeased. Yet, deep down inside, she was steaming. *The nerve of this bastard. At least have some fucking respect. Oh God, please give me the strength not to curse him out. I don't know how much more I can take,* she thought.

The waiter came by and asked if they were ready to order, and just as Christina was about to say no, Tony returned.

"Are you ready?" Christina asked him.

"Give us a few more minutes," he responded, looking up at the waiter.

Trying so hard not to give Tony an evil eye, Christina just smiled at the waiter.

"So how was Los Angeles?" he inquired, while glancing at the menu.

Christina quietly exhaled. "It was great. You know today is our anniversary, right?"

"Word? I've been so busy I completely forgot. I'll pick you something up tomorrow."

Christina glared at him and nodded. "Don't bother," she muttered.

Tony shot an evil stare her way and ignored her snide remark. "So are you ready to order?"

Oh, so you wanna play the ignoring game? she thought. "Actually, I am."

After the waiter came over and they placed their orders, Tony glanced around the room, waving to a few fans. He then turned his attention back to Christina. "So how does it feel to be the hottest chick in the game?" he asked in a sarcastic but playful tone.

"Hmmm, I don't know, but I'll tell you once I find out," she retorted.

"Come on, ma. If Tony Flowers says you're hot, then that's what it is." He winked.

"Oh, just because you said? Interesting," Christina said, sipping her water.

"What's so interesting? That I chose you?"

Christina's eyes widened. "You chose me? Wow! Thank you, Tony," she smiled.

"Anytime."

"Well, Elisa has some others thing lined up for me. In fact, she thinks she may have another endorsement deal coming my way and some movie scripts," she told him, smiling.

Tony smirked. "Big moves."

"I'm trying. I mean, since you've labeled me the hottest chick in the game, I wouldn't wanna disappoint you."

"Hope not."

"So tell me about London," Christina said, changing the subject.

"London was great! Hopefully, when I get back from L.A.

in a couple of days, I can shoot my next video."

Christina's eyes widened. "You're going to LA?" she asked in an inquisitive tone.

"I'm actually leaving the day after tomorrow," he said in a nonchalant voice.

"Oh, when were you going to tell me? I rushed back here so we could spend some time together."

"What the fuck are you talking about? You knew this months ago," he barked.

"You know what? Fine," she snarled.

"Ay yo, what's your problem now? You know my album just dropped, so I have to make some guest appearances. What the fuck? Aren't you doing the same thing?" Tony chided, tossing his napkin on the table.

"Why are you cursing at me? I completely forgot. Like I said, I was hoping we could spend some time together, that's all. But, forget it. It's not like you care. You forgot our anniversary for Christ's sake!"

"Aren't we spending time together now?" he replied.

Christina smirked. "You know what, Tony? You're right."

To avoid an argument, Christina didn't say another word to him. Frankly, she could care less if his bitch-ass got up and left. The way he was acting she would rather eat alone. After the waiter brought their food over, Christina pulled out a magazine to read while Tony chatted on his cell phone. Periodically, they engaged in small conversation, but for the most part, they didn't say a word to each other. She glanced over at him hoping he would acknowledge her presence. However, Tony paid her no attention. He was too deep into his conversation, even excusing himself a few times.

It was fruitless, she thought. Christina was hoping this dinner would be civil. Instead, it was turning into a disaster. Tony was completely humiliating her in public. Trying to hide her pain, she looked around and smiled at some of the other customers. *Where the fuck is he?*

When Tony came back, he asked, "How's your food?"

Oh, now you wanna talk to me, muthafucka, she thought. "It's fine," she mumbled in a dry tone.

"What's wrong with you?"

"Nothing. I'm ready to go," she said, putting her magazine away.

"A'ight." He reached in his pocket and tossed some money on the table.

After giving him a look of disgust, she got up and left him sitting there. She didn't bother waiting for Paul to escort them out. Moments later, Tony came out and got into the car.

Unable to tolerate his shit any longer, Christina faced him. "You know what, Tony? I'm sick of your shit. If you don't wanna be with me, then tell me. All night you've been acting up, saying slick shit out of your damn mouth, and I'm tired of it."

Tony sighed and disregarded Christina's ranting. One thing Tony never did was fight in front of anyone, which is something his father taught him years ago. Once Christina realized she was being ignored, she became hysterical. "So you're gonna ignore me? Well, fuck you!"

SMACK!

Christina hauled off and slapped the shit out of Tony, sending his head flying against the window. Mike was so shocked that he almost ran a red light. It took Tony tenth of a second before he realized what had happened. Stunned and embarrassed, Tony smacked her back.

"Fucking bitch!" he yelled, swinging on her. "You smacked me?"

Christina swung back while trying to block her face at the same time. "Get off of me!"

Paul quickly jumped in and grabbed Tony's hands. "Yo, Tony, chill!"

"Nah, this bitch has lost her mind!"

Christina franticly tried to free herself from his grip. "Get off me, muthafucka!"

Instead of releasing her, he grabbed her shoulders and shook the shit out of her, causing her body to make snapping sounds. "Little bitch!" he yelled. "I told you about acting out in public!"

Paul desperately tried to pry Tony's hands off Christina's shoulders, while yelling, "Tony, let her go!"

Mike, who was stunned by all of this, pulled over to the side of the curb. "Tony! Chill, man!" he yelled

After three minutes went by, Tony finally let Christina go, throwing her ass back in the seat. "Next time you hit me, I'm gonna break your fucking neck."

"You bastard," she cried, catching her breath. "I hate you!" she yelled, then jumped out and ran down the block.

Paul glanced at Tony, who was breathing heavy.

"Fuck," Tony grumbled, then rolled his eyes and sat back.

Paul hopped out and went after Christina. "Chris!" he called, hoping they weren't being followed by the media. "Christina, stop! Please," he said, getting closer.

Christina abruptly stopped and faced him. "I don't wanna hear it, Paul. I had enough. He thinks he can treat me like shit. It stops tonight. I've been nothing but good to Tony. I love him, but you think he cares? If he doesn't wanna be with me, then he just needs to tell me," she blurted out before collapsing into Paul's arms.

Paul sighed. *This shit is crazy.* He looked around, praying no reporters were out there. Even if Christina and Tony were heated, neither of them comprehended that they had an image to uphold.

"Chris, chill. You know how Tony gets."

Christina furiously pushed Paul away. "I knew you would say that. I forgot he's your friend," she said as tears ran down her flustered face.

She started walking away, when Paul gently grabbed her arm. "Nah, it's not that." He took a deep breath. "Listen, get back in the car. You don't want this shit to end up in the papers.

You have too much going on for ya."

Christina stared at Paul, with her eyes puffy, arms folded, and lips poked out. "He better not say shit to me."

Paul giggled. "A'ight, I'll make sure."

Snap! Snap!

"Gotcha!" someone yelled.

Their eyes widened. It was too late. The paparazzi already had a picture. Paul smoothly ushered Christina back to the car. Tony had already told Mike to drop him off at Joe's Sports Bar in the village. He needed some time alone before he did something crazy. When Christina got back in the car, they didn't say a word to each other. Tony glared at her a few times from the corners of his eyes. He was still fuming inside. Actually, Christina was lucky that Paul and Mike were in the car because Tony would've seriously hurt her.

"Thanks, fam. Don't worry, I'll be good," Tony said, after Mike pulled up to the bar.

Christina didn't bother to acknowledge him leaving. *Fuck him,* she thought.

To avoid another fight that night, Christina stayed in the guestroom. However, it was after midnight and she could not sleep. So many thoughts were running through her mind. She remembered how Tony was once so gentle, kind, and treated her like a queen. Now, he was a monster. Christina chuckled when she thought about the look on Tony's face when she slapped him. He probably didn't think she would ever swing on his ass, but he had it coming. While happy to finally stand up to Tony, a part of her was sad. She never wanted her relationship to turn into an abusive one.

Christina got up and sat over by the window. The view was beautiful and hypnotic, with different shades of purple and black and glistening stars. While gazing up at the sky, Rashid popped into her head for some reason. Maybe it was because she found herself feeling lonely. She ran downstairs to look for her bag. She hoped she hadn't thrown away his number.

Searching through her bag...Bingo! She found it in her wallet stuck to one of her credit cards. *Ironic,* she thought.

She pulled out her cell phone, dialed his number, and let it ring two times before hanging up. *What am I doing? I can't talk to him.* Christina felt her phone vibrating and glanced at it. It was Rashid. *Oh God!* At first, she was going to let it go to her voice mail, but then he would know it was her because of her greeting. Therefore, she decided to just answer it.

"Hello."

"Hello. Did someone just call me?"

Christina exhaled. "Uh, Rashid, it's Christina Carrington," she said coyly.

"Oh Christina! Hey, what's up?"

Christina smiled at the sound of his sexy voice. "Nothing. I came across your card and decided to call. Did I wake you?" she asked in a shy tone.

"Nah, ma, how are you? I wondered if you were ever gonna call."

Christina could tell from his voice that he was smiling.

"Yeah, whatever," she said, blushing like a schoolgirl.

"So where are you and why are up so late?"

Because I'm in love with an asshole and we had a fight tonight. And instead of being here with me working it out, he's off fucking some groupie, she thought. "I couldn't sleep," she whispered, fighting back tears.

"Are you okay?"

"Yes. Why you ask that?" she snapped.

"Just making sure, Christina," he replied, trying to comfort her.

Wow, why can't Tony be this caring? she wished. "Sorry. It's been a crazy night, Rashid," she mumbled as the tears fell and ran down her cheeks.

"Well, I'm here if you need to talk."

Christina did want to talk, but not over the phone. She needed a shoulder to cry on.

"Rashid, are you in New York?"

"Yeah…why?"

"I wanted to know if you feel like taking a walk. Maybe we could meet in the park and talk," she responded in an unsure tone. *What am I doing? If this story leaks out, my relationship with Tony will be over for sure.*

"Okay. Where would you like to meet?"

Christina didn't know. She hadn't thought that far ahead. "I don't know. Some place private where we can't be seen."

Both laughed.

"Alright, meet me on 14th Street and Twelfth Avenue. We can walk the pier. It's late, and I doubt if anyone will be out there at this time of night."

Christina sat there a moment thinking about what she was about to do "Okay. I'll wait for you in the little park area. Please don't take long."

"Yes, ma'am. I won't even put on any makeup," he teased.

Christina busted out laughing. "You're so crazy. Goodbye"

"Later."

Click!

Afraid of being noticed, Christina wore black jeans and a matching top, with her hair pulled back into a bun and Tony's black fitted Yankee hat. She threw on her black butter leather crop jacket and all-black Air Max. In the elevator, she chuckled to herself. She was dressed as if she was going to rob someone.

Though Tony lived walking distance from the pier, Christina still hopped in a cab. She couldn't afford for anyone to see her. When she got into the cab, she lowered her head and prayed the cab driver wouldn't recognize her. Once the cab driver pulled up to the corner, Christina glanced around looking for Rashid. When she noticed him standing across the street, she paid the driver and got out. As she was crossing the street, she suddenly started sweating and her stomach was in knots.

She walked up to Rashid. "Hello," she said bashfully.

He leaned down and kissed her on the cheek. "Christina."

They started walking along the pier. "So what's up?" Rashid asked, breaking the ice.

Christina stared up at the beautiful sky and took a deep breath before responding. "Rashid, can I ask you a question?"

"Sure."

"Do you have a girl?"

"I used to."

"What happened?"

"That depends. Are you friends with her?" Rashid responded, causing them both to laugh.

"No, for real, silly. Why did you break up?"

"We just grew apart. Basically, she didn't trust me and I didn't trust her."

"Did you cheat on her?"

"I'm not gonna front. Yes, I did. Christina, you know how it is in this business. Chicks are loose, but I stopped."

"Okay. So what happened?" Christina pressed.

"She started cheating…partying, hanging out, listening to her girlfriends. In the end, we just broke up."

"So you're single?"

Rashid laughed again. He felt like he was being interrogated. "Yep, and you?"

"And me what?" she stated in a high-pitch tone.

"Are you single?" he asked.

Christina sighed. "You know I'm not single, Rashid."

He nodded. "So where is the infamous Tony? Why aren't you snuggled up under his arms?"

Holding back tears, Christina remained quiet because she really didn't know where he was.

Rashid peeked over at Christina, who was in another world. "Are you okay?" he asked.

With tears rolling down her face, she continued to be silent, while Rashid took her into his arms. At that moment, Christina sighed and began to sob uncontrollably. Uncertain of what to do, he just held her. After a couple of minutes, she pulled herself together.

"Sorry," she mumbled.

Rashid lifted her head up by her chin. "It's cool. I'll send you my dry cleaner's bill," he told her, making Christina laugh. "Are you okay?" he asked seriously, letting her go.

Still unable to speak, she just nodded. Guiding Christina over to the bench, Rashid put his arm around her for comfort. He stared so intensely into Christina's eyes that it caused her to look away.

"Why are you staring at me?" she asked, avoiding eye contact.

Rashid handed her a piece of tissue from out of his pocket. "Because you're so beautiful."

Blushing, Christina looked away. "I'm serious."

"So am I. You are beautiful. That's why I can't image why he would hurt you."

Christina's eyes widened. "It's that obvious," she muttered.

Nodding, he said, "Yeah. So what happened?"

"We had a huge fight."

"About?"

"Everything, Rashid. I don't know what has gotten into him lately. He's been acting funny, like he doesn't wanna be with me," she stated, as she began to cry again.

"Did you talk to him? I'm not making any excuses, but you know how we men are. Maybe he's stressed out about something."

"Well, if that's the case, he should talk to me. I'm supposed to be his girl. What's so hard about confiding in me?"

"Because that's not what men do, Christina."

She shot him a wicked look, causing Rashid to rephrase it. "I don't mean that." He chuckled. "Some dudes, like Tony, have a lot of pride. They don't like expressing their problems, especially to their girl. They believe it makes them look weak."

"And you? What do you think?"

"I'm not like that. I don't mind sharing things that are

troubling me with my girl."

"I wish Tony was like that. But, I don't think it's that. I truly believe he has someone else."

"Oh. So if you know this, why are you still with him?"

Christina sighed and wiped the tears from her face with the tissue. "Because I love him."

Rashid stared at her. "Yes, but are you happy with him?"

Christina was caught off guard by his question. "Some days."

"Well, is that enough for you?"

"No."

"So what are you gonna do about it? Tony will only do what you allow him to do."

Christina's eyes watered up again. "You're right, but…"

"But what? Christina, if he's treating you like shit, why stay with him? You know whether you stay or go is up to you."

"There are days when we are happy," Christina proclaimed.

"If you say so," he responded, leaving the subject alone.

Christina sat there thinking. Rashid was right. She hadn't been happy with Tony for months. Their relationship was deteriorating right before her eyes. It used to be they would argue and immediately make up. Now, it had gotten worst. Their relationship had become a physical one.

"Well, listen, it's going on three o'clock in the morning and I have to get up," he said, standing up.

Not wanting to leave, Christina stood up, too. "Rashid, I hear what you're saying. And I do thank you, but…"

"But what?" he interrupted. "Listen, ma, never give a person hundred percent of you. Always keep ten percent for yourself."

"I'll remember that," she said.

Pulling Christina closer, Rashid stared directly into her dark-brown puffy eyes. He gently caressed her face. Still not saying a word, he licked his lips, which caused Christina to blush. Then he massaged her lower back, sending chills through her body. Christina closed her eyes and exhaled. *Damn, his touch feels so good. I haven't felt this way in months. Only if Tony was this romantic things would be better.*

Enjoying his touches, Christina pulled Rashid closer and they stared into each other's eyes with desire, anticipating each other's next move. She lifted her head up slowly and kissed him, while he embraced and passionately kissed her back. As their tongues explored each other's mouths, Christina rubbed her body up against his. This was so wrong, but felt so right.

Christina moaned, "Take me home."

"Are you sure?" Rashid asked, bewildered by her request.

Not sure about nothing anymore, Christina nodded. "Yes. I don't feel like being alone tonight."

Smiling, he replied, "Let's go."

As they were walking to the corner to catch a cab, Rashid stopped and turned towards Christina. "Are you sure?"

She stared at him with sadness in her eyes. "Why? You don't want me?"

Rashid sighed and grabbed her by the waist. "More than you know. I just don't want you to do something you'll regret. Christina, I like you, and I know you're going through a rough time right now. I don't wanna take advantage of that."

Christina buried her head in his chest and took a deep breath. He was right. She just wanted to get back at Tony. While she found Rashid sexy as hell and wanted so bad to make love to him, her heart still belonged to Tony Flowers.

"Thank you," she said, staring up into his face.

"For what?" he asked with a smile.

"For being a gentleman. I know it's crazy, but I do love him."

"Yeah, I know," he replied, kissing her on top of her head. "Listen, let's get you home."

"Okay," she smiled.

In the cab, they snuggled and kissed. The cab pulled right in front of the building, and not caring who would see her, Christina got out. As she went inside the building, she smiled.

Rashid had just proved that all men are not dogs.

The next day, Christina made the decision that she would start staying at her place effective immediately. While she loved Tony with all of her heart, somehow she couldn't get Rashid's words out of her head. From now on, it was going to be all about her. *Maybe then, Tony will realize what he has and come running back to me... hopefully.*

Chapter Eleven
Denise

Denise rolled over and looked at her clock. April had rolled around fast, and she had to appear in court that morning. She got up and went into Morgan's room, but she had already left for school. Returning to her bedroom, she sat on the bed. *How in the hell did I allow myself to be put in this situation?* Denise hadn't been arrested in years, and she made a vow to herself that once this case was over, the judicial system would never see her again.

She walked over to her walk-in closet, and after browsing through it, she finally settled on a black, pencil skirt, white sleeveless blouse, red tailored blazer, and four-inch leather pumps. She thought about changing her bag, but chose not to. She was going to court, not a photo shoot.

Denise got dressed and headed to 100 Center Street. When she got there, the line was outside and around the corner. She pulled out her cell phone and called Mr. Rubin. It went to voicemail, so she left a message letting him know she was there. Once inside, Denise went to Part A where she was scheduled to appear. *Fuck! Do people wash their asses before coming to court? It smells like pussy, feet, ass, and bad breath,* she thought. Denise held her breath while walking through the hall. She went into the courtroom to see if Mr. Rubin had arrived, and when she saw that he wasn't there, she came back out into the hall and went over to review the board for the scheduled hearings. She was number twenty-seven on the list. Just as she was about to go back inside, she heard someone call her name. It was Mr. Rubin coming down the hall. She waved as she walked up to him.

"Morning."

"Good morning. Sorry I'm late. The fucking trains," he said, trying to catch his breath.

Denise grinned. "Yeah, I know the trains. Always a sick passenger when you're in a hurry."

Both laughed.

"So here's the deal. I'm going to get it dropped today. Depending on the judge, he may go for it or he will give us another court day."

Denise listened closely and nodded. Strangely, she was a little nervous. She didn't know why because she'd been through the system before. Maybe it was because she had a lot more to lose this time around.

They went into the courtroom, and Mr. Rubin signed them in while Denise took a seat on the bench. A few minutes later, they called her. Nervous and uncertain about what was going to happen, Denise walked up to the podium, placed her hands behind her back, and looked straight ahead as the assistant district attorney read off the charges.

"Your Honor, the defendant was pulled over with a loaded unlicensed handgun. Although she does have a gun registered in her name, that's not the gun the police found in her car," the ADA proclaimed.

The judge looked over at Mr. Rubin, waiting for a response.

Mr. Rubin retorted, "Yes, Your Honor, my defendant did have a loaded gun in her car. However, what probable cause did the police officers have to search my client's car? The gun was in the glove compartment, not in plain sight. My client wasn't speeding or drinking. So what extenuating circumstance did they have? The police illegally searched my client's car."

Denise tried not to smile. Along with the judge, everyone glanced over at the ADA.

"Is it true that the police illegally searched the defendant's car?" the judge inquired.

The ADA sighed. "Your Honor, the officer searched the car only because there were shots fired in that area and a black car was seen leaving the crime scene."

Mr. Rubin immediately interrupted. "Your Honor, my client does have a black car, but so do a million other people. There were no real reasons for them to pull my client over."

The judge glanced over at the ADA. "He's right."

"But, Your Honor, the defendant has a criminal history," the ADA complained.

"For the record, my client has been arrested before, but she was never convicted of anything."

"Judge, if I may. The defendant use to be a part of a notorious street…"

Before the ADA could finish, Mr. Rubin interjected. "Are you kidding me? Your Honor, my client is a tax-paying citizen. I never said she was perfect, so please tell the ADA to stick with the law. The police had no valid reason to search my client's car. Isn't that why we have the Fourth Amendment? I mean, I thought this was America!" Mr. Rubin yelled.

The courtroom erupted in laughter.

"Mrs. Murphy?" the judge said to the ADA.

"Your Honor, the police believe they had probable cause to search the car," ADA Mrs. Murphy explained.

"Unless something changed in the Fourth Amendment, they didn't have probable cause. If you look at the police report, the police officers didn't even hear the shots. They saw my client speeding by trying to catch a green light. When they pulled her over, she tried explaining to the officers that she was coming from home. I also have surveillance cameras from her luxury Manhattan apartment building showing the time and date she left. Your Honor, I ask that all charges be dismissed against my client."

Denise's eyes widened as she held her breath. Mr. Rubin was on a roll; he was worth every penny.

The judge looked over the police report and then said, "I agree with Mr. Rubin. Mrs. Murphy, the police didn't have probable cause to search the car. I am dismissing the case against the defendant. Mrs. Murphy, I suggest you tell those officers to read the Fourth Amendment."

"But, Your Honor..." Mrs. Murphy started, then paused when she couldn't think of a worthy response.

Denise wanted to jump for joy, but instead, she took a deep breath and whispered, "Thank you, Jesus."

After the judge threw out the case, the court officer handed her a piece of paper stating all charges were dropped against her. Denise grabbed the paper and walked over to Mr. Rubin. She wanted to squeeze the hell out of him.

He looked up, winked at her, and said, "Let's talk outside."

Once they were outside, Denise blurted out in joy, "Gotdamn! Mr. Rubin, you don't play."

He smiled. "No, I don't, kiddo. Especially with these cock-sucking ADA's always trying to lock someone up."

"Well, I'm glad you're on my team. Thank you, Mr. Rubin."

"You're welcome. Now do me a favor. Stay out of fucking trouble. You're too smart for that, Denise. Come on."

Denise sulked. "Trust me, I will."

"Well, kiddo, I have another client to defend. Call me if you need anything. Oh, how's Greg?"

"He's good; trying to come home."

"I've always admired him, very smart and a good person. Well, tell him if he needs anything, my door is always open."

"Will do and thanks again."

They hugged and Mr. Rubin rushed over to another

courtroom. Denise said a silent prayer before heading out the door. On her way down the stairs, she looked across the lobby floor and saw Morris. He was holding hands with some girl. Denise probably would've been upset if she wasn't seeing Derrick. Instead, she put on her shades and left the courthouse. Fighting over a man was something she never did and wasn't about to start now.

It was eleven-thirty when Denise arrived at work. She walked in her office and was about to close the door, when Maria ran up to her.

"Dee, Lauren from Human Resources called for you. She said to call her. It's important," Maria mumbled.

In a laidback way, Denise nodded and said, "Okay," while trying not to appear worried.

Denise picked up the phone and placed the call. "Lauren, it's Denise."

"Hey girl, I need to see you in my office now."

"I just got in."

"You heard what I said," Lauren responded in a stern voice.

Denise sighed. "I'm on my way."

As soon as she walked into Lauren's office, she was ordered to close the door. After doing what she was told, Denise took a seat.

"Why didn't you tell me that you were arrested?"

"Huh?" Denise sat there with a confused look on her face.

"You were arrested?"

"Okay. I didn't know I had to report it," Denise retorted.

"Well, you have to. All city employees have to report if they were arrested. It's a part of your contract."

"I didn't know that, so now what?"

"Why were you arrested?"

Denise stared at Lauren with her face screwed up. "Since you already know I was arrested, why don't you tell me?"

Lauren exhaled. She didn't feel like going back and forth. "Listen, Dee, I'm just doing my job. Now are you going to tell me about the case or do I have to contact the Inspector General's Office?"

"Is that a threat?"

Lauren glared at her and remained silent.

"Do what you gotta do," Denise replied angrily, shrugging her shoulders.

Lauren rolled her eyes. "Fine."

Denise got up and was about to walk out, when Lauren blurted out, "You need to humble yourself. You know I could care less about why you got arrested, but I have a job to do."

Denise rolled her eyes and sighed. "Okay, sorry. I was arrested for having a loaded gun in my car," she informed her and then looked away in shame. She peeked over at Lauren for a reaction, but there wasn't one. So, she continued. "I had to go to court today and the judge threw it out," she explained, sitting down again.

Lauren folded her hands and leaned across the desk. "Now was that so fucking hard?" she asked, making them both burst out into laughter. "Bring me the paperwork so I can file it away, and stop taking shit so personal. This is me, Lauren. We came here and got hired together. I know we all have our problems. Shit, you know my drama. That's why I called your ass down here myself."

"Sorry, you know how I think," Denise muttered.

They both giggled.

"Bring me the stuff and stay your ass out of trouble. What the hell you need a loaded gun for anyway?"

"Because this is New York," Denise winked and walked out of the office. *Whew!* She hated her job, but she knew she needed it. She went back into her office, responded to a couple of emails, and made a few calls. She also met with her two system analysts, briefing them on some project since she was going on vacation. In the meeting, they talked about work, but then always turned it into a gossip session.

It was almost six o'clock when Denise cleaned off her desk

and headed out to meet Derrick. Tonight, she was taking him to Nello's Restaurant and then they were going out dancing. Initially, she was going to cancel, but she really wanted to see him before she left for Italy. Although she still was involved with Morris sexually, she couldn't deny she was smitten with Derrick. He was the total opposite of what she was accustomed to. Surprisingly, they were compatible. Like Denise, he loved to read and write poems. He also loved black and white movies and Jazz.

Many perceived Denise as a tough, foul-mouth, ex-drug dealer; when in fact, she was very shy, sensitive, and insecure. Her insecurities were the reason why she attracted guys like Morris. However, Derrick was changing all of that. She was becoming more relaxed and less standoffish.

As she was walking out of the office building, Derrick stood there with a big bouquet of roses. Surprised by the gesture, she smiled.

"What are you doing here?" Denise asked. "I thought we were meeting uptown."

"I couldn't wait to see you," he replied, kissing her forehead.

Denise blushed like a little girl. "I missed you, too. Thank you for the roses."

After goggling at each other, they jumped in a cab and headed to the restaurant. In the ride over, Denise leaned her head on Derrick's shoulder. She felt so safe around him.

"How was your day?" she asked.

"My day was great. Closed a few deals and made a couple grand," he joked. "However, it's better now that I'm with you."

Denise's face lit up. "It better be," she responded, playfully pinching him.

As usual, the two laughed and talked over dinner. She was so fascinated by him. Not only was Derrick smart and sexy, he was very humble. He never took anything for granted and pointed out the little things in life to her. Not to mention, he was quite the romantic type. Sometimes, she had to pinch herself to make sure she wasn't dreaming about this man who seemed too good to be true.

"What are your plans for this weekend?" Derrick asked, kissing Denise on the back of her neck as they walked into the restaurant.

"Oh, I forgot to tell you. I'm leaving tomorrow."

"To go where?"

"Italy."

"Oh," he responded in an astonished voice.

"It's not for me. I'm taking my niece to see her dad. He lives there."

"Your niece is Italian?" he asked.

"Yes. It's a long story, but basically, she hasn't seen her father in years," she replied.

"That's very noble of you. You see, I knew there was a reason why I liked you."

Both laughed.

"That's not all you're gonna like." Denise winked and flashed a devilish grin.

"I bet," he said, yanking her to him.

Usually, Denise was uncomfortable with being affectionate in public, but there was something about Derrick that she couldn't get enough of. And while they were eating dinner, she prayed she would never get enough of him because she loved the insatiable feeling she experienced whenever they were together.

Chapter Twelve
Gabrielle

It took Gabrielle a couple of weeks to digest all the information Britney had given her. Baffled as to why her husband was the fall guy, Gabrielle reached out to Tommy. She was certain there was more to this story than Britney knew, and she was determined to find out. Still uncertain of Britney's motives, Gabrielle took all the evidence and stashed it in a safe place. This was about to get ugly, so she trusted no one.

She was meeting with Tommy at a private location that day. She pulled up to a motel off of I-80 West, arriving first to scope out the area and make sure she wasn't being followed. Paranoid, Gabrielle paced back and forth in the room while waiting for him.

"Where the hell is he?" she mumbled to herself, as she kept checking the time on her watch.

Knock! Knock! It was Tommy, the private investigator who she had hired.

"Girl, are you on the run? What's with the top-secret location?" he said, joking.

Gabrielle just looked at him. Once he saw she wasn't

laughing, he knew it was serious.

"Sorry, Tommy, but I couldn't afford for anyone to follow me."

"Are you alright?" he asked, looking worried.

"Yes, I'm fine, but I just discovered something," she said, while walking over to the small table in the room. Tommy followed her, confused.

"Gabrielle, talk to me."

Gabrielle sighed, holding back tears. "Remember that girl Britney Cox?"

"Yeah, the one you wanted me to find."

"Yes! Well, it turns out that she's part of the reason my husband is in prison. The ADA that prosecuted my husband was her mother."

"What! Are you kidding me?"

"No, Tommy. In fact, everyone was in on it, even Jake Lawrence."

"What? *The* Jake Lawrence?"

"Yes. Apparently, my husband was supplying judges, police officers, and other law officials with drugs and hookers."

"Damn! This is crazy."

"Tell me about it. Look at all of this. Tommy, there's tapes of conversations discussing my husband's case."

Tommy shook his head in disgust. "Why your husband, though? It doesn't make sense. Was he blackmailing them?"

"I don't think so. If he was, they would've killed him instead of sending him to prison."

"True. Which means something else is going on."

"Exactly! And that's what I want us to find out."

Tommy pulled out his glasses and started to review the information. He then listened to the tapes while Gabrielle made notes. In the middle of the tape, Tommy stopped it.

"I've heard enough. This was bigger than your husband's case."

"I don't understand."

"Gabrielle, what's on these tapes isn't about drugs or murders. This is about money. Always remember something. When you follow a drug case, you find drugs. When you follow a murder case, eventually you will find a body. But, when you start following money, you never know what you're gonna find. They're talking about money."

Gabrielle took a long, deep breath. "Tommy, I need your help. I can't trust anyone right now."

"Not with nothing like this you can't. What do you need me to do?"

Gabrielle sighed. "Follow the money."

"Now you're talking," he replied with a wink.

"Tommy, this is serious. I can't afford for you to drop the ball on this. These people are gonna come after us with all they got."

"How long have you been practicing law?"

"For a while now. Why?"

"Well, I've been in law enforcement for thirty years. I went up against criminals that would make these son-of-bitches look like queens. Gabrielle, I have never given up on a case, so like I said: what do you need me to do?"

Their eyes met briefly.

"I need you to help me bring them down and bring my husband home."

*****

Gabrielle spent most her weekends focusing on the case. When she wasn't doing that, she went back to the crime scene, hoping to interview witnesses. Then, she and Tommy would meet up and share information. Greg's case became her main priority. They had read Greg's case over ten times, and it seemed like every time they re-read it, they discovered something new. It was amazing how Greg had so many loopholes in his case. A first-year law student could have won it. Going over his transcripts, Gabrielle got angry and then sad. She couldn't believe he didn't allow her to help.

Tommy was a perfectionist. He kept playing the tapes over and over, finding something new every time, from the sound of a person's voice to the noise in the background. Every little clue mattered.

"Gabrielle, do you recognize the man on the tape talking to Britney's mother?"

She listened again. "No. Why?"

"Because whoever this guy is he's not on the other tapes."

"I don't understand."

"From what I heard so far, ADA didn't trust any of them: Larry, Jake, or the judge. That's why she probably secretly recorded and documented everything in case the shit hit the fan. Notice how she addresses them by their name on the tapes. But, on this tape, it's a different person; a man's voice whom she never identifies."

Gabrielle nodded. "Okay, so what does that mean?"

"I don't know yet, but I'm assuming this man is the one she's protecting."

"Okay, so now what?"

"Well, I have a few friends that owe me some favors. But, first, we are going to lock these tapes in a secure place. People and things have a funny way of disappearing."

"Already done."

He laughed. "Great! Now we're gonna tear them apart starting with the detectives. They're probably the weakest link, so I'll start with him."

"Tommy, I don't want us to go after these people unless we're prepared."

"You don't think I know that. Come on! I'm not gonna show up at their front door asking questions. No! I'm gonna tear his life apart first."

Gabrielle laughed. "Alright now, Kojack!" she said, causing him to laugh, too.

"I've been doing this a long time. Trust me when I say justice will be served."

*****

Business was picking up at her law office. Good thing Abigail was back in the office. She divided the work among her partners and hired two interns, as well. Gabrielle was rarely in the office, and when she was, it was to research information.

It was the day of her conjugal visit with her husband and she was tired. Instead of driving up to the facility in Elmira like she normally did, Gabrielle took the bus. That way, she could get some rest. Lord knows she would need it messing with Greg.

The bus hadn't even pulled out before Gabrielle was sound asleep. Six hours later, the bus was pulling into the station. With two hours before her visit, she decided to go food shopping. So, she went to the nearest supermarket and picked up Greg's favorites: shrimp, fish, and chicken.

Arriving at the facility, Gabrielle sighed. While she loved seeing her baby, it was depressing, and it didn't help that the CO's were nasty. As usual, she was processed and taken to meet Greg. She got there only to find Greg, along with a few other inmates awaiting their visitors, standing at the gate. Even with all the stuff that was going on, he still managed to put a smile on his wife's face. God she loved that man.

"Hey, boo," she said, kissing him.

He kissed her back, while grabbing the bags. "What's up, baby?"

"Hmmm, nothing."

After they were inside the trailer, Greg put the bags on the table, while Gabrielle put her things in the bedroom.

"Boobie," he moaned, while running up behind her.

Gabrielle giggled like a schoolgirl. "Boo, please stop," she said, pulling away from him.

"No. I missed you," he said, as he turned her around to stare into her eyes.

"I missed you more, but let me put the food away," she replied, then started to walk out of the room.

Greg snatched her back. "The food can wait," he said before kissing her deeply.

Before she knew it, they were having sex. There were times when she and Greg would fuck, and other times, they would make love. He said it was the only way to keep their sex life interesting. Either way, he made sure his wife screamed his name.

Afterwards, Gabrielle fixed breakfast, while Greg sterilized the bathroom.

"Boo!" he yelled.

"Yes, daddy?"

"Lawrence wrote me and said you're not returning any of his calls," he told her, coming into the kitchenette.

Because he's a lying bastard, she thought. "Oh yeah, I forgot. This case is kicking my ass," she replied, referring to the case she was working on for her client Myra and her deadbeat boyfriend, Malik. Unfortunately, Malik's warrant was what kept him from being released, but Gabrielle was diligently working to find a way to make it possible for him to return home to Myra.

"Word? Well, please give him a call."

"Yeah, I will" she mumbled.

Gabrielle turned around, looked at Greg, and wondered would he ever tell her about Britney.

"Babe," she said.

"What's up?"

"Was there anyone special before me? I mean, did you ever have what you guys call a ride-or-die chick?"

"Nah," he answered in a nonchalant tone.

"Come on, Greg. You never had a chick that was your right-hand girl?" she asked, staring at him with her hand on her hip.

"No," he replied.

Okay, this is not working. Time for a different approach, she thought. "Have you ever dated girls that weren't black?"

Greg shot her a confused look. "That weren't black?" he repeated.

"You know, Spanish or white chicks?"

"Yeah. Why?"

"I'm just asking. So how were they?" she inquired.

"What do you mean?"

"I mean, have any of them written you?" she pressed.

Greg laughed. "In the beginning, but they stopped. What's with all the questions?"

"Nothing. A client of mines is white and loves black men. It just made me wonder if you were ever in an interracial relationship."

"I fucked a few, if that's what you mean. But, I never was in a relationship with them. Boo, did you look into any real estate?" he asked, changing the subject. "It's a good time to invest, ya know."

Gabrielle sighed. "Actually, no, I haven't. I've been so busy with Denise's contracts that I forgot. You know she's buying some buildings around y'all neighborhood."

"Yeah, you told me. Boo, you can't go wrong with real estate."

"I know, baby. I promise to look into it."

She wanted answers, but knew if she pressed the issue about his other affairs that he would become suspicious. So she decided to leave it alone for the time being.

After breakfast, they made love again, which put her to sleep. Sensing his wife was tired, Greg let her sleep until evening. Gabrielle woke up to the smell of baked chicken, yellow rice, and broccoli. She went in the kitchenette to find her hubby setting the table.

"You're up, sleepyhead," he said, kissing her on the cheek.

"Babe, why didn't you wake me? I would have cooked," she groggily told him.

"It's cool, boo. I know you're tired. Your boy got this."

She glanced around the place and was impressed. He had the candles lit, soft music was playing in the background, and the food was almost done. "Wow! What's all this about?"

"I just wanna make my baby happy."

"Awww, babe," she said, hugging him "I love you and I'm happy." She kissed him. "Is there anything I can do to help?"

"Yeah, wash your hands and sit down. Daddy wants to serve his Queen."

After they ate, Gabrielle offered to clean up, but he said no. So, she went into the bedroom and laid back down. Minutes later, she heard water running in the bathroom. When he came into the room, he lifted her up off the bed. Not saying a word, he stared into his wife's eyes and carried her into the bathroom. Once he had removed her t-shirt and his clothes, they got into the hot bathwater with the scented oil. Greg pulled out a basket of fruit from underneath the towel. Gabrielle laughed and rested her head on his chest.

"Awww," was all she could say. *Just what the doctor ordered,* she thought.

While lying in the tub, feeding each other fruit, and enjoying the music, Greg started to massage his wife's neck.

"Baby, you're so tense."

"I know, babe. I have so much on my mind."

"You wanna talk about it?"

"It's this case, but I really don't wanna talk about work. Tonight is our night, Mr. Brightman," she replied, shoving a strawberry in his mouth.

"A'ight, but I'm always here."

"I know. I love you," she stated, staring him in the face.

"I love you more. You are my life."

She moaned before passionately kissing him. Greg held his wife by the back of her head, while caressing her body with his other. They started in the bathtub, but because they kept slipping from the oil in the water, Greg carried his wife into the living room. When he put her down, she told him to hold on a second, and then ran into the bedroom to get her six-inch Louboutin stilettos. Now she was ready. She bent over and touched her ankles. Greg laughed; his wife was a freak.

Thrusting inside her, Greg pushed in and out while gently smacking her on the ass. "Whose is this?" he asked in a zealous tone.

"Yours, baby. Fuck me. Fuck your wife."

Greg then pulled out, carried her over to the table, and yanked her to the edge of it. Still with her pumps on, Greg threw her legs over his shoulders and started pounding her.

"Greg, it's in my stomach," she moaned.

"That's where it's supposed to be. Throw it back to daddy."

After a few minutes, Greg was ready to please his wife orally. Gabrielle moaned so loud that she thought the entire prison heard her. Massaging his head and touching herself, she felt like she had died and gone to heaven. Greg ate her until she climaxed in his mouth. He got up and slid back inside her, thrusting slowly but forcefully, making her body jerk. When Greg went to push her back on the table, she hopped down and dropped to her knees.

Gabrielle looked up at him. "What daddy want?" she asked in a seductive voice.

"Put it in your mouth."

She started out by teasing the tip of his head with her tongue. Then she licked up and down the length of Greg's hard cock. Glancing up a few times at him, she started sucking it. By now, he was in paradise.

"Damn, boo," Greg moaned.

Wow! Sucking on a banana really paid off, Gabriel thought.

Unable to hold it, Greg busted inside his wife's mouth. She almost threw up from the hot, thick substance. She rolled it around in her mouth, hoping Greg wasn't looking at her, but when she looked up, he was staring her dead in the face.

"Baby, I want you to swallow it."

Oh God, that's so nasty. She wasn't a fan of swallowing babies, but this was her husband. *I guess this is what Ludacris meant when he said be a lady in the street and a freak in the bed.* She obliged and swallowed.

"Yuck," she grumbled, causing Greg to laugh.

"Yuck my ass. It should taste like pineapples."

In an attempt to wash the nasty taste out of her mouth, Gabrielle went into the kitchen to get a glass of soda. When she returned to the bedroom, Greg was lying on the bed ready for some more, and so was she. Gabrielle climbed on top and rode him into the wee hours of the morning.

It was almost daybreak and they were still up, lying in each other's arms. Everything seemed perfect.

"You know, I wish I would've met you earlier," he said.

"Why?"

"I don't know. Maybe things would've gone differently."

"What do you mean?" she asked.

"It's nothing, ma. I'm just thinking out loud."

"Greg, what happened?" she asked, hoping he would talk.

"What are you talking about?"

"I'm talking about the case."

"You know what happened. That faggot-ass nigga Alex lied on me."

"Is that all? It's just hard for me to believe that the ADA went to trial and won with only one witness. Is there something else? I mean, you had Jake Lawrence," she expressed, sitting up.

"That's what I thought, too. He told me I was gonna beat it."

Gabrielle stared at him, trying to see if he was lying. But, something about his words said he wasn't. Greg really believed he was going to get off.

"Don't worry, boo. We're gonna bring you home."

For the next couple of days, Greg and Gabrielle enjoyed

their time together. They watched a couple of movies, danced around the trailer, and even went outside to play some basketball. But, like they say, all good things must come to an end.

With the van waiting outside, Greg grabbed his wife and kissed her before walking her out. "Boo, make sure you call the counselor for another date."

Gabrielle laughed. She couldn't even get off the campus before he was bugging her about another trailer visit.

"I will, Greg."

"Before you leave," he requested.

"Alright," she huffed.

Smacking her on the ass, he said, "Stop frontin' like you don't want another one."

They kissed and said their goodbyes before Gabrielle got into the van. After the officer locked the gate, he came back to the van and pulled off. Gabrielle looked out the window, smiling and waving.

*****

That Monday, Nancy walked into Gabrielle's office and announced that Gabrielle's sister was on the line.

"Giselle, what's up?" Gabrielle said after picking up the phone.

"Hey, Gabby, are you still coming to Mommy and Daddy's house tonight?"

"No. Why?"

"Grace is coming home, remember?"

Oh shit! With so much going on in her life, Gabrielle forgot Grace, the youngest of the four girls, was coming home. She had surprised everyone by enlisting in the Navy straight out of high school. Gabrielle believed she did that just to get away from their parents.

"I forgot that was tonight."

"Yep, and you know she'll be disappointed if you're not there."

"What time?" Gabrielle asked.

"Seven o'clock."

"Okay. I'll be there, but I'm not staying long."

"See you then."

Gabrielle sighed and closed her eyes, not looking forward to dealing with her snotty-ass parents that night. When she looked at her cell phone to check for any missed calls, she noticed Tommy's number on her screen. *Oh shit! Tommy called me.* She immediately picked up the phone to call him back.

"Tommy, it's Gabrielle."

"Hey. Now you call me back."

"I was away. What's up?"

"I need to see you face to face."

"Oh God, is it something bad?" she asked in a leery voice.

"For them."

"Really? That's great!"

"Well, I'm in DC right now and won't be back until morning. Let's meet at the same spot."

"Alright, see you then, and be safe."

Click!

After finishing up at the office, Gabrielle headed to her parents' house. Excited to see her sisters, she couldn't wait. It's not that often they all got together. She pulled up behind the cars that were parked in the driveway, walked to the door, and rang the bell.

"Gabrielle," her father said in a deep voice after opening the door.

"Daddy," she responded dryly, kissing him on the cheek and walking in.

"GABRIELLE!" Grace screamed excitedly.

They ran up to each other and hugged.

"Oh my God! It's so good to see you," Gabrielle said, as her eyes filled with tears.

"I missed you, big sis," Grace replied, while wiping the tears from her eyes.

"Hey, sis!" Gloria and Giselle yelled, walking up to them.

As they stood in the foyer embracing each other, their father advised them to go into the living room.

Gabrielle glanced over at him and mumbled, "Yeah, we wouldn't want the neighbors to know we laughed in this house."

They all giggled at her comment.

"Gabrielle, you're so bad," Giselle said, as they went into the living room.

"Mommy," Gabrielle said, hugging and kissing her.

"Oh, Gabrielle, I didn't even hear you come in," her mother said, patting her hand.

While they waited for dinner, Gabrielle and her sisters laughed, joked, and reminisced about the days when they were younger. Once the meal was ready, they all went into the dining room and Gabrielle's mother blessed the food before they ate.

"Daddy, doesn't Grace look great?" Giselle said, breaking the silence.

He looked up. "Yeah, she does. Will your hair grow back?" he asked in a snide tone.

Grace frowned. "It did, but I cut it again, Daddy."

"Why? Aren't females supposed to have long hair," he asked in a scornful tone.

Everyone just glanced at each other, and as always, their mother put her head down, pretending not to hear what he had said.

"Daddy, nowadays women are cutting their hair. It's easier to maintain," Grace explained.

Her father glared at her and then replied, "Fair enough."

"Gabrielle, how's Greg? I wrote him a few times and sent him some pictures. Did he get them?" Grace asked.

"Yes, he did. He wrote you back, I believe," Gabrielle replied with a smile, while eating her string beans.

"Isn't it a security issue writing a convict?" her father stated.

Everyone sighed.

Gabrielle slammed down her fork. "And what's that suppose to mean?"

"Nothing. Isn't he a convict? I mean, he was convicted of murder." He widened his eyes and frowned up his face.

Gloria mouthed for Gabrielle to ignore him, but she couldn't. She and her father fought about Greg all the time.

"Just because he was convicted doesn't make him a criminal," she mumbled.

"You watch your mouth, young lady. Don't get mad at me because you married a lowlife."

"A lowlife?" she retorted.

Giselle interrupted. "So, Grace, how long are you here for?" she asked, hoping to diffuse the situation.

However, it was too late.

"Father, my husband isn't a lowlife. Oh wait! I should've married someone stuck up like your ass, huh?"

"You watch your damn mouth. Your mother and I busted our asses to provide you with the best things in life, and what do you do? You go and marry a drug dealer."

"Oh please! You busted your ass to maintain an image. Who are you kidding, Daddy? So just because you gave us life you have the right to choose who I marry?"

"Gabrielle, don't talk to your father like that," her mother yelled.

"What, Mother? I'm sick of justifying my life to him! So what I didn't marry a pillar of the community like Daddy wanted me to. But, I married a good man, and regardless of what anyone thinks, he loves me dearly."

"Keep telling yourself that. He was running around screwing everything in sight. You need to thank me," her father said.

Gabrielle stood up and threw her napkin on the table.

"Grace, I'm sorry, but I refuse to sit here and pretend to be one big, happy family. You know what's sad, Daddy? Even if I didn't marry Greg, I would have never married a self-righteous son-of-a-bitch like you. You're so busy trying to be white, marrying Mommy because she was mixed. Ashamed of your own damn family? Why? Afraid the skeletons might fall out?"

"Gabrielle, stop," Giselle pleaded.

"No, he needs to know. Did you know as soon as we turned eighteen, we couldn't wait to get out of this hellhole? Maybe if you were a better fucking father..."

"GET OUT OF MY HOUSE!" her father yelled, facing her.

"With pleasure," she spat. "Giselle, Gloria, Grace...I'm sorry." She glanced over at her mother whose head was down. *Figures,* she thought.

"Whoever feels the same, you can get out, too."

Giselle and Gloria got up and followed Gabrielle, leaving Grace sitting there confused.

"Hey, Gabby, wait!"

Gabrielle stopped in the foyer and turned around. "Don't start. I'm tired of it," she cried.

"We know." Gloria hugged her. "I don't blame you. Let's get out of here and have a drink."

"Yes, please," Giselle whined.

Just then, Grace came running down the hallway. "Guys, wait! Y'all are not leaving me here with them," she said, causing everyone to laugh.

"Alright, let's go!" Gabrielle took a deep breath. "Parents."

"Yeah, you can't pick 'em," Giselle said.

The four sisters busted out in boisterous laughter as they left; another intentional stab against their father.

Chapter Thirteen
Morgan

As the sunshine shone into Morgan's room, she smiled like a Cheshire cat. She hadn't seen Tony in a week, and in a couple of hours, she would be leaving to go visit her father. The night before, Morgan had spoken with her mother. Jasmine always became frightened when Morgan traveled to Italy, fearing someone would snatch and sell her. One would have thought Morgan was going to fight in Iraq the way her mother broke down crying over the phone.

Knock! Knock!

"Morgan, it's Denise. Can I come in?"

"Yes," Morgan said, glancing over at the clock. It was 5:30 a.m.

"Are you ready for Italy?" Denise beamed, taking a seat on the bed.

"Yes! Chloe and Julissa will be here by seven o'clock, and then we're off. When I told my friends my dad was paying, their parents asked could he pay for all of their vacations."

Both laughed.

"Well, I'm ready, and I'm sure you could use a vacation.

Have you been to Italy before, Auntie?"

"Little Italy in the Bronx." Denise laughed.

"Huh?" Morgan laid there with a confused look on her face.

Denise cracked up laughing. "No, this will be my first time traveling outside of the country."

"Well, I can't wait to see my father. I miss him so much."

"I know, and he loves you even more," her aunt replied.

Morgan blushed. She loved talking about her daddy. "Well, maybe Mommy will let me move to Italy with him."

Denise cut her eyes. "Are you crazy? Jas allow you to live in another country with your father? I don't think so. Don't think because you're living with me that your mother would allow you to live with your dad. Shit, I had to damn near twist her arm for you to live here. Hopefully, one day, he can sit you down and tell you why he's not living here, though. As for your mother, she only allows you to live here because it was closer to school. You know how she feels about your education. Other than that, your little ass would be in Brooklyn. Besides, if you moved to Italy, I would miss you." She winked and got up off the bed.

Morgan glowed. "Awww, Auntie, I would miss you, too. I used to think I was a burden to you."

Denise turned around. "Why did you think that? I love having you around. You remind me of all the things I should've done. That's why I'm so proud of you, because you want more out of life than most girls. You're just like Jasmine — focused."

Morgan flashed a fake smile, then narrowed her eyes and looked toward the floor. *Only if you knew what was going on. There's so much I wanna tell you,* she thought.

Since Denise didn't get a response from Morgan, she went over and kissed her on the forehead. "Get ready. We have a plane to catch," she said, then exited the room, closing the door behind her.

As Morgan picked out something to wear, she suddenly felt nauseous. She became lightheaded and had to sit down. Praying she wasn't coming down with the flu. Morgan lay across the bed. After a couple of minutes went by, she felt better and continued getting ready.

*****

Thirteen hours and two flight connections later, they were in Venice, Italy. They retrieved their luggage and headed to catch a cab. As they walked out to the waiting area, someone yelled, "There's my princess!"

Morgan turned around, dropped her bag, and ran towards her father, leaving her aunt and two friends behind. "DADDY!" She jumped into his arms and wrapped her legs around him, almost knocking him down. After five minutes of hugging, she got down. "Daddy," she cried.

Felix embraced her. "You look good, Princess."

"Hey, Felix." Denise waved and kissed him on the cheek after finally catching up.

"Denise," he replied, while laughing because Morgan still had her head buried in his chest.

Overwhelmed, Morgan almost forgot to introduce her friends. "Oops, sorry," she laughed. "Daddy, these are my friends Chloe and Julissa."

Felix reached out and hugged them. "Nice to meet you."

They smiled back and said, "Hello."

Upon arriving at the house, they were greeted by Felix's family. All of Morgan's relatives were at the house waiting for her: cousins, aunts, uncles, and grandparents. It was around dinner time, and Morgan's grandma had prepared a feast. Following dinner, Morgan and her cousins went to the living room, while Denise and Felix took a stroll in the yard.

"Denise, thanks for bringing Morgan out here. You know she's the only thing that keeps me sane."

"You're welcome. I know how much you love her."

"I do. She's the only thing I have good going for me."

"Tell me about it."

As they strolled through Felix's manicured garden, he said, "Can I ask you something? And please don't lie to me."

"Sure," Denise responded, while holding her breath because she didn't know what to expect.

"Is Morgan living with you?"

Denise exhaled. "Yes, she is, but it's only because I live closer to her school," she explained. "How did you know?"

"Just because I live in Italy doesn't mean I don't have eyes and ears in New York."

Denise giggled. "I know Jas didn't tell you because she knew you wouldn't have approved of it because of my past. But, trust me, I'm not into that anymore. Morgan is like a daughter to me. I would never put her in danger. I'll lay down first."

He nodded. "I respect your honesty. I just wish your sister would include me when she makes decisions like this. Morgan is my child, too."

"Well, you know Jas."

"Do I! I know Jasmine is still upset about me being deported. But, that doesn't give her the right to exclude me out of Morgan's life. At the end of the day, that's my daughter, and if something happens to her..." He paused and took a deep breath. "Let's just say it would be problems."

Denise nodded and sighed. "I completely understand. Trust me, she's in good hands. Felix, I will never let anything happen to her."

"I know, and I'm glad she's with you. Overall, how is she doing? Does she need anything? Do you need money for her?"

She frowned and rolled her eyes at him. "No! Come on, Felix! This is me. Morgan is fine. I tell you one thing, though. I don't know what you and my sister did, but the two of you made a beautiful, smart, young lady. She's so focused it's not even funny. Sometimes I have to beg her to have fun."

Felix beamed. Just as he was about to respond, Morgan ran

towards them.

"Daddy!" she shouted.

Denise and Felix looked at each other and laughed. Morgan was definitely daddy's little girl.

"Daddy, Aunt Isabella said she's gonna take me to get my hair done," she said with excitement.

Her father shook his head and grinned. "That's not all we're gonna do for you. This week is Morgan's week. We're going to take you to a lot of places."

"Damn, you look just like your father...Italian," Denise commented, taking notice of Morgan's long eyelashes, flawless olive skin, and jet-black silky hair while she stood next to Felix.

The three of them laughed.

"That means you look good, Princess," he said with a smile and a wink.

*****

The next couple of days, even though she was still battling what she thought was a stomach virus, Morgan had a blast with her friends and family. When anyone would question why she was throwing up, she blamed it on the food. There were times when she just didn't eat.

Her visit was thoroughly planned out. In the morning, her cousins took her and her friends sightseeing. In the afternoon, they shopped with her aunts and uncles, and the evenings were spent with her father.

Morgan had gotten so sick that she almost fainted at her birthday party. Everyone assumed it was because she was surprised. At her party, she wore a peach strapless dress, gold sandals, and a wet and wild ponytail. Since she was only fifteen years old, Felix and Denise didn't allow her to wear makeup.

The party consisted of friends and family, who were dancing and having a ball. Morgan laughed at her father when they were dancing the Salsa. She was having such a good time,

179

she hesitated to go and talk to her mother and siblings when they called to wish her a happy birthday.

After the party, Morgan laid awake in bed feeling dizzy. She went into the bathroom and threw up again. *What is going on? I've been sick over a week now. If this continues, I'm going to see a doctor when I get back home, s*he thought. On her way back to the room, Tony popped in her head. It had been almost two weeks since she'd seen him. She really hoped this break would convince him to leave her alone.

When her grandma walked by the room, she was sitting up in the bed crying. "Bella, are you okay?"

Morgan's beautiful bluish-grey eyes were red and glossy. "Yes," she sniffled.

Her grandma went in the room and sat on the bed. "Then why are you crying?"

Morgan sighed. She didn't want to ruin her trip. "Because I'm happy. I don't wanna leave," she responded with a weak smile.

"Awww, Bella. We don't want you to go either."

"I wanna stay out here with Daddy where I'm safe."

"What do you mean *safe*? Is someone bothering you?"

"No. I mean...I love my daddy."

"And he loves you. I'll talk to him in the morning. We'll work something out."

"Thanks, Grandma."

"Now get some rest," she said and kissed her on the forehead.

"Okay, good night."

Morgan laid there and cried herself to sleep.

*****

Since it was her last day there, Morgan and her dad spent the entire day together. Felix took Morgan out to lunch. He wanted her to meet someone.

"Princess, Grandma told me that you were upset the other night. Are you okay?"

Morgan avoided eye contact with him. "I'm fine. I was just happy, that's all. No biggie."

"Morgan," he said with a serious tone and look, "tell me the truth. Are you okay? Grandma said something about you feeling safe here?"

Staring directly into his eyes, she replied, "Daddy, I'm fine. I meant safe like being with you."

Felix stared back into his baby girl's eyes. "Alright! You know I'm always here for you."

"I know." She smiled.

"Listen, I have a surprise for you."

"What?" she asked, beaming with excitement.

"I have someone I want you to meet."

Morgan was confused. "Meet?"

"Yeah," he responded, then looked over Morgan's shoulder and signaled for someone to come over.

When Morgan turned around, she saw a gorgeous, six-foot-tall, dark-skin model. She looked back at her father who was smiling.

He stood up. "Morgan, this is Mayla. Mayla, this is my daughter Morgan."

"Hello." Morgan waved to be polite and then looked at her dad again.

"Hello, Morgan. Wow, Felix, she's beautiful," Mayla proclaimed.

Morgan blushed.

"This is my baby."

Mayla sat down at the table, joining them. "I have heard so much about you. Your father talks about you all the time."

Morgan glanced over at her dad, smiling but confused. "Really? It's funny he hasn't said anything about you."

Stunned by Morgan's comment, Mayla gave a weak smile and sipped on some water.

Felix looked over at his daughter with a puzzled expression on his face. "Mayla, can you excuse us for a second."

"Sure. I'll just go to the ladies' room," she said, then walked off.

"Princess, are you okay?"

"I'm great," she responded in a snobbish tone, while cutting her eyes.

"Morgan, what's wrong?"

She sighed. "Is that your girlfriend?"

"Ummm, yeah. Why?"

"And you're just telling me about her today?"

"Well, I wanted to make sure Mayla and I was serious before introducing you to her. What's the problem?" he said in a worried tone.

She sighed once more. "Nothing. I was just hoping you and Mommy would get back together so we could be a family again."

Felix took a deep breath and moved his chair closer to her. "Morgan, your mother and I...we are not getting back together. But, that doesn't mean I don't love her. She moved on with her life, and I'm moving on with mines. We will always be together...because of you."

"Daddy, can I ask you something?"

"Sure."

"Did you and Mommy break up because of me?"

Felix's eyes widened. "What! No! Your mother and I had problems, and not because of you," he said, putting his hand on her shoulder. "Princess, I love you so much."

Morgan's eyes filled with tears. "I just feel like...I don't know...alone."

Felix nodded. "I know, Princess, but you're not. I tell you what. How about I talk to Mommy about you living out here with me?"

Her face lit up. "For real, Daddy?"

"Yeah."

"Please convince her," she begged.

"I will!" he said, kissing her on the forehead.

"Daddy...Mayla is beautiful," she told him, blushing.

"She's alright! You're the one who's beautiful." He winked.

Morgan laughed and did a little dance in her seat.

*****

Later that evening, Felix and Morgan went for a stroll through the garden and then took a seat in the sunroom. Felix rested his head on his daughter's head. He didn't want her to leave. For some strange reason, he worried about her. Despite the fact she lived with Denise, he felt like something wasn't right.

"Morgan, you know Daddy loves you, right?"

"Yes, I know."

"Are you sure you're okay?"

She stared off into space. She wanted to reveal what Tony was doing to her, but she made a promise to herself that she would keep her family safe.

"Daddy, I'm great," she lied, holding back tears.

"Can I ask you something?"

"Sure."

"Do you have a boyfriend?"

Shocked by his question, she blurted out, "Daddy! No!"

Felix giggled. "You're a beautiful girl and you're fifteen years old now. I know boys."

"Well, no!"

"Would you tell me if you did?" he asked with a serious expression.

Morgan looked away and then turned back toward him. "Yes, but what would you do?"

"I would sit down and talk to him. Tell him the rules for dating my daughter."

She nodded. "What if I told you that he hurt me?"

Felix took a deep, long breath. "Then…" He caught himself. "I would ask him why."

Morgan laughed. "You would ask him why?"

Felix tickled her. "Yeah," he replied. *Before I blow his fucking head off,* he thought. "Princess, you're the best thing that ever happened to me," he said with tears in his eyes.

"Daddy, what's wrong?"

Felix shook his head. "Nothing. I'm just upset because I can't be there for you. I'm missing out on the important things in your life."

Morgan hugged him. "It's okay, Daddy. I understand."

"It's not okay. There's not a day that goes by that I don't worry about you. Morgan, I will die if something happens to you. You are my life."Unable to hold it in anymore, Felix broke down in his daughter's arms.

Unsure of what to do, she tried her best to console him by hugging and patting him on the back. "Daddy, please don't cry. I'm fine."

"Princess, I'm so sorry for leaving you, but you have to believe me when I say I had no choice. Daddy is working day and night to come back, though."

Morgan wiped her tears away. "I know. Listen, I'm coming to visit you this summer."

Felix chuckled. His baby girl was growing up to be a beautiful young lady. "I can't wait," he said, pulling himself together.

They hugged each other and stared up at the sky. Morgan felt so safe in his arms. After gazing into the sky for a while, they went back into the house. As Felix was walking her upstairs, his mother called him into the other room.

"Princess, go upstairs. Let me see what Grandma wants," he said, kissing her on the cheek.

"Okay," Morgan replied, then ran upstairs to join her friends and cousins.

Felix walked into the room. "Yes, Momma?"

"Felipe, I'm worried about Morgan. Something isn't right."

"What do you mean?"

"She's been sick all weekend."

"Maybe it's the food. I know she doesn't have a boyfriend, if that's what you're implying."

"No, but I have this gut feeling that something isn't right."

Felix sighed. "I know. I have that same feeling."

"Felipe..." she said, walking up to him. She was so close he could smell the garlic on her breath. She pointed a finger. "I don't care what you have to do, but you bring Morgan home. She's a Marciano and needs to be with us. Not over there living with those people."

"Momma, those people are her family. Don't start that again," he snapped.

"Those people treat my grandchild like shit. She doesn't belong with them. You understand me? I don't know why you didn't take her when your ass was deported," she grumbled.

"You know why I couldn't. It would've killed Jasmine. Besides, Morgan needs her mother."

"And what about her father?"

Felix took a deep breath. His mother was right, but he didn't want to get into a bidding war with Jasmine over Morgan. "I'll talk to Jasmine and see if Morgan can move here with us."

"You do that. That's my grandchild up there. My blood runs through her. I don't feel comfortable with her living out there without protection. You bring her out here by any means necessary. If Jasmine don't agree, you make her understand!"

He nodded. "Understood, Momma."

"Felipe, if anything should happen to her..."

"I'll kill everything," he finished.

"You better," she said, leaving the room.

He picked up the phone and dialed a number. "Johnny, it's Felix."

"Felix, how are you doing?"

"Listen, I need a favor. I want you to follow a girl for me."

"Who?" Johnny asked.

"A friend of mine. Just follow her for a couple of days and let me know if something seems strange."

"Alright..."

"Thanks. Oh and, Johnny, if something does seem out of the ordinary...kill it."

"You got it!"

Click!

The next day, Morgan kissed her father goodbye and headed back to the States.

Chapter Fourteen
Tony

It's had been sixteen days since Tony last saw Morgan, and he was going through withdrawal, being very snappish and curt to his staff. Whenever someone asked him what was wrong, he would lash out at them, but Christina got it the worse. He was so rude and obnoxious, she moved back to her place. Tony had developed a disease, and Morgan was the cure.

Even after finding out Morgan went to visit her father, he still wanted to see her. He wanted to back off and forget her, but he couldn't. Tony should've feared what would happen to him if Morgan told her father, yet he still yearned for her. He had become so infatuated with Morgan that he cut off all his groupies.

Being that Tony couldn't see Morgan, he forced himself to rebuild his relationship with Christina. A part of him felt terrible because Christina was a good girl, but she just wasn't the girl for him. Tonight, they were scheduled to attend a movie premier and then a romantic dinner. Since Christina had been staying at her home, they arrived in separate cars. By the time she got there, he was already inside. They greeted each other and took their seats. During the movie, Morgan popped into his head, and he glanced over at Christina who appeared to be in another world. He wanted to cancel dinner, but knew all hell would break loose. So, he just went along with the plans.

After the movie, they went straight to dinner. In order to avoid an argument, Tony made causal talk with Christina, asking her about her day and how she felt about going on her first tour. Without her noticing, Tony kept checking the time on his watch. Afterward, Tony told Christina that he was going back to the studio to work on some tracks. Once he dropped her off at his house, he headed over to Denise's place.

He looked at his watch, praying they were still up. Tony was going to call her, but decided to surprise her instead. He pulled in front of Denise's place, walked in, and greeted the doorman. "Hey, Jimmy. Is Dee here?"

"Hey, Tony. Yeah, she's upstairs. You want me to call her?"

"Nah, thanks," Tony replied, as he walked past him. Reaching her door, he rang the doorbell.

"Hey you!" Denise said, letting him in.

"Sis," he chimed, kissing her on the cheek. "You know that's that bullshit, Dee. Your ass goes on vacation and don't tell your brother."

Denise giggled. "Excuse me, I didn't know I had to get permission." She waved her hand. "You must have me confused with Chris. In fact, where is your boo?"

He shrugged his shoulders. "I don't know."

She shook her head. "You are too much. Your ass needs an older chick to keep you in check," she said, walking back into the kitchen to finish cleaning out the refrigerator.

Tony laughed. "Yeah, whatever. Hey, what happened to your gun charge?"

"Oh, the case was dismissed. You know Mr. Rubin don't play."

Tony nodded and smiled. "That's great, and how about the trip to Italy?"

Denise looked out from the fridge. "They gave Morgan a surprise birthday party that was nice. She looks so much like her father. The pictures from the party are on the table if you want to see them," she said, pointing in the direction of the photos.

Thirsty to see his baby girl, Tony ran over and picked them up. He then sat in a nearby chair so he could concentrate on the photos. Morgan was so gorgeous. Tony peeked up at Denise to make sure she was not looking. He was beaming on the inside; he missed her so much.

"The pictures are nice. You're right. Morgan looks just like her father," he commented.

"Yes, she does. Felix loves that girl. He was tight when he found out Morgan was living with me," she said, walking over to him.

"Why?"

Denise frowned. "Because he thought I was still in the streets. You know he don't play that when it comes to Morgan. He told me straight up that nothing better not happen to her. I told him that he doesn't have anything to worry about. "

Tony sat there with a poker face, while she started walking back into the kitchen.

She suddenly stopped, turned around, and asked, "Tony, do you know if Felicia had any brothers?"

The fact that Felicia tried to set her up still weighed heavily on her mind. Denise was aware of Tony and Felicia's strained friendship, but she felt he may have known something she didn't.

"Nah, but I'll find out. Why?"

Since he didn't know about the setup, Denise played it cool. "Nothing. I just thought she had a brother or something," she replied, then continued walking into the kitchen. "Damn, I threw out a lot of shit. Now my ass has to go to the damn supermarket."

Completely ignoring her comment, Tony walked over to the

window. He couldn't get that picture of Morgan out of his mind. Feeling an erection coming on, he jiggled his leg. "Dee, I'm going in the family room to catch the playoff. A'ight?"

Denise nodded. "Okay."

While walking to the family room, he peeked up the stairs, wondered if Morgan was up there. He then went to the family room, turned on the TV, and started flicking through the channels while trying not to think about her. At the same time, he prayed she would come down the stairs. A couple minutes later, Denise entered the room.

"I'm about to go shopping," she announced.

Tony looked up at her. "Now?"

"Yes, because there's nothing here to eat."

"Well, let my driver take you so you don't have to pull your car out of the garage," he suggested. "He's downstairs."

"Aren't you coming with me?" Denise asked.

Tony screwed up his face. "Nah, I'm chillin' right here. I wanna watch the game. Shit, I might fall asleep."

Denise pondered on the suggestion for a second. "Okay. Well, call your driver and let him know I'm on my way down."

"Okay, and don't give him any problems either," Tony stated jokingly.

"Shut the hell up and give me some money," she said in a nasty tone with her hand out.

"I'm not your man. Ask Morris. He's the one blowing your back out."

Denise glared at him and rolled her eyes. "I'm not your chick, but your ass stays over here."

Tony reached in his pocket and was about to peel off some twenties, when Denise snatched them out of his hand. Tony looked up and they both laughed.

"Your ass still hasn't changed," he said with a smile.

"Glad you know that," she stated. "By the way, Morgan is upstairs probably sleeping. If she wakes up, tell her I went food shopping and will be right back," she told him, then left out the apartment.

Tony pulled out his phone to call Al. "Take her to a grocery store and call me when y'all are leaving to come back. Take her some place that's not too close because I need some time."

"You got it," Al replied.

Not wasting any time, he went up the stairs with his heart beating fast. As he got closer to her room, he could hear the sound of her television. Tony giggled; she was watching the game, too. Since Morgan's back was toward the door, she didn't hear or see Tony come in. *Damn, she looks good,* he thought while admiring her shape in the little t-shirt and boy shorts.

When Morgan turned around, she jumped from being startled by his presence. He was the last person she wanted to see.

Tony stood there with a big smile on his face. "Baby girl, what's up?" he said, sitting on the bed.

Morgan frowned and cleared her throat. "Nothing." Terrified of what he might do, she started to explain. "Tony, I'm sorry I didn't tell you that I was going away. I wanted to, but I didn't see you," she said, shaking while sitting up on the bed.

"It's cool, baby girl. I'm happy you went to see your pops. I saw your birthday pictures, and you looked lovely." Suddenly, his smiling face turned into a glaring one. "Did you say anything?"

Morgan was scared to death. "No, Tony, I didn't. I swear."

Tony grinned. "That's good. Well, I missed you"

Morgan dropped her head and pushed her hair behind her ear. *What does he want?*

Tony leaned over and touched her legs. "You're so sexy. Can I have a kiss?"

Morgan sat there in a daze, hesitating. "Where's Denise?"

"She went to the supermarket. Can I have a kiss?" he repeated, staring at her.

Taking a deep breath, Morgan leaned forward and kissed

him.

Tony pulled her closer to him. "I missed you so much," he moaned.

Palming the back of her head, he shoved his tongue down her throat while caressing her body. Out of the ordinary, Morgan became a bit aroused. Usually, she didn't like it, but today, it felt different.

He got up and went to the foot of the bed. "Come here," he ordered.

Morgan crawled to him on her knees. Tony took off his shirt and threw it across the room. He lifted Morgan face up and gazed into her eyes.

"You got me open," he whined, gently kissing her face.

Morgan whispered, "What if Denise comes back?"

"Shhh, baby girl. Denise isn't coming back for a while."

Morgan cried inside. *Where the hell is Denise?* she thought.

Tony pulled off her tank top, exposing her breasts. He then leaned down and started sucking them. Morgan, stiff as a board, closed her eyes and tried not to enjoy it. He laid her down on the bed and licked her from her neck down to her stomach. Morgan trembled while staring up at the ceiling. *This feels so good,* she thought. It didn't help that Tony was a good kisser with soft, juicy lips, gently and passionately licking and kissing every inch of Morgan's body. His touches sent chills up and down her spine. She felt his hot breath down near her vagina, causing her stomach to jerk.

"Tony," she moaned.

Tony pulled off her shorts, flinging them across the bed. He softly parted her two lips and teased her with the tip of his tongue. When he glanced up to see her reaction, she was looking up at the ceiling like she was on cloud nine. Tony grinned and licked it again. He wanted to continue, but couldn't risk Denise catching them. So, he flipped Morgan over on her stomach, positioning her on all fours. He pulled down his pants; he was rock hard. Before entering her, he stuck his finger inside her. *She's so wet. She's never been this wet before.*

He removed his finger and replaced it with his dick. "Damn, I missed you."

He closed his eyes and lost himself in paradise. She was so tight; this was the feeling he missed. Excited, Tony pulled out and teased her asshole with the tip of his tongue, causing her body to quiver.

"Tony," she moaned.

Thrusting back into her, in the heat of passion, he gasped and continued saying, "Baby girl, I missed you so much. Damn, I missed you."

Not wanting to cum yet, Tony pulled out, huffing and puffing. He turned her around and shoved his tongue down her throat. Then he grabbed the back of her head. "Suck it."

Flabbergasted, Morgan stared at him. "Suck it?" she asked in a confused tone.

Horny as hell, Tony groaned, "Yeah, I want you to suck it."

Morgan looked at it and then up at Tony, who had a tight grip on her head.

"Suck this dick," he mumbled, massaging it.

Morgan closed her eyes. *Oh God, please tell me this isn't happening.* She stuck her tongue out and licked the head, then looked up to see Tony staring directly back at her. Since he had made her watch those porno movies, she knew what to do, but just didn't want to. She licked the head again, hoping he would be satisfied.

"Yo, stop playing with me."

Morgan gazed into his eyes and did what she was told. Tony thought he had died and gone to heaven. He pushed her head back. "Chill, ma, you're gonna make me cum."

He carried her over to the dresser, threw Morgan's legs over his shoulder, and thrust inside of her, only to last five minutes. "Ahhh!" he screamed before busting off. He collapsed on top of Morgan, trying to catch his breath when he heard his phone ringing.

"Yeah, we are ten minutes away."

"A'ight, cool."

Tony looked over at Morgan, who was still on the dresser, and went over to her. "I wanna see you tomorrow. I have to see you."

"Tomorrow is Sunday. I can't. I have to study."

"A'ight. You can study at the crib, but I wanna see you tomorrow. Tell Denise you're going out with your friends. I'll pick you up around ten in the morning, and we can spend the whole day together."

Morgan threw her head back. "Tony, I can't"

He walked over to her. "I'm picking you up at ten o'clock down the block. You better be out there," he said, then went to the bathroom.

Morgan nodded.

Tony came back in the room and held Morgan. "Listen, it's gonna be fun. I gotta go. I'll see you in the morning," he told her, then tongue kissed her and left

As he was walking out of the family room, Denise was walking in the front door.

"You need some help?" he asked, going over to her.

"Yeah, thanks. Is Morgan up?"

Tony shrugged his shoulders. "I don't know."

After helping her put the groceries away, he kissed her on the cheek goodnight and went home.

*****

It poured down raining the next morning, but Tony Flowers woke up with a smile on his face. He would be spending the day with his baby girl. After throwing on some sweats, a hoodie, and a pair of uptown sneakers, he left. Instead of calling Al, he decided to drive.

As he waited for Morgan down the block, he thought about Denise and why she hadn't told him that she went to see Greg.

Something wasn't right. Denise went to see Greg, and then a couple days later Felicia was killed. *Did Denise kill Felicia?*

Deep in thought, Tony didn't see Morgan running towards the car with her book bag. She was about to get in the back seat, when Tony rolled down the window.

"Morgan."

She looked and noticed he was driving. Somewhat surprised, Morgan got into the front passenger seat. Tony leaned over and kissed her. Morgan flashed a weak smile. Before she knew it, they were on the highway. Tony played slow songs and periodically glanced over at her, while she sat there with her eyes closed and prayed it would be over soon.

Upon reaching the house, they went through the normal routine of things. Morgan cooked while Tony relaxed in front of the television. After they ate, Tony cleaned up the kitchen while Morgan went in the living room to study. Once finished, he came and sat next to her.

"You are so beautiful," he said, while touching her cheek.

She felt like smacking his hand away, but instead, she mumbled, "Thank you."

Tony stood over Morgan, intensely staring at her. She took a deep breath, closed the book, and placed it on the side of her. She knew what time it was; she could only pray it wouldn't last long. This time was different, though. This time, she experienced her first orgasm ever.

*****

Instead of going home, Tony drove to his old neighborhood that he hadn't visited in years. He pulled up in front of the infamous grocery store where he used to chill with his friends. Many didn't know that all of Tony's songs were inspired by that corner. It's where he found his voice and the first place he spit a verse.

That was ten years ago.

Damn, its crazy how times flies, he thought.

Tony wanted to get out and walk the hood, but didn't want to be bothered. After sitting in his car for a couple of minutes, he decided to go into the store.

"Abdul!" He smiled and gave him a pound.

"Oh my God, Tony Flowers! What's up, man? I thought you forgot about us."

"Nah, man. You know I've been busy," he chuckled.

A few customers were in the store. Once they noticed it was Tony Flowers, they smiled and waved.

"Yo, Tony, you heard what happened to Felicia, right?" Abdul asked.

"Yeah, that's fuck up."

"I know. Felicia was a good person."

When a few people started gathering outside of the store, Tony decided it was time to bounce. He gave Abdul a pound and left. On his way to the car, he bumped into Bruce and Joe.

"What's up, young blood?" Bruce smiled, nodding.

"What's good, fam?"

"Chillin'. I haven't seen you since your cousin got killed," Joe said.

Tony nodded. "Damn, it's been that long, Joe?"

"Yeah. Hey, did they ever find out who killed him? What was his name again?"

"Marion was his name, and nah, they never found out."

"That's strange because I remember him going into the building with Perry and them just before he died.

"What? In the building with Perry and who?" Tony asked to make sure he heard him correctly.

"Umm, it was Perry, Paul, and Mike. There was someone else, but I can't remember his name. They were all in the big park. Then, when your cousin came, they all walked into the building."

"Did you see them come back out?" Tony asked.

"They could have, but I didn't see them because I left not

long after they went inside. When I came back, they told me someone got thrown off the roof. It wasn't until a month later that I found out it was your cousin."

"Was Dee with them?"

"No," Joe told him.

"A'ight, fam. Thanks," Tony said, handing them a hundred dollars apiece.

"You don't think they had something to do with your cousin's death, do you?" Bruce asked.

"Nah, but thanks for the info though," Tony mumbled, before heading over to his car.

On his way home, he thought about that night. He was out of town with Stevie when he got the call Marion was murdered. They told him someone from out of town had killed him.

Were they lying? Did they kill my cousin?

Chapter Fifteen
Christina

The last few months Tony had become Dr. Jekyll and Mr. Hyde. Some days, he was so loving and caring, and other times, he was a cruel bastard. Christina didn't know what to do with him. At times, she considered leaving him, but deep down inside, she loved the hell out of him. She figured if she stayed at her apartment, Tony would come to his senses and act right. They said absence makes the heart grow fonder, but in Christina's case, the saying "out of sight out of mind" applied.

Having been aware of Tony's philandering ways, Christina knew it was different this time. Tony was in love with someone else. However, she was determined to stay with him and win his heart back. Sitting in her luxurious living room, Christina was scanning through a tabloid magazine when she came across an article titled "Hottest Couples Most Likely to Get Married". Underneath was a picture of her and Tony at an awards show last year. She screwed up her face and threw the magazine across the room.

"Hottest couple my ass," she angrily muttered.

While walking into her newly remodeled kitchen, she thought about her parents. It had been a while since she spoken to them. She hated herself for not calling more often, but it seemed like every time she called, her mother would chastise her. Against her better judgment, she phoned them anyway.

After four rings, Christina was about to hang up, when her mother picked up.

"Hello."

"Mommy?"

"Christina, is that you?"

"Yes," she responded, as tears rolled down her face. Christina missed the close relationship she once had with her mother.

"Honey, what's wrong? Are you okay?"

"I'm fine, Mommy. How are you doing?"

"I'm great. Your father just left for the dry cleaners. How are things going with you? I see your video all over the television."

"I'm okay, just busy with work. You know my career is taking off now," she weakly cheered, while wiping her tears away.

"I see."

She was about to ask her mother if she received the gift she sent them, when her mother interrupted.

"Christina, must you be naked in your video?"

Christina sighed. She knew that was coming. "Mommy, it's a video and sex sells."

"Well, I don't like it. You're a pretty girl with a voice. You don't have to prance around like that. It was fine when you were modeling, but what's the excuse now?" she snapped "I don't know why you even got into that business."

Her parents were very angry when she dropped out of high school to pursue a modeling career. Her mother did not speak to her for years. It wasn't until her grandma had a stroke that they made an effort to communicate. Even then, their relationship was filled with animosity. Instead of visiting, Christina just sent gifts.

"Well, you made it clear years ago that you weren't happy about my career choice. Still, that doesn't stop you from accepting my gifts," she said in a snide tone.

"Just because you bought us a house and paid off our debt doesn't mean we're supposed to look the other way. We're still your damn parents, and may I remind you that you were the one who wanted to buy us the house. If you're gonna throw it in our face every time we object to something, then you can take this house back. I don't like to see my child dancing across the stage half naked when she doesn't have to. Your father and I are proud of you. We never said we weren't. We're just concerned about your wellbeing. Don't let money motivate you, Christina. We raised you better than that."

"Money doesn't motivate me, Mommy. I wish you would stop downing me. Can't you just be happy for me?"

"Be happy for you? Is that what you just said? Chile, we have been happy ever since the day we brought you home from the hospital. The question is…are you happy? Yeah, I know, you have your rich, thuggish boyfriend with the fancy cars, clothes, and big house, but are you happy, Christina?"

Her mother had just dropped a jewel on her, and Christina had no retort.

"Hopefully, one day, you will go back and get your G.E.D. Do not let money be the deciding factor in your life. I mean, if you do something, do it because you want to and not because of the dollar signs that come behind it. Just because sex sells doesn't mean you have to be the one selling it. Baby, you are talented, but if you sashay around naked, who would know that if all they see is your ass? Listen, I have to run. When you're in town, stop over so we can have dinner. Okay?"

"Okay."

Click!

Christina didn't like what her mother said at times, but she had to admit she was so right. Ever since she became a model, people were more interested in her looks than her mind. Guys only wanted to be with her because she was pretty; they didn't care if she was smart. That was the main reason why she fell in love with Tony; he was different. Whereas he complimented Christina on her looks, he seemed to genuinely love her. Allowing her to leave the runway outside of their relationship, he exposed her to finest things in life.

The more Christina thought about the conversation with her mother, the more she realized she was right. Just because sex sells doesn't mean she had to be the spokesperson. Actually, it was Tony's idea to create her sexy image; Christina had wanted a more conservative look. Because Tony was the King of Hip Hop, she went along with the transformation. After talking with her mother, though, she decided it was time to go shopping for clothes that would display her sexiness in a classy and not trashy look. Christina knew her mother always had her best interest at heart, which was something she now questioned when it came to Tony and his love for her.

It had been two days and Tony still hadn't called her back. She thought about surprising him at his place, but she knew he wouldn't be home. On her way upstairs, her cell phone rang. She ran into the living room to pick it up. It was Rashid.

"Hello."

"Hello, Ms. Christina Carrington."

"Hey Rashid." She giggled.

"Are you busy tonight?

"Ummm, that depends."

He laughed. "Well, I have a game at The Garden tonight, and I wanted to know if you can come support you boy."

Indecisive for a second, Christina asked, "What time does the game start?"

"Eight o'clock."

"Hmmm, okay, but I have to bring a friend."

"That's cool. The tickets will be at the Will Call window."

"Alright. Bye," she said in a girlish voice.

"Later, babe."

Immediately, she dialed Asia number.

"Asia…"

"Hey Chris."

"Listen, girl. Remember Rashid, the basketball player? Well, he invited me to his basketball game tonight."

"Oh shit! For real?"

"Yes, girl, and I need you to come with me as a cover."

"WHAT!" Asia screamed, her eyes widening.

"I need you to come," Christina repeated.

"Are you fucking crazy? Tony will kill you."

"FUCK TONY! I'm sick and tired of everyone worrying about Tony's feeling. What about mines? This bastard is out there fucking everything, and I'm supposed to sit home and wait? Well, the waiting game is over. Are you coming with me or not?"

Christina didn't know it, but if this got out, her career would diminish quickly. While everyone adored her, it was her relationship with Tony Flowers that they loved more.

Asia sighed. "Alright, girl. You know I got your back. I just don't want you to do anything stupid. Rashid is sexy and all, but let's face it, he's not Tony Flowers. What time are you picking me up?"

"Around seven-thirty."

"See you then."

"Okay."

Christina jumped up and down. She knew everyone thought Tony was responsible for her career. He was the one who put her on the map, and that bothered Christina. While grateful for Tony's input and support, it was time she branched out on her own. She would show the world she could survive without him.

*****

After a long day of shopping, lunch at Sylvia's Famous Soul Food Restaurant, meeting with the stage director for her tour, and being interviewed at the local radio station, Christina was exhausted. But not enough to miss going to Rashid's game. It was six o'clock when she got in the house. Checking her phone, she had several missed calls from Tony. She smirked. *How does it feel, asshole?*

Christina headed up to her bedroom. Not wanting to be overly dressed, she pulled out a pair of dark blue jeans, a white fitted t-shirt, and her Brian Atwood green pumps. While heading toward the shower, she thought about calling Tony. *Maybe it's something important.* She was about to pick up the phone and call him, but then suddenly changed her mind. *Fuck him. Let him sweat.*

She showered and dressed. Tonight, she would break the rules by only applying a little mascara, some lip gloss, and pinning her hair up in a bun. Christina looked so much better without make-up. Actually, she looked younger. She hated that the industry required you to be "perfect" all the time. Sometimes she regretted getting into this business. While the money was great, it wasn't worth your sanity.

The game had started by the time they got there. Rashid had already scored ten points. It was playoff season, and Garden was packed. Once Rashid noticed Christina in the bleachers, he winked and smiled, causing her to blush. Asia looked over at Christina and thought, *She's playing with fire.*

"He's so sexy."

"He's alright," Asia replied.

"What do you mean? He's fine."

"He's alright. Still wet behind the ears, if you ask me. He's not on Tony's level, that's for sure."

Christina exhaled and rolled her eyes. She was sick of everyone praising Tony like he was a God. "Well, what level are we talking about, Asia? Oh wait. Let me guess…money-wise," she sarcastically replied.

"Girl, you have a rich, powerful man. Do you know how many women would kill to be in your shoes?"

Chris sighed. "There's so much more to life than money, Asia. What about love and respect?"

"And you think Rashid isn't the same? Please! Rashid just wants some pussy, girl, so he can brag to his teammates. Christina, every man cheats…"

Christina stared at Asia from the corners of her eyes. "Not all men. Maybe you should be with Tony then."

Asia rolled her eyes and ignored the remark. *Too late, honey. Been there, done that.* Asia and Tony had a sexual relationship that started out as a one-night stand, but turned into a secret affair. When she started catching feelings, he ended it abruptly.

After the game, Christina wanted to wait for Rashid, but she knew it wouldn't look right. So, after dropping Asia off, she went directly home. She wasn't in the house a good five minutes before her doorman called to announce that Tony was on his way up. Christina sighed. She really didn't feel like being bothered. They hadn't spoken in a couple of days.

When the doorbell rang, she walked over and opened it up.

"Hello."

"What's up? Sorry it took me so long to get back to you, I got kinda caught up," he said, brushing past her.

Christina stood there with door open. "Well, come in," she mumbled. Normally, she would be happy to see him, but tonight, she could care less about his ass.

"Wow! We remodeled the place. It looks great," he said, while looking around and taking in the changes Christina had made to her apartment.

She looked around with him. "Yeah, I had it done since I started staying here again," she spitefully said.

Tony totally brushed off her sarcastic comment. "So what's up? I've been calling you all day. Are you too busy to return my calls now?"

"Actually, I was. You know how it is Tony. I got *caught up*," she mockingly replied, flashing a fake grin.

Tony giggled. Christina had been feeling herself ever since that little fight they had a couple of weeks ago. Truthfully, he was kind of turned on by it, but she had better not get it twisted.

"So where were you?" he asked, following her into the living room.

"I was out. I'm going on tour, remember? So, I have a lot of things to take care of in regards to that."

"Oh yeah, so how's that going?" he asked, taking a seat on the sofa.

Why are you here? she thought. "Great! I actually just got back in the house, though. I was at The Garden watching a basketball game," she beamed, waiting to see his reaction.

Tony smirked. Christina had a lot to learn. *Doesn't she know nothing is a secret in this business?* He already knew she was at the game, just like he knew she met Rashid in the park. Little did Christina know Tony was parked down the block getting some head from one of his groupies.

"Word? That's great. So what do you feel like doing?"

She shrugged her shoulders. "Nothing really. I'm exhausted."

"So am I," he said, kicking off his shoes and pulling her onto his lap. "You know I miss you, right?" He planted a kiss on her neck.

Christina wanted to pull away, but instead, she stared into his eyes. "Yeah right!"

"I do, ma," he moaned in her ear.

Before she could say anything, they were having sex.

As they lay on the couch together, Christina said, "You know the awards show is in two days, and they are expecting us to show up. Are we still going together?"

"Yeah, why would you think we weren't? In fact, I was thinking maybe we could do a surprise performance together. Now that would be hot," he boasted.

Excited, she sat up. "Really, baby?"

"Yeah! Let's lock the game down."

Christina leaned over and kissed him. "I love you."

"I love you, too."

*****

They spent the next couple of days preparing for their show at the awards ceremony. Christina was on cloud nine. Finally, she had her man back and the media loved them. She made sure the paparazzi got plenty of photos of them together. If Tony was seeing someone else, he wouldn't be after that week.

It was the night of the awards show, and Christina and Tony were getting ready in a hotel suite. Though the last couple days had been great, Tony's behavior suddenly changed. He became distant and curt with his answers.

"Baby, how do I look?" Christina asked.

"You look good," he said, while fixing his shirt.

"You didn't even look at me," she whined.

"I don't have to. I know you look good."

"Gee thanks, Tony. You're such the perfect boyfriend."

"So I've been told."

Christina stared at him. "I'll be in the other room," she said, walking off. *Asshole!*

She wasn't aware, but Tony was going through withdrawals. He missed Morgan so much. No matter how hard Christina tried to please him, she wasn't Morgan.

When Tony entered where Christina was waiting, she was looking herself over one more time.

"Are you ready?"

Christina turned around and said, "I thought you were gonna wear the white suit so we could somewhat match."

"I changed my mind. I wasn't feeling that look. This is more me."

"Very well!" She picked up her clutch purse and then

blurted out, "You know, you're such an asshole. I don't know why I stay with you."

Tony grinned. "I don't know either," he said as they left out the door to go downstairs to the limo that awaited them.

When they pulled up to the red carpet at Radio City Music Hall, Tia and Joyce got out first.

Tony glanced over at Christina. "Are we ready?"

Christina sighed. "Please! I'm always ready."

He chuckled. "Then let the games begin."

Tony got out first and then helped her out. They held hands while walking down the carpet. They were never affectionate in public, so the fans went crazy. Both smiled and waved.

Christina whispered, "You're something else. Now you wanna hold my hand."

Tony threw up the peace sign and waved to the crowd. "This is want you wanted, baby girl. Don't front. You love the attention."

That's when she leaned over further to ensure no one could hear. "That's where you're wrong, Tony. I don't love the attention. I just love you."

He looked her in the eyes and was about to respond, when Tia and Joyce walked over to them.

"Guys, we need to break you two up for a second to conduct some brief interviews," Tia told them.

While many asked about their albums, the media also asked about their personal lives. Whenever asked if they were getting married, they always declined to comment.

After a couple of interviews, Tony and Christina met back up on the red carpet. While on their way inside, Christina saw Rashid. She almost fainted. She peeked over at Tony to see if he saw him. Needless to say, he did. Because Tony was such a bastard, he waved for Rashid to come over to them. Even though Christina had on make-up, you could still see her face turning red.

"Rashid, my man, congrats on your NBA title and MVP of

the year," Tony boasted.

"Thanks, man. You know it's been crazy."

Christina tried so hard not to look at Rashid. In fact, she wanted to snatch her hand from Tony and run. Rashid looked so good in his powder-blue linen Sean John suit.

Tony glanced over at Christina, noticing her fidgeting. "My bad, Rashid, this is Christine...but you already know that since the two of you have already met."

Christina forced a smile. She knew Tony was doing this shit on purpose. *Alright, Tony, two can play.*

"Indeed, we have. I went to game five at The Garden. Congratulations on your win, Rashid."

"Thank you, Ms. Christina Carrington." He smiled.

Just then, Rashid's publicist came over to them. "Rashid, we have to go. You have a few more interviews before we go inside."

Rashid nodded. "Excuse me, guys. Nice to see you again, Christina. Stay cool, Tony," he said before walking away.

"You are such a bastard," Christina mumbled.

"And then some. Stop frontin'. You wanna fuck him," Tony stated with a smirk.

"You know that's not a bad idea...since you're not. Just remember something, Tony. It's hard to replace a girl like me."

"You think so?" He smiled as they walked inside.

Although Christina and Tony weren't speaking, they made it through the evening with everyone thinking things were just dandy between them. Christina won the Best New Artist Award. While they were on stage performing, their chemistry was intense. Too bad it couldn't be as intense in their private lives as it was in their public one.

When the awards show was over, Christina wanted to go home immediately. She didn't feel like being around people. "Where are we going?" she asked, as the group of them headed to the awaiting limo.

"We have to make a couple of appearances at some parties,

remember?" Joyce said.

Christina sighed. She wasn't up to flashing a phony smile all night. "Do I have to go. I really just wanna go home."

"What's your problem now? This is part of the job, Tony snapped.

"Was I talking to you? I know it's part of the job. I'm just tired. You know what? Forget it. Let's go!" Christina yelled.

After they made some appearances, their final stop was the TP Production party. Everyone was there. Upon their arrival, they were led to a private table. Tony ordered Cristal and Grey Goose, while Christina sat there in a sad mood.

She looked over at Tony, who was occupied with a group of people. *Look at him. He doesn't even acknowledge my presence unless it benefits him.* Since it was also her night because of the award she had won, Christina decided to have a couple of drinks and loosen up by dancing around in the VIP section.

Feeling a bit tipsy, Christina went over to Tony and whispered in his ear, "You haven't dance with me all night."

Tony looked her up and down. "You know I don't dance. Why don't you go over there to Tia or Joyce and dance?"

Christina sulked inside. As she walked back over to her seat, while sipping on her glass of Cristal, she looked up and saw Rashid, who was across the room in another section dancing with some chick. Christina's face lit up, and she silently wished it was her that he was dancing with. She looked around to make sure no one was watching her stare at this man, especially Tony.

Christina then pulled out her phone and sent Rashid a text message: *I guess you found a new dance partner.* She looked up to see if he would respond. He pulled out his phone and looked at the text. After he read it, he looked around, laughed when he spotted her, and then texted back: *Well, I can't dance with you.* As she watched Rashid and his date have fun throughout the night, Christina grew more and more jealous, wanting to be with him instead of Tony.

By two o'clock in the morning, she was ready to go. So, she went over to Tony. "I'm ready to leave."

Tony stared at her, then said, "Yo, I'ma check y'all later, fam," and walked back to his section with Christina.

Assuming they were leaving, Christina grabbed her bag. However, Tony sat down and poured himself another drink. "We'll leave after this drink."

Christina rolled her eyes and sat next to him. Tony bopped his head to the music, while Christina sat there like a pretty girl. She was about say something to him, but her phone vibrated. It was a text message from Rashid: *I see your Prince Charming is back.* Christina busted out laughing and texted back: *Oh please! Why do you care when you're over there chatting with some chick?*

Tony peeked over at Christina, he said, "Let's go."

Rolling her eyes, she didn't want to leave now that she had Rashid's attention. "Now?" she asked.

"Yes," he replied, then walked out of the VIP section.

She grabbed her bag and followed behind him. Tia and Joyce remained at the party. Checking her phone, Christina hoped Rashid would text her back, but he was too busy talking to his friends. Once in the limo, she requested the driver to take her to her place instead of Tony's.

After they pulled up to the front of Christina's loft, she hopped out, thinking Tony would at least walk her upstairs. However, he stayed in the car.

Before she got into the building, he yelled out to her, "Oh Chris, tell ya boy I'll be here tomorrow. So, no sleepovers."

"Fucking asshole," she muttered, as she walked in her building.

Chapter Sixteen
Denise

Denise hadn't seen her parents in a while. Although reluctant to go over there, she decided to stop by after work. She thought about taking Morgan with her, but knew it wouldn't be a good idea. Denise hopped on the train to Harlem, where her parents now lived. On the ride uptown, she pulled out a book to read. She giggled to herself when she glanced at the first line inside: Appearances are deceiving. How ironic. She, herself, had transformed into a model citizen.

"Next stop 135th Street!" the conductor announced.

Putting her book away, Denise got ready to get off. Her parents lived only two blocks from the train station. She smirked as she strutted through Harlem. *Nothing's changed,* she thought. People were still walking around with that "Money-Making Harlem" pride.

Arriving in front of parents' one-family brownstone house, everything appeared to be in order. However, as she was coming up the steps, two young guys were walking out from the basement. Denise glanced at them, but then assumed her parents had rented out the extra space since her mother had mentioned it the last time they spoke.

Denise rang the doorbell and waited for about five second before ringing it again. She finally heard someone coming. It was her mother.

"Denise, what brings you here?" she asked with a surprised look.

"Actually, nothing. Just thought I would stop by. Well, are you gonna let me in?" Denise asked, as her mother continued to stand there blocking the doorway.

"Oh, I'm sorry. Come in."

What the hell! Denise thought. The place looked like a pigsty. There were clothes and food all over the place.

Her mother turned around and said, "Sorry, we didn't have a chance to clean up."

Denise nodded. "I see. What happened to all of the nice furniture I bought you?"

"It's here."

"Where?" Denise inquired.

Her mother sighed. "Did you come over here to inspect the damn place or visit?" she snapped.

"Actually, both," Denise retorted.

Her mother shot her an evil stare and Denise gave her one back. As they went into the kitchen where Betty was preparing dinner, Denise looked around in disgust. Dishes and garbage were everywhere. Once Denise found a clean spot on the counter, she put her bag down and started cleaning up.

"Ma, did you see my fucking hot pink shoes?" De'shell, Denise's sister, yelled from upstairs.

"No!" her mother yelled back.

"People are always touching my shit!" De'shell shouted out.

Denise glanced at her mother from the corner of her eye and shook her head in disgust. "Anyway, Ma, how have you been doing?"

"I can't complain. These bills are kicking my butt, but what else is new?"

"What bills?"

"The light, water, and mortgage."

"Mortgage?"

"Oh, we refinanced the house," her mother informed her.

"Why?'

Before Denise's mother Betty could respond, Shameka walked in the kitchen and looked Denise up and down. "What are you doing here?" she asked in a snide tone.

Denise turned around. "Excuse me?"

"Watch your mouth, Shameka!" Betty snapped.

Shameka cut her eyes and sucked her teeth. "Now you wanna act brand new," she mumbled before storming out.

"That's how they talk to you, Ma?" Denise asked.

Betty took a deep breath. "She's just a kid…"

"That's the problem, Ma. You keep thinking they're kids, but they're not."

It was quiet for a second before Denise heard moaning coming from the basement. She glanced at her mother, who pretended not to hear the sounds.

"Ma, what's that?"

"What's what?" Betty replied, while placing the chicken in the over.

Annoyed, Denise stormed out of the kitchen and downstairs to the basement. "WHAT THE FUCK!"

She couldn't believe her eyes. Her nieces Shameka and Ronisha were down there having sex with several guys. They were so caught up in the moment that they didn't even hear or see Denise standing there.

When one of the guys finally looked up, he yelled, "Oh shit!" causing everyone else to look up.

"Oh, it's just my aunt. May I help you?" Ronisha asked in a nasty tone, unfazed by Denise's presence.

Still flabbergasted, Denise stood there silent, but after snapping back to reality, she calmly told the guys, "Get out."

As the guys started to gather their clothes, Shameka blurted out, "Don't get dressed. She doesn't fucking live here."

Surprisingly, the guys looked up at Denise's face and continued getting dress.

Shameka turned towards Denise and yelled, "Bitch..." However, just as she was about to say more, Denise punched her in the mouth.

"Who the fuck are you talking to?"

Stunned at Denise's reaction, Shameka tried to charge her, but was unsuccessful. Denise hit her again, this time knocking her flat on her ass. "You wanna show off, huh?"

Ronisha glanced over at her aunt. She wanted to jump in, but was scared. Once the boys witnessed that, they didn't even bother to finish putting on their clothes.

Angry yet calm, Denise went back upstairs.

"What happened?" Betty asked.

"I knocked the shit outta Shemeka's grown ass."

"You did what?" her mother screamed.

Before Denise could respond, Shemeka came flying into the kitchen "I'm calling the cops on you, bitch! You think you can come in here and put your hands on me?" she cried, as blood dripped from her mouth.

Betty looked over at Denise with a look of disbelief.

"Call them," Denise responded.

Anita and De'shell came running down the stairs. "What the fuck is going on down here?"

"That bitch put her hands on me, Ma," she cried, pointing to Denise.

Anita, Shemeka's mother, looked at her daughter's face. "You put your hands on my child? Are you fucking crazy?"

"Fuck you and your child. Tell that little bitch to have some respect. She's fucking in my mother's house."

"So what? It's not you're fucking house!" De'shell said.

"But I bought it. Now what? And if she ever talks to me like that again, I'm going to dog walk her little ass all through this house."

"Denise, leave it alone," her mother cried in the background.

"You see, Ma. That's why I didn't wanna fuckin' come here. She thinks just because she bought this house with her drug money, she can tell us what to do!" Anita barked.

"You ain't nothing but a drug-dealing bitch…a fucking murderer! I hope someone kills your ass!" Shameka cried.

Denise smirked. "If you know of anyone, send them."

"Denise, shut up!" her mother screamed.

"I wish it was your ass that was murdered instead of Felicia," Ronisha stated.

All hell broke loose then. Denise went berserk. "You know what? Get the fuck out! All of y'all get out!" she said, charging toward them. "Since I'm a murdering, drug-dealing bitch, get the fuck out of my house."

"Denise, what are you doing?" her mother cried.

"What am I doing? Ma, are you crazy?"

"Denise, this is my house. You can't come in here putting no one out!" she yelled, grabbing her arm.

Denise forcefully snatched it away. "Get off of me!"

"I bet if it was that little white bitch Morgan, she would not have said shit," De'shell stated.

"Shut the hell up! Morgan would never do any shit like that."

"How do you know?" her mother asked.

"Because I know. You know what, Ma? Just because you fucked up, Jasmine and her kids shouldn't have to suffer."

"Don't talk to me like that in my damn house. How quickly you forget what you were like growing up."

"No, Ma, I don't. You won't let me. Regardless, I never disrespected you like they are doing."

"I guess selling drugs and killing people weren't disrespectful, huh? I prayed every night that someone didn't run up in that apartment and kill us for your bullshit."

Denise's eyes filled with tears. "And I prayed for a better

mother. Guess God didn't answer any of our prayers."

"Get out!" her mother screamed.

"I'm not going anywhere. You're gonna hear what I have to say. You don't like to hear the truth. That's the reason you tolerated this bullshit. Now you're a prisoner in your own home. Whether you agree with my choices in life or not, I never put my family in harm's way. Unlike you, I owned up to my mistakes and admit I'm not perfect. NO ONE IS! But instead of seeing the good in me and the progress I've made, you only see the negative. No matter how much I've accomplished, you never ONCE said you were proud of me. It used to bother me. For years, I asked myself why. But, you know what?" she said, fighting back tears. "No fucking more. It's not me, Ma; it's you. You blame everyone for YOUR mistakes. You won't even see your other grandkids because of the mistake YOU MADE! I forgive you, Ma, but you need to forgive yourself."

Betty stood there with her lips tight. "I did the best that I could…"

"You should have done better."

"You did, Ma," Anita said.

Denise turned around and gave her look that said for her to shut the fuck up.

"This is my house, and you have no right to come in here and put them out. You bought this house for us…"

"That's right," a man's voice interrupted from the back of the house. It was Roger, Denise's father. "I may not agree with everything Denise does, but she's right this time. She bought this house for us, not for y'all."

"Daddy…" De'shell whined.

"Daddy my ass. I have watched y'all turn my home into a whorehouse."

"Roger!" Betty yelled.

"Be quiet, Betty! Denise is right. Get the hell out!"

"Daddy, you're putting us out?" Anita asked.

"Yes, and I should've done it a long time ago. My kids may

have done a lot of things, but they NEVER disrespected me the way Ronisha and Shameka does. I want all of you out NOW!"

"Mommy!" Anita cried.

"Roger, they have no place to go," Betty said

"There's a drop-in shelter on the Grand Concourse," Denise snidely said.

"Betty, please! For the past three years, we have been prisoners in our own damn house. I can't even sit in my damn living room any more. Well, it stops tonight. I want y'all out of my house and take your fucking kids with you!" he screamed.

The room was silent. It was the first time their father ever got involved. While Denise always thought her father never paid attention to his kids, surprisingly, he did. She guessed he just needed some support. Anita and De'shell stood there praying their father would change his mind or that their mother would do something. Sadly, Betty had enough, as well. She was just too afraid to say something. She wanted them out a long time ago. Once Anita and the others realized Roger was serious, they stormed upstairs, collected most of their belongings, and left.

Roger faced Denise. "I know you probably think we aren't proud of you, but we are. Denise, you have transformed yourself into a beautiful woman. Now I know I haven't been exactly the greatest father in the world, and I'm working on that, but I just wanna say thank you. I love you."

After thirty years, Denise finally heard the words she needed to hear.

Her father reached out and hugged her. "I'm sorry," he whispered.

Denise smiled on the inside. "I am, too."

Betty, who had been standing there with tears in her eyes, stormed up the stairs while saying, "Roger, I can't believe you put your own damn kids out."

Denise and her father looked at each other and shrugged their shoulders.

"I don't know what's wrong with your mother."

"You, Daddy! Mommy has worked so hard to please you."

Roger took a seat in the living room. "Me? I don't understand."

"The night you found out Jasmine wasn't your child, you changed. It's like you didn't love us anymore. You became cold and distant."

He just stared into Denise's eyes, nodding acknowledgment. "Denise…"

She quickly interrupted him. "Daddy, do you know why I sold drugs or did the things I did? It's because I felt like nothing I did mattered. So, I turned to the streets. I'm not making excuses for my behavior, but as your child, I needed to hear you loved me. I needed to know you cared."

Roger sighed. "I agree. Your mother and I are to blame. Denise, I know I've made some bad choices in my life. For instance, taking out my anger on my children and cheating on my wife. But, I'm working on them, and all I can ask is for you to forgive me. Jas did."

Denise eyes widened. "Jas did?"

Rogers smiled. "Yeah, she came by one day and we talked."

Denise laughed. *Oh, so this is what Jas was talking about.*

Denise and her father chatted for another thirty minutes before she left. On her way to the train station, she ran into Perry.

"Denise, what the hell are you doing around here?"

Denise chuckled. "My parents live over on 137th Street."

"Yeah, I see Anita and De'shell on 140th all the time. What's good with you?"

"Same shit different day. How's the job with Tony?"

"It's cool. I don't really see dude like that."

"Well, that's good. I'm glad things are working out," she said.

"Ay yo, you heard what happened to Felicia, right? That fucked me up!"

Denise looked the other way to hide her *"she got what she deserved"* expression. "Well, you know Felicia…always into some shit. It was bound to happen."

"Damn, Dee, y'all were comrades," Perry replied, shocked at her response.

"You're right. We were. Felicia was still my girl, but she pulled some sucka shit," Denise snapped, rolling her eyes and shaking her head.

"Oh, I didn't know that. What happened?"

Denise really didn't feel like talking about it, but knew she needed to. Until now, she tried to forget about it, but couldn't. Something about Felicia's last words haunted her. *Who was Felicia talking about?* In order to get answers, Denise needed to ask questions.

"Perry, you got a minute?"

"Yeah, what's up?"

As they started walking towards the park, she took a deep breath. "Do you know if Felicia had a brother?"

Perry shook his head. "Nah, why?"

"Before she died, Felicia tried to set me up."

Perry stopped walking. "What! Felicia, say word. That's why you were riding around with your gun?"

"No, no, that was for something else. Anyway, she claimed it was payback from her father and brother."

He stood there surprised and confused. "Who's her pops?"

"Some bum ass from back in the day. He's a nobody," she said, not wanting to reveal too much information. "Anyway, a couple of weeks before she was murdered, she tried to kill me."

Perry shook his head in disgust. "You know, I hate when I hear sucka shit like this. It's always the ones we love that cross us."

"Tell me about it. She and I went way back. I can't figure out why. From what I heard about her father, he wasn't shit. He never took care of her."

"Who knows why people do the things they do? She was

my girl and all, but real talk...Felicia fell off. She still had a hood mentality. When she started fucking with them young cats, something was bound to happen. You know she thought you and Greg were fucking around?"

Denise frowned. "What? Get the fuck outta here. She had a thing for Greg?"

Perry laughed, clapping his heads. "Hell yeah. You know I was fucking her for a second. Anyway, Greg and I was chillin' one night, and we ran into her. She was coming from Spanish Rob's crib. We pulled up on her and were like, 'What's good?' She hopped in the whip. We're talking and shit. Then when we get to the block, she tells me to bounce because she needed to talk to Greg. He told me later that she asked him what was up with them and why hadn't he fucked her yet. Greg was like, 'What?' Then she told him, 'I know you're fucking Dee, so why not me, too?' Greg was like, 'Nah, it's nothing like that with Dee,' and she was like 'Whateva!'

Denise stood there with her mouth open. She could not believe Felicia would do that. "Perry, stop playing."

"She was loose like that, Dee. Felicia was my girl, but she got around. We all fucked her except for Tony. She couldn't stand his ass. She wanted to murder him plenty of times."

Denise chuckled. "Wow! You never know a person, huh?"

"Yeah, and that's why right now, I'm not playing with dudes. After seeing what Greg went through, my guard is up. If I even think a nigga is playing games, I'm pushing his shit back. Feel me? I'm not giving these niggas a break. Dudes force you to be a gorilla. But, damn, I can't believe Felicia did that shit. She went out like a sucka."

A dead one, Denise thought. "Yeah, she did. I just hope what she said wasn't true about her brother."

"You worried?"

Denise looked at him for a second. "Not really, just baffled."

"You know I'm all for change, ma, like I said when I first saw you. You've came a long way, and I'm proud as a muthafucka to see my sis doing big things. But, let's be real. We did a lot of shit. Now don't get me wrong. I'm not saying it was right what she did. But, that shit will come back to haunt us. Real talk! And the fucked-up thing is it's probably by someone close to us."

"I know. After that sucka shit Felicia pulled, I don't trust anyone. One thing for sure, Perry, what doesn't come out in the wash always comes out in the rinse. "

"If it's true, we will find out, and you already know how I get down. Say no more!"

Denise flashed a fake smile, but inside, she really didn't want to revert back to that lifestyle.

*****

Denise walks into her apartment, put her purse on the counter, and proceeded to the kitchen. As she poured something to drink, she thought about her father's heartfelt words. They seemed so sincere and genuine. She wished her mother was more forthcoming. Maybe then they could become a family again. She had finished her drink and was headed upstairs, when her house phone rang. It was Morris.

"Hello."

"Denise, what's up? You don't love me anymore?"

"Hi, Morris."

"What's good, ma? I wanna see you."

"See me?"

"Yeah, tonight."

"Morris, I just walked in the house and I'm tired."

"So? Pack some clothes and sleep over at my crib."

"No."

"Yes. I'll be there in a couple of minutes."

Click!

Denise threw her head back and took a deep breath. She really didn't feel like being bothered, but she was too weak to say no. When she went upstairs to let Morgan know that she would be out for the night, she was sound asleep. *I'll just leave her a note on the fridge,* she thought, while closing Morgan's bedroom door softly. While in her bedroom throwing some things into an overnight bag, Derrick popped into her head. She hadn't spoken to him all day, and that was not like them. Ever since they started seeing each other, they spoke at least once a day. Denise decided to call him. She picked up her cordless phone and dialed his number. It rang about four times before it went to voicemail.

"Hey, Derrick, it's Denise. I'm just calling to hello. Call me when you get a chance. Miss you."

She hung up the phone and finished packing. As she was walking out the door after leaving the note for Morgan on the fridge, Morris called and told her that he was waiting downstairs. Still hesitant to go, Denise locked the door and left. Strangely, she wasn't happy to see him. Unable to explain why, she wanted to go back upstairs.

Still upset at her for running out on him, Morris engaged in small talk while driving. "What's with you?"

"What do you mean?" she replied in a nonchalant voice.

"I mean, you bounced on me the last time we were together. You haven't called. What's good?"

Denise sighed and suddenly felt disdain for him. The sound of his voice started to irk her. "I've been busy. I do work, you know," she snapped.

Morris glanced over at her from the corner of his eye. *Yeah, okay. I know what you need,* he thought.

They pulled up in front of his building. Annoyed, Denise got out and went upstairs to wait for him. Once they were inside his apartment, she went and placed her bag on the couch.

Morris came up behind her. "Here," he said, handing over her watch that one of his jump-offs had taken from his place.

"Thanks," she said, putting it in her bag.

Normally, they would have been all over each other by now, but Denise was playing hard to get. She went into the bedroom and removed her clothes to take a shower, while Morris headed toward the kitchen. As she was washing up, Morris entered the bathroom butt-naked. When she turned around and saw him standing there, she tried not to stare at his sexy chocolate body, but it didn't help that Morris' penis was fully erect. Minutes later, they were fucking. Screwing throughout the apartment, Morris had Denise screaming his name before putting her ass to sleep.

*****

The next morning when Denise got up, Morris was already gone. She showered, dressed, and headed to work. Usually after a good orgasm, she would be smiling from ear to ear, but today, she wasn't. In fact, something was different. On her way to work, she realized the only thing she and Morris had was great sex. He never asked her how her day was, and they never went anywhere together, whereas Derrick treated her like a lady. In fact, she knew more about Derrick than Morris. *So why am I even still seeing Morris?* she silently asked herself.

When Denise entered her office, she found a huge bouquet of red roses on her desk. She read the card; it was from Derrick. Denise giggled to herself. *He's such a gentleman.* She smelled the flowers and then picked up the phone to thank him.

"Hey you!" he answered.

"Hi. Thank you. That was so sweet of you." She smiled.

"You're welcome. I got your message last night. I was in a meeting."

"It's okay. I was just thinking about you."

"I'm always thinking about you," he replied, causing Denise to blush. "Can I see you tonight?"

"Sure," she said, despite being tired.

"Alright. Listen, I have something special planned, so I'll pick you up around seven o'clock at your place."

"Okay. See you then."

"God willing," he said.

Just as they were about to hang up, Denise yelled, "Wait! How should I dress?"

"Sexy as usual," he responded, making her giggle.

Denise hung up the phone with a big grin on her face. When she looked up, Maria was standing in her doorway.

"Morning, chica! I just wanted to remind you about the monthly operations meeting today. Valerie called in sick, so you will be leading the meeting."

Denise dropped her head on the desk. Whereas she knew the material, she had a phobia about public speaking. "Great! What else is new?"

"Nothing. I see we have flowers today," Maria teased.

Denise giggled. "It's from this guy I'm seeing. He's a real winner."

"They all are in the beginning," Maria warned.

Denise glanced over at her. She never thought about it like that. *Will Derrick change?*

"Not all men, Maria," she responded hopefully.

"Um, the ones I dated did."

"That's because you're not me."

Both laughed.

Denise went about her daily routine, from meetings to conference calls and back to meetings, before heading home. Since Derrick was picking her up at seven o'clock, she left exactly at five. This way, she would have two hours to fumble through her closet. Hopefully, Morgan would be home by then. It had been two days since she had seen her niece. They rarely saw each other since they came back from Italy, so Denise decided they would spend the upcoming weekend in Jersey.

Once at home, Denise was searching through her closet for something to wear, when a shoebox fell on her head. She picked up the box and opened it. Inside was her gun. *How did it get in there?* She didn't remember putting it in there. She took it out to closely examine it. Yep, it was hers. While relieved to have found it, she couldn't help but to wonder whose gun that had been in her safe. *Damn, was Felicia right? Am I slipping? Nah, fuck Felicia,* she thought, while putting the gun back inside the safe. Denise never second guessed herself before and wasn't about to start now.

Morgan walked in the room. "What are you doing?"

"I'm looking for an outfit to wear tonight."

"You're going out?"

Denise poked her head out of the closet. "Yes, mother. Is it okay with you?"

Morgan giggled. "Yes, it's fine. Just make sure you come in at a reasonable hour."

Denise laughed. "What's wrong with you?" she asked after coming out of the closet.

"Nothing."

"You look a little pale."

Morgan walked over and looked in the mirror. "I don't know. My stomach has been acting up. I can't keep anything down. Maybe it's the food I ate over in Italy."

"That might be it. Are you gaining weight, though? Your ass and titties seem bigger."

"No, they're not. In fact, I lost a couple of pounds. Thank you very much."

"Not in that outfit. Now, which one of these outfits should I wear tonight?" Denise asked.

"I like the black dress. It's very chic and black goes with anything."

Denise took a step back, looked at the outfits she had laid out on her bed, and then said, "You know what, niece? I think you're right. I like the black dress, and I have some satin Lavin pumps that would look great with it."

Morgan blew her finger like it was a smoking gun. "I'm too

good. I need to be a stylist." She smirked.

Denise walked over and started tickling her. "You do, huh?"

Morgan fell on the floor laughing. "Stop," she yelled, while laughing.

Glancing over at the clock, Denise realized she didn't have much time to get ready since it was already 6:10 p.m. She ran into the bathroom, wrapped her hair, and jumped in the shower. Generally, she would stand under the water for a minimum of fifteen minutes, but tonight, she washed her ass and got out. After applying lotion and dressing, she grabbed her shawl and headed out. When she reached the lobby, she saw him on his cell phone. *Damn, he's handsome.*

"Hello," she said, walking up behind him

"Hello. Wow, you look stunning," he complimented after turning around to face her.

Denise blushed. "You don't look too bad yourself."

"So are we ready?"

"Yes. Where are we going?"

"Actually, we're going over to the Lincoln Center. I got some tickets to the Opera."

"Opera?" Denise inquired with a confused look.

"Yes, the Opera. Have you even been to an Opera show?"

"No. The closest I've come to seeing an Opera show was *Pretty Woman.*"

Derrick laughed. "Well, tonight, you're my pretty woman. Come on. You'll love it."

Against her will, Denise said, "Fine, but next time, I'm picking the place."

Both laughed.

They entered the Lincoln Center and Denise was amazed. It was so beautiful and elegant. The architecture was astonishing. She had never seen anything like it in her life. It was so breathtaking. Even the people were beautiful. Derrick noticed Denise's expression and smiled to himself.

"I was like that the first time I came here."

"Oh, it's that obvious," Denise said, giggling. "This place is gorgeous."

"Yes, it is."

The usher led them to their seats. At first, she didn't understand it, but after an hour in, she caught on and ended up enjoying the performance.

On their way out, Derrick whispered, "How was it?"

"It was beautiful. I really enjoyed it."

As they stood on the steps outside of the center, Denise reached out and pulled Derrick close to her. "Thank you," she said before kissing him.

After kissing her back, he replied, "No, thank you. Are you hungry?"

"Yes."

"Let's go eat."

"Where?"

"That's a surprise, too." He smiled.

Denise shook her head. "Aren't we full of surprises tonight?"

They hopped in a cab, and Derrick told the driver to take them to 34th on the FDR Drive.

Denise glanced over at him. "Derrick, are you sure you have the correct address. There's no restaurant over there."

"Yes, there is," he simply replied.

Denise twisted up her face and remained quiet. A short while later, the cab pulled up to a parking lot where people were boarding a boat. She was about to say something, but Derrick was already out of the cab.

"Ready?" he asked, extending his hand to help her out.

"I guess so," she mumbled.

Derrick led the way aboard. It was the grand opening of the *New York City Steak House Boat,* which sailed up and down the East River. Denise stood with her mouth wide open. It was spectacular. Everyone was dressed in a cocktail outfit.

She looked over at Derrick. "This is nice."

The hostess asked for their name and then escorted them to their seats out on the deck.

Denise smirked. "Any more surprises, Mr. Johnson?"

"Not tonight," he replied with a chuckle.

After a night of dinner, drinks, and dancing, Derrick dropped Denise off in front of her building.

"I had a wonderful time. Thank you," she told him.

"You did? Even at the Opera?"

"Yes, even at the Opera." Denise giggled.

"Well, I'm glad. You're worth it."

Denise blushed and gazed into his eyes. "So are you," she said, then leaned forward to kiss him.

While they stood there outside of her building, someone yelled, "Get a fucking room!" while driving by.

They both looked at each other and laughed.

"Yeah, that's New York for ya," Derrick said and smiled.

She was about to walk away, when he pulled her toward him again and kissed her more passionately.

"Good night," he mumbled, before walking out into the street to catch a cab.

Denise smiled. "Good night," she whispered, while licking her lips and walking into her building.

Chapter Seventeen
Gabrielle

To kill time, Gabrielle listened to the tapes again in her office. Something about the voices on the tapes bothered her. As she was listening to them, Nancy knocked on the door.

"Boss lady, your mother is here to see you."

Gabrielle looked up. "My mother?" she responded in a puzzled tone.

"Yes."

"Send her in."

Gabrielle was so shocked that she forgot to turn off the tape.

"Gabrielle," her mother said, while entering.

"Mother." She rose from her seat to kiss her on the cheek. "What brings you here?"

"I can't visit my daughter?"

Gabrielle chuckled. "You know I don't mean it like that. I'm just surprised, that's all," she said, playfully patting her mother's arm.

"So, Mother, what's up?" Gabrielle asked after they had taken a seat at the conference table.

"I wanted to talk to you about your father."

Instantly, Gabrielle cut her eyes and twisted up her face. "If you came here to tell me I was wrong, you're wasting your time."

"Gabrielle Dodson!"

"It's Gabrielle Brightman!" she retorted.

"You know what I meant."

"No, Mother, I don't. I've been married almost ten years now, and you can't even acknowledge my last name."

Sadie sighed. "Gabrielle, I didn't come here to fight with you." Then, she paused. "Who's that on the tape?"

Gabrielle jumped up. "Oh, it's for a client. Sorry. Let me turn it off." She ran over and stopped the tape. "Sorry," she mumbled again and sat back down.

Sadie looked around. She was so proud of her daughter. Even without their support, Gabrielle had established herself as a well-known lawyer. "I see you have a Biscoe painting in here."

"Actually, that's Greg's painting. It came out of his apartment."

"Greg was into art? I didn't know that."

"Well, there are a lot of things you don't know about him," Gabrielle snidely replied and cut her eyes.

Sadie grinned and nodded. Gabrielle didn't take shit from no one, the same way Sadie used to be years ago. Sadie was once feisty and outspoken like Gabrielle, until she met her husband. She was so in love with him that when he told her that women are supposed to be seen and not heard, she never commented about anything again.

"So, Mother, what's up?"

"I wanted to tell you how proud your father and I are of you."

"Really? Why do I smell a 'but' coming on?"

"Gabrielle, would you hush and stop being so defensive. Your father is just hurt…"

"Hurt? For what? Oh wait, let me guess. Because I didn't

marry some guy from Yale, Princeton, or some other Ivy League college."

"Your father and I worked hard for our children. We strived to make sure y'all had the best."

Gabrielle jumped up and started waving her hand. "The best? Let's define the best. You provided us with a nice house, and I use the word house because there was no love in it. So, the word home would be inappropriate. You sent us to a school where five other black kids attended, whom you forbade us to play with. Oh, let's not forget how Daddy didn't want me to hang out with his own family. Why? Because they didn't fit into his family portrait? He's a racist. He doesn't like himself. So, don't come in here with that 'we provided the best for you' bullshit, Ma. It takes more than a fancy home and private school to raise a child. "

"You are so ungrateful. You know how many kids would've killed to have your life?"

"No, but I do know kids that have killed their parents because of that life," Gabrielle shot back. While most kids would've killed to have her upbringing, she would've killed to have normal parents.

"Yeah, well, I know some people will always blame others for their mistakes. Don't blame us because you married a lowlife."

Gabrielle chuckled and shook her head. "A lowlife?" She nodded in frustration. "Greg may be a lot of things, but he's not a lowlife. But, what do you know? You can't even think for yourself. I may not be happy with my current situation, but at least it's my choice. Mother, I have a man who loves and respects me. I can't say the same about you."

Sadie had enough. She stood up and stormed over to Gabrielle. "How the fuck would you know? He's been locked up your entire marriage. Let me tell you something, Gabrielle. You may not like your father, but you damn sure will respect him…and me too for that matter. We busted our ass for our kids while most parents would not have given a shit."

Gabrielle turned her head, which sent fire through Sadie. She grabbed her by her chin. "You listen to me, dear. I came here to apologize, not to be insulted. So, watch your damn mouth. Whether you like it or not, you're standing here in this office because of us. Self-perseverance is learned not given," Sadie said, then pushed Gabrielle's face back.

Sadie turned around and started to exit, when Gabrielle yelled, "Ma, wait!" Gabrielle paused. "I'm sorry."

Sadie turned with tears in her eyes. "You don't know how proud I am of you. You have accomplished so much." She sighed. "I guess a part of me envies that."

Gabrielle gave her mother a confused look. "I don't understand."

She exhaled and took a seat back on the sofa. "Before I met your father, I wanted to be a pediatrician. I was actually in medical school, but I got pregnant. Your father, along with my parents, convinced me to drop out. He didn't exactly use those words; according to him, it was taking a break. Because I loved him so much, I did. When I wanted to go back, your father's career had just taken off, and before I knew it I was pregnant again. So, I just got my Master's and settled for being an Executive Director."

"Ma, I'm so sorry. I didn't know."

Sadie patted Gabrielle on the knee. "It's not your fault. I have a great life and a beautiful family. That's why I'm so proud of all my girls. You guys had the courage to do what I didn't do. Gabrielle, I know your father can be an ass at times, but he's still your father. You don't have to like him, but you do have to respect him. He only wants what every father would want for their kids…to be happy."

Gabrielle lowered her head before responding. "But, Ma, what makes you think I'm not? Yes, my marriage to Greg is challenging, but isn't all marriages? I just wish Daddy acted like a father instead of a sponsor. Greg is a good guy and he loves me to death."

"I know, sweetie. He would be a fool not to."

Sadie reached out and embraced her daughter, which was something she hadn't done in years. And it sure felt good. They ordered lunch, laughed, and talked until Nancy informed Gabrielle that her next client had arrived.

"Well, let me get going," Sadie said, cleaning off the table.

"Awww, Ma, I'll do that."

"Don't be silly," her mother replied.

Gabrielle walked over to her and hugged her. "I had a wonderful time."

"So did I, and I promise we will do this more often."

"Deal," Gabrielle giggled.

They kissed and hugged again before Sadie left.

After Myra entered, Gabrielle informed her that she finally got the ADA and judge to give Malik a bail. However, once they caught drugs in Malik's cell, they gave him a higher one, which Myra's dumb ass agreed to post. In addition to posting his bail, she agreed to provide him with a place to stay. All Gabrielle could do was shake her head. It was pointless rationalizing with Myra. Deep down inside, Gabrielle understood the power of love, but in Myra's case, it was the power of dick.

Gabrielle took care of a few more things before heading out to meet Tommy. That evening, Britney would be joining them. Tommy thought it would be a good idea to bring her along. Besides, he wanted to screen Britney to make sure she was on their side.

Tommy had them meet him at a hotel off the Garden State Parkway. A paranoid Gabrielle arrived there first, even though Tommy assured her that they weren't being followed. While waiting for Tommy and Britney to arrive, she paced back and forth. With so many thoughts cluttering her brain, she had forgotten to tell them what room she was in. So, she pulled out her cell phone to call them. Afterwards, she attempted to get comfortable by kicking off her shoes. While reading over some papers, her mother popped into her mind. Out of all days, she wondered why her mother showed up. Clearly, Gabrielle and her father had fought before, so why did Sadie stop by? *Maybe it was to make amends. After all, everyone is born with a conscious,* she thought.

Knock! Knock!

It was Britney. "Hey, am I late?"

"No, no," Gabrielle said, letting her in. "Actually, I'm early."

A few seconds later, Tommy knocked on the door. This time, Britney opened it.

"Hello."

Caught off guard, Tommy backed up. "Is Gabrielle…"

Before he could finish his question, Gabrielle emerged.

"Tommy."

Tommy laughed and then entered the room. "Sorry, I wasn't sure if I had the correct room number."

Once everyone was acquainted, they got down to business. Britney had brought some more tapes that had that same voice recorded. Gabrielle asked her if she knew the person on the tapes, but Britney said no.

Meanwhile, Tommy reviewed some documents he had gotten from one of his ex-CIA buddies. It appeared Robin Cox had been slammed by the Second Circuit Federal Court system for omitting evidence.

Tommy also found out that Robin was quickly promoted after Greg's trail. They also thought it was odd that a high-profile case like Greg's wasn't handled by the district attorney. Secretly, Robin leaked information to the media. Gabrielle read that a thousand times and it still burned her up.

"Now that we have all of this, how do we bring this bitch down?" Gabrielle snapped, and then after realizing what she had said, she looked over at Britney. "Sorry."

Not offended, Britney shrugged her shoulders. "Don't be.

She's a bitch."

Both laughed.

After going back and forth, they finally decided on a plan. Actually, Britney came up with a great plan to confront Robin. For Britney, it was personal. In the beginning, she was angry at Gabrielle, but after talking to her, she realized Gabrielle was just a victim.

It was getting late, so they decided to call it a night. As they headed to the parking lot, Britney turned to Gabriella and asked, "Do you think we're gonna win?"

Lost in her thoughts, Gabrielle didn't hear her. "What did you say?"

Britney sighed. "Do you think we're gonna win?" she repeated.

Gabrielle shook her head, wondering the same thing. "I don't know. But, I do know that all wars are won before they are even fought. With that being said, I think we're in good hands. Why? Are you having second thoughts?"

Britney looked down at the ground. "Not about the case. I just can't believe my mother. Gabrielle, I looked up to her so much."

Gabrielle reached out and touched Britney's hand. "I learned something today. I learned that our parents are human. Yes, we love them and we're supposed to look up to them. That doesn't mean we have to like them."

"I just don't understand," Britney said.

Gabrielle started to walk away. "And you probably never will. Goodnight, girl, and get some sleep," she said before getting into her car and driving off.

*****

It had been three weeks, and they still hadn't confronted Robin. Tommy advised them to hold off because he was researching some additional information and leads, which translated to Gabrielle that he had dropped the ball. *It's bad enough I've been a nervous wreck ever since Britney gave me all this information. Now, Tommy pulls this bullshit. He had better have some great news.*

"Boss lady," Nancy said through the intercom.

"Yes?"

"A Mr. Tony Flowers is here to see you."

"Tony Flowers?" Gabrielle repeated.

"Yes."

"Okay. Send him in."

Gabrielle took a deep breath. She couldn't stand him.

"Mrs. Brightman," he walked in and said cheerfully.

"Mr. Flowers," Gabrielle replied snidely, flashing a phony smile.

Tony leaned over and kissed her on the cheek. "How's my sis doing?"

Oh please, Tony! Cut the bullshit, she thought. "I'm doing well, and you?"

"Life is great," he said, taking a seat.

Being that both of them disliked one another, there was a brief moment of silence.

Tony looked around her office. "Nice digs. Why don't you let me hook you up with some office space in my building? You'll have a panoramic view of the Hudson River."

Gabrielle glared at Tony for a second. "Awww, thank you, but I'm perfectly fine right here in my little Bronx office. Besides, there are too many self-centered people in Manhattan."

Tony smirked and bit his tongue. "Well, the offer is open if you ever change your mind. On another note, Stevie said she sent my file over to you."

"Yes, she did." Gabrielle called Nancy and asked her to bring Tony's file in. "So what else is new?" she asked, pretending to care.

Tony knew Gabrielle didn't care for him, but the feeling was mutual. "Nothing much. Just came back from promoting my album in Europe."

Gabrielle nodded.

Nancy walked in and handed the file over to Gabrielle, while smiling at Tony, who smiled back.

Gabrielle looked at both of them and shook her head. "Thanks, Nancy."

Once Nancy left, Tony asked, "You think you can hook me up with your assistant?"

Gabrielle twisted up her face. "Aren't you with Christina?"

"Yeah, but what she doesn't know won't hurt her. You of all people should know that."

"What do you mean by that?"

"Come on, Gabby. You can't tell me you've been faithful to my man all this time."

Gabrielle took a deep breath. She knew where the conversation was going. Tony was deliberately trying to piss her off, which was something he had done in the past. However, this time, Gabrielle wasn't going to give him the satisfaction.

"When did my personal life become so important to you?"

"It hasn't. Just like mines shouldn't concern you."

Gabrielle flashed a grin. "It doesn't, but when you asked me to hook you up, you made it my concern. Tony, let's be clear about something. The only reason why I tolerate you is because of your friendship with my husband. Personally, I think you're a narcissist bastard who hides behind his image. You may have my husband fooled and my cousin, but I know you're full of shit."

"And you aren't? Gabrielle, you wouldn't be shit without my man. Yeah, let's talk about it. My man dicked you down something crazy. He took you out of that miserable little perfect life of yours."

"You believe that. You know what they say about men that abuse women. They only do it because they are lacking in other places. It makes them feel like a man...figuratively speaking. Stevie told me how you liked to beat her and then have sex.

Maybe that's why you're jealous of Denise...because she has a bigger set of balls than you. To the world, you are known as Tony Flowers, but to your team, you're nothing."

"You might be right, but look at them and look at me. Who's laughing now?"

"Laugh now, cry hard later."

Tony's blood was boiling. Luckily for her, she was married to his man, or else Tony would have that bitch's face cut. Tony always felt Gabrielle thought she was better than him.

Her words must've hit a nerve, because he sat there for a minute collecting his thoughts before speaking. "Listen, Gabby, I didn't come here to fight with you. I'm sorry if I was out of line...real talk. You have been nothing but good to my man, so you're alright with me."

Gabrielle slowly cut her eyes, as if she saw something outside her window. "It's not a problem, Tony." She handed him the papers for his signature.

"Gabrielle, you know I really regret losing Stevie. Every day I kick myself in the ass for treating her like that. She was the best thing that ever happened to me. She forgave me, and hopefully, one day, you will, too."

Gabrielle turned her head toward him. Tony was right. Stevie had forgiven Tony and moved on with her life. Maybe she should forgive him, too. In truth, he did help her a lot with her career, but her gut kept telling her that he was a snake.

"Listen, I know it's been years since you and Stevie have been together, and yes, she has moved on. Still, that doesn't change the fact that you abused her. Tony, I've seen the black eyes and busted lips. You terrorized her. Stevie may have moved on, but she will never forget. Mentally, you ruined her for life, whether you like to admit it or not."

"I know. I was young and immature. That was the only way I knew how to control her, make her stay with me. But, I've changed."

"Only time will tell."

Tony nodded. "Fair enough."

After signing the contracts, he handed them back to her along with a large envelope that contained some papers.

"What's this?" Gabrielle asked.

"I want you to look over this contract and make sure it's secure."

Gabrielle read it. "Christina signed a 360 deal with you?"

Tony smiled. "Yep, it was her idea."

"Interesting," she replied with a raised eyebrow. "So, no matter what, you will get fifty percent of her entire earnings for the rest of her life."

Tony smirked and nodded.

She handed it back. "Everything appears to be in order. Smart move, Mr. Flowers."

"Thanks." Tony kissed her on the cheek again before leaving.

Gabrielle shook her head as she watched him walk out the door. *Poor Christina.*

*****

Once Tommy delayed the plan, Gabrielle became suspicious of him. Therefore, she followed him around for the next couple of days only to find nothing. She started thinking the case was making her crazy. She even started taking a different route home every day and refused to answer calls from unknown numbers. In Gabrielle's eyes, everyone was starting to look like a suspect.

To get her mind off of the case, she called Denise.

"Hey Dee!"

"What's up, Gabby?"

"What are you doing after work?"

"I was thinking about going for a jog."

"Really? Damn, I haven't worked out in months. I should join you."

"You should."

"Alright! Where are you going jogging at?" Gabrielle asked.

"Central Park."

"Central Park! Are you trying to get raped?"

Denise chuckled. "Girl, please, ain't nobody tryna rape my ass. Meet me in front of my building. Is seven o'clock okay?"

"Alright."

Click!

After hanging up, Gabrielle instructed Nancy to run out and pick up something for her to work out in. When Nancy returned, she interrupted Gabrielle meeting with her staff to inform her that Tommy was waiting for her. Instantly, Gabrielle ended the meeting. Her heart skipped a beat. *This bastard better have a good explanation for not returning my calls,* she thought.

Gabrielle stood up and brushed off her skirt, as Tommy entered her office. By the look on her face, Tommy knew she was annoyed

"Gabrielle, let me explain."

Raising her eyebrow, Gabrielle stared at him.

"I know you're wondering why I haven't returned your calls."

"You damn right!" she blurted out.

"I wanted to make sure Britney was on board because she seemed too…willing."

"What do you mean?" Gabrielle asked, confused.

"Doesn't it seem odd to you that she's willing to help us destroy her mother's life? Her mother could go to prison."

Gabrielle's eyes widened. She never thought about that. She had to admit, Britney willingly gave them a lot of information. Even though Gabrielle's mother pissed her off, there's no way she could send her to prison. *Is this a setup?* she thought. Nauseous, Gabrielle took a seat.

"So what did you find out?" she asked in a disappointed voice.

"Nothing. She's clean as a whistle. I followed her everyday;

she's clean."

"Okay. So what's the problem now?"

Tommy intensely stared at Gabrielle. "Let's bring them down."

She laughed. "Tommy, you're something else, you know that? But, I need to ask you something."

"Alright."

"Can I trust you?"

"Can you trust me? Where did that come from?"

"You changed the plan and didn't return any of my calls. You did all that because you were tailing Britney?"

"Yes!"

"Really? Well, I was tailing you. Tommy, let's be clear about something. If I can't trust you, you're no good to me. So, can I trust you?"

Angry, Tommy exhaled. *Is this bitch crazy?* he thought. "You have balls asking me that."

"No, you're the one with balls."

Tommy giggled. Dean was right; Gabrielle was a something else. Actually, Tommy was glad she asked him this question. It showed she was focused. "Yes, you can trust me."

"Alright, because next time, I will not ask."

"I hope not."

Momentarily, they looked at each other before Tommy broke the silence. "Now that we cleared the air, not only have I been following Britney, but I've been following her mother, as well."

Gabrielle shrugged her shoulders and leaned back in her chair, allowing Tommy to continue.

"Robin was just appointed back to the Bronx district attorney's office. I was thinking we give her a couple of weeks to get settled before approaching her."

"What! Why?"

"Gabrielle, understand something. Robin is nothing to play with. She's a dangerous woman."

"And I'm not?"

He nodded. "All I'm asking for is a couple more weeks. We're still gonna go ahead with the plan, just pushing it back. I wanna make sure we don't leave any rocks unturned," he explained.

"Tommy, my husband has been waiting damn near ten years. You have two weeks."

"Thank you! Please let Britney know," he said before exiting.

A part of Gabrielle wanted to throw a glass up against the wall. "Shit!" she screamed.

Cooling off, she went back to editing Thomas' brief. *Robin's dangerous. Shit, what am I?* Gabrielle thought before releasing a giggle. After a couple of meetings and conference calls, she got dressed in her workout attire and headed out to meet Denise.

When Gabrielle arrived, Denise was in front of the building. "Wow! Aren't we ready?" Denise laughed.

"Yep."

Not wanting to waste any time, Gabrielle and Denise went into the park and stretched.

"Now go easy on me, Denise. I haven't jogged in months."

"Shit, that makes two of us. You're lucky Morgan is not with us. She would run our asses in the dirt," Denise warned, making Gabrielle laugh.

A mile into their run, Gabrielle's legs started cramping. "Oh wait, Denise," she said, huffing and puffing. "Damn, I'm out of shape."

Happy, Denise stopped. "Are you okay?" she asked.

Limping over to a bench, Gabrielle replied, "Y-e-a-h."

Denise followed her, laughing. "I know the feeling."

In pain, Gabrielle smirked and then sat there praying for the pain to stop. When she noticed Denise staring up at the sky, she asked, "What are you thinking about?"

Denise slowly shook her head and simply replied, "Life."

"Funny, I was thinking about the same thing. Isn't that something?"

"At times. How's Greg doing?"

"He's good. Denise, how do you feel about Jake Lawrence?"

Denise faced her. "What do you mean?"

"I mean, do you like him?"

"Personally, I would have retained Mr. Rubin. Jake is good and all, but Mr. Rubin loved us. He really adored Greg. We were more than drug dealers to him. I mean, just a couple of months ago, he got my ass out of jail."

"What! You were in jail? When?"

"Remember that night I told you about Britney. Well, after that, my ass got locked up.'"

"For what?"

"My gun?'

"Why were you caring a gun, Denise?"

Denise sighed. "It's a long story, Gabby, that's not worth discussing."

Gabrielle glared at Denise from the corner of her eye. "You've come too far…"

"I know," Denise quickly replied, cutting her off. "I'm not going to lie. I was scared as shit in there. Years ago, I didn't give a fuck, but the thought of being in jail now scares the hell out of me."

"I hope so. So when do you go back to court?"

"The case was dismissed."

"That's great. You know, Denise, it's easy to get in trouble, but hard to get out of it."

"Shit, tell me about it."

"Denise, can I ask you a question?"

"Another one? Sure?" She winked and laughed.

"What if you would've found Britney? Would you have killed her?"

Apprehensive, Denise looked at Gabrielle. "Why are you

asking me that? Are you working for the police...trying to get an indictment?"

Gabrielle busted out laughing. "No, silly, just answer the question."

Looking Gabrielle straight in her eyes, she replied, "Now...no. Back then...probably."

"Why?" Gabrielle questioned.

"Well, if it was back then, I loved my friends so much that I would've done anything for them. If she was a threat, she would have been taken care of immediately. But, now, I'm in a different frame of mind."

"Yeah, but...kill?"

"Yep! That's the name of the game," Denise responded. "You know, no one is born a killer. It's situations we are put in that causes us to kill. Mine was my first boyfriend."

"Come on, Denise. Science has proven that some people are born that way. They are born with a chemical imbalance."

"Maybe so, but think about it for a second. It's situations that force you to kill. When a mother kills her kids, nine times out of ten it's because of her situation. However, I agree some people are mentally disturbed. Shit, I know I am."

Chuckling, Gabrielle nudged Denise. "Fool! I guess you're right, though. So you really killed your first boyfriend?"

"Yep! Just the thought of watching him gasp for air made me feel good. He deserved it. He had ruined too many lives."

"And what about the others?"

"What about them? Gabrielle, I didn't just go around killing people just because. No! Someone had to act and then I would react. Our lives had to be directly threatened. That's the difference between us and a lot of crews out there. We just didn't go around beating up or killing people. You know how some people will kill a crackhead because they shorted them just to prove a point? Greg didn't do that. According to Greg, you don't get points by doing sucka shit like that, because they aren't a threat to you. That doesn't mean a scared person won't kill you first, but to answer your question, we just didn't kill *anyone*; you really had to push us. That's why we're still here. You're only as good as your leader."

"Greg was different," Gabrielle agreed.

"Yeah, and I guess that's why all of us were able to make a smooth transition out of the game. With Greg, he was real. He only wanted the best for us. He wasn't insecure like most leaders."

"Hey, have you heard anything else about Felicia's murder?"

"No. Felicia was an ass," Denise commented, looking away.

"Wow, Dee, she was your friend."

"More like a frienemy."

"Huh? Y'all two were tight back in the day."

"Exactly, back in the day. Felicia changed. You know what's sad. It's always the one you love that hurts you," Denise emphasized.

"Yeah, but I don't think she meant to hurt you."

"Really? She told you that," Denise snidely responded.

"Hush!" Gabrielle playfully pushed her. "No, silly, I'm just saying you guys grew up together."

Annoyed, Denise replied, "So? Just because you and a motherfucker used to play hide and seek doesn't mean that same motherfucker won't blow your brains out. Do you know how many crews crumbled because of shit like that? It's always someone close to you. That's why I won't blink twice when it comes to my friends now."

"You think any of them would cross you?"

Denise stared into Gabrielle's eyes. "Didn't Felicia?"

As they headed out of the park, Denise stopped to face Gabrielle and said, "In life, everyone has what I like to call a defining moment. A split second will change a person for the rest of their life. For me, my defining moment was meeting Greg. Yours may have been something different. But, we all have one."

Gabrielle nodded her understanding.

They hugged and kissed each other on the cheek before Gabrielle jumped into a cab. Little did Denise know, Gabrielle had already experienced her defining moment. Still, the best was yet to come.

Chapter Eighteen
Morgan

It was seven o'clock Monday morning and Morgan was still asleep. Denise knocked on the door.

"Morgan, are you up?"

Morgan rolled over and looked at the time. She had overslept. Actually, she had been sleeping a lot more than she normally did. In addition, she had felt ill while she was over her mother's house that weekend.

"Now I am," she said, jumping up out of the bed.

Denise opened the door. "Are you okay?" she asked, aware that Morgan hadn't been feeling well lately.

"Yeah," she said, smiling weakly.

"Alright. If you don't feel good, stay home and get some rest. I'm off to work. I'm going to pick up some vitamins for you before I come home. You've been up early in the morning and coming home late. It's probably starting to take a toll on your body. So, maybe vitamins will help you to feel better," Denise said, then went downstairs.

Morgan walked in the bathroom to turn on the shower, when suddenly, she felt dizzy. She threw some water on her face, hoping that would relieve her dizziness. Then she decided to get a glass of orange juice. She went downstairs and poured herself a glass of juice, but on her way back upstairs she felt nauseous. *What the hell is going on?* Unable to reach the bathroom, she threw up right there on the stairs. She ran up to the bathroom and continued throwing up. After flushing the toilet, she rinsed her mouth out and stood there looking at her reflection in the mirror. That's when it hit her that she hadn't seen her period in months. *Oh, no! Could I be pregnant? Please, God, no!*

Morgan hurried and got dressed. She remembered Chloe's sister had gone to a place on 149th Street in the Bronx to get a pregnancy test done. They offered this service to those who were uninsured.

Not sure how to get there, Morgan asked the token booth clerk for directions. Then she jumped on the number two train going uptown. On the subway ride there, Morgan felt nauseous again. She went between the cars and threw up. She couldn't believe this was happening to her. She prayed it was just some kind of bug. The last thing she needed was to be pregnant, especially by Tony.

After getting lost a few times, she finally walked into *Planned Parenthood*. Morgan looked around to make sure no one recognized her.

"Hello. May I help you?" the receptionist asked.

Ashamed, Morgan mumbled, "I need...um, a pregnancy test," with her eyes lowered.

"Okay. Well, just fill out your first and last name on the sign-in sheet, have a seat, and complete this form," she told her, while handing her a clipboard.

After reading the questions, Morgan felt like walking out. She feared they would notify her family. However, when she got up to give the clipboard back to the clerk, she was assured that everything was confidential and that her parents would not be notified.

Morgan sighed and frowned. "Sorry, this is my first time." She took the clipboard and proceeded to fill out the questionnaire. After completing it, she handed it back to the receptionist and sat down. There were many girls waiting to be seen, and most of them were pregnant.

Her eyes filled with tears. *Why is this happening to me?*

"Morgan Marciano!" a nurse yelled.

Morgan looked around and got up.

"Follow me, honey," the nurse said.

She took Morgan into one of the examination rooms. "So you want a pregnancy test?" she asked her after closing the door.

Embarrassed, Morgan shook her head yes.

The nurse reached into the drawer and pulled out a small plastic container. "The bathroom is on your left. Pee in this cup, make sure you tighten the lid, and bring it back to me. Leave your things here," she instructed.

Morgan did as she was told and brought the urine back. The nurse put on a pair of gloves and grabbed the container from her. Then she pulled out a pregnancy test strip from the top drawer and dipped the stick into Morgan's urine.

After what seemed like an eternity to Morgan, the nurse looked up and said, "You're pregnant."

Morgan broke down. "No, that can't be true."

She just sat there and cried, while the nurse tried to comfort her. "Sweetie, when was the last time you had your period?" she asked, so she could help determine how far along she was.

Morgan thought back and remembered it was about three months ago. The nurse pulled out a pregnancy chart and told Morgan that if what she said was true about her period, she was between eight to twelve weeks pregnant. Morgan sobbed even more; she could not have this baby. The nurse told Morgan there were options, but she would have to wait outside for a social worker to discuss them. She then handed her a paper with her name, test results, and due date.

Morgan waited in the seating area, but when she looked up at the time, she saw that it was almost ten o'clock. *Dag, I have to get to school.* Going up to the receptionist's desk, she told them she would come back after school.

Throughout the day, Morgan was in a daze. She couldn't believe she was pregnant with Tony's child. Although she didn't have an appetite, Morgan forced herself to eat at lunchtime, but it came back up. On her way from the bathroom, she bumped into the career counselor.

"Hello, Morgan. Don't forget we're having an orientation for the Harvard Law School Summer Program."

Morgan's eyes widened. She had completely forgotten. "It's today, Mrs. Davis?"

"Yes, Morgan, it's at three o'clock. It's a forty-five minute session, and I look forward to seeing you there," Mrs. Davis said, then walked off.

Since Morgan and a few other students were scheduled to be at orientation, the math teacher allowed them to leave class five minutes early. She tried to rush to the auditorium, but kept getting lightheaded. When she got there, it was already packed with excited students.

As Morgan sat through the presentation, all she could think about was how she was going to get an abortion. She needed some advice, but who could she confide in? Chloe would call her a hypocrite, and she wasn't close to the other girls. She wouldn't dare tell Denise or her mother. Her eyes filled with tears. *Why did this have to happen?*

Morgan looked down at her watch and saw it was almost four o'clock. *Oh God, I have to meet Tony today*, she remembered, while grabbing her bag and rushing out. Unable to run because she felt dizzy, she walked briskly, while praying Al was still out there. The car was just about to pull off when Morgan yelled, "Wait!"

She jumped in only to find Tony wasn't in the car. When Al got to a red light, he called Tony. "Yeah, I have her."

When they pulled up outside of the house, Morgan jumped out and ran inside. Afraid that Tony would be upset, she dropped her bags and went straight to the kitchen to prepare his food.

Tony came into the kitchen walked over her. "What's up?"

Frightened, Morgan glanced over at him. "Hi. Sorry I'm late. We had Career Day at school."

Tony nodded. "I don't see you for days and all you have to say to me is hi."

Morgan froze. She wasn't sure what she should do. Then it dawned on her what he wanted. She went over to him and gave him a peck on the lips. "Sorry."

Tony yanked her back over to him and shoved his tongue down her throat. "Don't you ever kiss me like that again. Now start cooking," he said, slapping her on the ass.

Morgan turned around and was about to start cooking, when she saw Tony pick up her book bag and unzip it. She ran over and tried to grab it from him. "Tony, no!" She didn't want him to see the papers from the clinic.

Tony pulled it away from her and held it in the air. "What did you say to me?"

Morgan stared at the floor and mumbled, "Please, can I have my book bag?"

"What's in here that you don't want me to see?" he yelled.

"Nothing."

"So if it's nothing, then why the fuck are you coming over here?"

Morgan looked up at him. "I just don't want you to mess up my papers, that's all."

Tony didn't believe her. "Get the fuck outta here. Do you think I'm stupid?" he shouted, slapping the shit out of her. "You're trying to be sneaky!" he yelled, striking her again while Morgan blocked her face. He tossed the bag across the room and grabbed Morgan by her hair. "Since you don't want me to see what's in your bag, I'm gonna make you tell me," he grumbled.

"Tony, please," she cried.

"Please my ass..." He flung her on the couch. "Now are you gonna tell me or do I have to beat it out of you?"

Trembling and crying, Morgan replied, "It's just papers…nothing else. I swear."

"So ya gonna sit there and lie to me," he said, raising his hand to strike her again.

Morgan blocked her face and screamed. "I'm pregnant!"

Tony froze. "What did you say?"

"I'm pregnant." She exhaled "I found out today. I'm about three months."

Tony almost passed out. He put his hand down, then started pacing back and forth before taking a seat on the couch next to her. "So that's why you've been so sick and tired lately?"

Morgan nodded, then jumped up and grabbed her bag. She took out the paper the nurse had given to her and handed it to him. After reading it, Tony placed his hands over his face. He felt like a real sucka.

"Baby girl, come here."

Still terrified, she backed away from him.

Tony got up and walked over to her. "I'm so sorry. I didn't know," he whispered, hugging her.

"Tony, I'm sorry. I didn't mean to get pregnant. I really didn't."

"I know. It's cool. We'll handle it."

Tony embraced the mother of his child, while she stood there with her arms at her sides. He then guided her back over to the couch.

"How do you feel?" he asked, rubbing her cheek.

"I feel okay," she said, twiddling her thumbs from nervousness.

Tony lifted her head towards him. "Don't worry. We're gonna be okay. I will take care of you and my child."

Morgan's eyes widened. "Tony, I can't keep this baby."

"What do you mean? It's ours. You think I'm gonna allow you to get an abortion?"

Morgan sighed and closed her eyes. "Tony, I'm only fifteen years old. I can't have this baby. My family would kill me."

"Fuck your family! You're carrying mines right now. We won't tell them."

He is really crazy, she thought. As she got up to walk over to the window, she explained, "Tony, we can't keep this baby. I'm too young."

Getting frustrated, he said, "So what you're young. You know how many chicks have babies at a young age? Many of them don't even have a fucking father for their baby. Morgan, we are not getting rid of this baby."

Tears rolled down Morgan's face. She couldn't believe this. "Tony, please, I can't keep this baby."

"You can and you will!" he shouted. In the Bible, I'm pretty sure them girls were younger than you when they married and had children."

Morgan glanced over at him. *Was that supposed to make me feel better?*

"Can we just think about it?" he asked, calming down a bit as he walked over to her. "All I'm asking for is a chance to prove to you that I'm a good dude. Do you think I would leave you? I won't. You're carrying our child. Doesn't that mean anything to you?"

"Tony, you don't understand. I have goals planned. I wanna go to college and become something in life. This is not what I wanted. I don't know anything about raising no child."

"So what? Neither do I, but we can learn together. As for you finishing school, you still can. That's why they have nannies. I want my baby, Morgan."

Morgan sighed. *There is no way I'm keeping this baby by this rapist.*

Tony reached out and touched her stomach. "You're gonna look gorgeous pregnant. You're already beautiful. They say

Italian women are stunning while they're carrying."

Morgan frowned; she wanted to tell him to shut the hell up.

Tony hugged her from behind. "You know pregnant pussy is the best pussy because it stays wet."

With that, he led Morgan to the bedroom so that his baby's mother could please him sexually in every way imaginable.

*****

When Al arrived to pick them up, they headed out to the car with Tony holding Morgan's hand. Sadly, he really did believe they were a couple. On the ride home, Morgan slept while he conducted business on the phone. During the ride, he reached over and rubbed Morgan's stomach a few times. When they got down the block from Denise's apartment, Al got out as normal to give them some privacy.

"Baby, it's going to be fine," Tony reassured her.

Morgan sighed. "Tony, I can't keep it."

"Why?"

Morgan wanted to say, *Because you raped me! Do you really think I wanna have a child by a rapist, you sick bastard.* But, she didn't. Instead, she replied, "I can't. I'm too young."

Tony rolled his eyes. He's always wanted a baby, and Morgan would be the perfect mother for his child. "I don't understand why you can't have it. It's not like we're ever leaving each other. You're mine."

Morgan's eyes widened. "I'm yours?"

Tony glared at her. "Yes. I'm marrying you."

She really became depressed then. "Tony, I'm not marrying you."

He frowned. "Well, tell that to your family when you visit them in the graveyard."

Morgan closed her eyes. "Why are you doing this to me? What have I done to you?"

"No! Why are you doing this to me? Do you know how I

feel about you? Why can't you be with me?" he retorted, not being realistic in his demands.

She looked away. "Tony, don't do this, please."

"Don't do what? I'm the one for you, Morgan. Me! I'll take care of you."

"I don't need you to take care of me."

"Either you're gonna be with me or else," he threatened. "If I can't have you, no one will."

"What do you want from me? I haven't said anything," she sniffled, with tears rolling down her face.

"I want you. I want you to be all mines and mines only. Don't worry. You will be taken care of, but I want you, Morgan Marciano," he said, forcing her to look at him.

Morgan wept. "I'm doing what you want. Isn't that enough?"

"I want you. Tell me that you're mine and we can move on. Because if you're not, it's gonna be a problem...and not for me."

She looked away and ran her fingers through her hair.

Tony grabbed her by the arm. "I didn't hear you. Are you mine?" he whispered in an angry tone.

With fear in her eyes, Morgan faced him. "Yes, I'm yours, Tony," she cried.

"A'ight, so I don't wanna hear anymore bullshit out of you. You're my girl. Understand me?"

Morgan nodded.

"I'll see you tomorrow"

"But I have dance practice tomorrow."

"No the fuck you don't, not with my child in you. That running and dancing shit is dead. See you at two, and don't be late."

Morgan was about to get out the car, when Tony grabbed her. "What did I tell you about that?"

Remembering that she had forgotten to kiss him goodbye, she leaned over and planted her lips on his. "Goodnight."

While walking to her building, Morgan broke down in the middle of the block in tears. There was no way she could be with someone that brought her so much pain. Most of all, she couldn't have his baby. Feeling nauseous again, she started throwing up. Morgan leaned on a parked car hoping the sickness would stop. When she looked down the block, she saw that Tony's car was still parked there. She pulled herself together and headed inside the building.

Thank God when she got home, Denise was sleep. Morgan was so tired that she didn't even bother to shower. She just washed her face, got in the bed, and prayed to be saved from her life that had turned into a never-ending nightmare.

Chapter Nineteen
Tony

Morgan had dropped a bomb on Tony. He couldn't believe she was carrying his child. On his way to the studio, all he thought about was the baby. Tony always wanted a child, and he had been crushed when Stevie lost their baby. He believed it was the reason why he started cheating on her, because he blamed her for miscarrying. While Tony was thrilled with the fact that Morgan was pregnant with his child, the reality hit him that if Felix and Denise found out what he had been doing to their beloved daughter and niece it would be the end of life as he knew it. He would certainly be signing his own death certificate should their secret ever be revealed.

When Tony pulled up to the studio, Mookie, who he had called and instructed to meet him out front, was standing by the curb waiting for him.

"What's up, fam?" Mookie said, after jumping in.

"What's good?" Tony replied in a tone that let Mookie know his mind was many miles away.

Sensing something was wrong with Tony, he asked, "You

a'ight?"

Tony sighed. "Yeah, I'm good. Yo, Mookie, I need a favor, but the shit stays between us. A'ight?"

"Tee, this is me. Of course, it does," he said, throwing his hand up.

"Nah, I'm serious about this."

"Tone, I got you. Damn, you act like I'm some fucking stranger."

"A'ight. Well, you remember Denise's niece Morgan, right?"

Mookie sat there for a second trying to picture the face. "Nah, I don't."

"Remember shorty at the photo shoot? I used to mess with her mom who is Denise's sister? It's Jasmine's daughter," he explained, hitting Mookie on the leg.

"Oh yeah, she was doing that modeling shit. Oh son, she's crazy. Shorty is gonna be a heartbreaker when she gets older."

Boiling inside, Tony didn't appreciate Mookie talking about his boo like that. "Chill, Mookie. Damn."

Mookie laughed. "Yo son, it's true. Shorty is straight up gorgeous." He could tell Tony was getting upset, so he decided to stop with his comments. "A'ight, fam, what's up?"

Tony rolled his eyes. "She called me last night asking if I could help her. She's pregnant and the dude that got her pregnant bounced," he said, sounding sincere.

Mookie shook his head. "Word? Damn, that's fucked up. How old is she?"

"She's around fifteen or sixteen years old."

"Damn, dude bounced? How old is the dude? Is he young, too?"

Tony glared at Mookie, growing irritated with his questions. "Dude is over eighteen years old."

"Wow, that's statutory rape for real, my man. That's why I don't fuck with them young chicks, because even if they agree to have sex with you, the State will still charge you. That's a mandatory seven years in prison."

Tony's eyes grew larger than quarters. He had forgotten about that. If Denise or Felix didn't kill him, Jasmine would surly make sure he went to prison. "Damn, I didn't know that, but anyway, I need you to take her to have an abortion."

Mookie screwed his face up. "Me? Come on, fam. Why don't you take her? She called you, not me."

"I would, but you know that shit would be all over the papers. Mookie, she's like a niece to me. Just do this solid for me this one time. Come on, fam. I've been there for you many times."

Mookie gave it some thought and then shook his head. "A'ight, son. I'll make some calls tomorrow, set something up, and let you know. But, tell shorty to keep her legs closed and stop fucking with them lame-ass dudes. She's too pretty for that."

"I will. Thanks, fam," Tony said, while reaching over to give him a hug and a pound.

After Mookie jumped out the car, Tony found himself both sad and relieved. True, he really wanted this baby, but he valued his life more.

*****

The next day, Mookie arrived at Tony's office just as he was finishing up the discussion with Tia regarding the details of his upcoming nine-month tour. He was wrapping things up when Mookie walked in.

"Tony, you wanted to see me?"

He nodded. "Yeah, Mookie, have a seat," he told him, and then turned his attention back to Tia. "So is everything a go-ahead with the tour? I don't want any hiccups while on the road."

"Tony, we're good. I spoke to all the other artists and they know it's your show. I went over the rules with their camps."

"A'ight. Well, that's all for now."

Tia got up to leave.

"Oh, and Tia!" he said before she walked out. "Don't schedule anything for me this week. I'm tryna chill before I head out. And one more thing, please close the door behind you."

Tia nodded.

Once she was gone, Mookie leaned over and said, "I made some calls about that thing we spoke about yesterday, and if she can do it on Sunday, that will be good."

"Sunday?"

"Yeah, Tony, I can't been seen with her either. So, he said Sunday is a good day."

"Yo man, I don't want some chop shop doing this."

"Damn, Tony, you really think I would do that? There will be other clients there, too. Tony, come on. I wouldn't do that. She's gonna be good. Tell her that she has to meet me at seven o'clock in the morning."

"Okay, I'll let her know. So, Sunday she has the appointment. Mookie, this is strictly between us. I promised her that I wouldn't tell anyone."

"Tony, I know already."

He gave Mookie a pound. "Thanks."

After Mookie left, Tony conducted his regular business routine, while thoughts of Morgan ran through his head and he counted down the hours until he would see her later that day.

When 1:30 p.m. rolled around, Tony called Al and instructed him to place an order for some Italian food that could be picked up once they scooped up Morgan. He made one more call, used the bathroom, and then headed out. Before leaving the office, he told Lisa, his receptionist, to forward all his calls to Tia and Mookie, and if anyone asked, he was gone for the day. By the time he got downstairs, Al was parked out front waiting for him. Tony waved to a few fans that passed by and then jumped in the car.

Before he could get settled in his seat good, he felt his cell phone vibrating. It was his sister Tammy.

"What's up, Tammy?"

"Hey, Brother. Listen, when are you going on tour?"

"I'm flying out this Sunday. Why? What's up?"

"Mommy wanted to know. She thought it was next Sunday. She was gonna cook you a going-away dinner."

"A'ight, that's what's up. I'm booked like crazy, though. Why don't y'all fly to see me? Bring the entire family and Mommy can do the dinner there."

"Okay, we can do that. I'll let her know."

"By the way, how is Mommy? Every time I call her, she's busy."

"Don't feel bad. She's like that when I call."

Both laughed.

"A'ight, Sis. Just call Tia and tell her what day y'all are coming so she can arrange a place for us."

"Will do, Bro. Talk to you later."

As Al and Tony pulled up, they saw Morgan leaning against a car. She looked sick. Tony shook his head. *It will soon be over,* he thought. When she saw it was him, she dragged her bag on the ground and got in the car.

"Hello," she said, leaning over and kissing him.

"Damn, baby, you sick like that."

"Yes, it's killing me," she replied

Tony wanted to share the news with her, but didn't want Al to know. "I have some good news for you. I'll tell you later."

Morgan didn't even look at him. She just closed her eyes and prayed for some relief.

Tony rested his hand on her lap. "Don't worry, ma. Daddy will take care of you."

After Al pulled up in front of the Italian restaurant and jumped out to go inside to get their food, Tony turned toward Morgan. "Listen, I thought about what you said last night and…" he hesitated for a moment. "You're right. You are too young to have this baby. So, I've arranged for you to have an abortion this Sunday. My man is gonna take you."

"You're not taking me?" she asked, staring into his eyes.

"Baby, I wish I could, but I have to leave for my tour that morning. Even if I wasn't, I don't think I could take you to kill my child. Morgan, a part of me doesn't want you to get an abortion, but I know it's best. You just don't know how I feel inside."

Morgan stared at the floor. Deep down inside, she didn't want to abort the life growing inside her either, but how could she keep a baby by the man that raped her?

"Listen, I meant what I said about you being my girl. One day, I'm gonna marry you and you will have my kids. Remember what we said yesterday."

Damn, I thought he forgot about that. She was about to respond, when Al got back in the car. So, instead, she just nodded and remained silent.

By the time they reached the house, it was 3:30 p.m. Tony grabbed Morgan's book bag, while Al carried the food inside.

"Same time, Tony?" he asked before walking out.

"Yeah, Al." Tony went over and locked the door. "Baby girl, go and lay down. I'll fix our plates."

Morgan removed her camisole and pinned up her hair. "I'm fine. I'll fix the food."

Tony went over and grabbed her by the waist. "Ma, I got this. You can chill. You think I can't fix a plate of food?"

Morgan smirked. "I didn't say that."

"Well, go and chill. Daddy got this," he said, then kissed her on the nose.

Morgan picked her bag up off the floor and pulled out her homework. Tony peeked in the living room at her; she was glowing. Tony stood there in a daze. She was his dream wife.

After fixing their plates, he walked over to her and asked, "Ma, are you ready to eat?"

Morgan looked up at him. "Yes, thank you."

When he went to help her get up, she stated, "Tony, I can walk."

"I know, Ma. I just don't want anything to happen to you."

You should've thought about that before you raped me, she thought.

As she sat down at the table, Tony noticed Morgan's earrings. "Ma, are your earrings real?"

Puzzled, she asked, "What do you mean are they real?"

"I mean, are they platinum balls?"

"They are sterling silver," she replied, while eating.

"Well, I don't want you wearing that. I'm gonna get you some diamond earrings, maybe three karats."

Morgan rolled her eyes. "I don't need diamond earrings, Tony. I like my earrings. My grandma bought me these when I was a little girl."

"That's the problem. You're not little anymore."

She sighed and let the subject die.

After they finished eating, Morgan returned to the living room to finish studying since Tony insisted he would clean up. When he finished, he joined her.

"How you feel, ma?"

"I'm fine."

"The baby is good."

Morgan frowned. "The baby is fine, Tony."

"I'm getting on your nerves, aren't I?" he asked, laughing.

Still afraid of him, she didn't want to say the wrong thing. "No, you're not," she mumbled, while continuing to read her book.

Tony placed a kiss on top of her head and played in her pretty, long hair. "What are you reading?"

"It's a book about famous black artists."

"Am I in there?" he asked.

"Not that kind of artists. It's about famous painters, like Elis Wilson, Ernie Barnies, and Jean Michel Basquiat," Morgan replied in a sarcastic tone.

Tony smiled. She was way beyond her years. Most females he dated had never heard of these famous painters and were doing good if they knew of Pablo Picasso.

"Excuse me, babe. Damn, you were ready to bite my head off. I'm just sayin'. You're so smart it's crazy. I've never met anyone like you. Smart, pretty, sexy, and humble. Everything I need in my life. By the way, since I'm going on tour next week, I want to spend this weekend with you. So, come up with some excuse to tell Denise so you can get away."

Immediately, Morgan felt sad again. *He's never going to let me go.* She thought about asking him why he raped her, but petrified that he would act out, she remained silent.

For some strange reason, Tony didn't want to have sex with Morgan that day, which surprised her. Though he loved making love to her, he really enjoyed talking to her. She was so intelligent, which was something he missed since he broke up with Stevie. So, for the next few hours, instead of being satisfied by her sexually, he found pleasure in having his mind stimulated by Morgan and her knowledge.

*****

Normally, Tony would let Morgan out down the block and drive off. However, for some reason, he decided to go upstairs. He waited about five minutes before going into the building. On his way inside, he ran into Perry, who was standing on the side of the building smoking a cigarette. "Oh shit, Perry. What's up?"

"What's good, Tony?"

"You and the things you do. I'm about to go upstairs to visit Dee."

"Me too!"

As they went into the building together, Tony decided to ask Perry about his cousin. "Perry, remember that night Marion was killed?"

"Yeah."

"Did you see him that night?"

"Yeah, he came through looking for you. Why?"

"I was just thinking about him, that's all," Tony replied. "It's crazy how someone could've done that shit to him on Greg's turf."

"Yeah, that's what we all said."

"It still bothers me because I wasn't there to save him."

"Sometimes it happens like that," he responded in a non-caring tone.

"I guess you're right."

Denise opened the door. "Let me find out," she laughed, giving them both a kiss on the cheek. "What brings you guys here?"

"Oh, I was just in the neighborhood," Perry said.

"Same here. I figured since I'm about to go on tour that I needed to holla at my sis."

"Well, it's always a pleasure." She smiled while leading them into the living room.

"Damn, Dee, you did your thing. The crib is nice," Perry cheered. "I can't wait to get my money right."

"Thanks," Denise said.

Perry noticed a picture on the wall of all of them at a party back in the day. "Oh shit, Dee, you kept this pic?"

Denise and Tony looked in his direction. Denise giggled. "Of course. Just because I live downtown doesn't mean I forgot where I came from. I have all of our pictures. They keep me grounded. Funny how time flies."

"Tell me about it," Perry mumbled.

Noticing that Tony was quiet, Denise asked, "What's up, Tee? Why are you over there so quiet?"

"I'm just chillin'. I got a lot on my mind."

"Anything I can do to help?"

"Nah, but thanks. Yo, did they ever find out who killed Felicia?" he asked, while looking in Perry's direction.

Shocked by Tony's question, she replied, "No, but I haven't been asking. I've been so caught up in my own little world, you know."

"So have I. Shit, some days I don't know if I'm going or coming," Tony mumbled with a little chuckle.

Perry was about to respond, when Morgan came down the stairs.

"Denise!" she called out.

"In here."

Morgan almost shit on herself when she saw Tony sitting on the couch. She wanted turn around and run back upstairs. "Umm, I'll ask you later."

"Are you alright?" Denise asked.

"Yes," Morgan responded, ignoring Tony and Perry's stares.

As she turned around to walk out, Denise said, "Morgan, aren't you going to say hello?"

Morgan sighed. "Sorry. Hello."

"What's up, Morgan?" Tony smiled.

"Oh, Perry, you never met my niece. This is Jas's daughter Morgan. Remember?"

Perry remembered when she was just a little girl. "Oh shit! Damn, I'm getting old. Excuse me; I just remember when you were born. We were all at the hospital celebrating. You grew up to be so pretty."

Morgan blushed. "Thank you."

Tony glared at Perry from the corner of his eye. Inside, he was fuming. Before he blurted out something stupid, he got up and went into the kitchen. "Dee, I'm gonna get a bottle of water. Anybody else want one?"

Denise and Perry shook their head no, while Morgan ignored the offer. On his way out of the living room, Tony stared in Morgan's face and mouthed, "Bring your ass in the kitchen."

When Tony got in the kitchen, he pretended to be on the phone just in case Denise started to look for him. Five minutes later, Morgan walked into the kitchen.

"How do you feel?" Tony asked, trying to stay calm.

"I'm feeling okay."

"I see that. You're smiling all up in Perry's face," he replied, letting his jealousy show.

Morgan looked away. "I wasn't…"

Tony grabbed her by the arm. "Don't play with me."

"You're hurting me," she said, pulling away just as Perry walked in.

"Oh, sorry," Perry said, as he started to walk out.

"Nah, it's cool, Perry. Come in."

"I just changed my mind and decided I wanted a bottle of water," he told them.

"I'll get it," Morgan offered

After handing Perry a bottle of water, she bolted out of there. Before Tony could say anything, Perry shot him an "I know you're not fucking with her" look.

"Tee…," Perry started.

"Nah, fam, it's not what you think. I was demonstrating to her the little incident Christina and I had a while back. Remember that bullshit the tabloids printed a couple of weeks ago about me grabbing Chris by the arm. Well, Morgan loves Christina, and she asked me about it. So, I was just showing her how it all happened. Trust me; I would rather die before I do some sucka shit like that to Dee."

"A'ight. I know shorty is beautiful and all, but she's still our sister's niece."

"Of course," Tony responded before walking out.

Perry stood there for a second. Now that he thought about it, he could've sworn he saw Morgan getting out of a black Benz like Tony's earlier. He felt that maybe he should say something to Denise, but what if he's wrong? He needed to do a little more investigating.

Tony knew Paul wasn't buying that bullshit, so he kissed Denise goodbye and left. On his way home, he thought about what would happen if it got out about him and Morgan. Not only would it ruin his career, but Denise or Felix would kill him. And Tony couldn't allow that to happen.

Chapter Twenty
Christina

Since Tony was still acting like an ass, Christina threw herself into her work even more. Her career had skyrocketed since the awards show. She was offered movie deals and seven-figure endorsements. In addition, her tour was about to start. Trying to spend some quality time with Tony before she left seemed impossible. Every time she suggested they hang out, he made up some excuse. So, she stopped asking.

In truth, Christina really didn't have the time either. She was up early in the morning doing talk shows and then off to the gym. From there, she would go to the dance studio and put in eight hours of non-stop rehearsing. She didn't realize rehearsals could be so strenuous on her body.

It was nine o'clock in the evening, and they were still practicing. Christina was a perfectionist, something she learned from Tony. If something wasn't right, she would go over it again and again until it was one hundred percent.

"Good job!" Jamela, the choreographer, clapped and yelled.

"Thank God," Christina said, trying to catch her breath.

They had just finished the last dance routine. Everyone was beat and Christina could barely walk. It was one thing to strut on the runway in six-inch stilettos, but to dance in them was another. She was certain after this tour she would need foot surgery.

After Joyce helped Christina grab their things, they headed to the car where Paul and Mike were waiting.

"Tony called. He wanted to know if you were coming over," Joyce said.

Christina glanced over at her. "Why?" she grumbled.

Joyce shrugged her shoulders. "I don't know."

"Where to?" Paul asked.

Christina sighed. "His place."

"A'ight. So we're dropping Joyce off first, right?" Mike said.

"Yes, please," Joyce replied.

Once they pulled off, Christina leaned over and whispered to Joyce, "I'm thinking about leaving Tony."

It's about time, Joyce thought, while nodding her head.

Tony had completely changed. Joyce remembered when he called Christina several times a day. Now she was lucky if he called her twice a week.

"Well, Christina, you have to do what's best for you. If you feel like it's hopeless, then don't continue to hang on. Either way, I'm here for you," Joyce mumbled back.

"It is," Christina muttered, then turned her head to look out the window.

Joyce glanced over at her. She didn't understand how someone so pretty would tolerate that abuse. Being that Joyce wasn't all that good looking, she always assumed pretty girls had it made in the love department. *I guess I was wrong,* she thought.

After they pulled up in front of Joyce's building, she opened the door and before exiting she said to Christina, "Cheer up. Everything's going to be fine. Call me if you need to talk."

Christina didn't bother to turn around. She just nodded.

The sky was clear with stars shining bright and a full moon. She leaned her head back and hummed her song. Maybe going on tour was the best thing for her, because right now, all she thought about was Tony Flowers.

After arriving at Tony's place, Christina passed a few people in the lobby. She smiled and wave to them. God, she hated being a celebrity sometimes, always having to smile even when you're hurting inside. Once they were on the elevator and heading upstairs, Paul glanced over at Christina, whose head was down.

"Always remember, a man is only gonna do what you allow him to do to."

Christina slowly raised her head and looked around. Who was he talking to?

"Yep, you're right, but love makes you do crazy things," she replied.

"Yeah, that's true, too, but it also makes you stronger," Paul said, while ushering her out of the elevator.

Christina was surprised at Paul's comment. He had never spoken to her. In fact, she thought he didn't like her.

She started giggling. "I thought you didn't like me since you never say anything to me."

Paul blushed. "It's not that, Christina. I have a lot of respect for you, but I was given a job to do and that's to protect you. Just because I'm not yapping with you doesn't mean I'm not digging you," he said, while staring deeply into her eyes before looking away.

Chris smiled and playfully tapped him on the arm. "Yapping?"

Both laughed.

Paul knocked on the door and Carmen answered.

"Good evening, Señora Christina."

Christina was still staring at Paul, when she heard Carmen's voice that snapped her back to reality. "Oh sorry, Carmen.

Hello. Is Tony home yet?"

"Yes, he's in his office."

Paul and Christina stood there gazing at each other, feeling awkward.

"What's good, my boy?" Tony said, starling them.

Paul turned around quickly, hoping Tony hadn't seen them staring at each other. "You, playboy," he replied, giving him a pound.

"What's up, Chris?" he said, leaning over to kiss her.

Christina flinched. "Hi, Tony." She, too, wasn't sure if Tony had seen her looking at Paul.

"Damn, did I miss something?" Tony asked, feeling like he had interrupted something.

"No," both said simultaneously.

"Well, Chris, am I picking you up at five in the morning?"

Christina widened her eyes and glanced over at Tony. "Yes, Paul, five o'clock will be good. Thank you," she said before running upstairs.

Before leaving, Paul gave Tony another pound.

Tony headed upstairs to the bedroom, where Christina was coming out of the bathroom. "So how's the tour rehearsal coming along?"

Chris looked around the room. *Is he talking to me?* Normally, he would just take a shower and go to sleep without saying a word to her. So, this was a surprise.

"It's going great," she replied in a wary voice.

"Are you nervous? I know this is your first time out."

Tony has a heart now? He cares about my feelings? It's gonna shit pigs tomorrow, she thought. Usually, Christina would be thrilled at the fact that he wanted to communicate with her. It reminded her of when they first got together. How they would stay up all night talking. However, now, she could care less. She didn't have time for his bipolar ass. She was tired and wanted to get some rest.

"Of course, I'm nervous, but I'll be okay," she said, while

removing her makeup. Then she got up and went to take a shower.

*****

It seemed like five minutes after Christina closed her eyes, it was time to get up. She was dead tired, but rolled out of bed with a smile on her face. She glanced over at Tony who was sleeping. *Why can't I leave you?* she thought. Christina strolled into the bathroom. She had fifteen minutes before Paul showed up, so she had to hurry. On her way down the stairs, Carmen was opening the door for Paul.

"Good morning, Paul," she mumbled.

"Are we good?" he asked.

Christina twisted her face. "Actually, I'm great." She flashed a devilish grin, and both of them laughed.

"That's good to hear."

"Let's go," she said, playfully pinching him.

It was weird how Paul and Christina had become friends after last night. She didn't know it, but Paul had a major crush on her. Still, Paul was a loyal dude. Therefore, he would never disrespect Tony like that.

They picked up Joyce before heading over to Starbuck for her usual frappacino and then to the Reebok gym that catered to athletes and celebrities. Christina dragged Joyce along for support. Even though Christina was in shape, Elisa recommended she work-out with a personal trainer.

As usual, Christina's trainer Mark would make her stretch first and then run on the treadmill for forty-five minutes before working her out. Normally, she would be tired and in a nasty mood, but today, she was so energetic.

"I thought about what you said last night," she said, while running on the treadmill.

"Okay," Joyce replied, running at a lower speed next to her.

"And I decided that after my tour, I'm ending my

relationship with Tony."

"Why after the tour?"

"Because I'm too weak to leave him now. I figure since I'm gonna be away from him for a couple of months, I will have gained the strength by the time I return."

"That makes sense. What about your business?"

"I haven't thought that far ahead. I'm taking it one day at a time."

"Sometimes that's all we can do."

"Oh girl, I have to tell you something else. Paul is so cool," she gushed.

Joyce almost fell off the treadmill. "Paul?"

"Yes. We were talking last night. He's kinda cute."

Joyce frowned. "That's nice. Just remember he's Tony's friend."

"Yep, but he's on my payroll," Christina stated, slowing down the treadmill.

"You're too much."

"So I've been told," she replied, then giggled while strutting off the equipment.

*****

After leaving the gym, Christina had the desire to go into the studio. So, she called up the producer who had worked on one of her albums and told him to expect her. Then she instructed Paul to drop Joyce off and then come back to pick her up.

She had been going through so much and wanted to translate it into a song, but Christina wasn't a writer. However, once she arrived at the studio, her producer encouraged her to give it a try...to just allow her heart to convey the words that she wanted to say.

Christina didn't realize how easy it was to write a song. After she and the producer talked and jotted down some things, they created a title, *Love Me or Leave Me*. Once they finally got the lyrics for the song, Christina stepped into the booth and took singing to another level. She sang her ass off on that track. All the producer could do was shake his head while experiencing history being made.

Usually, artists would have to do a song three or four times, but Christina nailed it on first take.

"Oh my God, ma! You took it to another level."

"Really?" she said, smiling.

"Yes. No artist out right now can fuck with you, and that's my word. You was feeling that shit."

Both laughed.

"Yes, I was."

"Well, it's a banger. Trust me on that. I'm gonna get it over to your record label first thing in the morning."

"Okay. You really like it?"

"Chris, you just changed the game. Real talk, you don't really need Tony anymore. I mean, he's your man and all, but, ma, you are crazy talented."

Christina blushed. "Thanks. Well, I better get going. I have an early day tomorrow."

"A'ight. I'll handle this. In fact, I'm gonna hit some radio stations and have them play this. Trust, we're gonna kill 'em."

Christine laughed, gave him a hug, and then headed out with Paul. As she left the studio, she felt so good. She had just written her first song without Tony's help.

Instead of going to Tony's place, Christina decided to go home. She and Paul entered her apartment, and after he looked around to make sure everything was okay, he said, "See you in the morning," while walking toward the door.

"Wait, Paul." She hesitated for a moment. "Can you stay with me tonight? I don't feel like being alone."

Paul took a deep breath. "A'ight. Let me call Mike. I'll chill until you fall asleep. Is that okay with you?"

Christina nodded. She went upstairs to take a bath, while he went into the living room to watch TV. After tossing and turning in the bed, she decided to go downstairs.

"Do you mind if I join you?"

Leery, Paul nodded. "Sure."

Christina took a seat on the other end of the couch. As they were watching TV, she turned to him and asked, "Paul, do you have a girlfriend?"

Suspect about the question, he replied, "Nah, why?"

"I was just wondering because you're with me all the time. I know it would be difficult to have a relationship."

"I guess, but I'm not looking for a shorty right now. I gotta stack my bread."

"Is that all everyone thinks about...money?"

"Nah, but in order to have a girl, you gotta have money. Chicks don't want no broke dude."

"Well, I don't care about money."

Paul chuckled. "That's because you got your own. But, you can't tell me that you would date a broke dude."

"If he treats me good, yes, I would."

"Yeah, sounds good," he replied, causing them to laugh.

Christina stared at Paul. Something about him was very dangerous, yet sexy. While he didn't smile much, when he did, it was sexy. His chipped tooth and dimples were so cute, and overall, he had a nice body. *Girl, have you lost your mind? That's Tony's friend,* she thought

He sensed Christina checking him out, and while he was flattered, he brushed it off. He could never betray Tony like that.

"Paul, would you date someone famous?"

"Not really. What's with all the questions?" he asked in a stern tone.

"Nothing. I was trying to make small talk," she said.

Paul sighed. He really didn't want to be mean, but it was the only way he could control his feelings. He hated the way Tony treated her, but at the end of the day, Tony was his man.

"Chris, I'm sorry. I didn't mean to be nasty. It's just..."

"Just what, Paul? Did I do something wrong?"

"No, you didn't. Check this out. Let's drop it. I don't wanna say something I might regret."

She stared at him and thought, *What is he talking about?*

"Please talk to me. I feel like I'm losing my mind," she said, her voice cracking.

He took another deep breath and closed his eyes. *Why the fuck did I stay here?*

"Tony is cheating on me, right? You know it and everyone else knows it."

Paul, who was unable to respond, just sat there with a blank expression on his face.

"Oh, so now you're gonna ignore me? You know what? Forget it! See you in the morning!" Christina yelled, as she got up to storm away.

Paul jumped up and snatched her by the arm, holding her by the waist. He stared into her eyes, then leaned over, wiped her tear away, and passionately kissed her. There they stood exploring each other's mouths. He removed Christina's robe and tore open her nightgown, while staring lustfully into her eyes. Not knowing what to do, she stared back. She wanted to say no, but couldn't. His touches felt so good. He had dreamt about this for so long. He kissed and licked every inch of Christina's body. Then he lifted Christina up against the wall and placed her legs around his neck so he was face to face with her vagina. Paul tasted her, bringing her to a climax. Christina thought she had died and gone to heaven.

Paul then carried her out to the foyer, laid her on the floor, and continued to taste her. Christina looked up at the ceiling and prayed, "God, please forgive me," before releasing her juices in his mouth. Next, he carried her to the bedroom, where he removed his clothing. *Good lord, this man is packing,* Christina thought.

Paul gently massaged her inner thighs. "I've wanted you for

so long," he moaned.

Lying there kissing and touching each other, Christina whispered, "Show me how much."

Paul flipped Christina on her back and thrust inside of her.

"Yesss," she moaned.

Although Paul was packing, it didn't hurt like Tony did. Like Tony, Paul was very aggressive in the bedroom. Before Christina knew it, he flipped her over on her hands and knees and started fucking her doggie style, causing her to let out a guttural moan. Paul had Christina screaming in ecstasy.

After pulling out, he carried her over to the chaise. "Ride it," he told her.

At first, Christina wanted to stop because she didn't know how to ride. She had only rode Tony a few times since they had been together, and he seemed displeased whenever she did it.

"Paul...umm, I'm not good at riding."

"Let me be the judge. Tonight, you're gonna learn," he said out of breath.

He grabbed Christina by the waist and guided her on top of him. Before she knew it, Christina was bouncing up and down on him. For the first time, she felt good having sex.

"You like that?" she asked seductively.

"Yes, you feel so good," he replied.

Minutes later, they reached their climax. Afterwards, they moved over to the bed and laid there in each other's arms.

"Paul, what happens now?"

"What do you mean?"

Christina lifted up to look at him. "I mean with us. Where do we go from here?"

Paul looked into Christina's eyes. He knew what he was about to say was wrong, but he couldn't help how he felt about her.

"Christina, I don't know. But, I do know that I care for you a lot. Tony doesn't deserve you. I've wanted you for so long. You don't know how much I wanted to hold you in my arms and tell you everything is gonna be alright. But, I know you love Tony. So, if you choose to stay with him, I'll respect that." He started to get out of the bed. "Don't worry. This will stay between us."

This time, she reached for his arm. "Paul…" She crawled over to him and silenced him with a kiss.

They made love all night long.

*****

The next day, Christina was backstage with Joyce getting ready for her performance, when Tony popped up on her.

"What's up?" he said, entering the dressing room.

Stunned by his presence, Christina responded in a nonchalant tone, "Nothing. What brings you here?"

"Come on now, Chris. I'm always here to support you."

She stared at him from the corner of her eye. "Really?" she said.

As she was putting on her dress, Tony noticed a hickey on her breast. At first, he thought it was makeup, but when he got a closer look, he realized it wasn't.

"Looks like someone was having fun," he said, pointing to her tit.

Clueless as to what he was talking about, she went over to the mirror. She almost fainted when she saw the huge hickey on her breast. Trying to hide her shock, she screwed up her face.

"It's not a hickey. I hit myself this morning."

"Yeah, with someone's lips."

"You know what, Tony? Don't come in here accusing me of anything when your ass is out there acting like a…"

Before she could continue, Paul walked in, causing everyone to stare at him.

"Sorry. Did I interrupt something?"

Tony looked at Paul suspiciously. "Nah, fam," he replied snidely before walking out.

Paul looked at Christina and then at Joyce. "Did I do something?"

"No, Paul. Tony is just being an ass," she said before walking out to take the stage.

Tony sat on the sideline while Christina performed. As usual, she rocked the stage.

Paul walked up to Tony. "Fam, is everything okay?"

Being that Tony had on shades, Paul couldn't see the disgusted look in Tony's eyes.

Tony flashed a fake smile. "It's cool, Paul, but let me ask you something?"

"Shoot."

"Is Christina fucking around? I know she's been seeing that ballplayer."

Confused at Tony's comment, he just stared at him before responding. "Nah, Tee, I don't think she's messing around."

"Yeah, I guess you're right. Listen, what's good with Moe?"

"Oh, he doesn't want it. I spoke to him over the phone, and he's good. You will not be hearing from that dude no more."

Tony gave Paul a pound. "Good looking. Oh, remember that night when my cousin was murdered? Did you see him that night?"

"Nah," Paul responded with a serious look.

Tony twisted up his face and replied, "Okay. Yo, tell Chris I had to bounce." Then he started walking away.

"A'ight. You good, fam?"

"Oh course," Tony turned and said. *But you won't be,* he thought.

Chapter Twenty-One
Denise

In the last couple of months, Denise's life finally took a turn for the better. After that incident at her parents' house, she and her dad were on speaking terms. They talked almost every day. Instead of dwelling on the past, they worked on the future. While everyone in the neighborhood assumed they were perfect, they really had some deep issues. One important thing she learned about her parents is that they were never taught how to be affectionate when they were younger. That's the reason why they never said the words 'I love you'.

Once her father cleared up a lot of things, it was hard for Denise to be upset with them. While her mother was still upset with her for putting her sisters out, her father said he was glad because they finally had their home back. *Guess you can't please everybody,* Denise thought. She knew one thing for sure: death must be easy because life was hard.

It was five o'clock and she was meeting Derrick for dinner at Mexico Lindo, a small place on the lower east side. Surprisingly, she couldn't get enough of him. In fact, they couldn't get enough of each other. Their conversations were unique but informative.

"Sorry I'm late," he said, leaning down to kiss her.

"It's fine. I just got here myself. So how was work today?" Denise asked, sipping on her glass of water.

"Work was stressful, but it's better now that I'm with you," he beamed and then motioned for the waiter to come over to their table

Denise shook her head. Derrick was full of words, and she loved it.

"Yes, sir," the waiter said.

"I would like to order Matia. Denise, what would you like?"

"A Cosmo," she replied.

The waiter nodded and then left to get their drinks.

"So, Ms. Taylor, how was your day?"

"It was interesting….a few useless meetings."

Both laughed.

Denise was just about to say something, when the waiter came back over to their table and handed her a piece of paper.

"Sorry, this was left for you."

Denise reviewed the note: *I know what you did. Felicia knows what you did. Revenge is near.* She held her breath and tried not to show her emotions. She looked around trying to see if she recognized anyone.

"Is there something wrong?" Derrick asked, noticing the worried look on her face.

She silently sighed. "No. Derrick, please excuse me for a second." She got up and went over to the waiter. "Excuse me. Do you know who left this note?"

"No, Señora. He just pointed to your table and asked me to give it to you."

"Do you remember how he looked?"

"Sorry Señora, I don't remember. Oh wait. He was big and dark-skinned."

Quickly, she ran outside and looked around. When she looked up the block, she saw someone who resembled Perry getting into a black SUV, the same one that was at Felicia's gravesite. Denise closed her eyes and dropped her head. *It's always the ones you love,* she thought.

"Denise, are you alright?" Derrick asked with a concerned look when she returned to the table.

She flashed a half grin. "Yeah. Now what were you saying before we were interrupted?"

Derrick knew something wasn't right, but decided to let it go.

"As I was saying, I'm flying out this weekend to attend a seminar and would like for you to join me."

"I can't, Derrick. I planned to spend this weekend home in New Jersey."

"Alright. Well, maybe next time."

"Maybe."

"I thought you lived in an apartment?"

"I do, but I also have a house in New Jersey," she told him.

Derrick smiled. "That's great. Hopefully, one day, I'll get to see it."

"Hopefully." She blushed.

After dinner, Derrick dropped Denise off. That note had ruined her evening. As she was entering the apartment, her cell phone rang. When she looked at the Caller ID, it was a blocked number.

"Hope you had a nice time," the caller said when she answered.

"Who is this?"

"Your worst nightmare."

Click!

Her phone rang again, but this time it was Tony.

"Hey sis."

"Hey Tony," Denise said with a stern voice.

"What's wrong?"

"Nothing. What's up?"

"I was just checking on you, making sure you're good. You

know I go on tour in a couple of days, so I just wanted to know if you needed anything."

"I'm good. Listen, what's up with Perry? How is he doing with the job?"

"Hmm! To tell you the truth, he's not doing all that well. Perry has changed, sis. He's very envious of our success. When we were on our way up to your place, he made a slick comment about how you don't even come around anymore. Then he made a comment about you having doormen and shit. I ignored him, but real talk, he isn't the same. Why? Are you catching bad vibes, too?"

"Now that you mention it, I'm trying to figure out how he found out where I live. I never gave him my address. But, anyway, he's still a part of the team."

"Yeah, and so was Alex. Remember that?"

"You're right. Tony, let me go. If I don't talk to you before you leave to go on tour, have a safe trip."

"A'ight, sis. Love ya."

"Right back at ya, bro."

"Damn!" was all Denise could say as she hung up.

Perry was Felicia's brother. All that bullshit about them fucking around was a lie. If they were messing around, Felicia would've confided in me. Denise sat on the bed and went over everything. It wasn't until she saw Perry that Felicia called her with that bullshit. Also, Perry was the only person not at her funeral. *If he and Felicia were so close, why he didn't show up?* It was ironic that she bumped into him leaving the courthouse and her parents' house. It was all starting to make sense now. *I guess he'll be joining his family.*

She was so deep into her thoughts that she didn't hear or see Morgan standing in her bedroom doorway.

"Auntie, are you okay?"

"Oh shit, Morgan, you scared me. Yeah, I'm fine." Denise glanced over at the clock. "Why are you home so late?"

"I stopped off to grab something to eat."

"Oh okay. Well, how was school?" Denise asked, walking towards her.

"It's alright. Can't wait until it's over, though," Morgan said, letting Denise pass.

Denise laughed as she went down to the kitchen. "How have you been feeling? Is your stomach still bothering you?"

"Not really. Actually, I'm feeling much better," she lied. "Um, Auntie, can I spend the weekend at Chloe's house?" she asked while following her.

Denise looked at Morgan. "Spend the whole weekend out?"

"Yes, she's having a slumber party."

"For the whole weekend?" Denise inquired.

Morgan had to think fast. "No, not the whole weekend, but she asked could I stay the whole weekend."

Denise poured herself some juice. "Do you want some?"

Morgan shook her head no.

"Who's going to be at this party? And are Chloe's parents going to be there?" Denise asked.

Morgan frowned. She didn't think Denise would ask so many questions, so she wasn't prepared. "Well, it's going to be about five of us, and yes, her parents will be there."

Denise walked over and sat at the island. Though she had plans for them to spend the weekend in New Jersey, she was happy her niece was finally enjoying life. "Will there be boys at this slumber party?"

Yeah, Tony, Morgan thought. "No, just girls."

Her aunt rolled her eyes and smirked. "Alright you can go, but call me when you get there and give me Chloe's information."

Morgan giggled. "Anything else, warden?" she said, then kissed Denise on the cheek.

"Yes, have your ass home early on Sunday. Understand? Oh, and don't forget that I'm hanging out after work with your mother tomorrow. So, I'll leave money on the counter in the morning for you to get something to eat. "

"Yes, Auntie. Tell Mommy I love her and try not to have too much fun," Morgan whined, walking out the kitchen.

*****

Denise woke up early the following day; she really didn't get any rest. Tossing and turning all night, she couldn't believe it was Perry. His words seemed so genuine. Denise knew it was only a matter of time before Perry struck again. If he still operated like he did back in the day, it wouldn't be good, which meant she must strike first.

Throughout the day, she and Derrick played phone tag. He wanted to see her that evening, but she was meeting Gabrielle to sign the contracts for the properties she would be purchasing, and then afterwards, the girls were hanging out.

Tonight, Denise wanted to dress causal. So, she decided on a pair of dark blue vintage jeans, a white tank top, and a black blazer with a pair of Cesare Paciotti shoes. After dressing, she caught a cab to the Minsk Theater. When the cab pulled up to the theater, she saw Jasmine, Gabrielle, and Stevie standing there talking while waiting for her to arrive.

"I'm not late!" she shouted, getting out of the cab.

They busted out laughing.

"Stevie, it's good to see you." Denise flashed a phony smile.

"Likewise, Denise," Stevie replied, flashing one right back at her.

"Sis, what's up?" Denise said, giving Jasmine a kiss on the cheek.

"Nothing," Jasmine simply said.

They chatted outside for a couple more minutes before going inside. Denise sat in between Gabrielle and Jasmine. The show started on time, and it was great from start to finish.

"I know this great steak house restaurant around the corner. It's quiet and the food is great," Jasmine told them.

"Alright, let's go," Stevie said, as she started walking.

During dinner, the ladies reminisced. It seemed like only yesterday they were in their twenties. Afterwards, they caught a cab and headed over to a club called Marquee on 28th Street and 10th Avenue. It was a Thursday night and Marquee was pack. After a while of searching, they finally found a table and ordered some drinks.

"This club is nice!" Gabrielle shouted over the music.

"I know it's a long way from the Palladium days." Stevie giggled.

"I know, right? Remember Nell's, Cheetah, and the Mirage?" Jasmine fell back in her seat laughing.

"Yes," they all said.

"Damn, Jas, you just named some great spots. Back then, that's when it was fun," Gabrielle said.

Stevie sighed. "Back then, guys had class and style. They treated you like a queen."

"Yes, they did. It's funny. New York men are so different; they have a certain swagger about them. I guess it's their self confidence," Jasmine said snidely.

"Nah, it's their cock." Denise winked.

Everyone laughed.

"Leave it to Denise to lighten up the party." Gabrielle giggled, sipping her drink.

"It's true. Cock plays a huge part in our lives, and I emphasize huge," Denise replied.

Jasmine, while still laughing, said, "You're a mess, sis, but it's so true. If he's not packing, he will be sent packing."

"I know that's right…and quick," Stevie added, high-fiving Jasmine.

"But no, really, at the end of the day you want love and happiness," Gabrielle protested.

"Of course, we do, Gabrielle, but he better know how to fuck. Shit," Stevie said, laughing

"Stevie does have a point." Jasmine winked.

"You know, I miss New York so much," Stevie mumbled.

Denise glared at her. "Maybe you should've never left."

Gabrielle shot Denise a 'don't go there' look, while Jasmine tried to figure out what just happened.

Stevie giggled. "Is there a problem, Denise?"

"No problem, Stacey," she replied, using her real name. "Maybe if your ass didn't up and leave, you still would be living here."

"Dee!" Gabrielle yelled.

Stevie raised her hand up. "No, Gabrielle. Denise has something on her mind and I wanna hear it."

Both ladies glared at each other.

"I'm all ears," Stevie said.

"All I'm saying is you had it all, Stevie. Tony loved you. He treated you like a queen, even though you were a slut. To him, you were his everything, and you repay him by bouncing like that?"

"Denise, leave it alone," Jasmine interrupted.

"No, Jas. I wanna answer her. Is that what you know or is that what Tony told you? Because last I checked, only Tony and I were in that relationship. Now, I know Tony is your boy, but he's not perfect. How about asking me why I left before you start taking sides."

"I know why you left, because he was cheating on you. You knew the rules when got with him. Yet this didn't stop you from moving up here with him. You knew he was fucking around, but did that stop you from accepting his gifts and allowing him to pay for your education? So, please don't tell me it was because he was cheating."

Stevie glanced over at Gabrielle confused. She thought Gabrielle had told Denise the real reason why she left. "Is that what you think? If you believe I left because Tony was cheating, then you really don't know shit. But, one day, you will find out the real Tony Flowers. Tony is nothing but a manipulative, insecure, deceitful bastard. Take away his money and dick, and you have a fucked up boy trying to be a man.

Tony is all about Tony."

"Maybe to you, but he's dating the hottest chick in the game," Denise beamed, hoping Stevie would get upset.

"Denise, I left Tony. He didn't leave me. I could care less who he's dating. In fact, I'm happy for him. I have a wonderful life in Atlanta."

"Exactly! So why the fuck are you so mad?" Gabrielle yelled at Denise.

"Nobody is upset. I just feel like Tony took care of her and she deserted him. Stevie, I'm not saying Tony is perfect, but he was crushed when you left. Contrary to what y'all believe, he did love you. You were supposed to stay with him, but that's my opinion."

"Right, just like everyone has an asshole," Jasmine said, rolling her eyes "Dee, has it ever occurred to you that Stevie wasn't happy. So what Tony has a couple of dollars? Life isn't all about money, sweetie. So it's okay for him to treat her like shit because he's supporting her? If you feel like that, then God bless you. I'll take a loyal broke-ass man any day over a rich, cheating bastard."

"I know that's right," Gabrielle said, folding her arms.

"Denise, I'm not the enemy. I wish Tony the best, but he has some serious issues."

"We all do, but it's cool, Stevie. I know Tony can be an ass. Just don't turn your back on him."

"As long as he pays me not to," Stevie winked.

Gabrielle sighed and jumped up. "Listen, I didn't come here to talk about Tony's ugly ass. The music is slamming. Let's get our party on. Shit!"

"Wait, let's make a toast," Denise said, holding up her glass. "To money, power, and respect."

Jasmine twisted up her face. "Money, power, and respect? Sit your ass down. To love, peace, and happiness."

"Cheers!"

*****

Denise only closed her eyes for what seemed like only five seconds before it was time to get up for work.

"Shit, I'm getting too old for this."

She thought about calling out but remembered she had a meeting with her supervisor. So, she started to get ready. As she was washing up, she thought about Perry. *Damn, I would've never suspected him.* Denise headed out to work, and although her body was there, her mind was someplace else.

Not wanting to prolong it any longer, Denise decided to meet with Perry that night. It seemed like time was dragging. Every five seconds, Denise glanced at her watch. It was almost five o'clock when Denise headed home. Since Morgan was spending the night at Chloe's house, she had time to carefully plan her attack. As she was getting ready, her cell phone rang. It was Derrick. As she stared at the phone, her eyes filled with tears. She started pacing back and forth.

"God, why! I know I've committed many sins in my past, but it seems like they are coming back full circle to haunt me. Derrick is a good guy; he's like a breath of fresh air. Please help me like you did that night with Felicia. Lord, I'm asking you to walk with me tonight. I remember reading Jeremiah 29:11-14, and I'm asking that you please provide me with the answer," she proclaimed loudly, dropping to her knees.

As she laid there motionless, Denise heard another voice in her head. She closed her eyes and tried to block it out, but it kept getting louder. *My brother and I...You traded in your gun for a briefcase.* They were Felicia's word echoing in her head. She wondered if she should forget about it and leave it in God's hands.

Nah, I'll leave it in God's hands tomorrow. Tonight, it's in mine, she thought.

She waited until it got dark outside and then headed out. When she got three blocks from the projects, she pulled over to a payphone and called his cell. *Knowing Perry's criminal ass, he got a disposable one.*

"Yo!" he answered.

"Perry, what's good? It's Dee. I need you to meet me in front of our old junior high school."

"You alright?"

"Yeah, I'm good. Oh, and bring your hammer and silencer. Don't tell no one where you're going or who you're gonna meet," she instructed.

"Come on, ma. This is me. I'm on my way. See you in ten."

"Alright."

After they hung up, Denise rested her head against the phone. Something wasn't right. Either Perry was a great actor or he wasn't Felicia's brother. Hopefully, she could close this chapter in her life.

After driving to the location where she would meet him, she parked and popped open her trunk. She grabbed a bag out and started walking to the back of the schoolyard. She wanted Perry to think she had someone behind there. When she got to the back of the schoolyard, she knocked out one of lights, and then she quickly ran back to the front. She was shaking. Knowing who she was up against, mistakes were not an option. As she was coming to the front, she saw Perry standing there looking around.

"Perry," she softly yelled.

He turned around and started walking towards her.

"You alright?"

Denise just nodded. As they were walking to the back, Denise asked, "Did you bring that?"

"Yeah," he replied.

"Give me it."

Perry looked at her confused. "Why?"

"He's back there and I wanna do it. It's personal."

Perry nodded and handed her the gun.

"Does this have any bodies on it?"

"Hell naw. It's clean and the serial numbers are burned off."

"Cool. Let me use your phone. I gotta make a call."

"Of course."

Denise put on her black gloves and then pretended to use the phone. Anxious to see who the lucky person was, Perry kept walking towards the back. Once she saw that he was a couple of feet in front of her, she put the silencer on and removed the safety lock. When he noticed there wasn't anyone back there, he turned around only to find himself face to face with a gun.

"Dee, what's up?" he asked, baffled.

"Don't give me that shit, Perry. You know what's up."

Perry stood there with his hands up. "No the fuck I don't."

"You and Felicia tried to set me up."

"What! Get the fuck outta here. When?"

"Perry, don't pull that sucka shit with me. I know that's your sister."

"What the fuck are you talking about? Felicia is not my sister. I told you that I was fucking with her. Yo, where did you get that?"

"Knock it off, Perry!" she yelled, while keeping the gun aimed at his chest.

"Ay yo, stop with the bullshit, Denise. Tell me who the fuck said that."

Denise remained quiet and kept focused.

"Oh, so now we kill first and ask questions later? You believe someone else over me! Denise, this is Perry you're talking to…the nigga that washed blood off your face…"

"It's funny you should mention that, because the same nigga that washes blood off your face is the same nigga that will cause your face to bleed. It's motherfuckers like you who make it hard for people like me to change. I trusted you. We were like family," Denise said, her voice cracking.

"You trusted me?! Don't come at me with that bullshit. If you trusted me, you would ask me. Haven't you learned anything from us? Why the fuck would I set you up? Denise, if

I wanted you dead, you would've been gone a long time ago. You know how I get down. Shit, I taught you."

Perry did have a point. Killing people was his craft.

"I guess you want me to cop out and say that Felicia is my sister, right? But, even with the gun to my head, I'm not going to say that. She's not my sister."

Denise took a deep breath and tried to remain focused. She knew once she slipped it would be over.

"I'm not asking you, Perry."

"Yeah, well, I'm letting you know. I'm a fucking man, ma…all day. I don't give a fuck about dying. As Greg stated to us years ago, a man lives once, but a coward lives a thousand times." He raised his hands and then kneeled down. "You know there's no turning back after this, right? Remember that. Never draw your gun unless you intend on using it."

"I know," she replied, still pointing the gun at him.

"Denise, I swear to you on my life and my kids that I had nothing to do with that. Felicia is not my sister. I'm being set up. All I ask is that you get to the bottom of this. Find out who set me up and have them join me."

Perry was a real solider. Even on his deathbed, he was not going to admit Felicia was his sister. This could only mean two things: either he was telling the truth or he needed an Oscar for his performance. They stared into each other's eyes. She knew if Perry lived, they could never be friends again. The trust had been broken. *Fuck it,* Denise thought and lowered the gun down.

At that point, she didn't care if Perry killed her. In fact, a part of her felt like she deserved it. Everything that was instilled in her from the streets she had just violated. Perry was right. She should've confronted him first. There was no way Perry was Felicia's brother.

She turned around and started to walk away, when Perry blurted out, "Where the fuck are you going? You think you're gonna just pull out on me and walk away like that? WOW!

Corporate America has really changed you. The Denise I taught would've pushed my shit back already. I guess you're not a killer after all."

Denise paused and her eyes widened. Those were the same words Felicia had said to her. She quickly turned around to face Perry, who was walking up to her.

"So that's how we do? I'm supposed to go home now and forget everything that just happened."

"No, Perry, you're not."

"So where are we going?"

"I'm going home, but you? You're going to a family reunion," she stated before pumping seven shots into his chest. "Give the family my best." She then walked over to him and said a silent pray.

Back in her car, Denise rested her head back on the seat and broke down in tears. *God, why am I reverting back into this lifestyle?*

Once she finally pulled herself together, Denise drove off. Still shaken up by all of this, she decided to go to her house in New Jersey. After pulling into her driveway, she looked in the rearview mirror, leaned back, closed her eyes, and took a deep breath. She then walked into her house and silenced the alarm. After kicking off her shoes, she walked upstairs and headed straight for the bathroom, where she removed her clothes and jumped in the shower.

First Felicia and now Perry, she thought, while crying.

Right after turning off the shower, she heard someone pulling into her driveway. She ran to window and peeked out. It was Morris! She grabbed her robe, ran downstairs, and flung open the door.

"What are you doing here?"

"Hello to you, too! Since you're not picking up the phone or at your apartment in the city, I figured you would be out here," he said, brushing past her.

"Well, I don't feel like company tonight."

"Are you sure?" he asked, touching her nipple through the robe.

Denise sighed and smacked his hand away. "Yes, I'm sure."

"Or maybe it's not me that you want to keep you company," he responded, giving her a disgusted look.

"Probably. Either way, you need to leave."

"And if I don't?" he muttered, walking up to her.

Denise chuckled. "Boy, don't do it to yourself. Please don't" After tonight, she really didn't give a damn what happened. She stood there looking him up and down. "Morris…" she said in a calm voice and then opened the door. "I'm tired and really don't feel like being bothered. You can either…"

Before she could finish, Morris interrupted. "Or what? You're gonna call the police?"

Denise smirked. "Nah, more like the CSI team," she exclaimed, giving him a serious look.

Morris had never seen Denise upset like that before. He bopped out, then turned around and said, "Tell that nigga that pussy is mines. He can't make you cum like me."

"Is that what you think it is? You think a nigga is upstairs waiting to fuck my brains out? You know what? Get the fuck out of my house and life. Don't come back here, you bastard!" she said before slamming the door in his face.

As he stood on the other side of the door calling out her name, she thought, *you better leave, asshole, or you will be joining the list of the unfortunates.* Luckily for him, he left without a further incident.

Chapter Twenty-Two
Gabrielle

After three months of investigating, Gabrielle was going to finally meet Robin Cox, the woman who indirectly ruined her life. With the help of Britney, Gabrielle was finally getting answers. As she laid there unable to sleep, she thought about how tomorrow would change her life. While she was happy, a part of her was scared. What if Robin revealed something she couldn't handle? What if Britney got cold feet and backed out of deal. Better yet, what if Greg found out? They promised never to keep any secrets from each other. Would he forgive her?

It was the night before Stevie was scheduled to fly back to Atlanta and they had thoroughly enjoyed the entire weekend together by clubbing, going to the spa, shopping, and even attending church.

Knock! Knock!

"Gabby, are you sleeping?"

"No, Stevie, come in," Gabrielle responded.

"Can we talk?" she asked, opening the door.

"Sure, Stevie. What's up?"

"You didn't tell Denise the truth about why I left Tony?"

Gabrielle sighed as Stevie sat down on the edge of the bed. "No, I didn't think it was my place. That was something you confided in me."

"Yeah, I know, but maybe if she knew the truth, she wouldn't be so quick to judge me."

"Who cares if she doesn't like you? Denise doesn't even like herself!"

"But a part of me wants her to know the truth about him. Gabrielle, I went through hell with Tony. When we first started going out, he was perfect, but after a year or so, he changed. Some days he would come in and wouldn't say a word to me. When I asked him what was wrong, he'd snap at me. Until you came along, Tony didn't allow me to have any friends. Then the beatings started. First, it was a push, a slap, then black eyes and busted lips. The sick part about it is he would make me have sex with him afterward. If I didn't, he raped me."

Even though Gabrielle heard this all before, it still sent chills through her body. How could someone be that cruel? Tony was a disturbed person.

"Stevie, you're better than me, because there's no way I could be friends with him."

"I know. At one time I felt the same way, but I had to forgive him...for myself."

"Whatever! Not me. He would be six feet under. And I would just have to deal with God on judgment day."

Both laughed.

"The sad part about it is Tony has the world fooled. People consider him the Pillar of New York, and the more money he makes, the more untouchable he will become."

Gabrielle shook her head in disgust. "You think so? Trust me, every dog has their day. We might not see it, but his day will come. You can mark my words. I wonder if he beats Christina."

"Not physically because she's in the spotlight, but he has

probably abused her mentally. Tony needs help. I don't know what happened to him when he was a kid, but he's a sick person."

"Shit, I'm starting to think none of us are normal."

"Now that's true, but you know what, Gabby? I'm so blessed. God didn't bring me to the water to drown me, but to cleanse me. I have a wonderful family. I guess that's why I still talk to Tony, because I'm so blessed...and he pays me for my advice." Stevie winked.

Gabrielle laughed. "I know what you mean. When he sent those contracts over for my review, I sent him my bill. Shit, he's Greg and Denise's friend, not mine," she said, rolling her eyes.

It was going on five o'clock in the morning, and they were still up gossiping when Stevie feel asleep at the foot of the bed. Since Gabrielle had to get up in another two hours, she decided to go downstairs and get some work done.

While in her office drafting up a brief for one of her cases, Greg popped in her head. She thought about how lucky she was to have a man like him. While many called her crazy for being with someone in prison, she felt special. Greg was very supportive and loving, while most men probably would've been intimidated by her. In a strange way, they complemented each other.

She glanced over at a picture of them that was on her desk and smiled. Greg was so sexy, and his laidback attitude made him even sexier. She couldn't wait for them to start a family. Although the doctor said nothing was wrong with her, she decided to take fertility drugs anyway to help increase her chances of getting pregnant on their next family visit.

It was going on seven o'clock, and since she had started to get sleepy, she headed upstairs to get ready for another long day in the office. Though Gabrielle could've called in, she didn't like rescheduling her clients' appointments. It was bad business.

Gabrielle looked over at Stevie who was sound asleep.

"Bitch," she mumbled, while walking out the door.

*****

"Morning, Nancy. Please get me some coffee," Gabrielle said, while walking into her office.

"Yes, Mrs. Brightman. Did we have a good weekend?"

Gabrielle flashed a weak smile. "Yes, a little too good."

Both giggled.

Gabrielle walked into her office and put her things down. Then she glanced over at the time; she was meeting Robin in two hours. While trying to concentrate on work, Gabrielle was nervous, praying she didn't fumble on her words. *Where the hell is Tommy with that wiretap?* She got up and started pacing back and forth, when Nancy walked in.

"Mrs. Brightman, someone is here to see you?

"Who?"

"Mr. Duncan."

"Mr. Duncan?" she repeated "Are you sure he's here to see me?"

"Yes. He said you're expecting him."

Gabrielle took a deep breath and walked back to her desk. "Well, send him in."

It was Tommy.

She chuckled and said, "Mr. Duncan?"

"Well, you never can be too careful. So are we ready?"

Gabrielle sighed. "Ready as I'll ever be."

"Don't back out on me now. We're almost there," he said, pulling out the wiretap equipment.

"I'm not."

As Tommy taped the wires to Gabrielle's body, he carefully went over the plan with her. Tommy was a perfectionist and hated slip-ups. After they went over the plan again, Tommy left so he could set up outside of the restaurant. Gabrielle looked at her hands that were trembling. This was the moment she had waited for, so why was she shaking? As she gathered her things, she thought about what if something happened. What if Robin called her bluff?

On her way out the door, Nancy blurted out, "Good luck," which was something she always said whenever Gabrielle met with new clients. Somehow, today, it had a different meaning.

Gabrielle turned around and flashed a phony smile. "I'm gonna need it," she said before exiting the office.

Even though she and Britney had rehearsed the plan over and over, Gabrielle still had mixed feelings about it. Though Robin deceived Britney, she was still her mother. Would Britney be able to go through with it knowing it would ruin her mother's career?

Gabrielle was meeting Robin at an Italian restaurant located in Riverdale in the Bronx. Tommy told her not to drive her car in case something went wrong, so she hopped into her awaiting car service. On the way there, she prayed to God, asking him to protect and forgive her. Gabrielle was in such a daze, she didn't realize they pulled up to the place.

"Mrs. Brightman, we are here," the driver said.

"Oh...sorry," she mumbled, then hopped out of the car.

As she started to walk in, she looked around and noticed Tommy parked diagonally across from the restaurant. She flashed a smile of relief before continuing to walk. Once inside, she looked around and saw Robin hadn't arrived yet. Since it was a beautiful day, she asked to be seated outside.

As Gabrielle waited, she started fidgeting. First, she fumbled with the napkin. Then, she started to tap her manicured nails on the table along with her feet. *God, what's taking her so long?* she thought. To calm herself down, she sipped on a glass of water. "Where the hell is she?" she mumbled.

Just then, a chubby white lady walked in. Oddly, Gabrielle knew that was Robin Cox.

She took a deep breath and said, "Ms. Cox," while waving for her.

Unaware of who Gabrielle was, Robin smiled and walked over to her. "Sorry I'm late. I got caught up in a case."

Robin and Gabrielle shook hands. She then unbuttoned her suit and took a seat. "So my daughter said you wanted to talk to me about a job?"

Gabrielle formed a puckish grin. "Not exactly. You see, Robin — if I may call you that — I'm here about a particular case you prosecuted eight years ago that involved Britney."

"What case are you talking about?"

Instantly, Gabrielle became upset that the bitch didn't even remember. "Gregory Brightman."

Robin's eyes widened. "Yeah, I remember that case. Excuse me, who are you again?"

"I'm his wife, Gabrielle Brightman."

Robin's face turned white as if she had seen a ghost. "You're his wife?"

"Yes, I am. I also know your daughter was messing with him and that she was supposed to testify on his behalf."

"Sorry, I wasn't aware..."

Gabrielle immediately interrupted her. "Robin, do not insult my intelligence," she said, grabbing a large envelope out of her bag and throwing it on the table.

"What's this?" Robin asked in nasty tone.

"It's all the evidence you presented in my husband's case. I thought you might like to review it." She reached in her bag and pulled out another envelope. "These are tapes of you discussing my husband's case."

Robin glared at the envelopes and then back at Gabrielle. "And? You think someone is gonna believe some drug dealer's wife? Sweetie, you better come stronger than that. FYI, honey, I'm an assistant district attorney," Robin boasted, then leaned forward. "Instead of shopping, you should've finished school."

Gabrielle grinned. "Unlike your daughter, I did. You're not the only lawyer at this table," she said, wiping the smirk off Robin's face. "Oh yes, honey, I'm not an ADA. They don't make enough for me. No, I have my own practice. So, I suggest you sit back and shut the fuck up! Like I said, I know you set my husband up by falsifying reports and evidence. I also know how you blackmailed Mr. Lawrence," she stated, while watching the fear in Robin's eyes. "And I know how you kidnapped your own daughter from exposing your dirty secrets. You even got Alex to lie on the stand."

Robin had heard enough. "What do you want?"

"First, I wanna know why?"

Robin sighed. "You don't know?"

"Know what?" Gabrielle said, causing Robin to look away. "Know what?" she repeated in a stern voice.

"It wasn't my idea."

"Yeah right! So whose idea was it?"

"Hopefully, one day you'll find out. What do you want from me?"

"I want you to file the 440 motion on Newly Discovered Evidence."

"You're insane. I can't do that. This is not *Law and Order*."

"You're right. This is someone's life. Either you file the papers today, or I go to the New York Bar Association."

"Big deal. I'm not afraid of losing my license."

"You're license isn't the only thing you're gonna lose. My second stop is to FEDS. You knowingly falsified evidence. Losing your license is the least of your worries."

She glared at Gabrielle and then smirked. "If all you have is some so-called evidence, then I'll take my chances," Robin scolded, as she got up to leave.

"Sit down, Mother." It was Britney.

"Britney, are you a part of this?" Robin asked, sitting back down.

Now it was Gabrielle's turn to smirk.

"Ma, how could you? You put an innocent man away. And for what? Because you didn't want me with him?"

"Britney, it wasn't that. It's complicated"

"What's so complicated? You lied," Gabrielle said.

Robin rolled her eyes at Gabrielle's comment. "Britney, can we talk about this someplace private?"

"Why? So you can kidnap me again? No thanks. I'm done with talking. It's time for you to start listening. Either you file the papers today or I will go on every major news channel. You know it's election year, so do you really wanna take that chance?"

Once Robin knew they were serious, she gave in. "There's no way I can draft up a brief in a couple of hours. I need more time," she begged.

"Here," Gabrielle said, handing her a prepared 440 motion. "I figured you would say that, so I took the liberty of preparing one for you." She snickered.

Robin slowly grabbed it. "I see we have everything planned out. I need to review the brief before I file it." She looked at Gabrielle. "No offense."

"Ma, cut the bullshit. Either you file the motion by tonight; or I'll start making my rounds."

"After all I've done for you," Robin cried.

"What have you done for me, Ma?"

"I don't know why you're helping her. It's not like he's coming home to you."

"You're right; he's not. But, at least he will have his freedom. I didn't have the courage to stand up to you eight years ago, but I do now. You ruined my life. The only person that cared about me and you took them away."

"Britney, I did it for you. I did it for the both of y'all. It's so complicated, but you have to understand."

"Forget it, Ma. I'm sick of all your lies. File the fucking papers today or I will personally make sure you join Greg in prison."

Gabrielle smirked on the inside. She didn't even bother to say anything. Britney was on a role.

"Fine, but it's gonna take some time to bring him out. You

should know that, Gabrielle. You're a lawyer."

"It shouldn't take more than a year. You're going back in front of the same judge. I'm pretty sure once you explain it to him about the newly discovered evidence, he won't have a problem releasing my husband. Or he, too, can join you."

"What assurance do I have that once Greg is out of prison you won't use this against me?"

"That's the problem; you don't. But, one thing I can assure you is you will never practice law in this lifetime again. After you submit the motion, you will report your *Prosecutorial Misconduct* to the Bar Association. People like you shouldn't be allowed to practice law. You're a disgrace. I also want you to report every case you fixed to the Bar. If you leave one out, I promise you will never see daylight again."

Once Robin realized Gabrielle and Britney weren't playing. she agreed to all of their terms and conditions.

As they were preparing to leave the restaurant, Gabrielle asked, "Robin, who else was involved?"

"Why?"

"Ma!" Britney blurted out.

"Judge Barron, Larry, Miguel, and Mr. Lawrence."

"Are you sure?"

"Yes!" Robin responded before grabbing the papers and storming out.

Britney and Gabrielle looked at each other, then busted out laughing.

"Girl, you were wonderful," Gabrielle beamed.

"Thanks. She had it coming. So now what? You think she got the picture?"

"Yeah. Either way, we have her on tape. Britney, I'm sorry…"

"It's fine. I'm happy I was able to help him. It's because of me that he's in prison. This was the least I could do."

"Awww! Thank you so much."

"Gabrielle, Greg could never know I helped him."

"Why?"

"Because he has a new life with you. Although a part of me will always love Greg, I'm so happy that he has someone like you in his life. Take care of him, and when the time is right, please let him know I kept my promise."

Gabrielle's eyes filled with tears "I don't know what to say. You know I could not have done this without you. Britney, I wish you all the happiness in the world. And yes, I will let Greg know you kept your promise. Hey, why don't you write him and tell him? I'm sure he would love to hear from you."

"Nah, I think it's best that I don't write. Hey, I have to get going. I'll make sure my dearest mother takes care of that. You keep in touch, and anything you need, just call me."

"I will and thanks again. Are you sure you're gonna be alright?"

"Yes, I'm sure."

They hugged and exchanged kisses before going their separate ways. As they walked in different directions, tears rolled down both of their cheeks. Over the past couple of months, they had gotten close. Not only were they in love with the same man, they had a lot in common. In fact, when they were little, they visited the same places.

On her way to the office, Nancy informed her that Mr. Lawrence could see her around one o'clock, which meant Gabrielle had to go straight there. *Perfect timing,* she thought. She informed the cab driver of the address. *One down; three more to go,* she thought.

As usual, Mr. Lawrence greeted her with a smile and a kiss. "It's so wonderful to see you," he boasted.

Gabrielle flashed a wicked smile but remained silent, allowing Mr. Lawrence to continue.

"I just wanted you to know that I'm doing everything in my power to get Greg home. But, I need a little more resources. Post-conviction requires a lot of time. I have this great investigator who I believe can bring him home."

She was burning up inside while listening to him. "Really? How much does he charge?"

"He'll want five thousand to start, but he's wonderful. We can't lose with him," Mr. Lawrence said, leaning back in his chair.

Gabrielle nodded and cut her eyes. "More money."

"If you want Greg home, it's gonna cost," he explained.

As he was talking, his private line rang. He ignored it and continued talking.

"Jake, I think you better get that."

"Why? Whoever it is will call back. It's probably my wife or kids calling for something."

Suddenly, his assistant barged in. "Mr. Lawrence, Ms. Cox is on the line for you. She said it's important."

"Tell her I'll call her back. I'm with a client," he snapped.

"Jake, you should take the call. She probably wants to tell you about my meeting with her. She's filing a 440 motion on Greg's behalf."

Instantly, Mr. Lawrence had a grave look on his face.

"What's wrong, Jake? You don't look too good."

"No, I'm just curious as to why Robin is filing a motion."

"Well, it seems that along with you and others, she falsely prosecuted my husband for a crime he didn't commit." He was about to explain, but Gabrielle cut him off. "Cut the shit, Jake. I know everything. I know they blackmailed you so that you could go along with it. I trusted you. Greg trusted you. And what did you do?"

"Gabrielle, let me explain."

"No, I don't wanna hear it. You sacrificed my husband's freedom to keep your skeletons in the closet."

Mr. Lawrence sat there rubbing his head. "What can I do to make it up to you?" he begged.

She reached into her bag and threw a large envelope at him. "Here's the brief you're gonna file to support her claim."

Mr. Lawrence nodded with relief. "Okay."

"I'm not done yet. In addition to that, you're gonna give me back the seventy thousand we paid you. And, like Robin, you're gonna report yourself to the Bar Association."

"Gabrielle, let's be realistic. I'll give you back your money and make sure Greg is home, but defending people is my life."

"NO!" Gabrielle yelled and stood up over his desk. "Making money is your life. You don't give a shit about your clients. All they are to you is accolades, another notch under your belt."

"That's not true! I bust my ass for criminals. Even when they are guilty, I still provide them with the best defense. So, don't come in here questioning my ethics."

"Did you have ethics when you sold my husband out? How many other clients are sitting in prison because you gave them "your best defense"?" she yelled. Then in a calm voice, she said, "You listen to me, you son-of-a-bitch, my husband sat in prison for almost nine years because his lawyer fucked him over. I know you don't give a shit about my husband. To you, he's just another nigga. But, you know what, Jake? Today you're gonna start. You're gonna bring my husband home and surrender your license. Or I promise you will spend the rest of your life in prison."

"Be careful, little girl. I don't take kindly to threats."

"And I don't make idle threats," she said, then started to walk out. As she approached the door, Gabrielle turned around. "It's really sad how you built your reputation on minorities. They believed in you, Jake. They put their life in your hands. A lot of people are sitting in prison because all you cared about was your image. Was it worth it?"

Gabrielle's words struck Mr. Lawrence like a sword. She was right. He preyed on the less fortunate; he built his empire at someone else's liberty. Many people, white and black, were in prison because of him. While the world labeled him one of the best in the business, deep down inside, he knew the day would come when he would be exposed.

"When you've been in the business as long as I have, you

will see I did my best. I defended murderers, drug dealers, rapists, scums of the earth. When no one wanted to defend them, it was me. So, before you accuse me of anything, I suggest you get your fucking facts straight, sweetie. And let's not kid each other. It's not like Greg was a pillar of the community. He sold drugs to his own kind. So you tell me who gives a fuck about whom. "

Turning back around, Gabrielle flew into a rage. "That's right he did, which makes you no better than him. The difference is he didn't pretend, unlike you. You think just because you drive a fancy car and live in a nice house that makes you better than the people you defend. Jake, these are people's lives we're talking about here! People who confided in you; they trusted you and what did you do? You sold them out. You were supposed to defend them. That's why you became a lawyer…to uphold the law, not break it. You are no better than the dealers and murderers you defend."

"I did the best I could!" he shouted.

"How, Jake? By making deals with the ADA behind their backs, giving them false hope, milking their families dry? That's what you did. You stinkin' bastard don't you dare tell me that you did the best you could. Because of you, my husband was sentenced to twenty-five years to life for something he didn't do. That's the best you could do? I don't give a damn if you took your oath in 1919 and I took mine yesterday, the rules still apply. You took my family away and now I'm about to take yours." She walked back up to him. "I want you to report every fucking case you fixed, and if you leave one out I promise I will do everything in my power to make sure you rot in prison. Motherfuckers like you shouldn't be allowed to practice law. You make me sick," she said and left.

With smoke coming out of her ears, Gabrielle stormed out of his office. *The nerve of that bastard, justifying his action. He's lucky I didn't have a gun. I probably would've shot his ass,* she thought. As she exited the elevator, Tommy was waiting in the lobby for her.

"Are you okay?"

Gabrielle wasn't okay. She looked at Tommy with her glossy eyes and broke down. He embraced her and led her to the car.

"Let's get you out of here, kiddo. You did good!"

Too shaken up to go back to her office and too scared to go home, Gabrielle decided to go to the office of her old law school mentor. Dean Miles' reputation was huge. He was known for exposing the legal system; a lot of people were freed because of him. Dean started out as a state prosecutor, then federal prosecutor before switching over and becoming a defense attorney. He used to say district attorneys and judges were the biggest criminals in the world.

Dean was coming back from court when he bumped into them standing in front of his office. "Gabrielle, what are you guys doing here?"

Gabrielle, her face red from crying, held her head down while Tommy flashed a fake smile. Once Dean saw that, he immediately took them inside. He dropped his briefcase and keys on the table before locking his office door

"What happened?" he asked, taking a seat.

With her too upset to talk, she allowed Tommy to tell him. "We did it! We confronted them."

Dean rubbed his chin in a subdued way. He was already aware of the situation because Gabrielle had placed a call to him months ago to discuss the matter.

"I see. How did it go?"

"It went great, Dean," Gabrielle blurted out. "But they don't care about these people's lives."

Dean went over and sat next to her. "Gabrielle, remember the first day in class when I said fifty percent of the students in my class will break the law and they will forget why they became a lawyer?"

"Yes, I remember," she replied, releasing a little chuckle.

"You asked us why we were there."

"Yes, I asked that question because people change. It's so easy for people to become corrupt. You know, money and power is the best aphrodisiac."

"Yeah, I know Dean, but..."

"But what, Gabrielle? There are a lot of Jake and Robin's out there. You think just because you took them down there aren't people waiting on line to take their place. It's called a chain reaction. There will be a day when your ethics with be tested. And while you may tell me what you will do, on that very day I guarantee you will do the opposite. It's life! "

"So what do I do now? They can't get away with shit like this."

"They won't. I told you months ago that I will do anything to help you, and I meant that. You worry about bringing your husband home. I'll take it from here."

Gabrielle looked at Tommy, who had a smirk on his face. "Dean, I couldn't..."

"Don't be silly. I insist. Besides, you're gonna be very busy when your husband comes home." He winked.

"Are you sure? Jake and Robin are..."

"Are what? Shit, you forget who you're talking to. Tommy, bring me all of the information. I'll take it from here."

It had been a helluva day and Gabrielle was mentally exhausted. On the ride home, she and Tommy stopped to get something to eat. She glanced at her cell phone and saw she had several missed calls from Greg and two from Stevie. She would listen to them later. Next, she called her office to check her messages. Nancy told her that she had five messages from new clients and one from Robin Cox who stated the paperwork had been filed. Gabrielle threw her head back and smiled.

"Tommy, she filed the papers," she beamed.

"I told you she would."

"Oh, what about those two officers? Do you think they will come after me?"

"You let me handle those two bastards. I have something special in mind. Gabrielle, I don't think anything will happen to you. We have them on tape, and even if something happens to all of us, they will not get away with that. Besides, tomorrow I'm gonna have two of my friends advise them that if something happens to you, they will disappear, too."

Gabrielle felt relieved. "Thank you, Tommy."

"No, thank you," he said, as he dropped her off. "Kiddo, get some sleep and don't worry about this no more."

"Alright."

She entered her house and smiled. Hopefully in a couple of months, her husband would be home. Since it was still early, she decided to relax and watch some TV. While lying in the dark watching her favorite television show *New York Undercover*, her phone rang. It was her husband, and she accepted the charges.

"Hey boo!" she beamed.

"Hey baby. What's up? Listen, I need you to call Denise for me now. I just heard Perry was murdered the other night."

"What? By who?"

"I don't know. That's why I need you to call her."

"Alright." Gabrielle clicked over and dialed her number.

"Hey Gab," Denise answered.

"Greg wants to speak to you. Hold on," she told her, then joined the calls.

"Dee, I just heard Perry was murdered. What the fuck is going on out there?"

"What! I didn't know that. Where did you hear that?"

"His cousin just told me. His wife didn't call you?"

"No."

"Well, go find out if that's true and send her my love if it is. I don't know what's going on. That's not like Perry to not have his hammer on him. Whoever did this knew him."

Suddenly, Denise got choked up. She wanted to tell Greg but couldn't. "Awww, man. I'll go around the way and find out what happened."

"Alright. Listen, be careful out there and find out who put our brother in the dirt ASAP. Boy, I can't wait to get the fuck out of prison. I swear niggas are gonna pay."

"Greg, calm down," Gabrielle said. "And what do you mean when you get out?"

"Nothing, Boo. Denise, just find out please."

"Alright. Talk to you guys later," Denise said before hanging up.

"Mr. Brightman," Gabrielle called him.

"Yes, Mrs. Brightman?"

"You listen to me. I'm sorry for your loss. I know you and Perry were close. However, you are my husband and I will not lose you again to some bullshit. We are so close to bringing you home."

"I know, boo."

"I'm not finished. You better not come home and do no bullshit. If you do Greg, I'm leaving you."

"You're never leaving me."

"Oh really?"

"Yeah," Greg replied with certainty. "Anyway, is there anything new with my case?"

This was the perfect opportunity for her to tell him everything, but she didn't. Knowing Greg, he would have interrogated her and then tried to take over. Not this time. Even though they vowed never to keep secrets from each other, this she would be taking to her grave. In this case, the ends justified the means.

"Boo, why did you get quiet when I asked about my case? What's up?"

"I didn't get quiet. You ask me about it every time I talk to you, and like always, nothing has changed."

"Are you even calling Mr. Lawrence to follow up on any new leads? Do you even care?"

"What is that supposed to mean?"

"Because I keep asking you if you followed up with Mr. Lawrence and you keep brushing me off. When was the last time you asked me about the case or offered to research new case law? It feels like I'm doing this by myself with my hands tied behind my back. You are a lawyer with access to certain shit, but it's like if I don't ask or tell you, you don't do anything."

Gabrielle took a deep breath and ignored Greg's accusations, mainly because he had just lost one of his closest friends.

"Oh, you gonna ignore me, huh?

"I'm not ignoring you, Greg. You're just being…well…GREG. If you feel like I'm not doing anything, then find someone else. I'm not gonna keep going through this. Eight years ago when I offered to help, you didn't want it. Now you're singing a different tune."

"Ay yo, Gabrielle, I don't have time to play games with you. Just because I didn't need you back then you don't wanna help me now?"

"I didn't say that. I've always been involved in your case. Anything you've asked me to do, I've done. So, don't start your shit. Look, I had a long freaking day and don't need this from you. Don't blame me for you putting all your eggs in one basket. I told you years ago to get another opinion about the case. But, you wanted to stay with Jake. Even when I questioned some of his decisions, you shot me down. So, if there's anyone to blame, it's you."

For the first time, Gabrielle shut Greg up. Both were silent on the phone for a second thinking about who should say sorry first. Greg finally broke.

"I'm sorry, boo. You're right. I didn't need you in the beginning, but I need you now. I'm sick of being in here for something I didn't do. This shit is getting to me. I can't see my wife and my boys are getting killed."

Gabrielle rested the phone against her chest. She wanted to

share the wonderful news with Greg, but couldn't. She knew if Greg ever find out, he would go ballistic.

"Boo, do you trust me?" Gabrielle asked.

"You know I do."

"With all your heart, mind, body and soul?"

"Yes, Gabrielle!"

"Then sit back and enjoy the ride. I promise you that I'm going to bring you home. Just like you got the streets, your wife got the Law. Let me do what I've been trained to do, and that means pushing Mr. Lawrence to the side. Yeah, I know he's a good attorney and all, but let me show you what I can do. Like yourself, I want you home more than anything in the world. Daddy, your wife got this."

Greg got an instant hard-on. Something about his wife's words was gangster. "Alright, ma, that's what daddy likes to hear. You know that shit makes my dick hard."

"Hmm, I wish I was there to ride it," she said in a seductive tone.

"So do I, boo. My hormones are fucking with me. I'm jerking off like crazy. I can't wait until our next family visit. I'm going hard," he boasted, causing Gabrielle to release a slight giggle.

"Oh, you're going hard next time?"

"I always do. So you better get your rest, because the next one it's on."

"Yeah, whatever."

They talked for a couple more minutes before hanging up. Gabrielle turned off the TV, laid on the sofa, and played back the entire day in her head. Something about Robin's words bothered her. *She kept saying it was complicated. What was so complicated and why didn't she tell us? Did it have something to do with the unidentified person on the tapes? Is he the mastermind behind all of this?* What bothered Gabrielle even more was the voice on the tape sounded familiar. Gabrielle wracked her brain until she fell asleep.

She woke up to a knock at the door. Glancing at the clock, she saw it was almost eleven o'clock. As she was slowly getting up, they rang the doorbell. *Who the hell is ringing my bell this late?* she thought. She was about to open the door when she noticed her motion lights weren't on. Something told her to peek through the side window. There were two men with police badges at her front door. Being that she had all the lights off, they didn't know if she was home.

She could hear one of them mumble, "I'm gonna fuck the shit out of her before I kill that bitch."

While the other tiptoed around the house to see if there were any lights on, Gabrielle ran and got her cell phone. She thought about calling the police, but they were the police. *Shit!* Instead, she called Tommy. It rang two times before he picked up.

"Tommy, it's Gabrielle. There are two police officers at my house. I think it's Larry and Miguel," she whispered in a scared tone.

"Alright, stay calm! I'll be there in ten minutes."

"Okay."

Click!

She peeked out of the window again and saw them driving off. "Whew," she mumbled. Nervous, she paced back and forth while waiting for Tommy. She thought about calling Denise, but knew she would ask too many questions and tell Greg.

Ding Dong!

She jumped and looked out of the window. It was Tommy. She ran downstairs to open the door.

"Thank God you're here," she said, pulling him inside.

"Did they leave?" Tommy asked in an angry tone.

"I think so. What if they come back, though? One of them said he's gonna rape and kill me."

Tommy cut his eyes. "They won't have a chance to do that. Listen, do you have someplace you can stay tonight?"

"Yes, I have an apartment in Riverdale that I can stay at for a while. Why?"

"I want you to pack a few things and stay there for a couple of days until I sort things out. I'll let you know when it's safe to come back."

"Tommy, I'm not leaving my house," she protested.

"Gabrielle, these people are gonna kill you," he warned.

She glared at him. She wanted to say something, but couldn't reveal too much information. Therefore, she played along and went upstairs to pack a bag. While she was getting ready, Tommy checked the house again and placed some devices inside and outside. When Gabrielle asked what they were, he simply told her, "Protection."

Tommy moved one of her cars into the garage and locked the gate to the backyard before they left. She drove her car, while Tommy closely followed her. It took them over two hours to get to her apartment. He wanted to make sure no one was following them. Once Gabrielle was secure in her apartment, Tommy left. It was two o'clock in the morning when she finally fell asleep.

The next morning, Gabrielle decided she had come too far to let a pair of corrupted-ass police officers stop her now, even if meant taking a life.

Chapter Twenty-Three
Morgan

A *couple more days and it will finally be over,* Morgan thought that Friday morning before leaving for school. While she was told having an abortion is a sin, there was no way she could have this baby. Sitting there rubbing her belly and looking out the window, she wondered if she kept the baby, who would it look like?

Morgan had already informed Chloe to cover for her just in case Denise checked up on her. She didn't reveal her true reason to Chloe. She simply said her family was having an outing and that she didn't feel like being around them. With Chloe's parents going away for the weekend, the plan was going perfectly.

At the end of the school day, Morgan glanced at her watch. She needed to get home before Denise. Tony said he would be down the block from her house at four o'clock waiting for her. While Morgan did not want to spend the weekend with him, she had no choice. It was the only way she could get the abortion.

Yes, Denise isn't home yet, she thought, feeling relieved as she ran up to her room and packed a few things. Knowing Tony, he was probably already there waiting. Sometimes Morgan wondered about Christina. *What excuse does he give her for his absence?* Before leaving, she jotted down Chloe's information, left it on the fridge, and ran out the door.

As she expected, the car was there waiting.

"Hello, Al," she said after getting in.

"Good afternoon. Tony is already at the house."

"Okay."

After Al pulled up to the house, he told her, "Enjoy your weekend."

Morgan flashed a weak smile. Tony must have already told him that she would be staying there for the entire weekend. "Thank you, and the same to you."

She walked into the house only to find Tony in the kitchen cooking. "Hey, baby, what's up?" he beamed.

"Hey," she said and then leaned over to kiss him.

"Mmm…that's what daddy likes. How's the baby?"

Morgan hated when he asked her that. "Fine," she simply replied, while taking off her sweater.

She offered to help cook, but Tony said he had everything under control. Therefore, she went into the other room to call Denise. It rang a couple of times before going to her voicemail.

"Hey Auntie, it's Morgan. I'm here. I left the information on the fridge. We're going out to the movies and then dinner. Love you."

Tony walked in. "Who do you love?" he asked.

"Huh?"

"Who did you say I love you to over the phone?" he asked again in an angry tone.

"I left a message for Denise on her cell phone to let her know I was alright," she explained, handing him her cell phone.

Tony sighed. "Oh a'ight, but why don't I have your cell number?"

Morgan turned away. "You never asked, but I'll give it to you."

"I shouldn't even have to ask for it, especially since you're carrying my baby."

That won't be for too much longer, she thought. "Sorry," she mumbled, hoping he wouldn't get violent.

Getting angry, Tony looked her up and down. "Put that shit on vibrate. This is my weekend," he snapped before walking out.

Morgan exhaled. *This is gonna be a long weekend.* She threw her cell phone on the bed and started to unpack.

Tony entered the room again and asked, "Is that what you wore to school today?"

Morgan looked down at herself before answering. "Yeah."

"Don't wear that shit again. It's too fucking revealing."

Puzzled, she walked over to the mirror to get a better look at what she was wearing. She had on a button-up blue dress with some flats. The dress wasn't tight. Yes, her ass stuck out, but it always did.

"It doesn't show..." she tried to respond, but Tony snatched her by the arm.

"I said it's too fucking revealing. That shit shows all of your curves and I don't like it."

"Okay, I won't wear it again," she said, frightened.

Tony released her. When he saw her cell phone on the bed, he picked it up and started scanning through her contacts list. "Who are Dave and Hassan?"

"They're in my dance class."

"Why do you need their numbers?"

Morgan dropped her head. "It's not like that..."

Before she could finish, Tony snatched her up by the neck. "If I find out you're fucking around..."

Terrified, she stared at him with her big, pretty eyes. "I'm not. They are just friends, nothing else."

"That's all they better be," he said, letting go of her neck.

Morgan stood there still frightened. She had to think fast. Judging by his looks, Tony was going to knock the shit out of her. So, she grabbed him by his waist and kissed him on the neck. At first, he rejected.

"Get off of me," he mumbled, but she pulled him closer.

"I don't wanna fight," she purred, flinging her hair back.

Feeble to her touches, Tony submitted and kissed her back.

"I'm sorry, ma. I just don't want anyone to touch you. You're mine."

Morgan frowned inside but continued to stroke him. "I am. Why don't you show me how much I'm yours," she replied, licking her lips.

Tony immediately forgot why he was upset. He carried Morgan into the kitchen and over to the table. Then he ripped open her dress, pulled out a knife from the drawer, and cut her panties off. Next, he grabbed a cucumber off the counter and slowly slid it up and down her body.

Morgan let out a yearning moan. "Uhhh…"

Taking the cucumber, he rubbed it on her clit, making Morgan jump. Then he slid it inside her. Tony had turned Morgan into a porno star. She played with herself and then shoved her two fingers in his mouth.

"Yes, let daddy taste it."

After thrusting the cucumber in and out of her, he pulled it out and stuck it in her mouth, wanting her to taste her own sweetness.

"Is it good, ma?" he asked, reinserting it inside of her.

"Yes, Tony," she moaned.

Horny, Tony went and grabbed a couple of ice cubes out of the freezer and rubbed them all over her body. Morgan knew what they were doing was wrong, but it felt so good. He removed the cucumber and placed in back in her mouth.

"Suck this," he moaned, while shoving the ice cubes inside of her.

Morgan threw her head back; she was in ecstasy. Tony then bent down and sucked what was left of the ice out of her.

"Oh yes," was all she could say.

Tony then threw her legs up over his shoulders and started eating her out, while staring at her vagina. It was so plump, pretty, and pink. The three P's he loved. Morgan rose up and pulled him into her.

"You're gonna make me cum."

Tony smiled. "Don't I always?"

She pulled off his shirt and kissed all over his neck.

"I love you, ma," he moaned.

Pretending she didn't hear him, Morgan pushed him down on a nearby chair and pulled out his cock. It was sad how he had turned her into his personal whore. Teasing him with her tongue, Morgan flung her hair back and looked up at him before she hog spit on his penis, making his body shiver as saliva ran down his erect member. Morgan slowly licked it off.

"OH SHIT!" he yelled.

Not only had Morgan mastered oral sex, but she looked beautiful doing it.

Tony played in her hair. "You're mine forever," he told her, then pushed her head back down.

Needless to say, they had sex the entire weekend. However, like the saying goes, all good things must come to an end. It was five o'clock Sunday morning and Al was picking her up in an hour to take her to the clinic. Mookie told Tony that he would meet her there.

When Morgan rolled out of bed and went to get in the shower, Tony followed her. "Baby, I want you to call me when you get home."

Morgan nodded. "Okay."

She was a little nervous, but Tony had already explained to her what was going to happen. She assumed he had been in this position at one time before.

After showering and dressing, she looked out the window and saw Al pulling up. So, she grabbed her bag and prepared to leave. Tony reached out and pulled her by the waist, squeezing her tightly.

"Baby girl, I love you. Everything is gonna be fine."

Morgan nodded.

"Listen, I'm leaving this afternoon to go on tour, but if you need anything, call me."

"Okay," she said, walking out the door.

Tony caught up to her and hugged her from behind. "I'm gonna make it up to you. I promise."

As Morgan went to get in the car, Tony yelled, "Morgan!" She turned around, and he walked over to her. "I want you to fly out to see me while I'm on tour."

"Tony, I can't."

"Well, I'll fly in to see you. Either way, I'm gonna see you. Do you need any money?"

"No, I'm fine"

Grabbing her by the waist, Tony kissed her one last time. "I love you so much!" he whispered.

Morgan took one last look at Tony and hopped in the car.

Al took Morgan to a place that looked like a brownstone apartment building, but it was a doctor's office. Petrified, she went inside.

"Ummm, excuse me, I have an appointment for...a-h-h-h abortion," she mumbled with her head down.

The clerk looked up. *They are getting younger and younger,* she thought. "What's your name?" she asked.

"Morgan Marciano."

The young lady reviewed the appointment sheet. "Oh yes. Have a seat. The nurse will be with you shortly."

Morgan nodded and sat down.

A couple seconds later, a nurse called her into another room to check her vital signs and do a sonogram. Afterwards, she told Morgan to have a seat in the waiting area again. This time, Mookie was in the waiting area. Morgan had never seen him before, so not knowing he was present, she sat on the other side of the room and took a deep breath. She glanced over in his direction, only to find him staring at her. He flashed a smile.

"Morgan?" he said with an unsure voice.

Afraid, Morgan smiled but remained silent. Mookie got up and sat beside her.

"Hey, Tony told me to make sure you're alright."

Morgan stared at him with big glossy eyes and then put her head back down. Mookie gave her a stumped look. He was about to say something, when the nurse called her again. She turned around and looked at him one last time before she vanished.

Mookie shook his head. *You owe me big-time, Tony,* he thought.

Morgan went into the room where she was told to remove her clothes. Afterwards, the nurse escorted her to what appeared to be a huge examination room. Morgan laid there motionless and incoherent as the anesthesiologist explained the medication he would be administering to her. As she lay there looking up at the ceiling and trying to stay awake, a single tear rolled down her temple. Before passing out, Morgan said a silent prayer to God asking him to forgive her and to help relieve her from this nightmare.

Chapter Twenty-Four
Tony

Tony watched as Al drove off with Morgan in the backseat. Once the car was out of sight, he went back into the house and broke down. This was the second time he had lost a child. He laid across the bed and thought about how beautiful their child would've been. He remained deep in his thoughts until he fell asleep. It was almost noon when he woke up. Immediately, he called Mookie.

"Yo, Mookie, what happened?"

"She's good. They did the abortion, but damn, shorty was pregnant with twins."

Tony almost fainted. "Twins?"

"Yeah, I overheard the nurse telling someone. That's crazy. Anyway, I left and told them to call me when she wakes up. Yo, shorty is banging. Her body is crazy. I see why dudes are busting up in that. Gotdamn!"

Tony's blood started to boil. "Watch you're fucking mouth," he snapped.

"A'ight, chill. Shit, she's fucking like an adult. Anyway, you ready for the tour?"

"Something like that," he grumbled, while still thinking about the babies.

"Well, it's showtime, play boy," Mookie chuckled.

Tony didn't feel like talking anymore. "I'ma holla at you later. Yo, thanks, fam."

Click!

He tossed the phone on the bed. "FUCK!" he screamed. This wasn't happening to him again. He dropped down on his knees and cried, "Oh God, what have I done?" After hearing that, he didn't feel like going on tour. He thought about how scared Morgan must have been. He needed to see her, to let her know he was sorry. Also, he wanted to make sure she was okay.

With tears rolling down his face, Tony was immobile. His phone rang, and it was Al.

"Tony, I'm about ten minutes away. Are you ready?"

"A'ight."

Tony gathered his things and washed his face. After going into the bedroom to get his phone, he stared at the bed and smiled, thinking about how they had made love that weekend. When Tony heard Al pull up in the driveway, he quickly scanned the house to make sure he had everything. Coming across Morgan's sweater, he picked it up and smelled it. *Damn, it smells just like her perfume.* Tony missed her already. He threw the sweater in his bag and left.

"Are you okay?" Al asked when Tony got in the car.

Still spaced out, Tony fought back his tears and replied, "Not today, Al."

Tony closed his eyes on the ride home. He couldn't believe Morgan was carrying twins. He had the urge to stop by to see her, but he didn't.

Once they pulled up to his place, he grabbed his bags, hopped out, and went inside. Still in a shock, he didn't notice Tia standing in the lobby.

"Tony!" she shouted.

"Damn, Tia, I didn't even see you."

"Yeah, I know. What's going on with you? You look like somebody died."

Tony glared at her with his glossy eyes. *Yeah, my kids,* he thought. "Nah, just have a lot on my mind. I'll be good. Is everything set?"

Tia pulled out some papers and handed them to him. "Yeah, here's your schedule. Our flight leaves in two hours, and your luggage was taken to the airport already. So, we need to get going. I'm going to run and grab something to eat before we get on the road. You want something?"

Unable to eat because he was worried about Morgan, Tony replied, "Nah, I'm good. Just bring me something to drink."

"Alright."

Tony hadn't seen Christina all weekend. Being that she was flying out right after him, he decided to stop by her place to wish her luck. He promised himself that once both of their tours were over, he was going to make it up to her. They pulled up in front of Christina's building and saw Joyce standing outside.

"Hey, Joyce," Tony said, giving her a kiss on the cheek. "Is Christina upstairs?"

"Hey, Tony. Yeah, she's up there getting ready."

Tony headed upstairs. Since she was getting ready, Christina had left the door open so Joyce could reenter without having to knock. Tony heard giggling as he walked in and noticed it was coming from the bedroom. He also heard a male's voice. *Oh, this bitch is up here with Rashid,* he thought.

He peaked through the cracked door and damn near fainted. Christina was fully clothed but laying on top of Paul. His biggest fear had just become reality. He slowly backed away from the door and went back downstairs. Pacing back and forth, he tried to collect his thoughts, when he heard Christina say, "Come on. We need to get going."

"Yeah, I have something romantic planned for us," Paul replied.

Tony quickly ran to the door and knocked. "Chris!" he

yelled.

"Up here, Tony!" she yelled back.

Pretending like he had just come in, Tony started up the stairs, when he saw Paul coming out of the room with some bags. They meet midway on the stairs.

"What's up, fam?" Paul said.

Tony was good at hiding his feelings, something he learned from Greg.

"Yo, playboy," he replied, then playfully tapped him on the shoulder and kept it moving. When he walked into the room, Christina was coming out of the bathroom.

"Hey," she said with a smile.

"What's up?" he replied.

"Nothing. I'm just about ready to leave."

"Me too. I thought your flight wasn't leaving for another three hours, though?"

"Yeah, but I wanna get there early and relax before hitting the stage."

Lying bitch, he thought. "A'ight, well have a safe tour and knock them dead." He was so disgusted with her. Before leaving, he gave her a friendly hug and a peck on the cheek.

*****

It was day three of his tour and everything was going great, until he got the call about Perry.

After the funeral service was over, Perry's wife walked over and thanked him coming. A few moments later, Christina walked up to him.

"Hey I tried calling you, but I figured you were too upset to talk," she said.

Tony smirked. *Bitch, you didn't come here for me. You came here to support my man. Get the fuck outta here,* he thought. "Oh really? That's strange. I didn't receive any calls from you. But, thanks for coming. Excuse me. Let me go holla at Denise," he said and walked away without saying anything to Paul or Mike.

After Tony and Denise got into his awaiting car service, he dropped her off at her place, hoping to see Morgan. He missed her so much.

Denise stared out of the window while Tony sat there in silence. He had never seen Denise so emotional. She didn't even react this way when Felicia died. When they reached her building, she didn't even bother waiting for Al to open the door for her. She just hopped out and went inside. Tony immediately followed her.

"Wait up, Dee," he said, running to catch the elevator.

As soon as they entered the apartment, Denise tossed her coat on the chair, headed straight to the bar, and poured herself a drink. She then walked over to the panoramic window and leaned her head on it.

"I'm sorry, Perry," she mumbled.

Tony poured himself a drink and took a seat on the couch.

"Denise, there's nothing you could've done. Yo, you gotta stop beating yourself up."

"I could've believed him. I've lost two of my closest friends in less than a year."

"I know…," Tony said.

Denise glanced over at him and took a sip of her Henny. She wanted to tell him; she needed to confine in someone, but remained silent. Until she found out who set up Perry, she decided to keep her mouth shut because right now everyone was looking like a suspect. Whoever was behind this was someone close.

Since Denise wasn't in a talking mood, Tony left. *Damn, I didn't even have a chance to see my baby girl.*

On his way to the airport, Christina popped in his head. *Fucking bitch,* he thought. Tony was more disappointed at Paul, who was supposed to be his friend. Greg had taught them

M.O.B. — Money Over Bitches. *With friends like these niggas, who needs enemies?*

Chapter Twenty-Five
Christina

It had only been a couple of weeks since Christina started having an affair with Paul, and although they were discreet about it, she couldn't help wanting to be around him all the time. They did normal things like taking long walks in the park, renting movies, and staying up all night talking, something she and Tony used to do. However, it was different with Paul. Being that he wasn't famous, it made Christina want him more. Not only was Paul patient with Christina, he encouraged her to better herself by going out and purchasing a GED study guide for her. When she didn't understand something, he took the time to explain it, even if he had to repeat himself over and over. He never got frustrated. If it was Tony, he would've cursed her out and left.

While Tony still had Christina's heart, she was starting to realize he wasn't the one for her. She knew deep down inside that he would never be faithful. At first, she turned a blind eye when he flirted and hooked up with other women in the business. Christina was also aware that Tony was sleeping with half of the women at his office. Still, she didn't care because she knew they were just flings. She even forgave him when she found out he was fucking her best friend. However, this new person was different. It was more than sex. Tony had fallen in love with her.

After the funeral service for Perry was over, Tony ran outside after Denise without even bothering to ask Christina how she was doing. *He's such an ass!*

Christina brushed it off and went over to Tia, who was talking to Perry's wife and handing her a check from Tony. *Typical Tony, always thinking money is the answer to everything.*

They headed outside to join Paul and the rest of the gang who were comforting Denise. *Oh bitch, stop making a scene. That wasn't your husband lying in the casket.* When they got over to them, Denise didn't even bother to say hello. She just jumped into Tony's awaiting car with Tony right behind her.

"Are we ready, Paul?" Christina asked.

"Yeah, babe," he responded, causing Tia and Mike to stare at him.

Back on tour, Christina could not help but think about how Tony acted, totally ignoring her. She was getting dressed when Paul came in.

"Are we ready?" he asked.

Christina jumped up, looked around, and then gave Paul a kiss. "Now I am."

Just as she was about to take the stage, Paul grabbed her by the arm and whispered, "I love you."

Christina was speechless. She gazed into his eyes, not knowing what to say. She did care about him, but wasn't sure if she loved him.

"Paul…" she mumbled.

He looked around and guided her over to a private corner. "Hey, I know you don't love me, but I just wanted you to know that I love you, Chris."

"Christina!" Joyce yelled. It was showtime.

Unable to respond, Christina walked back over to her crew

and said a little prayer before she rocked the stage.

Being Christina's first tour, she found herself extremely exhausted every night and would normally go straight to her room to sleep. However, tonight, Paul and Christina were having a romantic dinner. Joyce wanted to tag along, but Christina deliberately gave her something to do.

After they were seated, Christina took a deep breath. "Paul, I just wanna apologize for earlier. You caught me off guard."

"I know. I just felt like I needed to tell you. Christina, I know you love Tony…"

"Not like that. Tony and I are drifting apart; we have been for months now. I guess a part of me felt like I owed him for launching my career. But, he's not what I want anymore. In fact, I decided to break up with him after my tour. I made this decision before you came into my life. I realize Tony will never change."

"Chris…"

"Let me finish. Paul, for the first time in my life I can say I feel normal, and I owe that all to you. You have shown me happiness must come from within. I know it would be selfish to ask you to wait."

"Chris, you're worth the wait. Just be honest with me," he said, looking into her eyes.

"I will. Thank you for understanding."

That night, Christina fell in love with Paul.

A Year Later

Chapter Twenty-Six
Denise

After Perry's death, Denise sunk into a slight depression. She became somewhat introverted from the world. Blaming herself for his death, Denise was so overwhelmed with guilt that she visited his gravesite every Sunday for six months. At one point, she thought Derrick had given up on her because she was so snappish towards him. She had also become very paranoid and had even blown up at Morgan a few times for walking in on her. But, with the love and support from Derrick and her family, she was able to get through it. Although she was still haunted by Perry and Felicia's last words, she knew she had to move on because one day the truth would prevail.

It took some time, but things started to look up for Denise. Ever since she purchased those buildings, she spent every weekend with the contractors. She could have hired someone to oversee it, but she wanted to learn about the business. She had to admit working a full-time job during the week and then meeting with contractors on the weekends was becoming a bit much, though. There were days when she didn't know where she got the strength. With Derrick and Gabrielle's assistance, she was able to complete two of the buildings in nine month and rent them out.

She parked across the street from the building. "Stanley!" She waved.

"Good afternoon, Ms. Taylor," he said, walking up to her.

"Hello."

"Ms. Taylor, this is Ted. He's the foreman. Linda is his assistant and Joe is the manager. They will be on site everyday in case you have any questions. However, I will still be here if you need me."

After they finished doing the walk-thru and had walked back out to the front of the building, Denise heard a familiar voice calling out to her. She looked around and saw that it was Morris. She stood there in shock; she hadn't seen Morris in over a year. On her way to her Range Rover, Morris ran up to her.

"So it's like that? You're the black Donald Trump. You don't have time for dudes like me."

Denise rolled her eyes, then released a little chuckle. "You're right, Morris. I don't have time for cheating-ass motherfuckers like you. If you think you're gonna put me on a guilt trip, think again."

Morris reached out and touched her arm. "Dee, chill. I was just kidding. It's just fucked up the way things ended. You stopped taking my calls."

She stood there cutting her eyes. "Morris, we're on two different levels. It just wasn't gonna work."

He nodded. "Isn't this your old neighborhood?"

"Yes," she said, raising her eyebrow.

"It's good you're giving back."

"Thanks."

"You kept it official and I'm proud of you."

"I have to go," she said.

"Hold up. Damn, can we go somewhere and talk? I have some good news, too."

Denise sighed. "Morris, it's getting late, but maybe some other time."

"Dee, please, we can grab something to eat. I really wanna show you something. I've changed, too."

She threw her head back, knowing she would regret this. "Alright, but your ass better not be lying."

They hopped in Denise's Range Rover and took off. On their way to Morris' surprise, they stopped and pick up something to eat. She had a salad, while he ordered a burger with fries. Unsure of where they were going, Denise allowed Morris to drive.

"So can you give me a hint about the surprise?"

Morris glanced over at her. "I'll just say you inspired me."

Denise shook her head. "Yeah ...okay."

Minutes later, he pulled in front of a brownstone. "Come on."

She glanced out the window. "You think you're slick. I remember the last time we pulled up to this place. No, I'm not getting out."

Morris got out and walked around to her side, opening the door. "Trust me, it's not like that, Dee. I just wanna show you something."

She stared at him for a few seconds. "Alright, but I'm serious, Morris."

They walked up the stairs together and Morris opened the door. The place was beautiful inside.

Denise looked around. "Whose place is this?" she asked with her mouth open.

"Mine. I bought it last year."

She put her hand over her mouth. "Get outta here. How?"

Morris smiled. "I've been saving my pennies and got a great deal. You see, I do listen."

She strolled up to him and hugged him. "I'm proud of you, Morris. Do you have tenants occupying the other floors?"

"Yep, they just moved in, and once I finish the basement,

I'm going to rent that out, too."

"Wow! That's good. So you did learn something." She giggled.

There was a picture on the wall that caught Denise's attention. She remembered seeing it someplace else.

He reached out and gently grabbed her waist, distracting her from the picture. "I owe it all to you, Dee," he said, staring into her eyes.

"Morris, don't..."

Pulling her close to him, he said, "Don't what? I miss you."

Denise put her head down. "Morris...I'm...seeing someone," she mumbled.

Ignoring her statement, he leaned forward and kissed her.

At first, she turned her head. "Don't please."

Morris pushed her up against the wall, and she stared into his eyes. Damn, she missed him. They started kissing, but then she pushed him away. He reached out and grabbed her again.

"Fuck that. You're mine."

Denise pulled away. "Stop! It's over Morris. Please don't do this."

He snatched her by her arm. "You want it just as much as I do," he replied, yanking her arm.

She yanked it back and tried to walk out, but he snatched her again and without saying a word, he ripped open her coat and shoved his tongue down her throat. She tried to fight it, but she couldn't. She missed Morris' touch so much.

"Oh God, why are you doing this to me?" she moaned.

"Because you want me to."

Morris carried Denise up to the bedroom and tore off her dress. Denise wasn't wearing any panties and that turned him on even more. She laid there in lust, her eyes closed.

"I missed you, Morris."

"I missed you, too. I love you, Denise," he said, teasing her nipples with his tongue.

She tried to get up, but Morris kept pushing her back down.

He played in her vagina while kissing her from head to toe, driving her crazy. Before she knew it, Morris had fucked her all through the house.

It was three in the morning when Denise woke up, rolled over, and saw Morris sleeping next to her. She eased out of bed and grabbed her coat. She didn't even bother getting dressed. After throwing on her coat, she looked at the picture again on her way out. *Damn, where did I see this picture before?*

Once she was outside, she looked at her phone. There were ten missed calls, most of them from Derrick. Denise got in her car and broke down in tears. It was like déjà vu. She was an emotional wreck. She quickly called Gabrielle.

"Hello," Gabrielle said in a sleepy voice.

"Gabrielle!" she cried.

"Denise, what's wrong?"

"I need to talk…please!" she hysterically screamed. "Please, Gabrielle."

Gabrielle sat up in her bed. "Sure. Where are you?"

"I'm in Brooklyn. Gabrielle, please come."

"Alright, Dee. Can you drive?"

"Yeah, I think so."

"Okay. Meet me in front of my office. Is that too far?"

"No. I'm on my way."

Denise must've been doing a 100 mph on the FRD because she arrived there in twenty minutes. She got out of her car hoping to see Gabrielle, but she wasn't there yet. So, she paced back and forth, devastated about what just happened.

"Denise," Gabrielle said, walking up to her.

Denise was so distraught that she didn't even see Gabrielle pull up.

"Gabrielle," she collapsed into her arms crying.

"Dee, what happened?" she asked, rubbing her back.

She took a few moments. "Gabby, I messed up. I can't believe it," she wept.

Unsure of what she was talking about, Gabrielle suggested

⎯irs to her office.

⎯⎯ere, she turned to Denise and said, "You have to calm ⎯ ⎯n. You're scaring me."

Still hysterical, Denise continued to cry. Unable to talk, she sat down on the couch.

"Gabrielle," she huffed, trying to catch her breath.

"Take your time."

Denise took a deep breath. "Gabrielle, I had sex with Morris. I don't know why or how it happened..."

Gabrielle looked shocked. "What's happened?" she asked, handing her some tissue.

"Thanks. I had a meeting with the contractors and he was there. Well, he's working on the buildings. Anyway, we spoke. I was getting into my car when he came over to me. He wanted to show me something. He purchased his first brownstone. Gabrielle, you gotta believe me. I intentionally didn't go there to have sex with him. I love Derrick."

Gabrielle just shook her head. "I know it wasn't intentional. You and Morris have a history."

"That's the problem, Gabby. I should've known better. I can't believe this shit happened. Derrick's been so good to me and I pull this shit. What am I going to do?"

"Tell Derrick."

Denise twisted her face and shot Gabrielle a 'What you talking 'bout' Willis look.

"I can't tell him. He'll leave me. Gabby, Derrick and I agreed to abstain from sex for a year. And here my hot ass goes and gets fucked."

"Denise, do you love him?"

"Yes."

"Well, you owe it to him to tell him the truth. Don't start your relationship off with a lie because lessons can't be learned when lies prevail. If you do, your relationship will be full of scattered lies," she stated, sounding like a hypocrite.

Denise nodded. Gabrielle was right. She had to tell Derrick

what happened and pray he forgave her. "Alright, I will, but if he leaves my ass, I'm coming back to cry on your shoulder."

Both giggled.

"That's fine. Are you naked?" Gabrielle asked, noticing Denise only had a trench coat on.

Denise laughed. "Butt naked. I bolted out of there like a bat out of hell. What's left of my outfit is in the car."

Gabrielle busted out laughing. "You are too much."

After walking Denise back to her car, Gabrielle made sure she was capable of driving home.

"Dee, call me when you get home. And don't worry. Everything will be fine," she said, kissing her on the cheek.

"Thanks, Gabby."

"Hey, don't forget…my house Friday night."

"I won't," Denise replied, then pulled off.

*****

That day at work, Denise avoided Derrick's calls and tried to stay focused. After finishing up her monthly project report, she decided to call it a night. She was sleepy and her eyes were puffy from crying. She took the train home, and just as she was entering her building, Derrick jumped out of a cab.

"Denise!" he yelled.

Denise turned around. "Derrick?"

"Sorry to pop up on you like this, but I was worried about you. I've been trying to reach you since last night. Are you okay?"

She lowered her head. "I'm fine," she mumbled, as her eyes filled with tears.

Derrick intensely stared at her. "Denise, did I do something wrong?"

Yeah, meeting me, she thought. Shaking her head, she replied, "No…I have to go," and tried to walk off.

Baffled, he reached for her arm. "Talk to me, Denise."

When she turned around this time, tears were rolling down her face. "Derrick, we can't see each other."

"What? Where did that come from?" he asked.

She stood there without responding.

Derrick reached out and grabbed Denise's hand. "Come on. Let's go talk."

On the cab ride to Derrick's apartment, Denise sat with her head down while he stared out the window. After walking into his place, she went over and sat on the sofa. Derrick took a seat beside her.

"What's going on?" he asked in a stern voice

She continued to hold her head down, as if she was being scolded by her father. "Nothing, Derrick," she mumbled. "Let's just forget about it."

Not willing to let it go, he lifted her head up to stare directly into her face. "So we are lying to each other now? You're gonna sit here and tell me nothing is wrong with you? Denise, look at me. I love you, and no matter what it is, we will get through it. All I'm asking you to do is trust me."

She took a deep breath, got up, and started pacing back and forth, thinking about how should she say it. "Derrick, I had sex with my ex last night. It wasn't planned, trust me. It just happened. I bumped into him and one thing led to another," she mumbled, as tears rolled down her face.

This time, Derrick lowered his head. He was completely at a loss for words.

"Do you love him?"

"No, it just happened..."

Before she could finish, he got up and started pacing. "Dee, I need to tell you something. I slipped a few weeks ago. I had sex with my ex, also."

Denise stood there with her hands folded, trying to comprehend what she just heard. "You did what?" she yelled in an astonished voice.

After he repeated what he had just said, they stood in the

middle of the living room staring at each other. Then, out of the blue, they busted out laughing and walked up to each other.

"Damn, we're pathetic," Denise said, hugging him.

"Yes, we are, but at least we were honest. Denise, I wanted to tell you so bad," Derrick said, embracing her.

"What happens now?" she asked, burying her head into his chest.

Stroking the back of her head, Derrick stated, "I don't know. But, what I do know is that I don't want to lose you."

"Same here."

Gazing into each other's eyes, they started kissing. That night, Denise learned the difference between fucking and making love.

*****

As Denise entered her building, she bumped into several girls who were always lingering around. It was clear that they adored Tony because every time they saw Denise and him together, they would giggle and act silly. This time, since Denise wasn't with Tony, their reaction was different.

"I know that bitch is fucking Tony Flowers," one girl mumbled to another girl. "I saw his driver down the block several times last year."

Denise squinted up her face like she smelled something stank. "Excuse me?"

The young, white girl flung her hair back and put her hand on her hip. "I know you're messing with Tony Flowers because last year, I saw Tony's driver down the block a lot."

"Sweetie, Tony and I are not messing around. Unless you can see in my bedroom, I wouldn't say that out loud."

"Well, what was he doing around here?"

"Just because you saw his driver doesn't mean Tony is with him. Maybe his driver lives in the area."

The girls looked at each other. They never even thought

about that. They looked at Denise, who still had a nasty expression on her face. Then they giggled and walked away. Denise just shook her head and went upstairs.

Morgan was in the living room watching TV when she entered the apartment.

"Hey," Denise said, taking a seat on the ottoman.

"Hello, Auntie! Another glorious day with Derrick?" Morgan teased.

Laughing, Denise tossed a pillow at her.

Morgan was flipping through the channels when she saw Tony's video.

"Hold up. Is that's Tony's new joint?" Denise asked.

Morgan rolled her eyes. "I guess."

Denise looked at it for a second and said, "No wonder why these young girls are in love with him."

"Huh?" Morgan replied.

"When I was coming upstairs, these young white girls in the building swore that I'm messing with Tony."

"Why would they think that?" Morgan asked, trying to stay calm.

"According to them, they saw Tony's driver parked down the block a lot last year."

Morgan jumped up. "They saw his driver?"

"Yep, and with fans like that, Tony better be careful."

Little beads of sweat started to develop on Morgan's forehead. The nightmare was finally over, and the last thing she needed was for Denise to find out. Therefore, she decided to flip the subject.

"Aunt Denise, why didn't you ever mess with Tony?"

Denise screwed up her face. "Because Tony isn't my type."

"I thought he was everyone's type: rich and powerful."

"Tony may be rich, but powerful he isn't. Shit, I'll have to kill Tony's ass," Denise snidely said, then went upstairs.

While sorting out her laundry, Denise started thinking about the conversation she had with Gabrielle and how truthful the words were that she spoke. When you build a house with a deck of cards, it's only a matter of time before it starts crumbling down.

Chapter Twenty-Seven
Gabrielle

Victory was sweet! After Gabrielle presented all the incriminating evidence, the judge had no choice but to let her husband go. When the judge started dragging his feet, she threatened to go to the media. As for Jake, he was found shot to death in his house in the Hamptons. Police ruled it a suicide. The police were still looking for Larry and Miguel. Word around the precinct was that after sexual explicit photos of them were published in the papers, they vanished. Judge Barron suddenly got sick and was unable to return to work. As for ADA Robin Cox, she was charged with prosecutorial misconduct, lost her licenses, and in exchange for a lesser sentence, she agreed to go quietly. In addition, she had to give them a list of every case she fixed. Delighted that justice had finally prevailed, Gabrielle knew Robin was protecting someone else. As for Britney, she moved out to the west coast and started a new life hoping to forget about Greg.

God is good!, she thought. Gabrielle smiled while preparing breakfast for her hubby. It took a lot of work, but she finally had her husband home. On top of him having been home for about four months, they just found out she was three months pregnant.

Life is great! Greg promised he would make her the happiest woman on earth when he came home, and it's a promise he fulfilled. Gabrielle was on cloud nine, although it was hard keeping it a secret from her family and friends. When they asked why she was so happy, she would just smile. Greg was a very apprehensive person; he didn't want anyone to know he was home. When Gabrielle asked why, Greg stated he needed to do some investigating. The people he knew years ago might not be the same people. So, before he allowed them in his circumference, they needed to clear a background check.

He gave Gabrielle the green light for his birthday party. Since it was just going to be close friends and family, they decided to have the party at the house for a more intimate setting. As guests arrived, Greg waited upstairs. Once everyone showed up, he would make his grand entrance. Tony brought Christina; Denise and Derrick showed up together; Stevie and Jasmine came by themselves. Gabrielle's sisters came with their husbands, and Mike brought his girl while Paul came alone.

As everyone drank and reminisced about the good ole days, Gabrielle snuck upstairs to let him know everyone was there. Then she went back downstairs and yelled, "Hello," after turning the music down.

"May I have your attention? We came here to celebrate my husband and your friend's birthday…a man who has influenced all of us. Tonight, we celebrate his birthday. I just wanna say thank you for all your love and support," she said, getting choked up.

Denise reached out and hugged her. "It's cool, Gabby. Take your time."

Gabrielle took a deep breath. "Sorry…like I was saying, Greg has been there for all of us, and tonight, we celebrate his day. Please join me in raising your glasses to a man that words can't describe. I only wish he was here to see this."

"Thanks, baby," Greg said, walking down the stairs.

Silence filled the room, and everyone stood there in shock.

"GREG! OH MY GOD!" the room echoed.

Suddenly, the room was filled with tears and laughter.

"I can't believe this shit," Tony said in a state of shock.

Denise burst into tears. "Bro, your home!"

Greg calmed everyone down. "It's me, and yeah, I'm home for good. I've been home for about four months."

"Four months?" someone mumbled.

"Yes, and I owe it to my wife," he responded. "I had to make sure shit was correct. You know I've been gone for a long time because someone that I trusted put me there, and I refuse to give anyone a second chance to remove me from my wife. Don't take it personal. Anyway, I just wanna say thank you for coming out and being there for me and my family. As for my wife," he said, pulling her to him by her waist, "you are my life. I could not have done it without you. You brought me a glass of cold water when I was in hell, and I will forever be grateful to you for that. I thank you for loving me and giving me the ultimate gift, which is my baby." He touched her stomach.

With tears rolling down her face, Gabrielle whispered, "Babies..."

Greg's eyes widened and he smiled. "For real?"

She shook her head yes and kissed him.

"Okay, I just learned we're having more than one baby."

Everyone cheered.

Staring into each other's eyes, Greg kissed his wife. "I love you."

"I love you, too."

Everyone walked up over to them, hugging Greg and congratulating them on their new addition to the family. After a couple of drinks and dances, Gabrielle and Greg separated. The guys went into the basement to kick it with Greg, while the girls stayed upstairs.

"You stinkin bitch!" Denise screamed. "Why didn't you tell me that my brother was home?"

Gabrielle fell on the sofa laughing. "Girl, it was Greg's

idea."

"Please! Who are you kidding? You guys were making up for lost time," Stevie joked.

"I know that's right," Jasmine chimed in.

Having forgotten Christina was in the room, Gabrielle looked over her shoulder and saw her standing there. She walked over to join the conversation.

"How many months are you?" Giselle asked.

"I just made four months," Gabrielle beamed, rubbing her stomach.

"Well, I'm happy for you, sis. You definitely deserve it. I still can't believe Greg's home," Gloria said.

"Thank you. Girl, it's been wonderful. I mean, I was nervous when he first came home because we've been apart for so many years. It's one thing to be with a person but another to live with them. But, I can honestly say I'm so happy. It took almost ten years, but it was all worth it."

"Yay! Love is in the building," Denise clapped, walking out.

Everyone giggled.

"Denise is a mess, I swear." Jasmine shook her head.

"Well, sis, we're getting ready to go. I have to get up early. Gloria, are you ready?" Giselle said, grabbing her bag.

"Yes. I have to get up early, too. Well, sis, this was a special occasion and full of surprises. When are you gonna let Mommy and Daddy know?" Giselle asked, kissing her on the cheek.

Gabrielle sighed. "Let me tackle one thing at a time," she replied, while walking them out.

When Gabrielle returned to the other ladies, they all sat around having small talk. During this time, Christina had the opportunity to learn so much about them and their lives since Tony had always kept her from interacting with them in the past. A short while later, Paul came from downstairs.

"Sorry to interrupt, ladies. Christina, are you ready or are you gonna wait for Tony?"

Christina's face lit up. "No, Paul, I'm ready. I have to get up early in the morning."

"Okay. Are you gonna let Tony know you're leaving?"

"No, he's enjoying himself too much. I'll just let him be."

"Alright. Well, good night, everyone," he said, as he guided Christina out by placing his hand on the small of her back.

"Good night. Nice meeting everyone," Christina said, then left.

As soon as she was out the door, Gabrielle, Stevie, and Jasmine looked at each other.

"What's up, guys? Where's Christina?" Tony yelled, busting in the room.

"You just missed her. She left with Paul," Gabrielle teased.

"Without telling me? I wanted to introduce her to Greg. Did she say where she was going?"

"No," Jasmine stated.

"Oh," Tony muttered with a disappointed look.

Mike entered the room next. "Mrs. Brightman, it was a pleasure. Yo Tony, do you need me to drop you off?"

"Nah, fam, I'm good," he said, pissed because Christina had broke out like that.

"Tony, where's Greg?" Gabrielle asked.

Before he could answer, Greg walked in. "Hey, boo, where's Denise?"

"She's probably outside with Derrick," she replied.

Greg left out the backdoor to find Denise, who was relaxing in the yard with Derrick. "Hey you," he said, scaring them.

"Hey bro," Denise responded, smiling. "Greg, I want to introduce you to Derrick."

"Yeah, we were chatting downstairs. What's up?" Greg shook his hand.

"I've heard a lot about you," Derrick stated.

"Well, I hope it was all good." Greg laughed.

"It was," Derrick said, looking at Denise.

"Listen, can I speak to my sis for a second?"

"Sure, I'll be in the house," Derrick said, then kissed her on the cheek before going inside.

Once they were alone, Greg asked Denise to have a seat with him in the sunroom.

"So what's up, Dee?"

Denise felt like a little girl. "Nothing."

"Who is this guy?"

"We've been seeing each other for over a year now. He's a good dude. Why?"

"Nothing, just making sure my baby sis is happy."

Denise giggled. Greg hadn't changed; he was still protective as ever. "Yes, Greg I'm finally happy. You know I purchased some buildings over in the old neighborhood. The same thing you were going to do before you got locked up."

"Yeah, Gabrielle told me. I'm proud of you. You came a long way. I remember how we first met, sis."

Both laughed.

"All jokes aside. You did good for yourself." Greg smiled.

Overwhelmed with emotion, she replied, "I had a great teacher. I always knew you would come home. They can't keep a good dude down forever."

He blushed. "You know that's right. But, Dee, you were the strongest on my team. You had more heart than any of them dudes. That's why I knew you would make it."

"Thanks, Greg. I'm so happy you're home." She beamed little a proud daughter.

"That makes two of us. On another note, did you ever find out who killed Perry?"

Oh shit! Denise knew Greg was going to eventually ask her about it. The question was should she lie or tell the truth. If she lied and Greg knew it was her that killed Perry, he would never trust her again. However, if she told the truth, it could ruin their relationship forever. Denise took a deep breath before responding.

"Greg, there's something I have to tell you."

"What's up?"

She took another long, deep breath. "I know who killed Perry."

"Who?"

"Me."

Greg gave Denise a strange look. "What do you mean you killed him?"

"The night Felicia was murdered, she tried to kill me. There never were any dudes after her. It was all her idea."

"Why would Felicia try to kill you?"

"It was payback for her father...Grant."

"Grant was her father?"

"Apparently, but before she died, she said she had a brother and they decided to avenge their father's death."

Greg got up and started pacing back and forth, which was something he did when thinking.

"Where does Perry fit in?" he asked.

"I thought Perry was Felicia's brother."

"They aren't related. Did you ask him?"

"I know now they weren't, and yes, I asked him."

Greg sat back down next to her, but he was burning up inside. "Perry was like a brother to me, Dee. We came in this game together. I trusted him like I trust you. Why didn't you tell me this shit last year? You had me thinking it was someone else."

"I know. I wanted to, but I just didn't know how."

"You didn't know how? Perry's been dead for over a fucking year."

Denise remained quiet and stared at the floor. *Shit!* she thought.

"When you asked him, what did he say?"

"He said that she wasn't his sister..."

"And that wasn't good enough for you?"

"At that time, no, it wasn't. Greg, you've trusted Alex and many others, and look what happened. You know friends are nothing but enemies laying low. You taught me that. I wanted to believe Perry, but it was too late. I had already pulled the gun. And remember, you also taught me to never pull a gun out unless I planned to use it. After that shit Felicia pulled, I wasn't about to let anyone get another chance to take me out. Yeah, I'm sorry about Perry and Felicia, but if I had to do it again, I wouldn't think twice. It was me or them. And last time I checked, I loved me more," she snapped, then started walking away.

"Dee, chill out. I know you did what you had to do. I'm not disputing that. What I don't like is someone on my team hiding shit from me. You should've told me!"

"Yeah, you're right. I'm wrong for that. "

Both stared at each other trying to figure out what the other was thinking. Greg smirked inside. Denise didn't take shit from no one, and he respected that.

"I know Perry was your bother. So, it's only right that I ask this next question. Will I have a problem with you?"

"What do you mean?"

"Will I have to look over my shoulder?" Denise said with a serious glare.

"That depends. Will you?"

"I don't plan too."

"You're bold for asking me that."

"No! It's only right. Greg, only sheep get slaughtered in this world."

"And you are?"

"I'm the wolf."

"Perry was my man. He saved my life on many occasions. But, you..." he said, looking her in the eyes, "you are like my daughter. I know if you felt your life was threatened, you had no choice. To be real with you, I would've done the same. But, if you ever lie to me again...in your case, the wolf will get slaughtered."

Denise nodded. It was the first time she told someone about this, and it felt so good to confess.

"I didn't kill Felicia, though."

"What? I thought you said you took care of that," Greg replied.

"Yeah, I did, but it wasn't me. Someone was out there with us. Felicia was shot from a distance, sniper style."

"Word!"

"Yes. Maybe it was Perry."

"Nah, that's not Perry's style. Whoever killed Felicia probably set Perry up."

"You think so?"

"Think about it, Dee."

Denise never thought about it like that. "You know, he told me that he was being set up, and he asked me to find out who was behind it."

"Well, that's what we're gonna do."

"What if it's someone we know?"

"It always is," Greg replied.

On the way back into the house, he put his arm around her.

"I see Tony is making big moves for himself. Glad to see he gave the team jobs. You never forget the people who were there for you," Greg said, changing the subject.

"Well, you instilled that in all of us. There's no I in team," Denise explained.

"For sure...Love."

"Loyalty."

"Always."

"Forever."

After everyone left, Gabrielle and Greg went outside to the sunroom to look at the stars, something they did on beautiful nights like this one.

"Now this is the good life," Greg moaned.

"It sure is, baby. I didn't think love and happiness existed in this world."

They laid there gazing up at the stars, when Gabrielle heard the house phone ringing. She was about to answer it, but Greg told her to let it ring. Immediately, she heard her cell phone ring. *Whoever it is, they'll leave a message.*

Since she didn't pick up, Tommy's call was sent to her voicemail.

"Gabrielle, look, I need you to call me ASAP. You're not gonna believe this!"

Chapter Twenty-Eight
Morgan

I t was the day of Morgan's Sweet Sixteen birthday party. At first, she didn't want one, but her mother and Denise insisted. According to them, it was every teenage girls dream to have one. But, for Morgan, she could care less. In fact, she just wanted to stay home. The idea of dressing up in a ballroom gown was silly. However, once she told her friends and they convinced her it would be nice, Morgan agreed.

Jasmine flew in to help with the party. Morgan thought it would be great having her mother there, but quickly, she regretted it. Jasmine was like a drill sergeant. She made them rehearse every night from their entrance to the party to the first dance. Morgan was so fed up that she wanted to call the entire thing off. She truly believed Denise and her mother enjoyed it more than she did.

Denise surprised her with a *Queen for a Day* treatment at *Oasis Day Spa,* which included a facial, body scrub, manicure, and pedicure. Although Morgan's skin was flawless, Denise thought it would nice for her to experience a spa treatment. Once finished there, Morgan had an appointment at the hair dresser, where she sat in a chair for two hours for a so-called elegant bun. Morgan shook her head in disgust. She swore they would drive her crazy before the night was over.

Before going home, she stopped at Chloe's house. She needed a break from all this party crap. However, Chloe was out getting her hair done for tonight. So, Morgan headed home. On her way, Tony popped into her head. According to the radio, he was performing in Philly that night. She was happy. The last thing she needed was his ass popping up at her party.

Morgan walked in the apartment only to find no one was there. *Thank God!* she thought. She just wanted to relax before the big event. She went upstairs to her bedroom and found a box with a card attached. It was from her father. Morgan ripped open the envelope: *Dear Princess, I hope you enjoy your special night. Happy Birthday! Love, Daddy.*

She sat there as tears of joy rolled down her face. It seemed like only yesterday that they spent the summer together.

"Hey, baby, are you okay?" her mother asked, walking in.

Morgan flinched. "Hi, Mommy," she sniffled. "Yeah, I was just reading Daddy's card."

Jasmine walked over and took a seat next to Morgan. "I know you miss him, but hopefully, he will be at your next party," she said, placing her hand on Morgan's shoulder.

Morgan nodded. "Maybe, but not another party."

Jasmine giggled. "You don't like parties?"

Morgan screwed her face up. "Um, it's not that I don't like parties. It's the preparation I don't like. Last year, I wore a simple dress, washed my hair, and called it a day," she replied with a chuckle.

Jasmine laughed. "Well, you only turn sixteen once in a lifetime."

"Good! Mommy, can I ask you a question?"

"Sure."

"Are you ever gonna get married?" she asked, lowering her eyes.

"I don't know. Why? You have someone in mind for me?"

"No," Morgan giggled. "It's just that you're so beautiful. I just wanted to know did you ever want to get married."

"When I was younger, I did, but now…hmm, I don't know."

"Was it because of us that you didn't get married?"

"No. Actually all of your fathers wanted to marry me. I was engaged to Felix, Big Michael asked me to marry him, and Monique's dad popped the question, too."

"Why didn't you marry them?"

"Well, I was gonna marry Felix, but he was into too much stuff. As far as Michael and Monique's fathers, I didn't wanna marry them."

"But you have babies by them."

"Don't remind me," she said, causing them to laugh. "Sometimes things don't always work out the way we want. I wanted to get married and have all my children by one man. But, it just didn't work out like that. You know our lives are already planned out for us, from the day we are born until the day we die. That's why I don't question God's decision."

Morgan stared at her mother and flashed a weak smile. "I guess you're right."

Was it God's decision for me to get raped and pregnant? If so, why? Morgan thought.

Morgan was about to ask another question, when Denise came in the room.

"Hey, niece, are we ready for our big night?"

Morgan laughed. "I guess."

"I was just telling Morgan about life," Jasmine said, giving Denise an 'Oh God' look. "Never question God's decision. Remember that?"

Denise shook her head. "Shit, do I. I asked him plenty of times why me, but sometimes you have to say why not me."

Morgan looked up at Denise. "Really?"

"Yes, really!" they both yelled.

"Baby, I want you to read Ecclesiastes 3," Jasmine told her.

"Okay."

"And also read Isaiah 59. That's another good one. I read that when I'm going through something," Denise said.

Morgan nodded and smiled. "I will."

"Do you know how blessed you are? When your mother and I were growing up, we didn't have half of the shit you have. Sweet Sixteen party? Get the hell outta here! You were lucky if your parents said happy birthday to you. Trust me, niece, you have it made. Now, get ready."

Morgan sighed and rolled her eyes. "Do I have to put on the big wedding gown?"

"Yes, your little ass does," Jasmine snapped. "This party is costing me and your father a fortune. You better get dressed."

Morgan threw her head back and dragged herself into the bathroom.

Denise giggled. "That's your child."

Jasmine laughed. "That's your niece."

Both shook their heads and walked out.

*****

It was eight o'clock and Morgan was finally ready. As she came down the stairs, everyone watched up in admiration. She was stunning, looking like something out of *Vogue Magazine*. Jasmine stood looking at her with tears rolling down her face.

"Morgan, you look beautiful," Oliver, her date who was a senior at her school, said.

She blushed. "Thank you."

They took a couple of pictures before heading out. As rehearsed, they made their grand entrance into the dancehall. Morgan glanced around, amazed at how beautiful the place was decorated. The night was wonderful; everyone seemed to be having a good time, especially Morgan. She and Oliver were burning the dance up. At first, it was hard to boogie in that ballroom dress, but once she removed the hoop slip, she didn't leave the dance floor.

Taking a break to get something to drink, they were standing at the mini bar, when Morgan heard loud commotion coming from the other side of the room. She looked over and saw a crowd of people in a circle. Immediately, she assumed something happened. So, she went over to investigate. As she got closer, she heard someone say, "I can't believe he's here." When she realized it was Tony, Morgan backed away slowly. She was in shock. She thought he had a show in Philly. *What is he doing here?* she thought.

She needed to get some air. She felt as if she was going to faint. On her way out the door, Julissa grabbed her.

"Where are you going? Tony Flowers is here."

Unable to respond, Morgan smiled and kept walking. She was just about to exit the ballroom when Denise yelled, "Morgan." She tried to ignore it, but someone tapped Morgan on her shoulder to inform her Denise was trying to get her attention. Morgan exhaled and went over to Denise. She looked around the room for her mother, but Jasmine was in the kitchen. Morgan snatched Oliver by the hand so he could come with her, hoping Tony would think that was her boyfriend and leave.

"Yes, Denise," she said, ignoring Tony's presence.

"You're not gonna say hello to Tony and introduce him to your date?" Denise asked.

"Hi, Tony. This is Oliver," Morgan said, flashing a phony smile.

"What's up, man? You're a lucky dude. Ms. Morgan, you look gorgeous. Nice party."

"Thanks! Denise, can I go now?"

"Yeah, and, Oliver, keep your hands above Morgan's waist," she joked.

Morgan turned around and glanced over at Tony, who had an angry look on his face. She went back across the room and joined her friends. Even with his shades on, she could feel him watching her every move. While she tried to have fun, a part of her wondered why was he still there.

The party was coming to an end. Morgan and her friends had planned to hang out afterward. Instead of going home to change, everyone had brought a change of clothes. Morgan went upstairs to a private bathroom to change her clothing, and as she was coming out, she bumped into Tony who ironically was coming out of the men's room.

"Hey, baby." He looked around to make sure no one heard him.

"Hi, Tony," she responded in a frightened voice.

"You looked beautiful, just like a princess."

Morgan looked around hoping someone would come, but they were in the private section.

"Tony, I have to go. My friends are waiting for me downstairs."

He nodded. "A'ight. Where are y'all going?"

Morgan breathed out heavily. "I don't know…probably out to eat."

"Well, find out where they're going and I'll take you there."

Morgan's eyes widened. "NO!" she snapped.

Tony glared at her. "What did you say to me?"

"I said you don't have to. It's a group of us going," she mumbled, changing the tone of her voice.

Tony looked over his shoulder. He made sure they were alone and then leaned down to whisper in her ear. "You better watch your fucking mouth. I'll be down the block waiting for you. You have ten minutes," he said, staring directly into her eyes. Then he stuck a toothpick in his mouth and walked off.

Morgan eyes filled with tears. This was supposed to be her day. *Why is this happening to me?* That was it; she'd had enough. She wiped her face and decided to tell her mother and Denise. However, as she was storming away, she came to her senses. Tony would kill her entire family. She paused midway on the stairs and dropped her head.

"This can't be life," she mumbled, then put on a brave face and went to join her friends.

"Are you ready?" Julissa asked.

Morgan sighed. "Hey, guys, I have something to do. Can I meet you?"

"You're not coming?" Chloe said with disappointment.

"Of course, silly," Morgan smiled. "I just have something to do first, but I'll meet you. Where are y'all going?"

"That's the problem. We don't know," Chloe responded.

"Okay. Well, once you guys figure it out, call me."

"Cool," Chloe said.

Morgan went over, kissed her mother and Denise who were cleaning up, and thanked them for a wonderful time. Then she left to meet Tony. So no one would get suspicious, she chatted with her friends for another minute or two before walking down the block. She looked around to make sure no one was watching as she strolled to the car. At first, she was unable to find the car. That's when she assumed Tony had left. But then, a car flashed its headlights. When she got in, Tony was on his cell phone. Morgan sat there staring out the window. When he got off, he asked Al to give them some privacy.

"Was that your boyfriend you were dancing with?" he asked, turning toward her.

"No. He was just my date for the party."

Tony nodded. "I see. So where was y'all going afterwards?"

"Don't know, Tony."

"You were going out, but don't know where?"

"Yes. We haven't decided yet."

Tony nodded. "I see. So was Oliver going with you?"

"I guess. Tony, he's just a friend. There's nothing between us."

"Why are you acting so guilty? I didn't say anything. How old is he?"

"I don't know, probably my age or a little older," Morgan said, shrugging her shoulders. *God, I feel like I'm being interrogated.*

Tony could tell Morgan was getting a little frustrated with

his questions, but he didn't care.

"It's funny I haven't seen you in months and I don't get a kiss or hug. You gotta be fucking someone?"

Morgan looked the other way. *Here we go again! He's so insecure,* she thought.

"Just because I didn't greet you with a kiss, I'm sleeping with someone now?" she snidely replied, shaking her head in disgust.

"Watch your fucking mouth."

"I'm not sleeping with anyone. I didn't kiss you because we were at the party."

"We're not now..."

When she leaned across to kiss him, Tony pulled her on top of him. "Damn, I missed you," he moaned. "Let's get outta here."

"I can't. My friends are waiting for me."

Tony started to get angry. "So fuckin' what! I haven't seen you in months! You just spent about six hours with them!" he yelled, snatching her by the shoulders.

"I just promised them that I was gonna meet them," she responded in a frightened tone.

"Well, call and tell them you made other plans. Then call your moms and tell her that you're staying at your girlfriend's house."

Morgan stared into his eyes. She knew he was on the verge of smacking the shit out of her. Hence, she reached into her bag and pulled out her cell phone to place the calls. Tony tapped on the window letting Al know he was ready.

When they pulled up to the house, Tony told Al to pick them up in the next afternoon. He then held Morgan from behind as they walked to the house.

"I have a surprise for you," he told her.

When they entered, Morgan almost dropped to the floor. The entire place was filled with long-stemmed red roses and scented candles. On the table was a huge cake of Morgan in a white gown. Morgan turned towards Tony, who had a huge smile on his face.

"You like it?"

Morgan lowered her head. She was too scared to say something.

Tony walked over to her. "You thought I forgot about your birthday? I left my show early just so I could be with you. Baby girl, I missed you so much," he mumbled before sticking his tongue down her throat.

She wanted to turn away, but knew it would cause her to get hit. So, she submitted to his touches.

Tony took a step back. "You are truly beautiful."

Morgan looked into his eyes. "Thank you."

She walked over to the cake trying to seem grateful, but deep down inside, she wanted to leave. She really thought Tony had left her alone after she had the abortion.

Tony turned on some slow music. "May I have this dance?" he asked with his hand out.

Morgan hesitated for a second before taking his hand. She didn't know him to be a very romantic person. Tony was so happy to see her that he was singing Babyface's *Whip Appeal* in her ear. Morgan was astounded and nervous at the same time, but she played along. Tony even had a full-course meal prepared. Broil Sautéed Shrimp and Lobster Tail with steamed string beans and brown rice.

While other girls would've been happy, Morgan was depressed. After they enjoyed a candlelight dinner, Tony sang happy birthday to her. She had to admit it was sweet. She just wished it was someone else doing it. Once he was finished singing to her, they moved into the living room. Seeing a bible on one of the end tables, she picked it up and looked for the passage her mother told her about. Tony stared at Morgan like she was crazy, but he stayed quiet. Morgan opened the Good Book and turned to Ecclesiastes 3. Then she took a deep breath and closed it. She looked up at Tony who had a look of lust in his eyes. She leaned her head back and shut her eyes.

"What did you read?" he asked.

"Something my mother told me to."

Tony gently touched her face, then leaned over and kissed her. Before she knew it, they were in the bed having sex. Being that it had been many months, Morgan was extremely tight, which turned Tony on even more. Instead of fucking like they normally did, Tony wanted to make love. He wanted to tease every inch of her body.

As they stared into each other's eyes, Tony, overcome with guilt, whispered, "Morgan, I love you, and I'm sorry for what I did to you."

Morgan stayed quiet, allowing him to continue.

"These past few months have been crazy being without you. At first, I thought I could forget about you. But, after seeing you tonight, I realize I can't...and I don't want to. Morgan, I wanna be with you for the rest of my life. Just give me a chance to make it up to you, baby. I will die trying," he moaned, inserting himself inside of her again.

"Tony, please, I don't..." she said before he interrupted her.

"Morgan, please...I thought you said you were mine," he said, slowly thrusting in and out of her.

"Tony..." Morgan moaned.

He stopped and reached under the pillow. "Morgan, I have never loved anyone as much as I love you. Please, just me a chance to make it up to you," he said, pulling out a flawless, six-point, five-carat, pink heart-shaped diamond engagement ring.

"Morgan, will you marry me?"

She sighed. "Tony, I can't..."

"Yes, you can."

She gazed into Tony's eyes. Something was different; he was serious.

"I'm too young," she replied.

She thought about the conversation she had with her mother

and aunt. Was this the life God had planned for her? Was Tony the man she was supposed to marry, breed his children? Morgan closed her eyes. *Why is this happening to me?* She knew God doesn't make mistakes, but right then, she was questioning his decisions. How could she marry someone who caused her so much pain?

"I'll wait. You're not leaving me," he warned.

Morgan closed her eyes, and then opened them to stare into his.

I guess this is the life God has given me, she thought.

"Yes, I'll marry you," she mumbled.

Tony was ecstatic. "I promise I will make it up to you," he said, kissing her all over.

They made passionate love all night long.

Chapter Twenty-Nine
Tony

Isn't life wonderful, Tony thought. He was engaged to the love of his life and his mentor was home. While tabloids speculated that he and Christina were on the verge of getting engaged, Tony knew otherwise. When asked about the rumors, Tony would just laugh. As far as he was concerned, their relationship was over a year ago once he found out about Paul and Christina. There were days she would visit him while he was on tour and the sight of her irked him. They barely spoke when they were around each other. In fact, the only time they did speak was when attending public events together. Supporting each other's careers, it was more of a business relationship now.

Tony found himself more disappointed with Paul than Christina. He felt Paul could have at least come to him as a man. Tony knew a lot of the guys in the business hollered at Christina, but he never thought it would be someone close to him that would steal her.

Career wise, Tony had it all. His tour grossed over sixty million dollars; his album sold over seven million copies. He had just debut his clothing line. He also had a magazine out and just signed a deal to start his own movie company. According to Tony, it was the perfect time for him to settle down and Morgan was the one. In his eyes, even though it started off wrong, he felt sometimes good can come from a bad situation. Moreover, he was turning thirty-five years old soon, and sleeping with different chicks was getting played out. Watching Gabrielle and Greg proved that a monogamous relationship was good. Tony only hoped that one day he and Morgan could be like that.

Tony looked at his watch and saw that it was almost time for Greg to arrive. Tony had been trying to spend some time with him ever since the party. However, Greg was always busy. At first, Tony felt insulted when Greg kept canceling. But, finally, he was coming over. They had so much catching up to do.

Tony was upstairs when he heard Carmen say, "Mr. Flowers will be right with you."

He rushed downstairs. "Greg!"

Greg turned around with his trademark smile. "Tony," he said, and then they briefly hugged.

"Damn, man, I've been trying to holla at you for weeks now."

Greg took a deep breath. "Yeah, I know, fam. I've been busy. With my boo being pregnant and all, you know how it goes. She's got me on a tight leash," he said, chuckling.

Tony laughed. "Gabby doesn't play that. Come on. Let's go into the other room."

They went into the living room. Tony offered Greg something to drink, but he declined.

"I can't believe your home, bro."

"Yeah, man, neither can I. God is good."

"All the time," Tony added. "Yo! Wait right here," he said before running out of the room. He came back with an envelope. "Here," he said, handing it to Greg.

Confused, Greg looked at Tony. "What's this?"

"Open it." Tony stood there excited.

Greg opened the envelope, and inside was a check for twenty million. He looked up at Tony still confused. "What's this?"

"Your cut."

"Why?"

"I never paid you for the company. You once told me to owe no man anything, right?"

Greg nodded.

"That's what I'm doing. Fam, you could've deaded me on the company, but you didn't. Like I said before, I look up to you, so it's only right that you get what's yours."

Greg stared at Tony in admiration. "Tony, listen…"

Tony quickly interrupted him. "I know all the money could never make up for what you've given me, but I just wanted you to know I listened to what you said. You led by example, that's all, fam."

"I respect that, Tony, but you know I gave you that company, which means I don't want nothing in return but your loyalty. And you've given that one hundred percent. For me to accept this would go against everything I stand for, feel me? When I do something for someone, I never expect it back."

Tony nodded, but was disappointed. He should've known Greg was a man of his word. "You are just like Denise. Never want anything in return."

Greg chuckled. "You're not supposed to," he said, handing him back the check.

"Well, can we at least go shopping?" Tony joked.

"A'ight, man, we can do that today. Yo, is Taste of Seafood still on two fifth?"

"Yeah! We can hit that spot up after we finish shopping."

"Sounds like a plan to me."

Instead of using Tony's driver, they drove in Greg's BMW. Greg was leery about someone he didn't know driving him around. Because it was Greg, Tony didn't object. Besides, it felt like the good ole days. Trying to impress his big brother, Tony took him to all the expensive shops in the city. Little did he know Greg shopped at those place years ago. Still, Greg knew Tony was always looking for acceptance, so he went along. With the night still young, they went to The Village to drink some beer and shoot some pool.

"Yo, fam, I've been practicing, son," he said, racking the balls.

"Tony, please! I'll still bust that ass."

"You wanna put some money on that?"

"Holla!" Greg yelled.

"How about twenty million?" Tony stared at him.

"Tony, not with that shit again," Greg whined.

"Nah, come on! If I win, you pay me. If you win, I pay you. Scared?"

Greg nodded. "Scared money makes no money. A'ight, let's do this."

"I want all of my money, too."

"That makes two of us."

Both laughed.

Somehow, Greg knew Tony lost on purpose, and that night, he went home twenty million dollars richer. Persistent, Tony made Greg come back to his place so he could give him the check. In the car ride home, Tony decided to bring up Felicia. He wondered if Greg knew she was dead.

"Greg, you heard about Felicia, right?"

"Yeah, I heard. That's fucked up, but hey, shit happens."

Tony was shocked at Greg's comment since Felicia was a part of the team. "Damn, fam!" he said with disappointment. "What about Perry? How do you feel about that?"

Greg sighed. "I'm pissed off. Perry was like a brother to me. He was a good dude; he didn't deserve that."

Heated, Tony stared at Greg from the corner of his eye, but he knew better than to challenge his comment. *What did Felicia do for him to respond so nonchalantly about her death?*

Once they reached Tony's place, he went into his office and got the check, while Greg went into the living room. A few moments later, Greg heard Christina and Paul coming through the door. They had just come back from shopping.

"Tony, is that you?" she called out, walking into the living room. "Oh, I'm sorry. I thought I heard Tony," she said once she noticed Greg.

"Hey, Christina. He's in his office," Greg told her, then gave her a kiss on the cheek. "What's good, Paul?"

Startled, Paul replied. "Greg. What's good, playboy?"

Christina bumped into Tony as she went to search for him. There was a moment of silence, and then Tony grumbled, "What's up?"

"Nothing," she said, walking back towards the living room.

Paul and Greg were joking around when they reentered the room.

"What's good, Tony?" Paul beamed.

"Damn, nigga, do you ever get a day off? Go and blow a chick's back out or something," Tony blurted out in a condescending tone.

Greg looked at Tony sideways. Christina cut her eyes and stared at Paul.

Paul smirked and replied, "Oh, my girl is good. She has no complaints."

"It's hard to tell," he laughed.

"Anyway, Greg, how's Gabrielle doing?" Christina asked, changing the subject.

While still staring at Tony, Greg replied, "Boo is getting big."

"Well, tell her I said hello."

About ten minutes after Greg and Paul both left, Christina entered the living room where Tony was chilling.

"Why did you say that to Paul?" she asked.

"What?" he snapped.

"Why did you say that to Paul? You hurt his feelings."

"Fuck, Paul. Why are you so concerned about his feelings? Are you the one he's fucking?"

Christina fiercely looked at Tony. "You know what? You're an asshole," she said before storming out.

On her way up the stairs, she decided it was time to end their dysfunctional relationship. Moments later, he joined her in the bedroom where they both angrily stared at each other. Christina cut her eyes. *Dumb motherfucker,* she thought and jumped in the bed. Tony must've sensed what she was thinking because he called her a stupid bitch before heading into the bathroom. He was not as dumb as she thought, and she would soon learn this.

*****

The following day, while he was going up the stairs, he heard Christina in the other room talking to someone. It was Paul.

"Yes, Paul, I will marry you," she cried, overjoyed. Then there was a brief silence. Tony assumed they were kissing.

"Christina, I love you so much," he moaned.

"I love you, too, but we have to be careful how we tell him."

"I know. Let's tell him this week."

"Alright."

Fuming, Tony tiptoed into his bedroom fuming. "That stinkin' bitch," he grumbled to himself. He sat on the bed with smoke coming out his ears and devious thoughts invading his mind. Maybe he should bust in there and wild out on them. No, maybe he should ruin Christina's career. Better still, maybe he should have both of them killed. Tony reached into his pocket and pulled out his cell phone.

"Yo, I need a favor. I want you to take care of that nigga Paul."

"Alright."

Click!

"It's payback time," he mumbled.

As he was getting dressed, Christina came into the room.

"Oh, I didn't think you were here."

"It's my house," Tony snidely replied.

Christina ignored him. "Anyway, I need to talk to you about something when I get back. Paul is downstairs waiting for me."

"Paul is downstairs? Cool. I need to talk to him."

Before Christina could say anything, Tony was out the door, down the stairs, and into the living room where Paul was waiting.

"Good morning, fam," Tony beamed.

"What's up?" Paul replied in a guarded tone.

"Listen, fam, I was just joking last night," Tony said, extending his hand.

"It's cool," he replied, shaking it.

"On another note, I need you to take care of something for me."

"A'ight, talk to me."

"My man got a package for me. I need you to pick it up."

"Okay. Where and what time?"

"I'll have him call you."

"Cool."

"Thanks. Oh, I'll have something for you later. Don't tell anyone, especially Christina."

"Nah, I wouldn't do that. I got you."

Tony flashed a fake smile. "Like I got you," he whispered and then walked out to go about his day of business until he received the call he was waiting for, which came several hours later.

After Al pulled up to an abandoned warehouse in Staten Island, Tony instructed him to come back to pick him up in ten minutes. As Tony got closer to the warehouse's entrance, he heard crying sounds coming from inside. He opened the door with his shirt so he didn't leave his fingerprints on the knob.

"Tony, what the fuck is going on?" Paul cried.

"Fuck you, nigga. First, you killed my cousin, and now, you're fucking my girl."

Paul's bloody eyes widened. "What are you talking about?"

"You know what I'm talking about. You and Christina think I didn't know. You think I'm the same Tony from back in the day. Nigga, I'm gonna teach you to respect the kid."

"FUCK YOU, TEE! You're nothing but a bitch-ass nigga. You're alive because of us, and fuck your faggot-ass cousin. That punk-ass nigga deserved to die," Paul angrily stated, getting hit again with the gun.

Tony laughed. "I'm glad you feel like that, because now you're going to join my cousin. Yo, make sure you remove this faggot's phone, clothes, and I.D. I don't want them to find his ass."

"A'ight."

"Fuck you, Tony. I'll see you again. Bet on that. Oh, and tell Christina I love her."

Tony glared at him and then walked out. Next, he heard two shots. He smirked and thought, *Who's the fucking man now?*

Back at the crib, Tony went about his business. He had dinner with Morgan followed by passionate sex. After dropped her off, he headed home. When he got in the house, Christina was coming out of the kitchen.

"Tony, have you heard from Paul? I've been trying to reach him for over an hour now."

"Nah. Did you reach out to Mike and ask him?"

"Yes, but he's looking for him, too."

Tony shrugged his shoulders and went upstairs. Moments later, Christina, who was worried, entered the room.

"Maybe he fell asleep," she said. "I'll reach him in the morning."

He fell asleep alright, Tony thought, while lying there with his eyes closed.

Chapter Thirty
Christina

I f someone would've told Christina she would be in love with her bodyguard, she would have laughed her ass off. But, finally, she had found a man that looked past her glitz and glamour and saw the real Christina. It was as if God answered her prayers, Paul was everything she dreamed of. He was compassionate, nurturing, and funny. Most of all, he was patient and loving. As a result of his patience, she was able to obtain her GED while on tour. When things got to be too hectic in her life, that's when Paul stepped in and took charge. He kept her grounded, and she was extremely grateful for him.

So, after contemplating, Christina decided to end it with Tony. She was aware this decision could be the end of her career. However, it was a chance she was willing to take. Of course, she and Tony were the perfect couple in America's eyes. They had it all: the money and fame. However, for her, that wasn't enough. What good was having love without peace and happiness to go along with it? She would forever be grateful to him for believing in her, but it was time for their charade to come to an end.

Christina even stopped speaking to Rashid. As far as she was concerned, Paul was all the man she needed. Looking down at her three-carat engagement ring, her face lit up. She couldn't wait to start a new life with Paul. Christina Barnes had a nice ring to it. After they were married, she would take a break from her career and start a family. She was going to be the best mother in the world.

But, it had been two weeks since she heard from Paul, and she was losing her mind. No one had heard from him, and that wasn't like Paul. Tony implied that he probably snuck off with some chick for a vacation being that he worked so hard, but she knew better. Paul would never do that.

Christina was in her apartment alone, when Tony, Mike, and Joyce showed up. Instantly, she knew something bad had happened.

"Oh my God! What?"

"Chris..." Tony sighed. "Paul is dead. They found his body in the Hudson River."

Christina screamed at the top of her lungs, "NO! PLEASE, GOD, NO!" and fell to the floor.

Joyce ran over to her. "Chris...I'm so sorry."

Christina continued to cry hysterically. "What happened? Who did this?"

"We don't know," Mike said, getting choked up.

Christina got up and walked back into the living room. "How did he die?"

"He was shot in the head twice," Mike mumbled, as the three of them followed her.

Still in a state of shock, Christina just stood there while tears rolled down her face. "I can't believe this. We were supposed to..." Then she caught herself.

Tony glared at her. "Y'all were supposed to what?"

Christina shook her head. "Does his family know?"

"Yeah, his sister identified the body," Mike answered.

"Well, I wanna pay for his funeral. Anything she needs, I'll take care of it."

"Nah, Chris, I'll pay for it," Tony offered.

Christina shot him an evil look. "That's okay. I'll pay for it."

Right now, she just wanted to be alone. She was about to ask them to leave, when Elisa popped up.

"It's all over the news."

"What's all over the news?" Joyce asked.

"Paul's murder," Elise told them.

"And?" Christina snapped.

"And they are affiliating it with you," Elisa explained.

Her words instantly flew Christina into a rage. "He's not in the ground yet and all you're worrying about is the media!" she shouted angrily.

"Christina, this could affect your career," Elisa said.

"The hell with my career! A person was murdered. If they associate me with him, so what?"

"Chris, Elisa is just trying to protect you," Tony jumped in and said.

"Well, you know what? I don't need protection. The person who protected me is dead, and all you can think about is my career," she said, heaving. "Paul is dead!"

"I'm sorry. I didn't mean to upset you," Elisa said, while looking around at everyone.

Christina cut her eyes and stormed over to the window.

"Chris…" Joyce said in a worried tone.

Christina plopped down on the sofa. "I can't believe he's dead. I knew something was wrong when he said he needed to take care of something for an old friend."

"What? What old friend?" Mike inquired.

"He said one of his old friends asked him to do something for him. I knew something was wrong," Christina wept. She glanced at her engagement ring and cried even harder. "God, why!"

Noticing her engagement ring, Tony thought, *That's good*

for you, you grimy bitch.

Christina was so distraught that Joyce told everyone to leave and she stayed with her that night.

The next couple days were the worst of Christina's life. It was like she had lost a part of her soul, something she hoped to never experience. Christina walked around as if she was sedated. Barely sleeping, eating, and some days she didn't even have strength to get out of bed. She cancelled all of her scheduled appearances and did nothing but cry. She completely shut everyone out of her life. Tony stopped by a few times pretending to care, but Christina wasn't in the mood to be around anyone. Joyce practically had to beg to let her stay.

Paparazzi were in full force like hungry vultures when she arrived at the funeral service. They were dying to get that million-dollar shot. Normally, Christina would flash her trademark smile and wave, but today, she paid them no attention. She made it very clear to her team that this wasn't a social event, so they were to keep their mouths shut. Since Paul died, she was on a war path. Anyone that leaked information to the media would be fired. Anyone that questioned her actions was sent walking. Christina wore something simple because, knowing Paul, that's how he would have wanted her to come. Paul loved the laidback Christina. Therefore, she didn't bother getting all glamoured up. Moreover, she was not the famous Christina Carrington. That day, she was Christina Barnes, a grieving widow.

*****

It took weeks before Christina was able to get back into the swing of things. Often, she found herself drifting off thinking about Paul. To get her mind off of him, she threw herself into her work — signing major endorsement deals, movies scripts, and working on her second album. Being that she knew how to write, Christina took over the creative direction for her next album. Instead of using the hottest producer, she hired unknown ones. She flew to different states just to meet them and listen to their tracks. The record label she was signed under objected at first, but she threatened to leave if they didn't give her total control.

It was the night of Mookie's birthday party, and Tony thought it would be a great idea for Christina and him to attend it together. According to Joyce, the media and blog sites started speculating about their relationship. She figured that's why Tony asked her to go. Last year, he accused her of using their relationship for publicity, and now, he was doing it. Being that it was Mookie's party, she decided to go. Besides, she needed to get out of the house because she was getting tired of being alone with her thoughts.

However, there was one condition. She would arrive alone. You see, she knew Tony didn't want her, but he also didn't want anyone else to have her. That's why he started to spend time with her, called her, asked about her day, checked to see if she needed anything. He even offered to help her with her next album. But, he was a day late and a dollar short. As far as Christina was concerned, they were done. She was just waiting for the right time to drop his ass.

Tony was already there when Christina arrived. Putting on a façade, he walked over to her and planted a huge kiss on her lips. Christina gently glared at him before pushing him away.

"Where's Mookie?" she muttered before walking away, leaving Tony standing there looking like a damn fool.

Tony laughed it off and followed her. Throughout the night, Tony was very affectionate towards her. He whispered in her ear, got her drinks, hugged her from behind, and made sure they took pictures. Christina was astonished it took Paul's death to get him to act like a boyfriend. Maybe if he would have acted like this a year ago, they wouldn't have to pretend to be in love. Now, the thought of him touching her made her sick. At one point, she pulled him aside and told him to chill out. She liked it better when he ignored her.

After they sang happy birthday to Mookie, Christina called it a night. She was tired and really wasn't in the mood anymore. On her way to the car, Tony walked behind her.

"Are you ready?" he asked.

Not turning around, Christina replied, "What does it look like?" Then she turned to address her new bodyguard Roy. "Please make sure Mike is outside."

"Wait! I'll take you home," Tony offered.

"No, thanks. I'll be fine."

"Yo Christina, chill. I'll take you home."

Christina sighed. "Fair enough."

On the way to Christina's house, they rode in silence. When they pulled up in front of her penthouse, Christina blurted out, "Thanks," before hopping out and running into the building.

Tony immediately followed her. "Yo, what's your problem?" he mumbled, trying to catch up to her.

As she walked into the elevator, she responded, "Nothing."

Christina entered her apartment, tossed her bag on the table, and kicked off her shoes before heading upstairs.

"What's up with you?" Tony yelled.

Christina, who was midway up the stairs, turned around. "Tony, let's not pretend. Okay? Stop acting like you care. In fact, do us both a favor and get the fuck of my house," she said, then proceeded up the stairs and slammed her bedroom door.

A couple of minutes later, Christina's prayers were answered when he left. Once she heard the door slam, she waited a few more seconds and then went back downstairs to the kitchen. Lately, she had been eating like a pig. She had already eaten twice at Mookie's party, and now she was fixing herself a sandwich. Then it dawned on her that she hadn't seen her period in a while. Immediately, she ran upstairs, pulled out her emergency pregnancy test, and went into the bathroom. It was positive! Christina jumped for joy; she was pregnant.

"Yes, thank you, Jesus!" she excitedly shouted.

*****

The next couple of weeks, Christina walked around smiling. Although she lost the man she loved, he left her with a special gift. She prayed it was a boy, hoping it would look just like Paul. She was even nice to Tony, agreeing to have dinner with him at his house.

An hour went by and Tony hadn't showed up. Christina called his cell phone, and it rang five times before going to voicemail. She left a message for him to call her. Starting to get impatient, she poured herself a glass of water. It was going on nine o'clock, and still, no sign of Tony. So, Christina decided to call it a night. Just as she started to blow out the candles, the doorbell rang.

Tony probably forgot his keys, she thought, while going to open the door. However, it was Greg.

"Hi, Greg." She was completely stunned.

"Hey, Christina. Is Tony home?"

"No. I thought you were him. You wanna come in and wait. He should be here any second."

Greg hesitated for a second. "A'ight." After glancing around, he looked back at Christina. "Did I interrupt something?"

"No," she replied, leading him further into the house. "Your friend asked me to come over for dinner, and guess what? He didn't show up," she said in a sarcastic tone.

Greg sighed. *What the fuck did I walk into?* he thought. "Oh, he probably just got caught up."
He looked around again, hoping someone else was in the house with them. "Are you here alone?"

"No. I think Carmen is in the other room. You want something to eat or drink? There's plenty of food," she said, walking into the family room.

Greg waved off her offer. "Nah, I'm good."

Christina took a seat on the sofa while Greg sat on the

loveseat. "How's Gabrielle?" she asked.

"Oh, she's good. Getting big."

"Awww, that's so sweet. I hope I don't get that big," she blurted out.

"You're pregnant?" Greg asked, confused.

Christina put her hand over her mouth. "Did I just say that?"

"That's what's up. Does Tony know?"

She sighed. "Greg…Tony isn't the father."

He sat there with a poker face on. "Oh."

Christina took another deep breath. "Paul is."

"What Paul?"

"Paul…"

Greg rubbed his head and remained quiet.

"Paul and I started seeing each other before he was killed. In fact, we were engaged," Christina told him, showing off her engagement ring. "We never meant for this to happen, and now Paul is gone."

Greg was upset with Paul. Even though Tony probably treated Christina like shit, Paul should've never messed with her.

Christina got scared by Greg's silence. "Greg?"

"Sorry. That's crazy."

"What's crazy?"

He sighed. "Paul is my man and all, but he was wrong for messing with you. Regardless of what you and Tony were going through, you belonged to Tony. He was smiling in Tony's face and fucking his chick on the side. That's not right."

"Greg, Tony was out there fucking around, too."

"Yeah, but he wasn't fucking your friends. The worst things anyone can do to me are lie, cheat, and steal. Paul did all of that. Understand something, loyalty means a lot to me. If I can't trust you, then you can't be around me."

Christina lowered her eyes with shame. "Have you ever cheated on your wife?"

"Not after I married her. Why?"

"Then you wouldn't understand. Tony was out there fucking everyone, from my best friend to my sorry-ass manager. But, I guess he gets a free pass because he's Tony Flowers, your friend. Just so you know, Greg, it was more than just sex between Paul and I. We really loved each other, and he was gonna tell Tony. But, he died before he could get a chance," Christina cried.

Now, Greg lowered his head. He didn't mean to come at her like that. Maybe she was right. You can't help who you fall in love with. That's why Greg always made sure home was taken care of. He reached out and embraced Christina.

"Hey, I didn't mean to go off like that. I'm happy for you."

"Greg, you have to believe me. Paul and I were gonna tell Tony."

"I know. Listen, Paul was a good dude. With him, it had to be love."

Christina smiled. "Paul was the best thing that ever happened to me. You know, Greg, he looked up to you so much. The night of your birthday party, Paul said you and your wife represented real black love. You proved to him that true love does exist and that it's okay to express your love."

Greg flashed his trademark smile. "I wasn't always like this. When I first met my wife, I wasn't sure if she was the one. Like Tony, it wasn't cool for men to talk about our girl in public because of the environment we grew up in. We were taught bitches ain't shit."

"I know what you're saying, but at some point, don't you have to grow up?" Christina said, while trying not to stare at his strong features that attracted a lot of attention.

"Of course, you do, but sadly, it takes a bad situation for us to grow up. Even then, some don't. For me, it was prison. I married my wife before I went to prison, and I will keep it real. I was still tryna be a player. It wasn't until I blew trial that I realized what I have. My wife could've bounced on me. She didn't need me. Still, she stayed and rode it out with me. That alone made me grow up. Christina, a lot of men are afraid to reveal their feelings, thinking it will make them look weak. But, for me, it defines me as a man. I love my wife. She's the best thing that ever happened to me. That's what separates boys from men."

Christina smiled and her heart melted. "You sound like Paul."

"Paul was a good dude. Knowing him, he didn't set out to hurt Tony."

"And Tony?'

Greg exhaled. "Tony is…Tony."

Both laughed, as she walked him to the door.

"Christina, whatever you decide, I got your back. You don't have to worry about nothing. You're carrying my nephew." He reached out and hugged her.

"Or your niece."

Both chuckled.

"Greg, can you keep this between us?"

"Of course, but I think you should tell Tony. You owe it to him."

Christina nodded. "I will"

"Night," he said, while opening the door.

"Good night," she replied as he walked out.

Christina shut the door in awe. Greg was the definition of a real man.

She rubbed her stomach. "Baby, we are gonna be alright."

Since it was late, she decided to spend the night at Tony's. A nice hot bubble bath was what she needed. She listened to Prince's *Purple Rain* CD until she dozed off to sleep. When the CD ended, she woke up, grabbed a towel off the rack, and stepped out of the tub. Suddenly, she slipped and fell.

"Ouch!" she screamed.

Tony busted in the bathroom. "Yo, are you alright?"

"Yes, I just hit my elbow."

"You have to be careful," he said, helping her up.

"Thanks."

"Yo, I'm sorry about dinner. I lost track of time."

"It's fine! Greg stopped by."

"Oh, he did? I'll hit him in the morning. Are you sure you're good?"

"Yes," she said, while drying herself off.

"Damn," Christina grumbled, as she looked at her elbow that was turning black and blue.

Tony went back downstairs, while she went into the other room in case Tony tried to have sex with her. As usual, she talked to her angel Paul for a couple of minutes before dozing off.

Not much longer after falling asleep, she awakened to excruciating pain. Her stomach was cramping and the sheet was wet. Christina tried to jump up, but the pain was too intense.

"Tony!" Christina screamed.

Suddenly, it felt like she had just peed on herself. She turned on the light and touched herself; her hand was full of blood. She jumped up and tried to get out of bed, but fell to the floor. Lying there rolling on the floor, crying and gasping for air, she yelled out, "Someone please help me!"

With his hands in his pocket, Tony stood in the doorway watching as Christina laid there in pain. He smiled to himself. *Revenge is best when it's served cold.*

THE TRILOGY ENDS

SCATTERED LIES

"Finally, the Truth..."

Coming Soon
2011

Share your thoughts with the Madison by visiting her at
www.iammadisontaylor.com

Email: iammadison27@yahoo.com